D0686957

MIDNIGHT GRINDING

AND OTHER TWILIGHT TERRORS

Ronald Kelly

This special edition is limited to 1,250 signed copies.

MIDNIGHT GRINDING

GRINDING

AND OTHER TWILIGHT TERRORS

MIDNIGHT GRINDING

AND OTHER TWILIGHT TERRORS

RONALD KELLY

CEMETERY DANCE PUBLICATIONS

Baltimore
❖ 2008 ❖

The following selections were previously published: "Breakfast Serial" in *Terror Time Again*, 1988; "Miss Abigail's Delicate Condition" in *Noctulpa*, 1988; "Forever Angels" in *Cemetery Dance*, 1988; "Yea, Though I Drive" in *Cold Blood*, 1991; "The Web of La Sanguinaire" in *Deathrealm*, 1988; "The Cistern" in *Cemetery Dance*, 1990; "Papa's Exile" in *Deathrealm*, 1988; "The Hatchling" in *Tri-State Fantasist*, 1989; "Black Harvest" in *After Hours*, 1989; "Dead Skin" in *Grue*, 1990; "Consumption" in *Thin Ice*, 1989; "Dust Devils" in *2AM Magazine*, 1989; "The Boxcar" in *After Hours*, 1989; "The Dark Tribe" in *Tri-State Fantasist*, 1989; "Old Hacker" in *New Blood*, 1989; "The Winds Within" in *Cemetery Dance*, 1990; "Oh, Sordid Shame" in *Deathrealm*, 1990; "The Cerebral Passion" in *Eldritch Tales*, 1991; "Thinning the Herd" in *2AM Magazine*, 1992; "Blood Suede Shoes" in *Shock Rock*, 1992; "Tyrophex-Fourteen" in *The Earth Strikes Back*, 1994; "Scream Queen" in *Hot Blood: Seeds of Fear*, 1995; "Bookmarks" in *Gauntlet*, 1991; "Romicide" in *Cemetery Dance*, 1996; "Whorehouse Hollow" in *Dark Seductions*, 1993; "Depravity Road" in *Deathrealm*, 1991; "Beneath Black Bayou" in *Dark at Heart*, 1992; "Exit 85" in *Cemetery Dance*, 1996; "Grandma's Favorite Recipe" in *Cemetery Dance*, 2008; "Midnight Grinding" in *Borderlands 3*, 1992.

Cemetery Dance Publications
132-B Industry Lane, Unit #7
Forest Hill, MD 21050
http://www.cemeterydance.com

The characters and events in this book are fictitious.
Any similarity to real persons, living or dead,
is coincidental and not intended by the author.

First Limited Edition Printing

ISBN-13: 978-1-58767-182-1
ISBN-10:   1-58767-182-4

Cover Artwork © 2008 by Alex McVey
Interior Design by Kathryn Freeman

For my number-one fan and my best friend,
Rob McCoy.
Thank you for making me feel good about
myself and my writing once again.

TABLE OF CONTENTS

INTRODUCTION

WHEN first meeting you, folks down South are liable to ask you one of three questions.

"Are you kin to those no-account (insert your surname here) who live down yonder in the hollow?"

"What do you do for a living?"

"Do you attend church and—if you don't—why the hell not?"

It's that second one that usually trips me up.

"I'm a writer," I tell them. Then they get that look. You know, like when you crank up your motor on a frosty winter morning and discover a possum had cozied up against the warm engine block the night before, between the fan belt pullies. It ain't a pretty sight.

"What do you write?" they ask next.

"Oh, you know…horror. Scary stories."

The look on their face grows even more severe then. If it's a church lady you are talking to, it's even worse. *Uh-huh…devil worshiper*, their eyes gleam smugly. *Spawn of Satan.*

You wouldn't believe how many times that comes up in my line of work, although I'm as God-fearing as the next person, or maybe even more so.

Perhaps I ought to just tell them I'm a storyteller. That would simplify matters. Where I come from, folks understand the nearly-lost art of telling an entertaining story. They wouldn't ask if I was rich or famous; they would merely nod in understanding and leave it at that.

The South holds high regard for storytellers. Not that there are as many around as there once was. Like other rural arts—quilting, canning, whittling—its appeal has waned among the young in favor of television, video games, and the Internet. And that's a downright shame, in my opinion.

I had some hellacious storytellers on both sides of my family, before they went on to meet their maker...or that other fella with the forked stick. They could curl your hair and your toes at the same time, and stick a generous helping of goosebumps and belly laughs in between. Good storytelling deals with folklore and history, the Jesus-believing gospel and snipe-hunting bull. You hear everything from adultery, thievery, and vice, to tales of backwoods ghosts and things that creep unseen beneath carpets of heavy kudzu.

About the finest storyteller I ever came across was my grandmother, Clara Spicer. She knew how to spin a whopper of a tale, one after another, without stopping to catch her breath. I recall sitting on the front porch of her house when I was a young'un, listening to her for two or three hours at a time, enraptured, as though her words were a portal into a different—darker—time.

And the tales she would tell! The one about the simple-minded gent who carried his empty pinewood casket constantly across his back...the little girl she had played with who had fallen off a stone wall into a thick patch of devil's ear cactus and died three days later as the quills worked their way slowly toward her innards...the ghostly sound of kindling falling into a woodbox that drifted from a long-abandoned house and the knowledge that a woman had been bludgeoned to death by a stick of firewood there many years ago.

And then there was Green Lee.

My grandmother's uneasy memories of a deranged handyman with a skeletal hand and a fetish for honed steel were fact, which made the character that much more disturbing. It was that tale...more than any other...that sparked my desire to take on the art of storytelling myself...not vocally, but through the written word. Not that anything in this volume can be considered "high-minded" literature. No, they're just tales to haunt and mortify, and maybe even gross you out every now and then.

So kick off your shoes and sit a spell. Open your mind to the darkness that a Southern night might bring...out of the hills and hollows...the deep woods...the swamps and the places where shadow never gives way to daylight.

Let me tell y'all a story...

BREAKFAST SERIAL

I included this tale because it was the first story I had published and hardly anyone has read it. It is kind of fun, in a twisted sort of way. Just goes to show that you'd better be mighty careful who you share your ham and eggs with in the morning.

CHESTER Freely had been kicking around the dusty rural backroads of northern Alabama for many days and early that Saturday morning he sat down to breakfast with a charming farm family by the name of Johnson.

"Danged fine cook, my Emma...don't you think so, boy?" beamed Fred Johnson contentedly. He pushed away from the table and patted his swollen belly.

"Oh, yes, sir," Chester agreed. He gave Mrs. Johnson an appreciative smile. "Best home-cooked meal I've had in quite awhile, ma'am."

"Glad you enjoyed it, young man. More biscuits and molasses with your coffee?"

"No, thanks. I'm stuffed."

The twins, Randy and Rita, waved empty jelly-jar glasses at their mother. "Can we have some more chocolate milk, Mama? Please?"

Emma Johnson eyed them in a moment of indecision, then broke into a smile. "Well, maybe just one more glass for each of you." She walked toward the refrigerator at the other side of the kitchen.

"I sure appreciate you helping me mend that fence along the south pasture this morning," said Fred. He had already milked the cows and slopped the hogs, when Chester had wandered up the road and offered to lend a hand.

"My pleasure," nodded the lanky drifter. "Kinda hard to find good honest work when you're on the road as much as I am. Sure glad to help out folks whenever I can."

The Johnsons smiled at their guest, unaware of the secret he held. A secret that he concealed well behind a handsome, good-natured smile of his own.

Chester Freely was a serial killer.

He had been at it going on three years now and, by his count, had murdered nearly forty-two families; families very much like the Johnsons. He did one a month, sometimes two if he found the opportunity. And he never murdered in the same state twice in a row. He would do one in Minnesota, then one in California, another in Texas, still another in Maine. He staggered them out across the country, never leaving a definite pattern, never performing his atrocities in exactly the same manner. Perhaps that was why the authorities hadn't wised up to him yet. Either that or pure dumb luck.

Now he was sitting in a cheerful kitchen in a lonely farmhouse twenty miles north of Birmingham. He liked the South almost as much as he liked the Midwest, for it was there where his victims lived in great abundance. The requirements were always the same: a hard-working, God-fearing farmer and his modest family who lived on acreage so vast that his closest neighbor lived quite a ways down the road. In other words, a small group of people who were totally isolated in their everyday routine. Sometimes his victims were so far out in the sticks that they weren't discovered for several days. By then he was three or four states away, satisfied for the moment, but secretly contemplating his next massacre.

Chester was rarely treated to such a fine meal as the one Emma Johnson had prepared that morning. After saying grace, they dug in. Scrambled eggs, country-cured ham, big cathead biscuits, and all the black coffee he could drink. At first he had nearly considered letting this one pass, but decided otherwise. It was nearing the end of the month and he was desperately in need of the physical and emotional rush that wholesale murder gave him. The gruesome sight of blood and mutilation intoxicated him much like some potent drug, placing him in the same category as a junkie in constant search of a fix.

A faint whimper and a scratching at the back door drew their attention. Chester grinned. He had been mulling over his execution of today's bloodletting all during breakfast and now it came to him, suddenly and without warning, almost causing him to laugh out loud.

"Mrs. Johnson, do you mind if I carve off a slab of this ham for my dog?' Chester asked politely. "He hasn't had a bite since yesterday." He had started traveling with a dog during his second year. Mostly he would befriend some stray he came across while he was on the road. People seemed to trust a stranger more easily when they traveled with a dog. Besides, whenever he got tired of them and needed a cheap thrill, Chester just slaughtered the poor mutts, then tossed them in a ditch or stuffed them in a drainage pipe. But it was never the same as doing a human being.

Emma smiled at her guest warmly. "Why, certainly you can! But let me get you a sharper knife. That one there is kind of dull." She began to rummage through a counter drawer.

"I'd sure appreciate it," said Chester calmly. He was so wired now that he could barely sit still. He glanced around the table. Fred Johnson sat back, his belt loosened a few notches, thumbing through a copy of the local, small-town paper. The Johnson children giggled at the sad-eyed dog that peered through the screen door, chocolate milk mustaches splashed broadly beneath their pert, little noses.

This is going to be easy, Chester thought. *So damned easy.*

Emma Johnson started across the spotless linoleum floor, holding the large butcher knife by its wooden handle. "Here you go, young man."

He had it all worked out now. As soon as he had his fingers wrapped around the haft of the knife, he would turn and sink it deep into Fred's solar plexus, killing him instantly. Emma would stand there stunned for a second, long enough for him to grab that antique iron skillet that hung beside the knick-knack shelf and brain her enough to knock her flat. He didn't want her dead just yet. Emma was a drab, homely woman, but she had a nice body. She would be repeatedly raped and tortured before he allowed her to join her husband in death.

By the time their mother hit the floor, Randy and Rita would react in one of two ways.

They would either sit there in shock or they would run screaming for their lives. He hoped for the latter. It was always so much fun hunting children, like a hound running a coon. They all had the mistaken notion that they could hide from him. Sometimes it was under a bed, sometimes behind a tree outside or in the hayloft of the barn. The Johnson Twins had been so polite and loveable throughout his stay, that he figured they were deserving of something special. A beheading perhaps. Yes, either that or dismemberment.

As his perfect hostess approached the table, he reached out, the hairs on the nape of his neck tingling with anticipation. "Thank you very much, Mrs.—"

He didn't get a chance to finish his statement. With an upward swipe, sweet Emma Johnson slit his throat from ear to ear.

Chester Freely fell backward out of his chair, an expression of utter surprise dawning on his pale face. He hit hard, splattering blood across the linoleum tiles. His *own* blood!

He wanted to say *"What the hell is going on?"* but that was quite impossible. The blade had sliced clean through his larynx, as well as the major arteries. The only sound that he could make was a wet gurgling as blood engorged his severed windpipe.

Then the children were upon him. Little Randy and Rita laughed playfully, running around the leg of the oaken table with sharp implements. They attacked his abdomen with a bloodlust he himself had rarely possessed. Randy jabbed at him with a butter knife, while pig-tailed Rita impaled him viciously again and again with a fork from Emma's best silverware.

"That's enough, kids," laughed Emma, crouching down to hug her bloodstained babies. "He's dead now."

"Look, Papa!" the twins squealed as one. "Look, Papa, look!"

Fred Johnson arched his eyebrows and puffed on his pipe. "My, my, now ain't that a fine piece of work," he said proudly. "Couldn't have done it better myself."

Emma stared down at the butchered body lying across her kitchen floor. "Such a nice young man. Sure wish we could've let him go this time."

"Now, Emma," said Fred, stretching lazily. "You know very well if we let one go, it'd have to go for 'em all."

The woman sighed. "I suppose so. Where are we gonna put this one? The root cellar?"

"Nah, we've got them stacked like cord wood down there already. I reckon we oughta start stashing them in the smokehouse now."

Fred winked at his young'uns. "I'll tell you kids what. You two help me carry this fellow outside and we'll clean up and drive into town for ice cream afterwards. How does that sound?"

"Oh boy!"

"Yippee!"

The children's blood-speckled faces broke into broad grins as they each grabbed ahold of one of Chester's trouser legs and began to pull him toward the back door.

MISS ABIGAIL'S DELICATE CONDITION

I hate snakes. Whenever I see one I go into a blind panic. It's not just rattlers and copperheads, either. Big or little, dead or alive...I utterly loathe the things. I can't say why I react in such a way. Maybe it goes clear back to that nasty business in Genesis. Whenever I cast my eyes upon the serpent all I see is treachery and evil.

If you don't already have a fear of snakes, this story may leave you with one. It is based on a true medical account that took place back in the early 1900s...I just embellished the outcome a bit.

MOST folks in the little town of New Bainesville, Virginia were certain that Miss Abigail Beecher would go to her grave an old maid, even though she was now only nineteen years of age. It wasn't that Miss Beecher was terribly homely; on the contrary, she was quite lovely. And it was not that she came from a poverty-stricken home and had no dowry to interest potential suitors. No, the young lady came from one of the wealthiest and most respected families in New Bainesville. Rather, it was the nature of Miss Abigail's physical condition that made her a less than likely candidate for matrimony.

Since childhood, Abigail had been sickly, plagued with physical ailments galore. It was rumored that her problem began at the age of nine. Her family had been picnicking down beside the babbling swell of Chestnut Creek on the Beecher property, when young Abigail knelt and drank from the creekbed. The picnic went well, but upon returning home, the child became quite ill. She lay with a high fever for many days, unable to eat anything, before her temperature finally broke and lowered to normal. But much to her parents' dismay, her troubles did not end there. The fevers resurfaced regularly, accompanied by alternate periods of nausea, choking, and convulsive fits. It was believed that she had consumed some strange bacteria from the innocent swallow of creekwater. And it soon became necessary for James Beecher to employ a full-time nurse to watch over his daughter's fluctuating condition.

She grew into a young woman, inheriting her mother's auburn hair and hazel green eyes, but her skin was pale from lack of sun, as white as alabaster. She was also painfully shy and extremely nervous; her frail, white hands fidgeted constantly with one another. No wonder all the prim, gossiping ladies pegged her as a potential spinster.

So it came as quite a shock to many an old busybody when a handsome, young gentleman by the name of Jeremy Burke began to call regularly upon the reclusive girl.

Their paths had crossed by association with the New Bainesville Bank & Trust. Abigail was the sole beneficiary of her late father's estate, while Jeremy had recently returned from the war in Europe and had taken over his father's position as bank president. It was during the execution of the Beecher will that young Jeremy grew to fancy the demure young lady who seemed content to sit in her shaded parlor with her books and Victrola. Miss Abigail seemed equally taken with the outgoing gentleman with the smiling eyes and the slight limp, a battlefield injury he corrected with the help of a horsehead cane.

And so, in January of 1920, the courtship of the two began, to the surprise of many, but the well wishes of all.

It started with suppers at the Beecher home and, afterwards, quiet evenings of pleasant conversation before the big fireplace in the main room. When Jeremy grew to know her better and the weather began to warm, he suggested a picnic for just the two of them beside Haverstone Lake, which bordered his own estate. Being the recluse that she was, Abigail was reluctant at first. But unable to disappoint her beau any longer, she finally consented. Her nurse, Mrs. Henderson, also agreed, feeling that a change of scenery would do her mistress a world of good.

It was a sunny day in mid-March, a day of new spring, daffodils, green-budded trees and songbirds. They took a canoe across the lake, Jeremy in his straw hat and sleeve garters, Abigail wearing a sheer veil to shield her lovely face from the rays of the sun. Their trip to the far side was leisurely. Once, Jeremy had put down the oars and strummed a couple of popular tunes on his five-string banjo. His playing was atrocious and she laughed as she had not laughed in years. Encouraged that the day was off to a good start, Jeremy resumed his rowing and soon they had their lunch laid out upon the grass beneath a blossoming magnolia tree.

The two were engaged in small talk and a feast of fried chicken, roasting ears, and cornbread, when something from the direction of the lake drew the young lady's eyes from her companion. The man turned and, much to his surprise, saw a snake emerge from the water's edge. It was a cottonmouth, a snake common in the South that frequented the area's lakes and rivers. He watched, startled, for the serpent was so bold as to leave the safety of its waterhole and slither straight toward them.

"You need not worry, my dear," he assured, but when he turned to Abigail he found not fear in her eyes, but rather a strange fascination. She looked fairly hypnotized by the ugly reptile that crossed the spring grass toward them.

He stood and, with his cane, drove the black snake back to the lakeside. "Nasty devil!" he shouted, watching as it swam, head above water, into the quiet breadth of Haverstone Lake. "Now, dear Abigail, we shall finish our lunch and—" He was jolted from his train of thought as he turned back to find her face ghastly pale, her eyes wide with sudden shock. She began to choke, her breath escaping in shallow gasps, her slender arms trembling as she collapsed to the ground.

His heart heavy with fear, Jeremy carried his lady to the boat and oared to the far side. Halfway across, the cursed snake reappeared, craning its head over the edge of the bow. With a shout, Jeremy gave the serpent a vicious swipe with the broad end of his paddle, sending it darting across the rippling waters. By the time Jeremy rowed ashore and, with the help of the groundskeeper, carried her inside to the parlor sofa, Abigail Beecher's frightful seizure had run its course. It was at that moment, as she lay pale and scared before him, that Jeremy knew he truly loved this frail woman. He took her tiny hands in his own and gently kissed her.

He proposed to her the following evening, in her own parlor on bended knee. And, with tears of happiness in her eyes, Miss Abigail Beecher readily accepted.

They were married on the first day of April. It was a lavish church wedding and it seemed that the entire township of New Bainesville had attended. After the ceremony had proclaimed them husband and wife, they retired to the Burke estate, which would become their permanent home after Abigail's property was sold. Their love for each other was consummated that night, tenderly and with patience, Jeremy treating his new bride as gently as a china doll.

Abigail's nurse moved in to look after the lady's bouts of illness, which seemed to grow fewer as the weeks drew into months. Jeremy was pleased to see that his wife was spending more time outdoors and that she had even taken up oil painting. Many an evening he returned home from the bank to find her at work on the veranda, rendering a likeness of the lakefront. It was on one such evening that he glanced past her latest canvas and spotted a snake—another cursed cottonmouth—winding its way up to the porch from the direction of the boathouse.

Once again he chased it away with his cane. And once again, Abigail's apparent fascination with the poisonous snake transcended into a fit of coughing and convulsions. She was led to her room with the help of Nurse Henderson, and Old George, the caretaker, was sent to fetch the doctor.

After Doctor Travers had made his examination, he took Jeremy aside and told him that the fit had passed and that Abigail was resting comfortably. He also told the young husband something that took him by surprise. His frail wife was with child. Jeremy voiced his concern, thinking that her ill health might jeopardize the lives of both mother and child. Travers told him not to worry, that the pregnancy would go smoothly if she was kept in bed and protected from further agitation.

After the doctor had left, Jeremy called Old George into his study. "There is a disturbing abundance of cottonmouths venturing up from the lake lately," he informed the man. "Find their nest and destroy the lot. I will pay you a sterling silver dollar for each one killed."

■■■

During the following months of that summer, twenty-seven watersnakes were laid at Jeremy's feet and his money pouch grew lighter as Old George's grew heavier. Most had been killed down by the lake, yet, oddly enough, eight were discovered uncomfortably close to the main house.

Abigail's fever wavered over the days ahead, but her sickness seemed to quell with twilight and she slept peacefully. Jeremy, however, found his sleep fitful on those nights. Half of his insomnia stemmed from worry over his wife and their unborn baby, while the rest was due to the disturbing nightmares he had been having lately. He had been dreaming of snakes, but the dreams lacked substance or any sense of purpose. He dreamt of two serpents—male and female—lying in a bed of grass, entwined in a fitful throe of flailing heads and tails, engaged in an obscene act of copulation. Then amid the thrashing, the grass changed to white bed linens and he realized that the bed was their own, his and Abigail's. He would bolt awake, near hysteria, while his wife lay in a restful slumber beside him.

Summer passed into the cool nights of autumn and still the nightmare persisted. It was on a night in early September that he awoke abruptly with the eerie feeling that his awful dream had not yet ended. Frightened, he lit a lamp beside the bed and threw back the covers. There, lying between him and Abigail, curled a snake: a single cottonmouth, bearing its deadly needle-like fangs and the gaping white maw that gave the serpent its particular namesake. He had gone for his pistol, yelling for his wife to flee from its reach. But Abigail merely lay there, her breathing deep, her sleep undisturbed.

The gunshot awoke her as Jeremy knocked the serpent to the bedroom floor with his cane and blew its head apart with a single well-aimed bullet. Nurse Henderson rushed in just as Abigail began to strangle violently and lurch upon the feather mattress in a harrowing convulsion that traveled the length of her slender body. After a moment, however, she relaxed and returned to her dreamless slumber.

The next few months were the most difficult for Jeremy Burke. He sat in an armchair beside his wife's sickbed most nights, sometimes reading, but mostly watching her with heart-rending concern. The days since the incident had not been kind to dear Abigail. They were filled with nausea and fever and gut-wrenching cramps that Doc Travers had no diagnosis for. Relief came only with nightfall and it was then that Jeremy suffered, watching silently over his beloved wife, jumping at every little shift in her sleep, every little change in her breathing.

It was on a December night, during one of his nocturnal vigils, that the cause of Abigail's strange ailment finally became known.

Jeremy had been reading a book of O. Henry, when he unwillingly drifted into sleep. It was only when the hall clock chimed the hour of twelve that he awoke. Silently scolding himself for his goldbricking, Jeremy studied his wife's pale face in the soft glow of the bedside lamp. She slept as usual, on her back, her mouth open slightly, her breathing shallow. Then, as he returned his weary eyes to his reading, a hitch sounded in the woman's breath that caused him to glance up.

His heart began to race at the awful sight he was witnessing no more than three feet away. At first he thought it to be her tongue, somehow bloated and bruised, but in an instant, and to his growing horror, he realized that it was rather the triangular head of a *serpent* that probed inquisitively from between the petals of Abigail's parted lips.

He was gripped by indecision for only a fraction of a second. Then, without further thought, his hand shot out and fisted around the snake's slender neck. *"Oh dear Lord in heaven!"* he gasped as he stood over the bed. His wife awoke, eyes wide in alarm as the horrid thing within her squirmed and convulsed under Jeremy's firm grasp.

Nearly overcome with the terror of it all, he hesitated, then began to pull. One...two...*three* feet of the cursed thing he dragged from his wife's open mouth. It writhed in the cool air of the room, its hide blistered and raw from years of swimming in gastric and intestinal acids. Abigail's thin hands clawed at the bedclothes, panic bringing her close to the edge of madness as she watched her husband exorcise the demon she had housed since the age of nine.

Finally, the snake was out. Jeremy held the serpent aloft, watching its scarred head strain and turn, trying unsuccessfully to sink its fangs into the flesh of his hand. With a fury born of pure anger and loathing, he flung it against the oaken panel of the bedroom door. Then, retrieving his .45, he emptied the clip into its thrashing body.

■■■

Dawn brought the sound of Doc Travers' footsteps as he descended the stairs and joined a haggard Jeremy Burke in the kitchen. Silently, he poured himself a cup of coffee, then spoke. "I gave her something to quiet her down. Physically, I think she is all right. The awful shock of it all did the most damage, but she'll get over it. In time, we will all get over this whole damned ordeal."

Jeremy shook his head, reliving the horror. "But that... that horrid *thing* living inside her for all these years..."

"Indeed," sighed Doc Travers with a tired smile, "but I had best get back up there. My work won't be finished here for some time."

"What do you mean?" asked Jeremy with alarm.

"I mean, young man, that your wife is in early labor. The baby will be premature, but I have delivered many that way," he said, rising. "I wouldn't worry if I were you."

Jeremy buried his head in his hands. "I just pray that dear Abigail can make it through the strain."

The labor of Abigail Beecher Burke turned out to be a long and painful one and, by the eve of that winter day in 1920, it finally came to its end. Jeremy was there, despite the doctor's protest, to offer his young wife comfort and to see that things went well.

He watched silently as the birth of his child took place. First the infant's head appeared, followed by the tiny body and limbs. He watched as Doc Travers tenderly handed the newborn fetus to Nurse Henderson and carefully withdrew the umbilical cord from the womb. Jeremy felt a thrill of terror grip him momentarily for, at first glance, it appeared that the physician held a snake in his hands. That was not the case, but for some reason the link between mother and child was darkly colored and possessed a scale-like texture. He quickly studied his firstborn—a little boy—and relaxed. His new son was incredibly small, but appeared completely normal.

A big wink and a grin from Doc Travers assured Jeremy that everything would be all right as he lifted the baby by its heels and gave it a sharp slap across the buttocks.

Jeremy exchanged a weary, but loving smile with his darling Abigail, took her hand gently in his own and eyed his squawling son as he squirmed within the grasp of the doctor's experienced hands.

But as the infant began to cry, Jeremy noticed something that caused his newfound pride to swiftly rise toward horror. For the inner lining of the baby's mouth was not a tender pink in color, but rather a ghastly milky white.

And, just beneath the pale gums, a hint of tiny fangs.

FOREVER ANGELS

To me, the worst nightmare imaginable would be the death of a child. The devastating loss, the grief, the realization of a life unfulfilled, would seem to be more than one could bear. Folks in the South derive some comfort from the belief that children are incapable of going to Hell; that these earthbound angels are simply making the transition to heavenly ones.

I wrote this story when I was a single man and, back then, it really didn't bother me that much. But now that I am a father of two, it seems particularly disturbing.

DEANNA Hudson didn't believe her second-grade classmates at first. Not until they actually took her there and showed her that it was true.

The Glover County school bus let them out at the corner of Flanders Drive and Pear Tree Road at a quarter after three. Together, they walked the two blocks to the Milburne Baptist Church. The building had stood there for nearly one hundred and fifty years, always virgin white and immaculate, the lofty steeple rising in a pinnacle that could be seen throughout the entire township. Milburne, Tennessee was located on the very buckle of the Southern bible belt and the little church was a picturesque example of how very prominent religion was in that region of the country.

There were five in the youthful procession that walked quietly down the sidewalk, then crossed the well-mown lawn that separated the church property from the adjoining graveyard. There was Deanna, Jimmy Thompson, Butch Spence, and the Waller twins, Vickie and Veronica. They made their way through the cramped cemetery, past marble headstones and a scattering of lonely trees, their backpacks slung over their shoulders. Thunder rumbled overhead. The day had begun cheerfully enough, but by afternoon dark storm clouds had rolled in from the west, promising the threat of spring showers and perhaps a thunderstorm before the night ended.

"Well, there it is...just like I told you," said Butch with a sneer of triumph. "Can't call me a liar now, can you?"

Deanna said nothing. With the others, she slowly approached the little half-acre lot that was fenced in ornate wrought iron. An unlocked gate sported a couple of trumpet-playing angels overhead and a poetic inscription: *Those who are called to the Lord in innocence shall be, forever, angels.*

"Come on," urged Jimmy, pushing the iron gate open with a rusty squeal. Deanna followed the others inside, trying hard to suppress a shiver of cold uneasiness. Yes, it was exactly what it appeared to be; exactly what Butch and Jimmy had described so masterfully on the elementary school playground. It was a miniature graveyard.

A graveyard for children.

They began to walk among the rows of tiny tombstones, each a quarter of the size of their adult counterparts in the next lot over. "Don't be such a scaredy-cat!" Butch shot back in disgust when the fair-haired girl hesitated near the gate. Finally, she drew up her courage and

30

followed her schoolmates onto the gently sloping hill of the small graveyard.

At first the stones seemed fairly new, chiseled from pastel granite of pink and blue, bearing cryptic names like "Little Tommy" or "Baby Linda." Unlike the headstones out in the big graveyard, these seemed devoid of flower arrangements. Instead, long forgotten toys were scattered upon the short mounds: rubber balls, pacifiers, and rattles, their colors bleached by sun and rain, the plastic cracked and broken. A teddy bear lay on its side before the grave of "Sweet Andy Wilson," its eyes blank and unseeing. The stuffing had been burrowed from the fur of its matted tummy, strewn across the grass by some wild animal that had come foraging for food with no luck.

Further into the cemetery, as the little hill reached its peak and began to descend to the edge of a thick forest, the headstones grew older and the rows were choked with weeds.

The inscriptions were more difficult to read, the names sanded clear down to the bare stone by decades of wind and harsh weather. "My dad says these have been here since the 1800s," said Butch. "Said there was a big diphtheria epidemic back then that killed half the babies in Glover County. Most of them are buried right here...beneath our feet."

They stood there in reverent silence for a moment. The gentle breeze had grown blustery, stripping the leathery leaves off the cemetery's only tree, a huge blossoming magnolia at the very heart of the grassy knoll. Deanna began to back away, a creepy feeling threatening to overcome her. "I've got to get home," she said, her voice barely a whisper.

"Go on home, if you want," said Butch with a shrug. "But you ain't gonna be able to escape them, you know. Not as close as you live to this place." They all peered into the three-acre woods that separated the churchyard from the new subdivision that had been built to either side of Pear Tree Road. Through a gap in the pine grove,

Deanna could see her parents' split-level house, the one they had moved into only two months ago.

"What do you mean?" asked the girl, clutching her book bag tightly. "Who are you talking about?"

A devilish grin crossed Butch Spence's freckled face. "The babies, that's who. They crawl up from their graves at night, you know. Old Man Caruthers, the caretaker, he's heard them out here before…giggling and crying, crawling among the tombstones, trying to find their mothers. And on dark, stormy nights they hop the fence over yonder and crawl through the woods…to *your* house!"

It began to rain. "Stop it!" yelled Deanna. "You're scaring me!"

"Listen!" said Jimmy Thompson. "Did you hear that?"

The sound of something stirring in the high weeds on the far side of the fence reached their ears. "It's *them!*" yelled Butch in bogus panic. "It's the dead babies! They're in the woods already, Deanna, and they're heading straight for your house!"

"Stop it!" sobbed the girl. "Do you hear me? Just stop it!"

The Waller twins squealed and giggled with a mixture of fear and delight. The sounds in the forest grew louder. It sounded as though something was in the thicket, crawling on hands and knees.

"Mama!" wailed an infantile voice from out of the high weeds. "Dadda!"

"Gaah, gaah! Goo, goo!" cooed another from the same vicinity beyond the bordering fence.

"Run, Deanna, run!" called Butch, stifling the laughter that would come later when the grand deception was over and done with. Then his buddies, Hank and Jason—who had beat them there on their bikes by five minutes—would come out of the woods and they would all enjoy a big bellylaugh at the new girl's expense.

And the seven-year-old girl did run…through the open gate, across the graveyard, and past the old church to Pear Tree Road. By the time she reached home, the heavens had opened and delivered a drenching downpour. She met her mother at the doorstep, soaked to the skin and crying, the laughter of her playmates cruelly ringing in her ears.

She had seen one once before…a dead baby.

That disturbing experience had taken place at the funeral of Grandpa Hudson a couple of years before. Deanna had gone to the bathroom and, upon returning, lost her way among the many mourning rooms, the places where the deceased were displayed before the casket was moved to the chapel for the final service. She had entered an empty room very similar to the one her grandfather was in and, at first, she had the sinking feeling that her family had up and left her. Then she saw the difference in the flower arrangements and in the coffin that sat upon the shrouded pedestal at the head of the room.

The casket was very small, not over two feet in length. And it was the prettiest shade of baby blue that Deanna had ever seen. Although she was frightened, her curiosity was much stronger than her fear and she had climbed upon one of the folding metal chairs to get a better look. She nearly lost her footing and fell off when she saw what lay in the open box.

It was a baby boy, about the same age that her little brother Timothy was now. It was dressed in a blue jumper, its head covered by a knitted cap of the same pastel hue. Tiny hands clutched a blue rattle in the shape of a sad-eyed puppy dog. It was the round, little face that scared Deanna the most; a face devoid of color, despite a touch of undertaker's rouge at each chubby cheek. A face that was coldly deceptive in its peaceful slumber, an endless sleep that would never be disturbed by a middle-of-the-night hunger for warm milk or the discomfort of a wet diaper.

As Deanna climbed off the chair and started for the door, she had heard—or thought she had heard—the dry sound of the plastic rattle echo from the casket behind her.

Deanna thought of that as she lay in her bed that spring night and listened to the storm's fury rage outside her bedroom window. She drifted into a fitful sleep, then awoke to a violent clap of thunder and a flash of lightning that illuminated her entire room, if only for a second. She clutched her Raggedy Ann, cowering beneath her bedsheets at the awful thrashing of wind and rain. She tried to fall back to sleep several times, but her thoughts were too full of Butch Spence's nasty prank and the baby blue casket at the Milburne funeral home.

Then, when the disturbing images finally did begin to fade, something else sent her into a fit of near panic. It was a small sound, a sound nearly swallowed by the bass roar and the cymbal crash of the thunderstorm in progress.

It was the sound of a baby crying. Outside. In the woods.

Deanna pulled the covers up over her head and tried to wait it out, but that dreaded creature curiosity once again prodded her. *Go and look out the window*, it told her. *You will never know what it is until you do. Maybe it is just a lost kitten or the howling of the wind.*

Despite her better judgment, she climbed out of bed and did exactly what the little voice suggested. She padded in bare feet across her toy-cluttered room to the big window and peeped through the lacy curtains. And she saw exactly what she was afraid that she would see…but, no, it was much worse than that.

At first there was only darkness beyond the rain-speckled panes. Then a bright flash of lightning erupted, dousing the wooded thicket with pale light. There in the weeds down below, things moved. Initially, she couldn't quite make out what they were. Then a double dose of electrical brilliance revealed the startling tableau and she clutched at the curtains in horror.

Small, hairless heads bobbed through the tall grass and honeysuckle like dolphins cresting the waves of a stormy sea. The pale, hairless heads of a dozen lifeless babies.

She began to scream shrilly. Soon, the bedroom light was on and her mother was there to comfort her. Through her tearful hysteria, she tried to explain the awful spectacle she had witnessed. Her father, his hair tousled and his eyes myopic with sleep, peered through the darkness at the yard below. "There's nothing down there, sweetheart," he said, kissing her on the forehead before creeping back to bed. "Nothing at all."

Her mother tucked her back into bed, wiping her tears away. "You just had a nightmare, honey. A bad dream," Mom said. "Now, you just relax and this time you'll have a nice one." The girl followed her mother's advice and, before long, she was fast asleep.

She was awakened a few hours later, again by a baby's cry, but this time it was only her brother in the nursery, wailing for his three o'clock feeding.

■■■

In some Southern communities, Memorial Day is also known as "graveyard day." That had always been the case in Milburne.

It was a day of remembrance, a day reserved for re-spect of the dearly-departed; the recently deceased, as well as those long since past. At the Baptist church it began as a day of work and ended as a day of fellowship. The men would mow the grass and trim around the graves with weed-eaters. The women would tackle the stones, scrub-bing away grime and bird droppings with Ajax and warm water. The children also contributed in their own special way. Armed with baskets of plastic flowers, they removed the old arrangements and replaced them with the new. On the graves of veterans, they placed American flags.

After the congregation had finished sprucing up the cemetery for that year, they would spread blankets and patchwork quilts upon the grass and sit down to eat din-ner on the ground. The Hudson family found a spot near the wrought iron gate of the children's cemetery and, despite Deanna's protest, they laid out their picnic lunch. After the pastor's prayer, they began to enjoy a meal of hot dogs, potato salad, and cold iced tea.

It was during the churchyard meal that the town handyman, Old Redhawk, pulled his rickety pickup truck into the parking lot and staggered up to where the congregation sat eating. Redhawk was a full-blooded Cherokee, once a proud member of a local tribe that had made Glover County its home. But he had fallen on hard times and turned to drink. When he wasn't cleaning out someone's drainage gutters or roofing someone's house, he could be found down at Boone Hollow Tavern, indulging in his favorite pastime. From the looks of him that May afternoon, it appeared that he had downed a few shots of sour mash whiskey before arriving to speak his mind.

Deanna sat between her parents, gently holding little Timothy's hand, as the old Indian ranted and raved about things long since past. She couldn't understand a lot of what he seemed to be so indignant about…something concerning the desecration of sacred land and Indian burial mounds. Soon, Sheriff Harding and his deputy arrived and tried to talk Old Redhawk into leaving peacefully. The drunken man took a wild swing at the constable and, suddenly, they had him face down on the ground, not more than six feet from where the Hudson family sat.

The seven-year-old watched, appalled, as they handcuffed the old Indian and pulled him roughly to his feet. For a second, the Indian's eyes met Deanna's. Those bloodshot eyes seemed to hold a dark message just for her.

Better watch where you sit, little girl, they seemed to warn her. *There are things buried beneath you that you could never hope to imagine. Arrowheads and pottery and the dusty bones of many a brave warrior. And, on top of that, despite the protests of the tribe, others were buried. Innocent children whose foolish parents interred them in sacred ground. There are nights at certain times of the year when the magic of the great Elders raise those tiny bodies from their earthen slumber and return them to the world of the living. Never mind what that comforting inscription atop the cemetery gate might promise. Whatever crawl this hallowed earth in the dead of night...they are far from being angels.*

"Come on, you crazy old coot!" growled the sheriff as he herded Old Redhawk off to the patrol car. "Let's see if a week or two in the county jail will teach you to leave decent folks alone."

Mom handed Deanna a hot dog. "Just try to forget him, dear," she said, stroking her long blond hair. "People do and say crazy things when they are all liquored up like that."

The girl absently took the food, her eyes glued on the tiny stones that jutted along the hillside—or was it burial mound?—on the other side of the fence.

■■■

That night Deanna had the most frightening nightmare of her young life. She dreamt that she stood alone in the half-acre cemetery in the dead of night. A full moon was out, highlighting the tiny stones, making them look like bleached teeth sprouting from earthen gums.

She stood atop the small hill beneath the thick foliage of the magnolia tree, barefoot, her pink nightgown fluttering in a cool breeze. She watched as the iron gate opened and a tall figure stepped within. It was Old Redhawk, but not the same drunken old man that she had seen earlier that day. He was now a proud Cherokee chief with a feathered headdress and streaks of warpaint smeared across his ancient face and arms. Behind him filed a silent gathering of braves and squaws. Old Redhawk began to chant, lifting his hands skyward. The clouds boiled like the depths of a dark cauldron. Lightning jabbed downward like gaunt fingers of blue fire upon the horizon.

Before she could flee through the backwoods to her house, the ground beneath her began to buckle and heave. Clods of grass erupted, yielding a harvest of pale-fleshed

37

heads. Soon, they had clawed the smothering confinement of dank earth away and were there before her, some toddling off balance, others crawling on all fours. The maddening noise of old rattles and squeaky toys pressed against her ears. Her screams drew their attention and, with an infantile mewing, they started up the hill toward her. The only source of escape was the tree. Limb by limb, she ascended the magnolia, glimpsing the pale little forms between the clusters of thick leaves.

When she finally reached the top, she thought herself to be safe. But she was not. Hearing a faint stirring in the leaves above her, she looked up and saw her baby brother, Timothy...his chubby face ashen...his Winnie the Pooh pajamas soiled and dank with fresh earth. And, as he reached for her, she recoiled from his cold little hands...and fell.

Deanna awoke, drenched in sweat, and her mouth was cotton dry. Trembling, she turned on the hall light and crept downstairs to the kitchen for a drink of water. She was filling a glass under the tap, when she heard a noise on the other side of the back door. It was a dry sound, the sound of tiny beads clattering within a plastic shell. A sound much like dry bones rattling within a casket. Small bones inside a small casket.

Don't look outside, she told herself. *Just go back upstairs and crawl into bed and forget all about it.*

But that annoying little voice—Miss Curiosity—whispered insistently in her mind's ear. *It could just be an old newspaper blown against the screen door, maybe a jackrabbit scratching against the concrete steps, wanting a carrot from the fridge.* She walked slowly to the door and unlocked it. For a second, she simply stood there. *Remember what you saw the last time you looked,* she told herself. But she opened the door anyway.

Nothing was on the backdoor stoop. No crumbled newspaper. No bunny rabbit. Nothing but...a single pink bootie lying in the center of the newly-cast concrete.

Cautiously, she picked up the knitted article of baby footwear and examined it. It was old...very old. Its cotton threads were rotten and reeked of soil, like the peat moss Daddy had spread around the shrubs last Saturday. And there was something else...something alive. She tossed the bootie away with a cry of disgust.

There had been squirmy white things crawling between the interlacing fibers. Maggots.

Then, as she was about to step back inside, she heard the faint rustling of the high weeds at the far end of the house. It was pitch dark that night, no moon at all. She strained her eyes until she actually began to see them. Tiny, pale splotches against the deep shadows of the pine grove. Not emerging from the thicket, but retreating.

"Deanna," someone whispered behind her.

She nearly screamed, but recognized her mother's voice before she could. She ran to her, quivering in the warm comfort of her arms. "What's the matter, darling?" Mom asked, bewildered. "Were you sleepwalking again?"

Deanna said nothing. She just continued to cling with all her might.

Mom had come down to fix Timothy's three o'clock bottle. When the milk had been warmed and tested on the inside of Mom's forearm, the two mounted the steps to the upstairs hallway.

The nursery was strangely quiet as they stepped inside. Mom felt along the wall for the light switch. "Surely he didn't fall back to sleep," she told her daughter. "He was screaming like a little banshee only a few minutes ago."

A click and the light came on. The nursery was revealed: lacy blue curtains, dancing clowns painted upon the walls, and in the crib, beneath a dangling mobile of Sesame Street characters, lay...

Mom screamed.

The baby bottle slipped from her hand and rolled along the hardwood floor.

Deanna could only stand there and stare...and think about the magnolia tree.

■■■

The Milburne pediatrician said it was something called "crib death." Deanna didn't know exactly what that was…only that it happened every now and then in Glover County. Her baby brother's passing had been disturbing for the girl, as had his funeral— baby blue casket and all. But the most devastating thing was the place they had buried him. Deanna had screamed and cried when she found out, but the grownups had ignored her and buried Timothy there anyway. On the half-acre hill of stones…beneath that blossoming magnolia tree.

After that, Deanna found it hard to sleep at night. Her parents worried that the strain of her brother's death caused her bouts of insomnia. But it was not. It was something much more sinister.

What drove the comfort of slumber from young Deanna's mind were the nightly visits.

Visits by a single tiny shadow outside her bedroom window and the low cooing sounds that drifted from beyond the sash. She would lie with her back to the window, her thin body shivering and her eyes screwed tightly shut, until the first rays of dawn chased that awful presence from her midst. For she knew that if she listened to her little voice and turned to look, she would see his pale and bloodless face pressed against the panes. She would see those dark, liquid eyes, glazed and unseeing, burning in at her with some strange light…some unholy motivation torn between the restlessness of the living and the moldering of the dead.

And, the following morning, there would be another toy missing from the cool sheets of Timothy's abandoned crib.

YEA, THOUGH I DRIVE

Surprisingly, the practice of hitchhiking is still prevalent, even after years of well-deserved paranoia and tragic news reports about the perils of trusting strangers who travel the roads with their thumbs stuck in the air. Whenever I see a driver slam on the brakes to pick up someone holding a cardboard destination sign, I want to honk my horn and yell, "Hey, maybe you ought to give it a little thought first. Doesn't this guy look familiar? Jeffery Dahmer's second cousin, maybe?"

This tale of hitchhikers on a stormy Tennessee night takes place on the fictitious stretch of Interstate 53, where a grisly fellow by the name of the Roadside Butcher has been pretty danged busy lately...

THERE was a massacre in progress on I-53.

The interstate system stretched from Atlanta, Georgia, across Tennessee and Kentucky, clear to Cincinnati, Ohio. Until the autumn of that year, it was known mainly for its scenic beauty and the Southern hospitality exhibited at the restaurants and motels that served as overnight havens between the long miles of rural solitude.

Then the killings began.

In three short months, the "Roadside Butcher" had murdered seventeen travelers along Interstate 53, each one varying in degree of brutality and mutilation. Some drivers were found sitting in their cars or eighteen wheelers with their throats neatly slashed from ear to ear. Others were found lying at the side of the road, sliced open from gullet to groin, gutted like a deer at hunting season. And then there were the more grisly of the Butcher's victims...those who had been hacked to death, dismembered, or decapitated. The strange thing about the whole ordeal was that there was no definite pattern. The victims had been hitchhikers and drifters, as well as vacationing travelers and burly truckers who regularly frequented the five hundred mile stretch of southern interstate.

The Highway Patrol was out in full force, as were the FBI, but the increase in law enforcement did not seem to deter the Butcher from performing his fiendish whims. It got so that veteran travelers of the road began to carry pistols and sawed-off shotguns, secretly stashed in glove compartments and sleeper cabs. Most of the truckstops began to sell a rather popular bumper sticker which read "YEA, THOUGH I DRIVE ALONG THE HIGHWAY OF THE SHADOW OF DEATH, I WILL FEAR NO EVIL, FOR I AM THE MEANEST S.O.B. ON I-53!" However, at least a couple of those fearless motorists were found lying across their front seats with their throats cut down to the neckbone or their entrails dangling from the rearview mirror like strands of Christmas garland.

The sudden increase in freeway paranoia did not help Mark Casey's situation any. He had been a drifter for years, possessing a nagging desire for wandering and the freedom of the open road. Before the chaos on I-53, the long hair and beard had not hampered his ability to catch a ride, either from one exit to the next, or straight through to his intended destination. But these days, hitch-hiking was becoming one big pain in the ass. Whenever he hung out at a truckstop or stood at the roadside with his thumb in the air, he felt the eyes of potential rides appraising him negatively and noticing his uncanny resemblance to Charles Manson. Never mind that the wild eyes and swastika carved on the forehead was absent; the motorist would still see all that hair and the baggy field jacket that could easily conceal any number of sharp implements. They would see all that in one fleeting glance, shake their heads "fat chance," and drive on, leaving Mark frustrated, sore-footed, and cold.

If it hadn't been for his sudden pairing with Clifford Lee Gates, Mark was sure he would have ended up walking clear from Florida to Ohio that week in mid-December. Clifford Lee was a lanky boy of eighteen from Cloverfield, Georgia, a farming community that boasted a gas station, a general store, and a whopping census of one hundred and eighty-two citizens. Clifford Lee had high aspirations of becoming a country music singer. His constantly good-natured grin and overabundance of optimism were signs that he actually believed that he would make it big in Nashville, armed only with a beat-up Fender acoustic and his rural charm, despite his obvious lack of money and connections. Mark knew at once, upon meeting him at a greasy spoon called Lou's Place, that he should watch out for this wide-eyed innocent. The boy would be easy pickings with a psychopath like the Butcher on the loose.

Anyway, it was Clifford Lee's infectious charm that netted them a ride north with an overweight copier salesman by the name of A.J. Rudman. Rudman was returning home to Louisville from a Xerox convention held in Daytona Beach the previous week. They had overheard him talking to the truckstop waitress and, when he was paying his check at the register, Clifford Lee approached him with a big ole' country-bumpkin grin. The middle-aged salesman was apprehensive at first, eyeing the young man's bearded friend with immediate suspicion. But soon, the boy's benevolence won over the man's worries and he told them he would give them a lift that stormy winter night.

The long drive started out in silence, a silence born of tension and uneasiness. Mark sat in the front, while Clifford Lee took the backseat, upon Rudman's insistence. Obviously, the Kentucky salesman wanted the more suspicious of the two where he could keep an eye on him.

Mark suffered the blatant mistrust quietly, just thankful that he and the Georgia farmboy were inside a warm, dry car and not humping the dark countryside in the pouring rain.

By the time they crossed the Tennessee state line, the mood had lightened somewhat. Idle conversation had echoed between the three and Clifford had even picked some country tunes on his guitar. The hillbilly twang in Gates' voice grated on Mark's nerves, but he settled into the Lincoln's plush velour seat and tried to enjoy it anyway. A.J. Rudman seemed to be having digestive problems. He drove with one hand on the wheel and the other tucked into the mid-section of his tan raincoat over his prominent beer belly. *Probably has a bad peptic ulcer,* thought Mark, not without a flare of mean-spirited satisfaction. *I guess that's what you get when you're a part of the corporate rat race these days, right, Pops?*

"Where are you boys bound for?" Rudman asked out of pure boredom. His nervousness seemed to be gradually increasing for some reason. He was popping Rolaids like they were jelly beans.

"Well, I'm heading for Dayton," Mark replied, trying to inject a friendly tone in hopes of dispelling the man's distrust in him. "I'm going home to my parents' place for Christmas. Mom always has a big spread laid out: turkey, candied yams, the works."

"How about you, son?" the salesman asked over his shoulder.

Clifford Lee had been softly singing a medley of Dwight Yoakam songs. He looked up and grinned sheepishly. "I'm off to Nashville, Tennessee, to be a big country star. I grew up on country and western music. Me and my pa, we'd listen to the Grand Ole Opry every Saturday night. I got to singing and picking on the guitar here and the folks said 'Why, you're as good as any of 'em, Clifford Lee! You oughta head on up to Music City and try your luck.' So that's what I aim to do."

During the farmboy's longwinded explanation, Mark noticed his hand squeeze past the guitar strings and disappear into the hole of the Fender's hourglass body. He grinned. Surely Clifford Lee didn't have a secret stash hidden inside his guitar. Mark had been around enough potheads to know a few who hid their grass in strange places, including musical instruments. But, no, Clifford Lee Gates was no more a smoker of marijuana than Jesse Jackson was the Imperial Wizard of the Ku Klux Klan.

Still, the thought of a good smoke, straight or otherwise, brought out that craving for nicotine in Mark Casey. Since Rudman seemed to be a smoker himself, Mark absently reached into an inside pocket of his olive drab coat for a pack of Marlboros, figuring the guy wouldn't mind if he indulged. Suddenly, the big Lincoln Continental was whipping back and forth across the double lanes of the northbound stretch of I-53, shooting onto the paved shoulder on the far side and braking to such a sharp and screeching halt that the bearded hitchhiker would have butted his head against the windshield if his seatbelt hadn't been buckled.

A breathless silence hung within the car for a long moment. The pattering of steady rainfall on the roof was the only sound to be heard. Then Mark turned and regarded the pale-faced businessman. "What the hell did you do that for?" he yelled. "Are you trying to kill us or something?"

A.J. Rudman swallowed dryly, his right hand still pressed against his gastric woes. "What were *you* doing?" he croaked back. "What were you reaching for...inside your coat?"

"My smokes, man, that's all!" Mark pulled the cigarettes from his pocket and slammed them down on the dashboard. He stared at the businessman incredulously. "You thought I was going for a knife, didn't you? You thought that I was the freaking Roadside Butcher! That I was gonna pull a big knife outta my coat and carve your sonofabitching head clean off. That's exactly what you thought, wasn't it?" He snorted and shook his head in disgust. "Well, I ain't the damned Butcher...you got that? I may look like some drug-crazed devil worshiper to you, but I'm just a regular guy trying to get from point A to B and, believe it or not, I'm just as jumpy as you are where that butchering crazy is concerned."

"Well, I thought..." began Rudman in embarrassment. "It's just that you reached into your pocket without any warning and..."

"Yeah...yeah, I know, man. Just a big misunderstanding. Why don't you just loosen up and put us back on the road again, okay?"

The salesman nodded. He was about to shift back into drive, when Clifford Lee chuckled from the backseat. "Shucks, Mr. Rudman, ol' Mark ain't the killer. Shoot fire, he's one of the nicest fellas I've ever met," he said with a grin. "Heck, naw, he ain't the Roadside Butcher. But, you want to know something kinda funny? I *am!*" And, with that, the farmboy reached around the padded headrest and laid a pearl-handled straight razor against A.J. Rudman's flabby throat.

"What are you doing, man?" Mark asked. He looked at the goofy Georgian with the cowlicked crop of reddish blond hair and the slightly bucked teeth. Suddenly, as he stared into that freckled face, he realized that what he had initially interpreted as down-home naiveté had actually been a dark, underlying madness all along.

"What do you think I'm a-doing?" giggled Clifford Lee. The honed edge of the shaving razor glinted sinisterly in the pale glow of the dashboard light. "I'm fixing to kill this nice gentleman. Now, don't go looking so danged surprised, Mark. And don't worry...I ain't gonna hurt you none. You're my friend."

Mark Casey watched in numb disbelief as Clifford Lee made his victim shut off the engine, unbuckle his seat belt and, ever so carefully, climb out into the stormy night. As if in a trance, Mark left the car also, walking around the rear bumper to watch the inevitable bloodletting. Clifford had Rudman's head pulled back by the hair, the straight razor positioned at a deadly angle above the man's carotid artery.

"But *why*, man?" asked Mark, his stomach sinking at the dread of having to stand there and watch a crimson gorge open beneath Rudman's double chin. "Why are you doing this?"

Clifford Lee Gates gave his roadmate a toothy grin and shrugged. "Why not?"

Then something very strange happened. Something that neither Mark nor Clifford anticipated. A.J. Rudman still had his hand tucked inside his raincoat. It had been there all during the tedious transition from dry car to wet pavement. Mark had just figured the poor guy's ulcer was about to explode. But he saw now that hadn't been the case.

Rudman slowly withdrew his hand and—clutched in his pudgy fingers—was the biggest damned Bowie knife that Mark Casey had ever seen in his life.

He didn't know exactly why he did it, but he yelled "Look out, Clifford!" The razor-wielding musician leaped back just as Rudman turned and slashed in a broad arc that would have taken out most of the boy's abdomen if he had been standing in the same spot. The twelve-inch blade sliced through the cold misty air with a loud *swoosh*.

Rudman laughed. "The Butcher, like hell! You're nothing but a damned copycat... and not a very good one at that. Oh, slitting throats is just fine and dandy, but it shows a great lack of creativity." The middle-aged salesman passed the heavy knife teasingly from one hand

47

to the other. "Come on, farmboy, let me show you how I express myself."

Mark could only stand and watch as the two men squared off in the twin beams of the Lincoln's headlights. The guitar-picker stood poised and ready, the joint of the razor's blade and handle gripped between thumb and forefinger. The salesman crouched in a classic fighter's stance, the big Bowie held, long and perfectly balanced, in one chubby hand. Like a couple of duelists, they circled one another, appraising strengths and weaknesses, then came together in a violent fury of flashing steel and spurting blood.

Mark knew he should have run for his life, but he was transfixed. Grunts of pain and the ripping of clothing and flesh echoed across the empty lanes of Interstate 53. The frightened hitchhiker witnessed the awful blood feud, torn between revulsion and fascination. He rooted for neither man, although one had been a newfound friend until only a few moments ago.

The fight ended abruptly when the two men struggled to the pavement and rolled toward the front of the car, away from Mark's view. A torturous scream split the air, followed by a wet gurgle. For a moment, the headlights revealed only the glistening pavement ahead and the driving rainfall. Then a single form stood up.

"I won," grinned Clifford Lee.

Mark backed away as the young man started around the car for him. Clifford's denim jacket was in bloody tatters, his face criss-crossed with deep gashes. He had traded his razor in for the broad-bladed Bowie. "You know when I said I wouldn't hurt you, Mark?" asked Clifford Lee, brushing aside of flap of loose skin that hung above his left eye. "Well, hell, I lied. I'm sorry, buddy, but I'm gonna have to kill you, too. Can't leave no loose ends, you know. Hope you understand."

But Mark didn't understand. He leaped off the road and into the darkness. With a maniacal cackle, Clifford Lee was in hot pursuit. Unfortunately, there was no solid ground beyond the glow of the car's high beams, only a steep drop-off into a wooded hollow below. The two tumbled head over heels, landing at the bottom of the grassy incline. Mark was the first one up and that was to his advantage. Clifford Lee was groggy from bashing his head against a rock on the way down. He crawled toward his lost blade, but didn't quite make it. Mark reached the big knife first and, without a second's hesitation, drove it between his traveling buddy's heaving shoulder blades.

"What'd you do that for?" croaked Clifford Lee, blood spraying from his mouth and nostrils. "I thought we were pals."

"I thought so, too," replied Mark. "God help me, I really did." He withdrew the knife and buried it to the hilt one more time, just to be on the safe side.

Moments later, Mark was climbing back up the grassy face of the hollow for the interstate. His wild high of exhilaration and relief faded into confusion when he reached the lip of the thoroughfare. A dark form crouched beside the bloody body of A.J. Rudman, then stood and shucked a revolver from a side holster when he saw Mark stumble out of the darkness.

"Killed him..." Mark managed, trying to explain, pointing back into the hollow. "I killed him...stabbed him..."

The state trooper lifted his .357 magnum in a two-handed hold. "You just stop right there," he barked. "Drop it and don't move a muscle."

Mark couldn't understand why the lawman refused to listen. "The Butcher..." he gasped. "Dead...I killed the..."

"I said, *drop the knife!* This is my last warning!"

"But you don't understand..." Mark sputtered. He lifted his hands to reason with the man and there it was, the Bowie knife, completely forgotten until it flashed electric blue in the patrol car's cascading lights.

Three shots rang out. Three hollowpoint slugs obliterated the top of Mark Casey's skull and sent his body sprawling across the white borderline of the median. Clumps of brain and splinters of skull littered the dark pavement, but they were soon washed away as the black rains of the storm soaked Interstate 53 and scrubbed it clean.

Officer Hal Olsen holstered his revolver and walked back to the patrol car. He sat down heavily and picked up the mike of his radio. "Unit H-108 to headquarters. Send me additional back-up, will you? I've got one hell of a mess out here on I-53, two miles north of the Monteagle exit. I've just shot the Roadside Butcher, but not before he killed two others." When he was assured that help was on its way, the officer replaced the mike and turned his radio off.

He sat and stared at the body lying there in Army fatigue jacket and faded jeans. Shaking his head, he withdrew an object wrapped in canvas from beneath his car seat and walked over to where Mark Casey lay.

"I don't know who you were, fella, but you just got me off the hook."

Officer Olsen withdrew a long-bladed machete from the wrapping and hefted its comforting weight in his hand one last time, before tossing it as far as he could into the wet darkness of the backwoods hollow. Then he returned to the car and waited for his fellow officers to arrive.

THE WEB OF LA SANGUINAIRE

Spiders are another type of critter I'm not particularly fond of. The South is crawling with them. Black widows, brown recluses—we call them "fiddlebacks"—and we even have an aggressive "jumping" spider that will literally chase you.

I hear tell there is a nasty breed of spider that frequents the dark swamps of Louisiana...one that the Cajun folk speak of in hushed and fearful tones. An eight-legged monstrosity known as "La Sanguinaire."

L AROUSSE would not take him there at first. "It not safe to travel de swamp at night," the old Cajun warned in his heavy French accent.

But Douglas Scott Price was accustomed to having his own way. An extra hundred dollars laid across the old man's leathery palm soon changed his tune.

The last rays of daylight played through the Spanish moss hanging from ancient cypress trees when the two climbed into Henri Larousse's pirogue, a canoe-like boat used by many of the trappers and fishermen in the area.

"What's that for?" Price asked his guide when a double-barreled shotgun was laid across the center seat.

The elderly man shrugged. "De gators, dey would rather eat than sleep. Where we are going, dey be plenty of dem."

They began their long journey into the Louisiana bayou in silence. Price sat at the bow of the boat as Larousse rowed. Deeper into the swamp they drifted and deeper did the shadows gather, until the Coleman lantern next to the scattergun had to be lit. It cast an orange glow upon the two men. The lack of conversation was awkward, but they really had nothing to talk about. The only link between them was purely monetary.

A loon screamed off in the darkness, causing the young man to jump. The elder man chuckled softly and continued to row with slow, even strokes.

"So, what is it you do for a living?" the Cajun asked. Without conscious thought, he maneuvered the dugout across the dark waters, missing exposed roots and sandbars by mere inches.

"Oh, nothing really," Price replied with an air of pomposity. "I was born into old family money. Ever heard of the New England Prices? No? Well, I expected as much. Being independently wealthy tends to mean a lot of free time, but I manage to keep myself busy."

Larousse had a good idea what sort of luxuries occupied Doug Price's time. Ferraris, eighty-foot yachts, and million-dollar thoroughbreds; a wet bar always at hand and a beautiful woman waiting at every point of the compass. Larousse knew his mind as well as he knew his own. Men of wealth and influence...you could almost smell the good fortune exude from them like the odor of some cheap cologne. The Cajun had been born in backwater poverty and had lived that meager life for nearly eighty years. He could sense a rich man a mile away, like a bluetick hound catching the scent of swamp coon upon a midnight breeze.

Seeing Larousse's amused eyes in the glow of the lamp, the young man continued. "Despite what you think, old man, I do not spend every waking hour jet-setting with a buxom blonde on my knee and a martini in my hand. No, actually my interests are quite respectable. My passion has always leaned toward the biological sciences, most particularly zoology. I've contributed millions to various zoological societies; the Smithsonian, the Audubon, the Sierra. I've also devoted much of my time. I've traveled the world over collecting rare species of bird, mammal, and insect life, both for public exhibition and for my own private collection."

"And so dat be de reason we are here, rowing through the bayou at such an ungodly hour?" asked the guide. "To collect something or other?"

"Yes," said Price, a little peeved. "But don't complain. You're being well paid for this little foray. In an hour or so, you'll be back at your humble swamp shanty, stuffing that three hundred inside your mattress. And I'll leave this godforsaken place with what I came here to find."

"And that would be de creature you mentioned before?"

"That's correct," said Price. "A rare species of the order *Araneae*. The pronunciation of its Latin nomenclature would likely be way over your head, old man, so I won't even bother. Needless to say, the common name of the arachnid is the striped swamp spider. It has a pale underbelly, the upper shell pitch black with broad streaks of crimson on the hind section. I do hope this isn't a wild goose chase you're taking me on. You are sure that you've seen such a spider in these parts?"

Larousse nodded. "*Oui,* a very large and ugly thing. But only at night...never in de light of day."

"Yes, they are nocturnal in nature," agreed the collector. "And they are rather large; the size of a man's fist, or so I've heard. That is why I came prepared." He patted a ten-gallon aquarium at his feet.

The darkness grew thicker, the night sounds more varied, more mysterious to one unaccustomed to the swamps. They rounded a sharp bend between two water-logged stands of old cypress and came upon a tangle of heavy cobwebs, stretching from one side of the channel to the other. Price directed the beam of a flashlight upon the vast webs, the glow etching each silver strand upon the darkness beyond. Fat-bodied spiders the size of golf balls scuttled away from the silken centers, away from the probing light.

"Hoo-boy!" exclaimed the Cajun. He watched the long-legged things climb swiftly upward into the obscurity of the dark limbs above. "Dere be you some spiders, Mr. Price. Plenty o' them. Oughta take a bucketful back with you."

The young man seemed disinterested. "Common water spiders." He tore away the fragile network of webs with a swing of his arm and they continued on. "They've been an item of my arachnid collection for years. It is the swamp spider I'm looking for now."

They moved on into the bayou, into far reaches where the boldest of poachers dared not come, even in broad daylight. The roar of a bull gator rumbled to their left, but it was too far away to present any immediate danger.

"De thing you seek...de swamp spider...it has an interesting history, it do," Larousse said. The glow of the kerosene lamp highlighted every little wrinkle, every line and liverspot on his aged face. "Some of de Cajun people, dey still believe in de old ways, de magic and de beliefs of dere ancestors. When de French first settled de bayou, dey believed in such things. De spider of which you search, dey called it *La Sanguinaire*, 'The Bloodthirsty,' for it was said to be big enough to catch and devour prey larger than other insects. Birds, rabbits, dere was even a case of one trapping a wild boar in its awesome web. Some, dey say, dat even a man fall prey every now and again, and de Sanguinaire would crawl down out of de trees and drain him of his blood. Many thought, and still do, dat dey are de souls of de damned left upon earth as punishment, left as things repulsive to be loathed by man. Some think dat dey possess magical powers...dat if a man be bitten upon de crown of de head by a Sanguinaire, he is subject to dere very wishes for de remainder of his life...to watch over dem, to protect, to provide food, if it be necessary."

Douglas Price laughed out loud at the old man's story. "And do you, old timer..." he asked with a grin, "believe these stories of the Sanguinaire?"

"I do not so much believe or disbelieve, as I respect dem. Dere be many things, Mr. Price, that are unknown to us...many strange and awful things. If you are to travel in strange lands and deal with strange people, you would do well to learn to respect local customs and not scoff so easily."

"Enough of this mumbo jumbo," said Price. "Back to the business at hand." He flashed his light upon the routed trunks of the cypress, along the heavy thicket that grew dense on the mossy banks. The wide swath of light swept the shallow bank to the right, then settled there. Movement came from the shadows between a clump of gnarled, exposed roots. "Take me over there...quickly, man, before they get away!"

Larousse steered the pirogue to the far bank as his passenger prepared the glass tank. Price slipped on a pair of heavy, rawhide gloves and, when they reached the tangle of roots, handed the flashlight to the old man. "Shine the light on that opening there," he indicated. The old man nodded sourly, thinking the whole situation was somewhat ridiculous. All this fuss for a stupid spider! But he remembered the trio of hundred dollar bills tucked in the pocket of his goosedown vest and did as he was told.

The pale light revealed an entire nest of the spiders, great and bulky, glistening black with streaks the color of freshly-let blood crossing their hindquarters. They tried to escape into the webbed tunnels they had con-structed beneath the shelter of the cypress roots, but Price quickly dispatched two of the larger ones, placing their writhing bodies into the aquarium and clamping on the screened lid.

"Good Lord!" breathed the young man, his face livid with excitement. "Will you look at the size of these things? They're three times larger than the common tarantula." The two swamp spiders clawed at the glass walls, fairly the size of full-grown tree squirrels.

The Cajun laughed, his broad grin showing off raw gums and a few tobacco-stained teeth. "Aw, I have seen much larger than those," he said, handing the flashlight back to its owner.

Price stared at the old gentleman, unable to determine whether the swamper was serious or just pulling his leg. He studied the two monstrous specimens in the glow of the Coleman, then glanced at his Rolex. It was a quarter after nine. "You get us back to town by midnight, oldtimer, and I'll up your fee by another two hundred. Fair enough?"

Larousse nodded, his eyes hidden in the shadow of his oily fishing cap. "*Oui,* Monsieur Price. That would be most generous." He began to guide the low boat back into the channel from which they came.

For hours they traveled the labyrinth of channels that made up the stillwater bayou. For some reason the night sounds that had seemed so prominent before were now oddly absent. Price was aware of this, as well as the unfamiliarity of the swamp they now cruised, a swamp more densely overgrown than the one they had set into earlier in the evening. He wanted to mention the fact openly several times, but the elderly guide seemed so confident in his navigation that Price had let it go. *Probably just a shortcut back to the settlement,* he concluded. *For an extra two hundred, I bet the old geezer could find a shortcut clear to the gulf from here.*

Once, a curious gator crossed the dark waters and slammed his blunt snout against the side of the pirogue. The impact caused the lantern to topple off the center seat and over the side with a splash. When Price asked him why he hadn't fished it out, Larousse only smiled. "I can afford to lose a lantern. I have lost many to de swamp. But I can't afford to lose an arm. Look."

Price understood when he directed his flash upon the channel and saw half a dozen hungry gators floating like logs to either side of the boat.

They moved onward down the winding channel. The young collector was gradually aware that the darkness around them had thickened. The full moon that had hung overhead was gone, obscured by overlapping branches, heavy mats of gray moss, and something else.

He directed his beam ahead of them. A velvet wall of light mist choked the inlet a few yards ahead. "Looks as though a fog has rolled in," he said, gathering his jacket closer around him.

"*Oui,*" replied the Cajun. "De fog…it gets as thick as gumbo in de bayou. So thick, in fact, that you can reach out and grab a fistful of it, if you so wish." His passenger shook his head at the old man's tale. "Really, *monsieur.* Go ahead and give it a try."

They were upon a wall of white mist now and, just to show the old man how idiotic his idea was, Price thrust his hand over the bow. His smug expression melted into confusion as his hand sank into something unsolid, yet of definite substance. It was sticky and clinging and, when he attempted to pull his hand away, he found that he could not.

"Something has a hold of me, old man," he gasped. He batted at the adhesive strands with the aluminum flashlight, but it too became entangled. It dangled in the silky wall, despite its weight. "Help me, Larousse. Dammit, man, get me out of this confounded mess!"

Then he felt the distinct sensation of the boat sliding out from underneath him and realized that it actually was. With a curse, he lost his balance as he attempted to stand up and his entire weight lurched backward into the wall of unyielding mist. He was overcome with sudden terror when he realized that his body was now suspended over the dark water. He craned his head around and saw Larousse rowing the pirogue away from him, maneuvering to head back the way they had come.

"Where the hell are you going, old man?" Douglas Price screamed, his anger quickly passing into blind panic. "Come back here this instant! I'm paying you good money, do you hear me?" He struggled wildly against the gummy strands, trying to pull away. But he only managed to entangle himself more firmly amid the great web.

He watched as Henri Larousse began to row back up the channel. The flashlight bobbed crazily in its suspension, throwing light upon the retreating boat. Larousse totally ignored Price's pleas for help. He didn't even turn around. He absently removed his cap to scratch his balding head.

The shimmering glow of the battery-generated light revealed two deep indentations on the back of the old man's skull. Two ugly marks that seemed to sink clear past the bone to the brain, yet that had healed over many years ago.

Douglas Scott Price screamed loudly and fought furiously with the spiral of viscid silk that imprisoned him. But, of course, there was no escape. As the darkness swallowed the old Cajun and his boat, Price was keenly aware of movement in the trees above. When he finally saw the things creeping down the web toward him, as big as pit-bull terriers, his mind snapped and he began to shriek madly.

"*Bon Appetite,*" called old Larousse from out of the night.

But the young man was beyond hearing him. Only the *Sanguinaire* acknowledged his well wishes, before they resumed their feeding.

THE CISTERN

Every small town or rural community has some particular point of interest that is native to that region. It may be a natural landmark or a man-made dwelling, like a home or church. Many are based in solid history and tradition, while some have grown murky and mysterious with the passage of time. In the town of Liberty, Tennessee, not far from where I live, there is a painting of a mule fifty or sixty feet up on the face of a stone cliff. No one recalls who put it there or why. And when it grows faded, it somehow becomes magically repainted. No one knows who is responsible for that act, either.

The good folks of Jackson Ridge weren't sure how the stone cap of the old cistern came to be. But, as they were to find out, it was not only a local landmark, but a barrier that separated good from evil...

SURPRISINGLY enough, it was the same as he last remembered.

Well, *almost* the same. Of course there would have to be changes after twenty years. The old Ridgeland Theatre had been replaced with a new grocery store and the solemn gray-stoned front of the Cambridge County Trust & Loan now sported a thoroughly modern automatic teller. But everything else was there, unchanged and constant. It matched the vivid memories of his boyhood like a photograph that had somehow remained true in the passage of time, retaining its brilliance instead of fading to a disappointing drabness like he had dreaded it would.

Jackson Ridge, Tennessee had been Jud Simmons' hometown from birth until age twenty-one. He had spent a happy childhood in its peaceful, picturesque setting. But, like many had before, Jud left its comfortable niche of tranquility and had plunged headlong into the urban rat-race and a vicious cycle of stress, anxiety, and potential coronaries. In fact, Jud hadn't even thought of stopping in Tennessee on his way back from a business conference in Atlanta. He had been cruising down the interstate when the sign had loomed before him. NEXT EXIT—JACKSON RIDGE. Nostalgia had gripped him unexpectedly and he had turned off the exit, driving down the two-lane rural road, across the old bridge, until he was finally there.

Jud cruised slowly past Chapman's Feed CO-OP and the low brick building of Jackson Ridge Elementary, marveling at the sameness of it all. He drove along the shop-lined street until he reached the grassy expanse of town square with its ancient oaks, two-story courthouse, and tarnished bronze statue of the Reverend Caleb Jackson, the Lutheran minister who had founded the town in the early 1700s.

The main thoroughfare was unusually quiet, even for a small town, but the sidewalks were lined with cars as far as the eye could see. Jud was lucky to find an empty parking space directly in front of the courthouse.

As he cut his engine, he sat wondering if *it* was still there: the one point of interest he was most anxious to see again. But of course it was. It had always been there and always would be.

He left his Lexus and walked to the eastern end of the grassy courtyard, enjoying the crispness of the autumn afternoon. He approached a wide slab of smooth stone and mortar that lay beneath a state historical marker. The old cistern...there as it had been since the founding of Jackson Ridge in 1733. It had been no more than a simple underground reservoir that had collected rainwater for the few residents when the little town was no more than a trading post for those settlers brave enough to venture into the wilderness south of Virginia.

Jud walked around the vast slab of stone. The cistern...a source of legend and fantasy for young and old alike, a thing of mystery. SEALED IN THE YEAR OF OUR LORD—1765 was chiseled into the great, flat lid that the townfolk had, for some unknown reason, secured over the pit of the well long ago. Everyone had their favorite stories for exactly why the cistern had been sealed. Some said it had been covered when a typhoid epidemic poisoned the town's water supply, while others claimed that bodies were buried there: the remains of a French trapper and his nine Indian wives, violators of the Reverend Jackson's strict moral code. Almost every kid in town was sure that buried treasure had been stashed there—precious jewels and golden doubloons as big around as the face of Grandpa's pocket watch.

As Jud finish reading the historical marker and looked down at the gray expanse of ancient stone, he was shocked to find that, during his long absence, a long fissure had split the heavy lid. The crack was a good two feet across, musky darkness gaping from the depths within. He felt a sinking disappointment grip his heart as he crouched to examine it better. "Now what the hell happened here?" he muttered.

"Joe Bob Tucker got drunk the summer before last," came a child's voice from behind him. "Ran his four-wheel-drive up onto the grass and hit the thing a good lick. They tossed him in the county jail for a whole month just for putting that crack down the middle...I guess because it was a historical thing and all."

Jud turned and regarded the boy. He must have been around nine or ten, a short fellow in faded overalls, a striped T-shirt, and worn sneakers. He was a cute kid, all freckles and bright red hair. From the drabness and ill-fit of his clothing, Jud figured the boy must belong to one of the poor families who had always lived on Esterbrook Road, another unchanging constant in the little hamlet of Jackson Ridge.

"Joe Bob Tucker, did you say?" grinned Jud in fond remembrance. "I went to school with a Joe Bob Tucker... kind of lanky fella with buckteeth and a scar across the bridge of his nose?"

The boy nodded. "Yep, that's him all right." He studied the stranger with interest. "So you were from around here once, mister?"

Jud walked over and extended his hand. "Yeah, a long time ago. My name is Jud Simmons. I live in Chicago now. And what is your name?"

The boy took his hand proudly, delighted to be shaking with a real grownup. "Name's Calvin...but everyone just calls me Chigger."

Jud laughed good naturedly. "Well, it's mighty nice meeting you, Chigger."

The youngster beamed. "Same here."

The businessman cast his eyes along the street he had just traveled. "You know, I don't believe I've seen a single person since I drove into town. Where is everybody?"

"They're all down at the fairgrounds, mister." Chigger pointed to a colorful poster in a storefront window that proclaimed CAMBRIDGE COUNTY FAIR, SEPT. 8th-12th.

For the first time since his arrival, Jud heard sounds drifting over the wooded rise beyond the courthouse. The peppy notes of a circus calliope, the thunder, rattle, and roar of the rollercoaster, the steady hum of voices and loud pitches of the barkers on the midway.

"So how come you're not over there joining in the festivities?"

Chigger's smile faded. He stared down at his scuffed sneakers in shame. "On account I ain't got no money."

Jud frowned. "Not even enough for the fair?"

"I ain't got *nothing*! Papa says he can't afford to give me an allowance like the other kids, so I can't go." Then with a sudden burst of enthusiasm, he raised his eyes hopefully.

"That is, unless *you* treat me!"

Jud couldn't help but grin. "Well, I wasn't planning on staying long..."

Chigger was suddenly tugging at his hand. "Come on, mister...*please?* We'll have a real good time. There's all kinds of neat things going on down there. Mayor Templeton is judging the pie-baking contest, there's gonna be a tractor-pull, and after dark the Fire Department is having a big fireworks show. Come on, will you, mister? Please?"

Jud knew there was no need in arguing. "Sure, Chigger, let's do that fair up right!"

He took the boy's small hand and, together, they climbed the rise that overlooked the fairground. They were greeted by the sights, sounds, and smells of a genuine country fair. Swapping boyish grins of anticipation, man and child descended into the swirling activity of break-neck carnival rides and colorful sideshow tents.

As afternoon passed into evening and the evening into night, Jud and Chigger had the time of their lives. They rode all the hair-raising rides, played all the midway games, and gorged themselves on junk food. But, as the sun went down, Jud began to feel a little uneasy despite the excitement of the festivities. It was the people

RONALD KELLY

who milled around them that conjured the sensation that something was basically wrong. He found himself noticing their faces. Instead of the cheerfulness and joviality that should have been there, he witnessed only tension and underlying fear. But why? He could not understand why they would feel such a way in such a festive place. He recognized a few folks from his distant past and tried talking to them, but they merely nodded and moved on or did not acknowledge him at all.

And there were other things, like the vendor at the concession stand. Jud had been in the process of buying himself and Chigger a foot-long hotdog and an orange soda, when he glanced up and saw—or *thought* he saw—the vendor's face change slightly. One moment the man appeared normal enough, pudgy and middle-aged, and then the next his features seemed to be creased by some horrid torment, the flesh seared and blistered as if by some great heat. Then, abruptly, the puzzling sight shifted back into reality, returning the man to his former appearance.

"What's the matter, mister?" Chigger asked.

"Nothing," Jud told him. "Nothing at all." But there had been something and, from Chigger's sly grin, he gathered that the boy was somehow privy to it also.

They continued on down the bustling midway, Jud's suspicions growing stronger as everyone began to prepare for the big fireworks display. His apprehension came to a head when Chigger wandered from him for a moment to watch a parade of cavorting clowns, some riding unicycles, while others sprayed the crowd with seltzer bottles. Jud was standing beside a tent, when a woman's hand took his arm and drew him into the privacy of the fortune teller's booth. The gypsy who confronted him stared at him with the same expression of anxiety. "You must leave this place now," she warned gravely. "While you still have the opportunity to do so."

"But why?" asked Jud. Instead of being irritated at her rudeness, he regarded her with an interest born of creeping dread. "What could there possibly be here that could cause me harm?"

The fortune teller's fearful eyes stared out the open doorway. "The boy...the one called Chigger. Believe me, he is not what he appears to be."

"You're insane!" said Jud. "He's just a little kid." He turned and glanced absently out at the midway.

The dancing clowns were gone. In their place was a procession of naked humanity, writhing and wailing as they ran a gauntlet of hot coals and broken glass.

Jud turned back to the gypsy, his eyes questioning, then again looked outside. The clowns were back, walking on their hands, bombarding passersby with cream pies.

"I do not have time to explain," said the woman, pushing him toward the rear of the tent. "Just go. Get back to town as fast as you can, get in your car, and drive as far from this place as possible. And never return."

Jud was about to protest, when Chigger's voice came from out on the midway. "Mister? Mister, where'd you go?"

Jud almost answered, but caught himself before he could make that fatal mistake.

There was something peculiar about that youthful voice, some dark intent hidden beneath the innocence and boyish charm. And, for one fleeting second, Chigger's small form flickered like the waves of a desert mirage, giving a subliminal hint of some awful presence in his place. Something ominous and beyond human comprehension.

"Quickly, through the back way. You haven't got much time!"

Without hesitation, Jud took the fortune teller's advice, ducking through a flap in the canvas wall and making his way swiftly along the back lot of the carnival grounds. He ignored little Chigger's inquisitive calls and made it to the wooded rise undiscovered. His heart pounding, Jud topped the knoll just as the first of the fireworks shot skyward, filling the starry night with bursts of heavenly brilliance.

He looked back down at that swirling maelstrom of shows and rides and fun and felt as if he had just been had. *You're nothing but a damned fool, Jud Simmons!* he told himself. *You're just letting your imagination run away with you. There's nothing wrong...not with this place, not with these people, and certainly not with sweet, little Chigger!*

He was just about to go back down and rejoin his little friend, when he happened to glance over his shoulder at the town behind him. Jud's panic flared anew and he leapt down the steep rise, running toward the collection of quaint buildings that he had lived among so many years before.

In the eerie light of the skyward explosions, Jud witnessed what truly existed before him. The town of Jackson Ridge was in shambles. The picturesque storefronts were now dilapidated and decayed, their windows hanging in jagged shards. The paved streets were littered with debris and fissured with deep cracks. What few vehicles stood on the street were no more than rusted hulls, while the grass of the square was scorched an ugly brownish-black.

Jud felt as if he might pass out. *This can't be for real,* he thought, although he knew it was. Then he heard a voice call out from behind him, from the top of the wooded rise. It was the voice of little Chigger...but, then again, it was also the rumbling voice of something that could not possibly possess the soul of an innocent, nine-year-old boy.

"Hey, mister!" it thundered, the tone hitting highs and lows virtually impossible for the human voice to manage. "Where do you think you're going? Come back, will ya? Do you hear me? I said...COME BACK!"

Jud Simmons almost turned around and, if he had, would have surely been lost right then and there. He stood stone still for an endless moment, acutely aware of something coming down the rise toward him. Something very *big*, something very *evil*. A fetid heat prickled the nape of his neck and the sulfurous stench of brimstone and burnt flesh assaulted his nostrils. Jud knew that if he turned to face the thing, its appearance, perhaps even its very presence, would surely drive him insane. Resisting the overwhelming urge to commit mental suicide, Jud began to run as fast as possible up the cluttered avenue of Main Street for the town square and his car.

A hoarse roar shook the air around him, nearly shattering his eardrums. "WHERE ARE YOU GOING, MISTER? DON'T YOU WANNA GO BACK TO THE FAIR? EVERYONE'S WAITING FOR YOU...CAN'T YOU HEAR THEM?"

Yes, he could hear the sounds coming from over the rise, but it was no longer the toot of the calliope or the excited voices of the crowd. The awful screams of tormented souls drilled through the night air, enhanced by the crackling flames and explosive dishevel of wholesale Armageddon. It was the sound of an agonizing hell on earth.

As he ran past the battered shops and stores, a strange thing happened. The town began to *shift*. Brief flashes of normality replaced the devastation. Ben Flanders was giving Charlie Walsh a haircut in the big window of the barber shop, the elderly Stokes brothers were playing checkers outside the hardware store, and a teenager in a Future Farmers jacket was selling *Grit* papers in front of the post office. Then, just as swiftly as it had appeared, the deceptive camouflage returned to death and destruction. The clever and well-maintained illusion that had been conjured for the benefit of those outsiders who happened to visit Jackson Ridge from day to day abruptly bled back into grim reality.

Jud cut across the eastern side of the square for his car. *God, oh dear God in heaven, let me make it!* But what if he *did* make it to the Lexus? Would it make any difference?

He now saw the rusted wreck of Joe Bob's 4x4 pickup truck where it hadn't been before, hanging on the lip of the square, its front bumper stuck in the split stone of the cistern. It looked as though the windshield imploded from some terrible force. Jud suddenly knew that his car would be no protection whatsoever from the thing that pursued him.

"COME ON BACK, MISTER! YOU SAID YOU'D TREAT ME TO THE FAIR. YOU PROMISED YOU WOULD!" The horrid voice was strangely infantile, yet as old as time itself. And there was an underlying evil, a gleeful cruelty in every syllable it spoke. Whatever dark realm the demon had originated from, its very presence exuded a foul sense of utter depravity that made Satan's threat seem pale in comparison.

The thing was gaining on him. He could hear its approach, like a thousand pounding feet in hot pursuit, growing ever nearer. *It's going to catch me,* Jud thought wildly. *It's going to grab hold of me and...what? What in heaven's name will it do to me then?*

He could sense the thing's vast bulk as it shifted to his right. It was heading toward the car, trying to cut him off! Jud's legs felt like rubber. He knew he couldn't possibly beat it to the car. Abruptly, a crazy idea crossed his desperate mind and he acted on it. He veered sharply to the left, past the historical marker, and squeezed through the gaping crack in the lid of the cistern.

Cool darkness met him, as well as empty air. He fell for what seemed to be an eternity, before hitting the smooth hardness of the reservoir floor. The breath knocked from his lungs, Jud lay there for a long, silent moment. Even after regaining his senses, he stayed put, staring up at the fissure eight feet overhead. He awaited the inevitable, but it did not come. It appeared as though the demon was somewhat reluctant to enter the place that had entombed it for over two centuries.

Moments passed. Jud sat up, his eyes still glued to that jagged black slit with its sparkling backdrop of firework-filled sky. When the ogre finally appeared, Jud was not at all surprised to see the innocent, freckled-face of the boy staring down at him.

"Come on, mister," begged little Chigger. "Don't be an Indian-giver. You said we were gonna do the fair up

68

right. We can still have loads of fun, you'll see. We'll eat buttered popcorn and those big salty pretzels and we'll see the freak show and we'll ride the Wild Mouse and the Tilt-a-Twirl and..."

Jud listened to the innocent voice for a long time, reeling off the simple pleasures of the county fair. He could even hear the music and the crowd again, could smell the rich fragrance of roasted peanuts and sawdust. He wanted to go back, he truly did, but he knew what awaited him if he dared succumb. The crackle of hellfire would mask the pops of the firing range, the pungency of cooked flesh would overshadow the sticky sweet smell of cotton candy, and his screams would join those of the damned.

PAPA'S EXILE

Alcoholism was rampant in my family at one time. The demon liquor turned kind, good-hearted folks into sadistic, mean-spirited ones. This brought about violence and heartache, even resulting in one uncle killing another in a fit of drunken rage. That is why I've never taken a drink in my life. Not trying to sound judgmental; it was just a personal choice I made to avoid that horrible disease from sinking its thorny claws in me.

This story is short, but certainly not sweet. It deals with an alcoholic and the physical and emotional havoc he wreaks, as well as the way he is "cast out" from the family that he victimizes.

WILL Papa ever come home again?" asks Stephanie, her face staring hopefully from amid the snug safety of her pillows, blankets, and plush stuffed animals.

"No, baby," says Mother. "Never again."

Stephanie begins to ask why, but the dousing of the light curtails that simple question. "Sweet dreams," Mother whispers and leaves her with a kiss.

Thunder rumbles, echoes of a distant storm, as Mother walks the darkened halls of the old house. Her daughter's question brings a thin smile to her lips and she pauses by the parlor window. The persimmon grove crowds against the northern wall. Skeletal sentries stand tall and somber, as if ever watching.

No, never again. Not her dear, half-blind husband. Never again would his drunken voice resound within their peaceful household, eliciting fear and dread, nor would there be the fleshy blows of anger. And his mustachioed face would never glare hatefully across the dinner table, one eye livid, the other emotionless, unreal.

Never again will you rule us, she had told him that night long ago, a night laced with pain and the raw stench of liquor. *Never again will you find comfort before the warmth of the hearth, nor in the folds of our marriage bed. Never again shall you savor the scent of my perfume or relish the softness of my skin.* She had declared all of these things and they had come to pass. After that night, Papa no longer filled the gabled structure with his troublesome presence, no longer darkened the cobbled walk with his weaving, drunken shadow.

The storm comes, forceful and born of vengeance. Dark clouds boil overhead, advancing, engulfing the land with their surly discontent. Beside the house, the grove dances, swaying to and fro, trees animated. Deep in the torrid darkness, something winks in whipcrack flashes of heavenly brilliance. Then, as a violent thunderclap shakes the earth's very foundation, it falls like a lone hailstone, bounces, rolls across the sodden ebony carpet of night.

■■■

The following morning reigns supreme.

72

Young Stephanie skips cheerfully beneath the dripping branches, down the winding center path, through Mother's flower garden and into the grove. She jumps an obstructive puddle, then is teased by an earthward sparkle. Stephanie spies a glistening orb lying at the foot of an ancient tree, hollow and dead from the ravages of time. Picking up the peculiar object, she polishes it against the cloth of her blouse, marveling, a treasure to behold. She stares at it and it stares back. Familiar, yet unreal.

Curiously, the girl regards the old tree, for the trunk's gaping seam has been rent by the angry passing of the storm. As she draws nearer, something within the hollow shifts and falls forward.

Stephanie squeals, but not in delight.

Papa has come home.

THE HATCHLING

Back when I was a kid, dog-fighting was popular in the area where I lived. Before that, cockfighting was the favorite illegal pastime of my Grandpa's generation. I don't hear much about either anymore, but they are still around. Men with money to wager and a hunger for violence never grow weary of such a sport.

I'm sure there are those who participated in such dealings—including the training and competition of pitting one of God's creatures against another—who now regret those bloodthirsty days. The Lord forgives us of our sins, but the Devil isn't so quick to forget.

"Not so fast, hoss," he'll say with a chuckle, then heap the misery of those past actions upon you a hundredfold.

RECKON a couple of things could have brought it about. Maybe it was that new corn feed I bought wholesale down at the co-op or maybe it was simply some unforeseen deformity. Such things happen on the farm occasionally...two-headed calves and the like. But, then again, I always figured there was some strange and sinister intelligence behind the whole ugly business. Something unspeakably evil. Sometimes I wonder if old Lucifer himself hadn't seeded that hen and caused the sudden appearance of that godawful egg.

I've been a farmer here in Crimshaw County since I was fourteen and that was some sixty years ago. I've planted and harvested all types of produce: tobacco, corn, soybeans.

And I've dabbled in livestock, too, but most particularly chickens. Folks from all over the county drive for miles to buy my eggs and poultry. But when I was a younger man my association with chickens was not so innocent. There was a time when I had quite a reputation among the local sportsmen as a first-class breeder of champion fighting cocks. However, I sickened of that blood sport as I grew older and wiser and, much to the relief of my wife Margret, gave it up for honest work.

Anyway, it was a chilly morning in early spring when Margret hollered at me from the chicken coop. "Jake... come out here and take a look at this."

I had been slopping the hogs, so I set my pail aside and crossed the barnyard to the henhouse.

Margret was standing there in the shadowy coop, a half-full basket of white and brown eggs in her hand and a puzzled look on her face. I glanced down at her feet and saw one of our best laying hens stretched out on the earthen floor. I stooped down and picked at it for a while. At first glance, I thought maybe a fox or a weasel had gotten into the coop and laid waste to the poor critter. But, upon further inspection, I saw that it hadn't been eaten at all.

"This is mighty strange," I told the wife. "Almost looks like this hen was split in two...*from the inside out.*"

"No doubt it was," Margret agreed. "Take a look at what it laid here in its nest."

I stood up and regarded the long, laying bins that went three levels high along the back wall. In the nest that the Rock Island red had always occupied there was the damnedest egg I'd ever laid eyes on.

The thing was big, the size of a coconut. And it was as black as sin. It didn't have that flat, slightly granulated texture to it like a regular hen egg. Instead, it was slick as a black pearl. You could see your reflection in its surface, the shell was so shiny.

Well, now, I didn't rightly know what to do. At first I figured I oughta take it to the county agent down at the farm bureau and see what they made of it. But then I got to thinking. They'd just turn it over to some dadblamed scientist who would likely crack it open and study its yolk and, hell, what would that tell them? Besides, I was kind of curious as to what sort of chicken would hatch out of such a strange egg. So I decided to just keep the thing my personal secret for a while.

I went to the tool shed and dug out one of the boys' old incubators that they had used when they were in 4-H club in school. It was a homemade job; just a wooden box with chicken-wire windows and hay in the bottom. I screwed a sixty-watt bulb into the fixture at the top and, after setting that gigantic egg down deep amid the straw, put the whole kit and caboodle at the far corner of the henhouse.

Oh, another thing I oughta mention. None of those hens in that coop would go near that egg. Acted like they were scared of the thing. And I had me a couple of hearty roosters, too, who seemed even more leery of the egg than those hens.

For a week, I checked on the black egg, making sure it didn't get too warm or cold. I fussed over it so, Margret joked that I was so all-fired concerned with the blasted thing, why didn't I take to sitting on it myself. I had me a good laugh at that and said I surely would have but, with the size of the thing, it wouldn't do my hemorrhoids a speck.

A couple of nights later, I was awakened by the most harrowing racket coming from that henhouse. Such a fluttering and squawking it was, that I grabbed my shotgun and a lantern and went out there to check it out. I found the door ajar and figured, well, this time it was a fox or an egg-sucking dog. Stepping inside, I shone that kerosene lamp around. There didn't seem to be any damage done; no dead chickens or broken eggs.

Or so I thought. I walked over to the far corner and uttered a curse in spite of myself. That homemade incubator had been ripped apart. The wood frame was splintered in several places and the chicken-wire in the front had a hole the size of a good-sized cantaloupe torn in it. And, down in the hay within, was the shell of that black egg, cracked and lying in two halves.

I examined that hatched egg and was more confounded than I was to begin with. There was the most awful stench coming from the empty shell, like raw sulfur. And when I stuck my finger to the slimy residue that coated the inside, it burned my skin like battery acid. I had to run out and wash it off under the spigot of the long-handled pump, it blistered me so.

As I walked on back to the house, I had the strongest feeling that something was watching me from the dark woods beyond the barn. I checked the load in my Remington, but that didn't make me feel any safer. With a shiver, I ducked into the house and locked the back door behind me.

I had never, in all my years of living on that farm, locked the doors of my own house. I did that night, however, and I couldn't quite put my finger on why I had done so.

The next morning, over breakfast, Margret asked me about that black egg. I told her that some animal had gotten into the coop the night before and smashed it. I wanted to leave it at that, wanted to forget that it had ever existed...but something out yonder in those woods wouldn't let me.

I didn't think any more about it, until a week later when my redbone hound, String, came up missing. I searched my property high and low and finally found him down by the creek. Poor String was dead. At first I figured he had died of old age, for he was going on fifteen years. But when I got to checking, I found a single wound on his stiffening body...a tiny hole in his right temple, just beneath one floppy ear.

I couldn't rightly believe what I was seeing because, you see, I was familiar with that kind of wound, but not in a dog. If you don't know anything about cock-fighting, let me explain. Just before fighting roosters are thrown into the pit together, the owners attach these tiny, hand-made spurs to their feet. There ain't much to them; just a curved length of steel like a bent nail with leather ties to secure them. The victor of the two cocks is the one who strikes first, driving that metal spur into the side of the other's head. I told you before, it was a bloody sport and that was one of the reasons I took leave of it.

After burying String down in a honeysuckle hollow, I went to the tool shed out of pure curiosity. I went to my workbench where I knew a pair of those rooster spurs hung on the pegboard; sort of souvenirs for old times' sake. Well, you guessed it. Those steel spurs were gone. A cold fear hit me then and I figured maybe it would be wise to keep old String's death from Margret...and especially the disappearance of those spurs.

As it turned out, String wasn't the only victim. Those two roosters I'd bought to look over the hen-house...I found them out back of the smokehouse. They had died the very same way. A single, clean hole through the side of the head. I took my shotgun that afternoon and hunted the woods over...exactly what for, I have no earthly idea. Nevertheless, I found nothing. Not a track, nor a sign of anything.

Spring passed into summer without incident and then things took a turn for the worse. Someone—or *something*—tore the back door off its hinges one night and rummaged through the kitchen drawers. Margret took inventory of the utensils the next morning and swore that the only things missing were a couple of old ice picks she used to chip away freezer ice when she was defrosting the Frigidaire. I didn't grasp the significance of that late night theft until I discovered our finest Holstein milk cow lying in the south pasture a few days later. There was a deep hole in her temple, the wound reaching clean to the center of the brain.

Whatever had killed my cow didn't stop there. Farmers all over this side of the county began to lose cows and hogs in the same gruesome manner. No animal was ever eaten, just smitten upon the head and left lying there. A lot of crazy theories began to circulate. Frank Masters, who owns the farm down the road a piece, claimed that devil worshippers were to blame. I began to figure that, indeed, maybe there *was* something of the devil involved, but I didn't tell any of the fellas down at the grange hall that. I kept my mouth shut and hoped to God that things would die down.

But, of course, they didn't.

■■■

I was cleaning out the hayloft a couple of weeks later, when I came across something that chilled me to the very bone.

It was my pitchfork, the one I had bought at the True Value earlier that year. But something had damaged it, something very strong. Two of the four tines had been snapped off. My mind immediately flashed back to the fighting spurs and the missing ice picks.

That night I took extra precautions before I retired for the night. I checked every door and window in the house, making sure they were securely locked. I even locked our bedroom door and Margret said I was being downright silly for doing so. I wasn't so sure, though. I lay in bed for a long time before sleeping, turning my

suspicions over and over in my mind. *If that thing, whatever the hell it was, had graduated from dogs to cows,
then what did the missing tines off that pitchfork mean?
Did it intend on pursuing larger game now...of the human variety perhaps?* The thought so unsettled me that
I got up and swapped the birdshot in my scattergun for
double-aught buck.

The following morning I awoke and, much to my
surprise, found Margret still in bed. She usually rose an
hour before I did, so as to fix breakfast before we did our
daybreak chores.

I reached over and shook her gently. "Wake up,
dear," I said. "It's five o'clock. We're running a little behind schedule this morning."

She did not answer me, did not even move. When I
pulled my hand back it was covered with blood. With a
cry of horror, I turned poor Margret over and...

The doctor said the wound in her temple had been
made by a very long, very sharp object thrust downward
with inhuman force. "It looks like someone drove a railroad spike through the side of her head with a sledge ham-
mer," he told me after I demanded his honest opinion.

I had been a law-abiding, church-going citizen of
Crimshaw County for many years and so I wasn't suspected. But I still blamed myself for dear Margret's death,
blamed myself for not doing something to prevent such a
thing from happening. I grieved for many days after the
funeral and, so, I wasn't exactly prepared for that horrid
night toward the end of August.

Exactly why I awoke at two o'clock in the morning
was unclear to me. All I know is that I came awake suddenly, my heart pounding, my eyes straining against the
darkness.

I felt a strong presence there in the bedroom with me
and there was that unmistakable scent of sulfur.

"Who's there?" I croaked, but I knew very well what
had come visiting in the dead of night. The foot railing of

the big, brass bed creaked as something of great weight perched there, waiting for the right moment to strike.

It was moonlight that saved me. Moonlight filtered through the lacy material of Margret's hand-sewn curtains and it glinted upon that sixteen-inch spur as it stabbed for my head. I rolled aside, off the bed and onto the floor, as the steel tine ripped deep into the pillow my head had rested upon. I could see it against the light patch of the window then...pitch black and bristling with jagged feathers, its spurred feet clawing that bed to shreds like a grizzly mauling its prey.

I brought up my pump shotgun, jacked a shell into the breech, and squeezed off a shot. The force of the blast knocked that hellish thing off the bed and plumb out the upstairs window. By the time I reached the window, the moon had gone in behind a cloud and I could see nothing but darkness. Hurriedly, I struggled into my overalls and, shotgun and lantern in hand, went downstairs to check it out.

Nothing lay on the dewy grass but shredded curtains and shards of glass. I was beginning to think the awful critter had made its escape, when a noise caught my ears. It had come from the chicken coop.

The walk I took across that dark barnyard that night was the longest one of my life. When I reached the henhouse, I found the door open and heard nervous clucking and rustling inside. I gathered up my nerve, jacked a fresh shell into the scattergun, and, holding the lantern ahead of me, stepped inside. After a few moments, I realized that, except for the regular inhabitants, the coop was empty. Just bins of hay-filled nests bearing frightened chickens. I was turning to leave, when the trap was sprung.

It came through the open door, so tall that its fleshy comb scraped the top of the doorframe. If it had been knee-high, I would have said it was a rooster. But since it was well over six feet tall, I could only describe it as being something horrible and demon-like. It strutted into that henhouse with an arrogance that reeked of pure evil. Its wings and tail feathers were oily black, like that of a crow. In fact, it was pitch black from head to toe; the comb and beard, the scaled feet, even the beak was dark as sable. Only its eyes glowed in contrast, burning like red-hot coals. Its fury was unmistakable, as was its intent.

It came for me as I backed toward the far wall and, this time, its aim was more true. It struck savagely, the long spur piercing the muscle of my left bicep, pinning my arm to the weathered boards of the shed wall. The pain was horrendous. The lantern slipped from my fingers and shattered on the hay-strewn floor. The flames spread quickly and, soon, the henhouse became an inferno.

With a hoarse crowing that signaled its triumph, it reared back with its other talon, intending to pin my skull to the wall. I remembered the shotgun then and, raising it one-handedly, stuck the muzzle into that hellish rooster's belly and pulled the trigger. It lurched backward with the blast and the spur withdrew from my arm, releasing me.

I knew I had to get out fast. Flames lapped at the walls like dry tinder, catching the hay of the nests afire. Soon, the whole damned coop would go up. So I fired again and again, driving the horrid thing back into the far corner with a hail of buckshot. It slumped to the ground, flapping and hollering, but I didn't take any chances. I left the henhouse, bolted the door behind me, and stood a good distance away to watch.

The boards of that old henhouse were bone dry and the structure went up quickly. I could hear the demon bird inside, shrieking, battering against the locked door in desperation. But my buckshot must have weakened it, for the door held firm. I watched as the coop became a bonfire, completely consumed in flame.

I figured that was the end of the evil thing, when the corrugated tin roof exploded skyward. Like a great Phoenix that devil cock rose. Its feathers were ablaze, its crow of agony shrill enough to shatter a man's nerves and drive him to madness.

I raised my shotgun, but did not fire. I watched as the fowl climbed into the dark twilight as if trying to penetrate the very heavens. Then it swung off course, heading over the peak of the barn and toward the open pasture. I ran to the split-rail fence and, before my eyes, it seemed to disintegrate and break apart into a million tiny cinders. They drifted earthward like crimson fireflies, then vanished before hitting ground.

With a flashlight from the truck and my scattergun in hand, I searched the field over that night. I found nothing...nothing but a few scorched feathers.

And, by morning, they too were gone, like ashes upon the wind.

BLACK HARVEST

The rural South is steeped in tradition. Some of those traditions are observed solely within the confines of family gatherings, while others can encompass an entire community.

The tradition of finding the first red ear of the harvest dates back a hundred years or so, before John Deere and the concept of industrial agriculture turned the autumn harvest into something sanitary and impersonal. Back in those days, folks would come from miles around for a square dance and a corn shucking. It was a time of fellowship among friends and neighbors; a time of celebration.

And, every so often, it could also be a time of sacrifice.

WELL, there it is fellas," Elliot Leman said, gesturing toward a waist-high pile of newly harvested corn. "Get it done by midnight and we'll have us a late supper and a barn dance that'll ring long and loud throughout these Tennessee mountains!"

It was an old-fashioned corn shucking just like they'd had back in the olden days. In fact, there hadn't been a decent shucking in Cumberland Valley for nearly fifty years. But Elliot's yield had been so plentiful that year that he figured, what the hell, might as well make a celebration of it for the entire township. The Leman family had done it up right, too, orchestrating the gathering to the most authentic detail. The menfolk wore flannel shirts and denim overalls, while the ladies came in knitted shawls and ankle-length dresses of calico and gingham. Coal oil lanterns hung from the barn rafters, casting a warm glow over the nostalgic proceedings and putting everyone, young and old, into the mood for the hoedown to come.

Elliot stepped aside and the men lit into that pile of dried corn. They sat and peeled the shucks from the hard-kernelled ears, which they then tossed into a sturdy crib constructed of hand-hewn logs. Some of the women joined in, too, to speed the pace, while the rest prepared for the feast that would await at the end of their work.

One of those who took to shucking was Elliot's eldest son, Curtis, a strapping boy of eighteen years. Curtis was a senior at the local high school, a straight-A student and athlete who had hopes of winning a football scholarship and going away to college. He was an intelligent boy, Curtis was, but he had never begrudged his father his eccentric ways of farming: planting by the signs and such as that. No, Curtis enjoyed the ways of simple country living. He cherished the fellowship and warm feelings that abounded in his papa's barn that night as most of the tiny township of Cumberland Valley sat around the corn heap, just shucking and spinning yarns and tall tales, some of the men smoking cob pipes and chewing Red Man tobacco.

Halfway toward the midnight deadline, Curtis yanked the brittle husk off an ear and, much to his surprise, found the kernels along the cob to be a brilliant crimson red.

86

"Well, will ya'll lookee there!" called out their neighbor, Charlie Walker.

Pete, the youngest of the Leman clan, laughed in delight. "Look, Papa…Curtis found himself a red ear."

"Let me take a gander at that, son," Elliot requested. He took the ear in hand and held it in the light of the nearest lantern. He turned it slowly and a big grin split his face. "Why, it surely is…a pure red ear. No spotted pokeberry corn there…it's plumb blood red, through and through."

"You know what that means, don't you, young man?" asked Grandpa Leman with a wink.

"Yes, sir, I sure do." Curtis blushed as red as his newfound ear.

"Tradition has it that you get to kiss the prettiest girl at the dance later on."

"Who's it gonna be, Curtis?" pestered Pete, nudging his big brother in the ribs. "Louise Varney or Emma Jane Betts? All the Abernathy girls are here tonight, each one of them prettier than the one before."

"It's my red ear, brother." Curtis grinned, sticking the corn into his overalls pocket for safekeeping. "I'll do the picking myself, if you don't mind. Anyway, we've got a heck of a lot of shucking to do till we get to that bottle underneath."

"Amen!" echoed several of the menfolk and, in anticipation, they continued to shuck and toss.

It was a quarter till twelve that night when Elmer Baumgartner let out a hoot and a holler. In triumph, he withdrew a gallon jug of corn liquor from the midst of the dwindling pile. The jug was passed around until the very last ear was shucked clean and the celebration began. Everyone grabbed a china plate and piled it high with fried chicken, sugar-cured ham, and plenty of homemade fixings.

A few of the guys were warming up with fiddle, guitar, banjo, and mandolin, ready to pick a little bluegrass for the big barndance, when Curtis finished his meal and joined a couple of his friends near the hayloft ladder. He surveyed the impressive abundance of pretty young ladies who gathered at the far wall, waiting to be asked to dance. He tried his darnedest to determine the loveliest of the bunch, but was constantly perplexed by the next one he laid eyes on.

Suddenly, he saw the one who fit the bill. She stood alone beside the open double doors, a shapely girl near his own age, dressed in blue calico trimmed in lace. Her complexion was like creamy alabaster and her long, waist-length hair was of a silky, raven blackness.

"Hey, fellas...who's that gal over yonder by the door?" he asked, mesmerized by her beauty.

"I don't rightly know," said Hank Tyler. "Never seen her before. She ain't one of the Harrison twins, is she?"

"Naw, both those girls have hair as light as cornsilk," informed Teddy Dandridge. "That gal looks like she might have a touch of Cherokee in her."

"Whoever she is, I'm going over to ask for a dance." Curtis felt in his pocket for the lucky ear, then started across the spacious barn for the open doorway. Pastor Jones began to call a square dance, his baritone voice rising to the rafters. Most everyone there grabbed a partner and began to shake a leg to the tune of "Turkey in the Straw."

Curtis Leman mustered a charming smile and made his way through the milling crowd. The girl noticed his approach, however, and perhaps guessed of his intentions. She quickly ducked through the barn door and disappeared into the darkness beyond.

"Hey, wait up!" Curtis called out and followed. Stepping out of the warmth and activity of the autumn celebration and into the chill, motionless night was like crossing over into another world. He hesitated at first, thinking maybe he should find another girl from whom to receive his rightly-won kiss. But her dark loveliness haunted him. He continued on through the empty barnyard, past pickup trucks and cars, until he saw a fleeting movement ahead. The girl's playful laughter ran across the tattered ruins of his father's cornfield. He watched as a pale flash of calico flitted among the skeletal stalks, then vanished.

With a nervous grin, Curtis climbed the fence and entered the dark field. He pursued the sound of her footsteps and soft giggles through the maze-like rows, tripping over broken stalks and autumn pumpkins in his haste. A full moon etched the drooping, brown leaves in silver luminance, while the rutted rows of turned earth were swallowed in the shadow of the Smoky Mountains. The high swells of the range had always seemed to cradle Cumberland Valley like a babe nestled in the bosom of a protective mother. But that night, the mountains seemed cold and distant.

He had reached the center of the forty-acre cornfield, when he stepped into a parallel row and there she was. She stood as pale as a ghost, waiting for him.

Curtis was again stricken by her beauty, but the tedious hunt had sapped him of most of his bravado. He approached her, forcing the smile now. She did not turn to flee this time. She merely stood and regarded him demurely as he cleared his throat and stepped forward.

"I didn't mean to frighten you, miss," Curtis apologized. "I just wanted to talk to you for a spell." As he grew closer, he marveled at how porcelain-smooth her features were, like the face of an antique china doll. Her eyes were dark and striking despite her apparent bashfulness. For a moment, they appeared as deep and bottomless as the black of her wind-swept hair. But, upon further inspection, they returned to their former hue of soft earthen brown.

"You did not follow me out here to talk," she said, almost in a whisper.

Curtis grinned clumsily and produced the red ear from his pocket. "If you're not familiar with the tradition..." he began.

"Oh, but I am...quite familiar," she told him. She eyed the crimson cob as if it were the jeweled key to some wondrous treasure. "In fact, it was my people who originated the custom, long years before this valley was even settled."

The boy's apprehension eased a little at that assurance. "Then you'll grant me my kiss?"

A cloud passed overhead, obscuring the moon, leaving her only in silhouette. "Most certainly, Curtis Leman."

He was surprised. "You know my name?" he asked. "I'm sure that I don't know yours. I don't believe I've ever seen you here in the valley before."

"*Who* I am does not really matter. It is *what* I am that is most important this night." She extended pale hands to draw him closer. "For you see, I am the maiden...the maiden of the Black Harvest."

What do you mean by that? he wanted to ask, but held his tongue. He didn't want to spoil receiving his intended kiss by asking stupid questions. A lot of the mountain girls were odd sorts, possessing a strange sense of humor that usually went completely over his head. But that didn't bother him as he started forward and took her dainty hands in his. All that filled his mind was her dark and almost savage beauty. He moved in closer, embracing her, staring deeply into the liquid pits of that strange girl's eyes. He found none of the shyness she had displayed before. Instead, there flared a sultry flame of total abandonment.

"Kiss me," she whispered, her lips lush and irresistible. "You've won the right...now claim your prize."

Curtis intended to do just that. He swallowed dryly and brought his lips in close proximity to hers. The hoopla of the fall celebration seemed to be a thousand miles away. It was a mere distraction in the wake of this lady's hypnotic charms.

When he found her lips icy cold to the touch, Curtis knew something was horribly wrong. He grabbed her slender waist to push her away, but the fullness of her calico

90

dress seemed to crumple, as if the flesh beneath were slipping away. His fingers ripped through rotting cloth and slipped through the empty slots of her exposed ribcage. His knuckles scraped painfully against the pitted hardness of flattened bone, wedging there, denying his escape.

"Kiss me." Her lips moved like slivers of dead meat against his own.

Curtis tried desperately to pull away, but skeletal fingers clutched at him, dragging him nearer. A moan of horror rose in his throat as the lovely face of porcelain white seemed to yellow and crack with a hundred tiny fissures. The skin began to shatter and fall away like broken crockery, revealing stark white bone underneath. The sparkling brown eyes that had once smoldered with desire were now gone. Empty sockets glared at Curtis with an emotion akin to hunger, as the wretched thing pulled him closer.

Suddenly, he knew the meaning of her cryptic words. When Grandma Leman had fallen sick and passed away the previous year, Grandpa had sat before the hearth and, in a low, trembling voice, had said "The spring has bled into summer and the coming of autumn has brought upon us a black harvest."

Curtis had never been able to figure out what Grandpa had meant by that...until now.

The Black Harvest marked the finality of one's existence; the crop of youth planted, tended to maturity, and eventually reaped, the same as a field of summer corn or a base of Burley green tobacco. There is a balance between Man and Nature, equilibrium. And when the scales tip too heavily in one direction, compensation must be made.

"Kissss meeee," rasped the skeletal wraith. Her bony jaws clutched his lower face in a horrid kiss of eternal love.

Curtis began to scream wildly, his terror echoing through the hollow of ancient bones and the wind-whipped stalks of the deserted cornfield. But no one heard him. The sound of dancing feet and the rapid-fire staccato of banjo-picking drowned his weakened cries as the maiden lowered him to a bed of withered leaves and began to reap the ripened crop of that darkest of seasons.

DEAD SKIN

When I was three years old, I was playing reck-lessly—as most children do at that age—and pulled on an electrical cord that was draped across the kitchen doorway. One end of that cord was attached to one of those big ol' silver coffee percolators that were a common fixture in the '60s. Its contents missed my head by mere inches, but my left arm was scalded. I don't recall much about what followed, but I do remember my time in the emergency room. I remember that the walls were puke-green in color and that there was a 7-Up machine in the corner. I also remember screaming my head off while a kindly, old doctor gently trimmed the blistered flesh from my tiny arm.

I sometimes wonder what happened to that dead skin. Did they discard it...or did someone keep it?

LET me go! Let me go!!

It was strange how those words came to mind as Brandon Doyle held the squirming bundle of new-born life in his latexed hands. As the harsh squalling of the newly-liberated infant rang throughout the delivery room, the disturbing cry that had echoed within his mind's ear seemed to grow more focused. It seemed to be the whining, frantic voice of a toddler, perhaps three or four years of age. A youngster who was frightened-half out of his wits.

Let me go!

The doctor handed the infant to an assisting nurse. He tried to chase the bogus cries from his mind, but they seemed to linger, nagging at the dusty, cobwebbed corners of his subconscious.

After mother and child had been separated for the time being, Brandon washed up and headed downstairs, still dressed in his jade green scrubs. He caught the elevator just as Nurse McKeon did, which suited him fine. He and the nurse—Janet, as he knew her after professional hours—had become quite an item since he had started his residency at the Atlanta hospital nearly six months before.

"How did it go with Mrs. Powell tonight?" Janet asked him.

"I had to perform a Caesarian, but other than that, things went smoothly," he replied. "She had a nine-pound baby boy. A real screamer, too. The kind that will clean the wax out of your ears."

Let me go!

"Are we still on for Friday night?"

Brandon seemed distracted for a moment. "Oh yes, of course. Seven o'clock sharp at your place, right?"

Janet nodded. "You're in for the best home-cooked meal of your life, Dr. Doyle. I'll have you know I make the best chicken and dumplings south of the Mason-Dixon. I'll have it cooking by the time you get there."

You stay away from that stove, young man! Stay away or I'll tan your hide!

Brandon smiled at her and thought about stealing a kiss, but decided to leave the affection for after hours. "I'll be looking forward to it, Nurse McKeon."

Janet got off at the ICU on the third floor, while Brandon rode on down to the lobby level. It was well after ten o'clock. That day's visitors and most of the staff had already left. Jasper Ryan, the custodian, shampooed the carpeting in the main waiting room.

Brandon strolled down empty halls, past the cafeteria, and through doors that were posted STAFF ONLY. Soon he had reached his destination: the doctors' lounge. Just a quick cup of coffee and then home for a good night's sleep. At least, that was his intention.

He wasn't at all surprised to see Robert Cressler sitting at the corner table with his feet propped in a neighboring chair. Rob was one of the hospital's top anesthesiologists and was almost constantly on call. Beside him sat an overweight fellow with curly hair and John Lennon glasses.

"You look beat, my friend," Brandon said. He took a Styrofoam cup from a dispenser and filled it from the steaming glass pot. As he returned it to the coffee maker's warming plate, he felt the heat of it prickle the fine hairs of his forearm.

Oh, God! He's burnt...

Rob yawned and stretched to reinforce his colleague's observation. "You better believe it. One of my busiest days yet. Gall bladder surgery, a thyroid biopsy, and to top it off, a triple bypass." As Brandon took a seat at the table and began to doctor his java with sugar and cream, Rob introduced the mysterious civilian. "Oh, this is my brother-in-law, Arthur Quinn."

Brandon knew the name instantly. "The writer?" He shook the visitor's hand. "I've read your work, Arthur. I really enjoyed that piece you did on the fallacy of cryogenics for *American Science*."

Arthur seemed embarrassed, so much in fact, that he nearly knocked his coffee cup off the edge of the table. It teetered for a precarious moment, then jarred back into stability, sending a miniscule splatter of black coffee onto the linoleum floor.

It fell off the eye...Oh dear Lord, it just fell plumb off!

The writer smiled sheepishly. "Thanks. I get on certain kicks. Sometimes it's robotics, sometimes global warming, sometimes hardcore science fiction. I've been working on a book lately...about closet genetics."

Closet genetics. Brandon was familiar with the term. It referred to the increasingly common practice of performing genetic experiments on the sly, sometimes out of desperation, due to lack of grant money. Sometimes it was done unethically, behind the backs of hospital administrators who frowned on such research in their midst. It was a subject that bothered Brandon a bit; the very thought of young geniuses working feverishly behind closed doors, unsupervised and challenged with the unknown factors of human life. And, in the process, creating only God knew what.

"I've done most of my main research," continued Arthur. "All I need now is a good kick-off. An introduction that will knock their socks off."

"That's why I invited him down," said Rob. "I thought I'd show him Delcambre's old laboratory."

Brandon sipped his coffee and frowned to himself. "Delcambre. Now where have I heard that name before?"

"I'm sure you've heard him mentioned around the hospital from time to time. If not, I'll fill you in, since you're the new kid on the block. George Delcambre was a respected and brilliant surgeon here during the '60s and early '70s. But there was a dark side to the old boy. He was also the resident mad scientist. He had an unhealthy curiosity about things that most of his colleagues had put out of their minds after leaving med school. He was interested in experimenting with DNA, dominant and recessive chromosomes, and the cause and effect of cellular mutation. Of course, now it's called genetic

96

research. Back in those days it was considered screwing with nature."

Arthur already had his tape recorder going. "Well? Don't hold anything back, Rob. Tell it all."

His brother-in-law laughed and punched the Stop button on the mini-recorder. "Not so fast. I'll leave all the gruesome details for our visit to Delcambre's lab."

"Where is this laboratory?" asked Brandon, suddenly interested.

"Down in the basement, across the hall from the morgue. The place is locked up. No one's been inside for twenty-five years."

"So how are *we* going to get in?" Arthur wanted to know. His journalistic zeal was barely contained.

"I've made arrangements," said Rob. He drained the last of his coffee and chucked the cup at the wastebasket, but missed. "Old Jasper has every key to every door in this old building. We'll meet him down there around eleven."

"Great!" Arthur seemed more than pleased with the prospect of exploring some genetic pioneer's forgotten legacy. "How about you, Brandon? Are you going to take the grand tour with us?"

"I don't know, guys. I've just gotten out of surgery. I'm bushed."

"Come on, doctor. Where's your sense of professional curiosity? Don't you want to see what your elders were up to while you were running around in short pants and bruised knees?"

Brandon sat there for a long, bone-weary moment, regarding the two men's exuberant faces. They were like kids, anxious to go and see what Santa had left them.

The lounge was silent, except for the coffee maker. It sizzled and sputtered as it strained out a fresh pot.

He's burnt! Oh God, he's burnt real bad!

With a groan, he complied. "All right. But this better be good."

■■■

Old Jasper's key ring rattled as he searched for the right one. He found a brass one, tarnished green from age. The others slid down the ring, clinking, metal against metal.

Snip, snip, snip...

"Ain't nothing here but a bunch of sick specimens in mason jars," Jasper complained. "Things a man shouldn't ever have to lay eyes on, let alone *want* to see."

"We can handle it, Jasper," Rob told him.

The janitor smiled thinly around the stem of his pipe. "Well, if you say so, Dr. Cressler. I'll let you be the judge of that."

After jiggling the key in the old lock for a moment, a brittle snap signaled the disengaging of the tumblers. Jasper pushed the door open with a scraping of warped wood and a squeal of hinges. He reached in and fumbled for the light switch. The overhead lights—common sixty-watt bulbs, not modern fluorescents—drove away the shadows. The walls were painted pea-soup green, like some of the older operating and examining rooms upstairs.

Just hold still, young man. Everything is going to be just fine.

"Have fun, gentlemen," said Jasper, turning to leave. "I'll be back down later to lock up."

Rob thanked the old man, then turned to his two companions. "Well, my friends, I give you the laboratory of Dr. George T. Delcambre."

Tentatively, they stepped inside.

The laboratory indeed looked as if it hadn't been used in twenty or thirty years. Cobwebs hung abandoned from the ceiling and laced the contents of the shelves. The furnishings were unremarkable: a roll top desk, filing cabinet, a couple of hospital gurneys. The air reeked of mildew and age...as well as the faint, sweet-sour scent of formaldehyde.

Arthur went immediately to the roll top desk. He slid back the sectioned covering with some effort. The pigeonholes were all empty, as were the drawers. All that occupied the moldy desk blotter was a wooden rack holding two briar pipes and a framed picture of a man and a woman, both in their late sixties. The black and white photo had nearly faded out; Brandon's eyes centered on the man. He was tall and gaunt, with snow-white hair and spectacles with lenses as thick as the bottoms of soda bottles.

Oh, Doctor, please help him! You've got to help my baby!

The writer was about to dig into the filing cabinet, when Rob pulled him aside. "Plenty of time for that, Arthur. Come on over here and let's check out what the old gentleman left behind."

The three walked further into the cramped room. As they began to study the things that floated within dusty jars and beakers, it crossed their minds that perhaps Jasper had been right. Maybe Delcambre had left behind treasures best left buried and forgotten.

"Delcambre was a particularly curious individual," Rob began, imparting the information he had gathered over sixteen years of working at the Atlanta hospital. "His thirst for knowledge began during his medical education. Dissecting cadavers and examining the workings of the internal organs was only his first taste of hands-on research. Once he began practicing and had established a respected position on the staff here, he set up shop...in the basement."

Startled, Arthur stepped back a few paces. He had scrubbed away the coating of dust and spiderwebs from a five-gallon jar and found himself staring face-to-face with a severed human head.

"I'm not saying old Delcambre was a grave-robber," continued Rob. "No, he had plenty of opportunities to collect his specimens right here in the hospital. Of course, they were taken quietly and with discretion. No one on the staff really knew what he was up to. I'm sure that the administrators of this institution would have been shocked if they'd known precisely what was taking place down here."

Brandon passed a shelf of baby food jars. Each held paper thin slices of pale, bloodless tissue.

No need to worry. A third-degree burn, but not very serious at all.

"They said the old man did all types of weird experiments in this laboratory—gene-splicing, genetic mutation, tampering with growth and sexual glands in test animals, which created horrid monstrosities that Delcambre had to destroy immediately. There were even stories of him trying a little cloning. But it never quite worked out."

Goosebumps prickled Brandon's flesh. Everywhere he turned there were tiny, unfocused eyes peering at him from cloudy jars and vials. It was like looking past the thick spectacles of the man in the photograph and finding cold, dead fish eyes staring back at you. Not the warm, compassionate eyes of a man of healing, but the hard, expressionless orbs of an unbalanced fiend, brilliant in one way, but long past the bounds of madness in another.

Then Brandon Doyle turned around and knew that his suspicions were correct. He stared at the thing in the quart jar and held his breath.

You've got to help him! He's my baby! My only son!

It sort of looked like an aborted fetus. Sort of. There were differences. Horrible differences. Like the way the tiny body was twisted and gnarled, as if in terrible pain. Like the way the thing's skin was blistered and peeling, as if someone had immersed it in boiling water after its forced birthing. Like the way the oversized head was thrown back, the smooth toothless mouth stretched wide in a silent scream of gut-wrenching agony.

Brandon turned away, but not before his eyes locked with those of the horrible infant.

Dead blue eyes swam in cloudy, yellow liquid.

Just hold still now, son, and we'll fix you right up.

"That's really sick, man!" piped Arthur's voice over his shoulder. With a snort of disgust, the writer turned away and, heading back to the makeshift office, began to rummage through the file cabinet.

When Rob and his brother-in-law were about ready to leave, they found Brandon staring at the blankness of a cinderblock wall, his eyes averted from the jars that lined the dusty shelves. His face was pale, his eyes distant and glazed, like someone reliving a childhood dream. Or, perhaps, a nightmare.

"Brandon?" said Rob, "are you alright?" Concerned, he laid a hand upon his colleague's shoulder.

Brandon flinched at his friend's touch. He regarded Rob, his eyes suddenly clear and alert again. "Yes...I'm okay. Just got a little spooked, that's all."

Arthur laughed nervously. "Welcome to the club." He held up a manila envelope packed with yellowed papers. "At least I got what I came for. Hell, I might end up doing a series of books on this Delcambre guy."

"Just don't mention who gave you the lowdown," said Rob. "Delcambre might not have given a damn about ethics, but I certainly don't like having mine questioned."

During the elevator ride up, Brandon absently rubbed the place where the anesthesiologist had touched him moments before.

"Didn't mean to hurt you," Rob said apologetically.

"That's okay." He pulled down the collar of his greens to reveal the ugly patch of scar tissue that lay across his left shoulder. "It's always been a little tender."

Arthur grimaced. "When did that happen?"

Brandon shrugged. "When I was a little kid. I don't remember much about it. I was only a few years old at the time."

"Bad burn, huh?"

See, Brandon, nothing to worry about. Only a little dead skin...

He swallowed dryly and pulled his collar back in place. "Yes."

The elevator lurched with a dizzying motion as it reached the first floor. Just before the doors slid open,

Brandon Doyle caught his distorted reflection in the polished metal.

And stared into swimming blue eyes.

CONSUMPTION

For a kid, exploring the Tennessee backwoods is like stepping into another world. It can be lush, green, and beautiful. It can also be isolated, shadowy, and slightly unsettling. I remember when I was a boy, my cousins and I would wander through the dense woods behind their house. The wilderness seemed to stretch for miles and miles.

One creepy thing about the woods, though... much of the ground is covered by a dense carpet of wild ivy, sometimes a good foot or two deep. You never know what might lurk underneath: could be possums or weasels, could be snakes. But, of course, being boys we blundered through blindly, oblivious to the danger. I remember once, following a romp in the forest, I came home and felt something thrashing and wiggling in the leg of my jeans. A second later a black centipede nearly eight inches long crawled out! Just goes to show you what might be lurking beneath the underbrush.

Pap Wilson brought something home with him after a journey into the backwoods. Something much worse than a pesky ol' centipede...

PAP Wilson was returning home from a tedious day of digging ginseng down yonder in a backwoods hollow. His spirits were high and his sack held a good eighty dollars worth of the medicinal root. He was only a hoot and a holler away from the old log cabin his grandfather had built shortly after the Civil War, when his foot sank through the dense carpeting of wild kudzu and into what he first thought to be a sinkhole hidden from sight.

"Confound it all!" said the old man as a sudden jolt of pain shot up the length of his right leg. When he attempted to pull his boot from the opening in the round, a sensation of prickly discomfort gripped him, as if his foot had fallen asleep. However, his injury proved to be much more serious than that. Red-hot needles of agony stitched his flesh in a dozen places, causing him to moan aloud.

Pap, you damned fool! he told himself. *You've done gone and put your foot into a nest of copperheads!*

But snakes were far from being the source of his discomfort.

With a curse and mighty heave, Pap extracted his leg from the knee-deep kudzu and landed hard on his backside in the thicket. For a moment, all he could do was sit there and stare dumbly at his foot. Something had a hold of Pap Wilson. Something he had never seen the likes of during his seventy-odd years in the hills and hollows of Tennessee.

Tiny black eyes glared up at him, burning with an emotion that could only be described as intense hunger. What it appeared to be was a very large and stubby caterpillar, the wooly kind that built great transparent nests in the boughs of blooming dogwoods in the heart of springtime. But several disturbing differences separated that creature from any insect that Pap had ever encountered.

A thick coat of bristles covered the cylindrical body of the ugly thing. The old man poked at its back with the end of his walking stick. The cane emerged covered with long quills, five to seven inches in length, each as sharp and barbed as the end as a fish hook.

As the pain grew increasingly worse, Pap's attention was reluctantly drawn to the bloody, black maw that encircled his lower leg. It worked ravenously, awful sounds of sucking and tearing rising from deep within its gullet. The teeth were triangular ivory razors. The thing moved along flesh and bone in an odd circular motion, performing irreparable damage, funneling the chewed tissue and gristle into the dark tunnel of its throat. In sudden horror, Pap realized that the mouth had traveled upward a few inches, totally engulfing the swell of his ankle.

The thing was *eating* him!

Pap Wilson had always been a proud man. He forever balked at help offered by neighbors or kin, and staunchly refused any consideration lest acceptance be interpreted as a weakness on his part. But that evening, deep in that wooded hollow, he screamed long and loud for his life and prayed to the good Lord that someone would hear his frantic cries.

Someone did. Nate and Johnny, the old man's strapping sons, were in the barn unharnessing a pair of swaybacked mules. Their upper bodies were tanned and slick with sweat, for they had spent all day plowing the hillside acreage that bore their meager crop each year. The two brothers looked at one another. "That sounded like Pap," said Nate.

They ran out of the barn and down the slope of the hollow. They found their father lying in a tangle of briers and bramble, trembling in a palsy of torment, his life's blood flowing freely now.

"Good God Almighty!" gasped Johnny, the younger of the two.

The boys stared in disbelief at the thing that pulsated along Pap's right shin. Nate crouched and curiously extended his hand toward it.

"Don't touch it, son!" warned Pap through clenched teeth. "The critter's got barbs as sharp as a porcupine's."

"What the hell is it?"

"Don't rightly know. Put my foot in a sinkhole under the kudzu and the thing latched onto me with a vengeance." Pap shuddered with another spasm, each more painful than the last. "Well, don't just stand there a-gawking like a couple of idiots...get me on up to the house!"

Fashioning their brawny arms into a makeshift chair, they carried their papa up the steep embankment to the ancient log house. "Ma!" they yelled as they approached the back porch. "Come on out here quick! Pap's been bad hurt!"

Mable Wilson rushed out of the kitchen door, drying her hands on her apron. "Lord have mercy!" she cried. "What's happened to him?" At first, all she could see was her husband's britches leg saturated with fresh blood.

Then she saw the parasite and nearly screamed.

Pap reached out and took her hand firmly. "Now, don't you go getting hysterical on me, old woman," he said evenly, trying to inject an element of calm into his faltering voice. "Ya'll just get me inside and we'll see about getting this ugly cuss off'n me."

By the time they carried Pap to his chair at the head of the kitchen table, the creature had crept to the bulge of the old man's knee. They tried two things, neither of which showed any positive results. First they tried pouring hot water on the thing. Mable had a kettle of water boiling on the woodstove, knowing that her husband enjoyed a mug of tar black coffee after his forays in the forest. Carefully, she tipped the kettle over the writhing body of jagged bristles. All in the room were silent, watching in nervous anticipation. Mable and the boys prepared themselves for the shrieking and thrashing of the scalded critter as it dropped away and the grisly sight of Pap's leg, flesh and bone whittled away to a point like a lead pencil. But the boiling water had no effect. If anything, it only riled the creature. It continued its gnashing and gnawing with renewed vigor.

Next, Nate took a carving knife from the kitchen pantry. Careful not to ensnare his hand in the quills, he jabbed at the thing's body, intending to skewer it. But, still, their good intentions proved futile. The knife's edge continuously struck a network of hard, interlinked scales, comparable to the chain mail of a knight's armor.

"Try its head," suggested Johnny.

He did. After chiseling for a few moments, the point of the blade broke off with a snap. "No good," sighed Nate. "The blamed thing is as hard as a tortoise shell."

"What're we gonna do now?" asked Johnny. He noticed the thing was halfway up his father's thigh and, amazingly enough, its toothy maw was expanding in width, accommodating the circumference of the morsel it was devouring.

Pap had no more answers. He merely sat there trembling, tears of rage and agony rolling down his leathery cheeks. Mable saw her responsibility and took control. "Carry your papa into the bedroom and make him comfortable." She followed them to the front room that she and her spouse had shared for over fifty years. After Pap had been laid gently on the big feather bed, Mable led her sons out into the hallway. "Nate...you've got the keys to your papa's truck, don't you?"

"Yes, ma'am."

"Now, listen to me, both of you," she said, trying to calm herself. "I want you to drive to town and fetch Doc Hampton. Bring him back here as fast as you can."

"But that thing on Pap..." Nate began to protest. "As fast as it's going...won't be nothing left of him by the time we get back."

"Don't talk such nonsense!" balked Mable, although her skepticism was half-hearted with dread. "Now get going. And put on a shirt, the both of you. I don't want you roaring into town looking like a couple of naked savages on a rampage, you hear me?"

"Yes, ma'am." They dressed hurriedl, and soon the old pickup was heading down the dirt road for town.

"Mable?"

After a moment's hesitation, she went in to see what Pap wanted.

"Mable?" Pap muttered weakly. His face, once ruddy with good health, now stared up at her as pale as baking flour. "Mable...I want you to do me a favor."

"Of course," she said, but there was wariness in her tone.

"I want you to fetch that old shotgun of mine from outta the hall closet and load it for me."

"Whatever for?" Mable exclaimed. Her mind raced, revealing reasons and quickly discarding them. She had a cold fear that she knew exactly why Pap wanted the gun.

The elderly man avoided looking her in the eyes. "The pain, Mable...oh, dear Lord in heaven, it *hurts!*" His white-knuckled hands clutched at the mattress, the nails digging deeper into the bedcovers. "Mable, darling...I don't know how much more of this I can stand."

Mable Wilson removed her apron and tenderly wiped the sweat from his pasty brow.

She was a God-fearing, church-going woman and, at that moment, knew she must draw on her faith to get them both through this terrible ordeal. "I'll not let you die, Pap Wilson," she declared, her own tears spilling freely. "Not by your hand or by this...this *monster* that's got hold of you!"

"So you refuse to help me?" Once again he was the rawboned mountain man, fearful of nothing and full of piss and vinegar; the man she had wed the summer of her eighteenth year. "Well, if that be the case, then just get the hell outta here! Get out and lock the door behind you! And no matter how badly I scream, woman, don't come in...do you understand what I'm saying?"

He stared down reluctantly at the quilled parasite. The thing was at the joint of his crotch and thigh now, blood pouring in torrents, more blood than he had seen in an entire lifetime of hardship. The appetite was what mortified him. Could the thing eat and eat and never gorge itself to capacity? Was its devilish hunger eternal? And who would it start on next, once it had its fill of him?

Mable obeyed her husband's demands. Swiftly, she closed the door behind her, locked it shut with the skeleton key. She stood at the front door screen and watched the evening bleed into twilight. She prayed softly, trying hard to ignore the awful noises of feeding that sounded from the next room.

In the course of a lifetime one rarely endures the kind of living nightmare that befell the Wilson clan that dreadful day in the wooded hills of East Tennessee. A nightmare so horrendous that it crumbles the very foundation of daylit reality, then pursues the tortured mind relentlessly into the realm of troubled sleep afterwards.

■■■

When Nate and Johnny returned with Louis Hampton M.D. in tow, darkness had fallen. They found their mother sitting in her rocker on the front porch, her face buried mournfully in wrinkled hands, her frail body racked with the force of her sobbing. "It was horrible!" she told them. "The screaming...I've never, in all my born days, heard such awful sounds as those that came from that room. Oh, your poor papa...how he must have suffered. And, Lord forgive me, I did nothing. I sat right here until the screaming finally stopped."

Nate left Johnny to look after Ma. Then, accompanied by Doc Hampton, he entered the house. Living so far back in the sticks, the Wilson household, like most of their backwoods neighbors', existed without benefit of telephone or electricity. In pitch darkness, Nate fished in the hall closet, found the old Parker twelve-gauge, and loaded it. Then, flashlight in hand, they unlocked the door and burst in.

The pale beam was directed at the brass-framed bed, as were the twin muzzles of the scattergun. But there was nothing to fire at. The big feather bed was empty.

Nate and Doc stepped closer and examined the spot where Pap Wilson had once lain in agony. The sheets were twisted and soaked through with blood. The only lingering remains of poor Pap appeared in ragged tatters of clothing and the upper plate of his mail-order dentures lying near a chewed and discarded pillow. As for the parasitic worm, the only traces of its horrid existence were a few barbed quills protruding from the mattress ticking.

Where is it? Nate's mind raced in panic. The beam of the flashlight followed a long smudge of fresh blood, like the slimy residue of a slug's trail, crossing the hardwood floor toward the open window. Nate caught a glimpse of movement out of the corner of his eye, but too late. He whirled and fired just as the thing disappeared over the sill and into the outer darkness, leaving only a smear of fresh gore and needles along the ledge...a taunting reminder of the horrible act committed therein.

■■■

Nate Wilson struggled from the clutches of that ghastly dreamscape, realizing that the grist of his nightmare had actually taken place several hours earlier. He hadn't intended on sleeping a wink that night. Since shortly after the hour of ten, when the windows of the house had grown dark, Nate had sat in the loft of the barn, gun in hand, watching, waiting for the first sign of that bristly little monster to emerge from the encompassing thicket. He knew that eventually its awful hunger would overcome its fear and it would inch its way across the yard in search of an easy entrance.

A full moon was out, splashing pale light upon the immediate expanse of the Wilson property. Nate quickly dismissed the moonlit patches; it was the dense shadows in between that worried him. From his vantage point he had a good chance of spotting the thing. If an elongated shadow started through the grass below, he could easily dispatch it with one well-placed shot.

Or so he had intended, before falling asleep. He was fully awake now, his mind alert and instantly suspicious. *Better safe than sorry*, he told himself. Nate left his nocturnal perch and climbed down the rungs of the hayloft ladder. After all, this wasn't exactly some chicken-hungry fox he was lying in wait for.

Moving swiftly, he left the barn and crossed the moonlit yard. He stopped at the long-handled pump near the back porch, set his gun aside, and cranked himself a dipperful of cold well water. Soon, he was stepping through the back door. His brother Johnny was fast asleep on the kitchen table, his breathing heavy and his slumber restless. The flashlight sat on the woodstove where Nate had left it. He now took it and started down the inner hallway. He flashed the light toward the front bedroom, but made no move toward it. The door was locked, the ugly tangle of blood-soaked bedsheets left untouched since Doc Hampton's confused departure. Tomorrow the county sheriff would be out to investigate the incident, but that was unimportant to Nate at the moment.

A faint noise from behind the adjacent door set his nerves on edge. He turned the knob quietly and stepped inside, sweeping the walls with the beam of the handheld light.

He had insisted that his mother sleep in the boys' room that night. She had agreed passively and he had tucked her in, concerned with her listless mood and the glassy look in her eyes. Pap's death had broken the old woman's spirit, causing her to withdraw somewhere into her mind, away from the surroundings that might remind her of her husband and set the horror into motion once again.

Nate walked quietly to the bed and directed the light on the fluffy goosedown pillow at the headboard. "Ma?"

he whispered. His mother's pale face stared, wide-eyed and unseeing, up at him, the muscles of her shallow cheeks twitching grotesquely. "Ma, are you all right?" Fear crept into the young man. Was she having a fit or was she in the throes of a stroke, a delayed reaction to the strain she had been subjected to earlier?

Nate's fear changed into the wild thrill of unrestrained terror when he shined his light further downward. The bedsheets were saturated with fresh blood, the lumpy folds shuddering and shaking rhythmically. Whatever it was that moved beneath the gory bed linen, it was not the body of his dear, sweet mother. Swiftly and without hesitation, Nate grabbed the edge of the sheet and pulled it aside.

He recoiled a few feet, the light shimmying wildly in his hand. He wanted to scream. Dear Lord in heaven, he wanted to scream with all the abandon of a madman, but he couldn't. He could only stand there and gawk, repulsed and frightfully fascinated at the sight his eyes were taking in.

Somehow the cursed thing had found its way back into the house. Exactly how was beside the point. All Nate knew was that it was here, in front of him now, and it had gotten hold of Ma. Why she had not screamed in agony like Pap had was beyond him. Perhaps it had been her state of grief and numbing shock that had kept her from crying out. It didn't really matter now. She was far beyond help.

Ma's body was *gone*. The spiny parasite had consumed her completely, clear up to the wrinkled neck, which it now sucked and chewed at with relentless fervor. Ma's face stared blankly up at her son, the jaw working, as if trying to utter some meaningful words of parting wisdom that would make her hideous death a fraction more tolerable. But no words rose from her open mouth...only a wet gurgle and a ghastly bubble of bloody spittle. A perfectly-formed bubble that abruptly burst when, with a great shuddering gulp, the toothy maw of the worm engulfed her head completely.

Nate stared at the thing and it stared back with tiny, coal-black eyes. Its prickly body squirmed, bloated to twice its normal size. Instinctively, he brought his right hand up, but it was empty. Suddenly, he remembered the awful thirst that had gripped him during his walk across the back yard. He ran into the hallway, screaming. "Johnny...the shotgun! I left it out by the pump! Get it...quick!"

He heard a frantic scramble, the slap of the back door, and soon Johnny was bolting down the hallway, shotgun in hand. "What's wrong?" he demanded breathlessly. "What happened?"

The awful look in Nate's eyes scared Johnny half to death. "It got Ma!" Nate sobbed, strangling on those dreadful words. "The ugly thing got her!" He traded his flashlight for the shotgun and turned toward the bedroom, every nerve in his body alive and on fire. Snapping back the twin hammers, he stepped back into the dark room. Johnny followed and directed the light of the flashlight upon the bloody bed. Nate braced himself, peering down the joined barrels of the antique twelve gauge.

The bed was empty. The petite woman who had raised them from infants to hardworking men was completely gone. But, worse still, so was the devil that had devoured her.

"Where is it?" cried Johnny. "Nate...*where is it?* Did it get out the window like last time?" They both looked to the room's single window. It was closed and latched from the inside. An awful feeling gripped them both. The thing...the caterpillar-like parasite with the ceaseless hunger...was still in there somewhere!

They stood stone still for a moment, but no sound alerted them to its whereabouts. No dry rasping of long needles grating one against the other, no gnashing of razor sharp teeth. Only silence and the ragged labor of their own breathing.

"Let's get outta here," said Nate, grabbing his brother by the arm.

"What're we gonna do?" Johnny moaned as Nate herded him into the hallway, then shut the door behind them, locking it and taking the key.

His brother's eyes were wild. "We're gonna burn that sucker out, that's what we're gonna do!"

Johnny was in no position to argue. Meekly, he joined his sibling in an act that some would have termed as pure madness. They first went to the tool shed and, toting two five-gallon cans of gasoline, returned to the log house they had lived in since birth. With a desperation that was almost wanton in its execution, the two splashed the outer walls with the flammable liquid, soaking the ancient logs. Nate dug a book of matches from his trouser pocket and, igniting the whole thing, pitched it at the dry brush near the eastern wall.

By the time Nate and Johnny reached the peach orchard opposite their bedroom window, the old house was wreathed in flame. Nate checked the loads in his shotgun and waited for the fire to get good and hot. It didn't take long. The hewn logs and chinking in between burnt like dry tinder and, before five minutes had passed, the structure was totally engulfed.

Nate took a firm grip on the gun. His attention was glued to that bedroom window, for that was where the horrid thing would attempt to escape. The inner walls of the cabin had ignited now. As the heat rose in intensity, the windows began to expand and explode like brittle gunshots. The bedroom window was the third to go.

He raised his shotgun, ready to let loose. The ruptured window stared at him like the empty eye socket of some fiery skull, but nothing moved along its sill except tongues of flame.

"Johnny," he called to his brother behind him. "Do you see it anywhere?"

No reply. Only the crackling of the fire and the crash of timbers giving way.

Nate was reluctant to turn away from the window, but he did so anyway. "Johnny?"

114

His brother was nowhere to be seen. Nate stared hard into the pitch blackness, his eyes more accustomed to the brilliance of flame than the inky depth of shadow. It was noise that alerted him…a soft rustle of wet grass. His eyes focused on motion at the base of a tree.

"Johnny…is that you?" He walked a few steps closer.

Yes, it was Johnny. His younger brother lay on the dewy ground, his arms flailing frantically, his legs performing a bizarre dance of torment. The flickering glow from the house reached midway into the orchard, shedding light upon the gruesome spectacle at Nate's feet.

The thing had somehow escaped the fiery barricade, unnoticed, and had crept up behind them, catching Johnny by surprise. It had a hold of his brother's head and was at work with the zealous craving it had exhibited at the expense of his ma and pa. Nate raised the shotgun and pointed it at the pulsating column of the critter's expanding body.

If Johnny wasn't already dead, he would be soon. There was nothing Nate could do for his brother…nothing but avenge his horrible demise. And Nate intended to take care of that right then and there.

The young farmer's eyes shone with a strange emotion that was a mixture of pleasure and agony, of elation and self-destructive rage. He brought the muzzles of the shotgun flush against the bulbous head of the wretched thing and smiled. "I got you now, you filthy little bastard!"

As Nate was about to exact his revenge, he heard a rustling in the leafy branches above his head. But there was no wind that night.

Before he could pull the trigger, they began falling out of the trees.

DUST DEVILS

Have you ever seen a dust devil? You know, those spontaneously-generated mini-twisters that you see every now and then. They aren't all that common, but they do materialize occasionally under the right conditions.

The idea for this story evolved one day when I spotted one making its way across my neighbor's yard...heading straight for his black lab. The dog rose to its feet and barked at the approaching cyclone of dead leaves, dust and debris. Right when it seemed on the verge of colliding with the dog, it abruptly changed its course and retreated. Almost as if by some conscious intelligence. I thought to myself, if one of these pockets of random wind currents could react out of fear and apprehension, couldn't it display other emotions...perhaps passion and love? Or something much stronger?

THE bruises were not so much painful as they were downright ugly. Stan had put them there when he discovered the green and gold cheerleader uniform hanging from the knob of her closet door.

"What do you wanna be? A slut or something?" her stepfather had bellowed in one of his drunken rages, which had seemed to grow in frequency since the death of her mother.

"Do you want them boys looking up your skirt whenever you do those somersaults and splits? Do you, huh? Cause you're a filthy, little tramp if you do. That's all cheerleaders are anyway, you know. Just slutty teases, wagging their pretty asses in your face, getting a man all worked up for nothing!"

She had opened her mouth to object and he had lit into her like a wildcat. Before she had made the safety of her bedroom, he had put a half dozen good-sized bruises on her arms and legs and given her one hell of a black eye. She had awakened that Tuesday morning hoping, praying, that it wouldn't look as bad as she suspected it would…but, of course, it did. She had stayed home from school that day, from the try-outs she had looked forward to for nearly three weeks. Tomorrow the swelling would be down, reduced to an ugly yellow-brown patch around her left eye, and she would sadly return the cheerleader outfit to Mrs. Petty, the girls cheerleading coach. She knew when she did, she would receive that awful look of pity—a look she had grown to hate like a poison.

Becky Mae Jessup spent the day in her cramped room at the rear of the house trailer. She lay in bed, watching the soaps on her black and white portable. A beautiful socialite was on the screen, downing martinis and Valium, crying her eyes out because her executive husband was across town bedding his boss's wife.

"What do you know about being lonely?" she spat at the actress. "*Truly* lonely?" The thought almost angered her to tears. Loneliness was a sixteen-year-old girl in west El Paso whose heart soared whenever a boy—*any* boy—smiled her way or just said "Hi."

Loneliness was crying yourself to sleep, thinking of the pretty clothes you would never own and the exotic places you could never hope to see.

She glanced over at her open closet door at the poster that hung inside, a poster of one the hottest pop singers around. He smiled at her with those perfect, white teeth and she smiled back with teeth that were not so perfect or so white. Stan didn't know that she had it. If he had, he would have pitched a fit. "You ain't old enough to be thinking of such things," he constantly told her. "Next thing I know you'll be knocked-up or have AIDS or one of them damned venereal diseases!"

She always ignored his senseless ravings, though, seeing past his grumbling guidance to the hypocrisy underneath. For a man who seemed so all-fired concerned with his stepdaughter's moral upbringing. Stan Jessup had no qualms whatsoever about the raunchy centerfolds that papered the walls of his own room or the women he sometimes brought home from the Diamondback Saloon. *Loose women,* her mother used to call them with dismay, *common whores.* Some nights Becky Mae had to bury her head in her pillow to drown out the sounds of dirty laughter and the jouncing of bedsprings.

She grew weary of the endless scandals of daytime TV and went outside, stopping by the fridge for a soda. Becky Mae sat there on the rickety wooden steps of the weathered trailer, staring at the drab surroundings she had known for six years. Her mother had married Stan Jessup in '83, a few years after her real father had died in an oil rig explosion. Stan hadn't seemed like such a bad fellow until her mother died of lung cancer in the spring of '85. Then he had ruled over her with an iron fist, and that fist hurt, both physically and mentally.

The trailer park on the far reaches of the West Texas highway was owned by Connie Ketchum, a bird-like woman with brilliant red hair. She lived in the little adobe bungalow that doubled as the main office with her seven-year-old son, Tony. Mrs. Ketchum had run the park alone since her husband went out for a pack of Camels one morning and never came back. That had been five years ago.

Mrs. Ketchum was pruning the cactus around her patio when an unpleasant memory came to Becky Mae. She had been twelve then, right after her mother had come home from the hospital that last time. Mrs. Ketchum's face had been deadly serious. "Becky Mae," she had said, "does your stepdaddy ever touch you...in a *wrong way?*" Becky Mae hadn't known what she was referring to and told her so. The woman's face had blushed as red as her firebrand hair. "Never mind, dear," she had muttered, dismissing it as quickly as she had brought it up. "Just forget I ever mentioned it."

But she couldn't forget. And now, four years later, she knew exactly what Mrs. Ketchum had been getting at. Becky Mae had become slowly aware of Stan's growing attention toward her in the past few months. A couple of nights ago he had reached across the table for the salt shaker and deliberately brushed her breast, chuckling at her sudden embarrassment. She was also aware of how his eyes followed her around the trailer when she wore a halter top and cutoffs in the summer.

A low whistling roused her from her place on the steps and she walked around back. At first she could see nothing but the back lot, littered with trash and the rusty junkers her stepdad tinkered with on his time off. There was the railroad tracks and, beyond that, the distant expanse of scrubby Mexican desert. The landscape appeared as desolate and lonely as she felt at the moment. The tears threatened to come then, but held off when the whistling sound grew louder, closer.

She could see it now, floating in from the west. A little whirlwind, a mini-twister, a *dust devil* as her mother called them. What was it her bedridden mother had warned her about dust devils? *Don't you ever go near one, girl,* she had said, cigarette jutting from between lips swollen by chemotherapy. *And for God's sake don't ever walk into the middle of one! Take it from me, they'll take a hold of you and tear your soul right out. It's true! I read it in the* National Enquirer.

She had never believed her, but now, watching the dusty funnel drift lazily toward her, bouncing over the steel rails and cross-ties into the backyard, Becky Mae almost could. She set her soda on the seat of a busted lawn chair and found herself walking directly into its weaving path.

The tears were flowing freely now. *Well, let's just see if it is true then,* she thought. *If it is, I don't care. Let it take my soul. Maybe I'll end up in a better place than the one I'm in right now.*

Slowly, erratically, the dust devil skimmed across the earth, drawing small pebbles and surface dust into its centrifuge. A mesquite branch was snapped off its bush, caught up in the swirling packet of air, then discarded. Becky Mae continued forward. Ten feet stretched between them, then only five. Before she could give her actions a second thought, she closed her eyes and stepped into the center of the sand spout.

Surprisingly enough, there was no great force that tore at her, no turbulent howling within. Only a strange calm, as the eye of a hurricane might be. She kept her eyes screwed tightly shut so as not to get dust in them and simply stood there. The twister did not move beyond her, but stood stationary, cradling her within its hollow.

Abruptly, a strong feeling gripped the teenager. It was as if—yes, there was—a *presence* of some sort there with her...inside the heart of the dust devil. A very lonely presence, one that ached for companionship. A decidedly *male* presence.

You're just imagining things, she told herself. But, on second thought, she didn't think so. The air currents swirled tenderly around her and, as she relaxed and let her troubles vanish, she strangely felt as though her clothing had suddenly slipped away.

Tiny breezes like gentle hands caressed her bare skin, running masterfully along her small breasts, the flat of her

121

stomach, the flare of her hips. An electric thrill traveled through her, from the base of her spine to the top of her head. *Is this how it feels to make love?* she wondered.

Then there was a pressure on her lips, a soft meshing of warm air against flesh...a spectral kiss from whatever haunted the spiral of dust. *Becky Mae,* a voice said as if coming from some great distance.

"Yes," she gasped. "That's my name...what's yours?"

Silence. Then the voice came again, but different this time. Distinctly familiar and edged in anger. *Becky Mae...where the hell are you, girl?*

Startled, she backed out of the center of the little whirlwind, tripping and landing hard on her backside on the barren earth. The dust devil hovered there for a moment longer, then retreated back in the direction from which it came.

Stan Jessup, dressed in greasy coveralls and toting a lunch box, rounded the corner of the trailer and glared at his stepdaughter hatefully. "What in tarnation are you doing down there?"

Becky Mae felt panic grip her, but when she looked down, she found her clothing to be intact. "Nothing. Just sitting here."

"Well, you ain't gonna have no butt left to sit on if you don't get on up right quick," Stan warned. "Now, get on in the kitchen and put some supper on the table before I give you an instant replay of last night."

She did as he said. Before following him up the steps, she cast her eyes back across the broken horizon with its endless miles of buttes and sagebrush. *Nothing but an old dust devil, that's all,* she thought in disappointment. *Just a daydream.* But, somehow, she could not convince herself that what had happened that afternoon had been a trick of the mind, rather than something intimate and true.

■■■

Becky Mae's one and only boyfriend had been Todd Lewis, but their relationship had been short-lived, spanning all of thirty seconds. The senior had showed up at the trailer to take her to the double-feature at the Skyline Drive-In, but Stan had chased him off with a shotgun. Her stepfather had blown out the taillights of the boy's Mustang before he could make the safety of the main highway. Since that incident, no guy in his right mind came near Becky Mae Jessup, no matter how cute she was.

Now she awaited a boyfriend of a different kind, one that she could only hear in her mind, that she could only feel in the currents of the wind. She awaited him that Friday evening as she had for the past two days, sitting on the hood of an old Plymouth Duster in the backyard. For two days she had watched the dusty desert along the Texas-Mexico border for a fleeting sign of the dust devil. Each evening after school she had stared across the sun-baked wilderness until darkness descended, leaving her depressed and disappointed once again.

This evening a new emotion joined the others. Fear sat heavy in her heart, not over the absence of the sand spout, but because of her stepfather. Mrs. Ketchum's cryptic words of four years ago came back to haunt her and she had a dreadful feeling that tonight would be the night that Stan would make his lurid move. Tonight he would finally try to touch her in that *wrong way*, or perhaps attempt something much worse.

She knew that it was so, the way he had acted over breakfast that morning, the way he had looked her square in the eyes over french toast and coffee. It was nearly six o'clock now. He had already clocked out from the garage and was on his way home. After supper, he would have a few shots of Wild Turkey to gather his nerve and then force his filthy self upon her. The thought of him close to her made her cringe in revulsion. Stan was a wiry man, but strong, and she was afraid that whatever he had in mind that night would take place, no matter how violently she struggled.

123

Tears threatened to come, but she fought them back. She didn't want her spectral lover to see her bawling like a baby. *You really are warped, you know that?* she scolded herself. *What happened the other day was just make-believe, just a fantasy.* But no matter how many times she told herself that, she still could not escape the feeling that the lone dust devil was exactly what she thought it was: a wandering ghost, a kindred spirit as hungry for love and companionship as she was.

The setting sun hurt Becky Mae's eyes as she continued to survey the brilliant hues of the darkening horizon. A western breeze blew through her strawberry blond hair, a kiss blown from a thousand miles away. She closed her eyes and tried to imagine the sensation of gentle hands upon her body, delivering thrills of delight. Then a harsh voice from behind her dispersed the calm, filling her with a cold dread like a heavy stone in the pit of her gut.

"Are you out here *again*, girl?" Stan asked incredulously from the rear door of the trailer. "I swear I'm beginning to think you're retarded, Becky Mae. Now you get on in here and fix me some supper. You hear me?"

Becky Mae said nothing. She just sat there and stared across the deepening desert, praying...praying for a miracle and knowing very well that miracles did not happen in Ketchum's Trailer Park on the outskirts of El Paso, Texas.

"Dammit, girl, don't make me come out there and get you!"

Again she ignored him and continued to wish for the impossible. *Please! Please come and take me away from this awful place. Come and sweep me away on the wings of the wind, away from El Paso, away from Texas, away from this world if you can.* She listened for the familiar whistle of the sand spout's approach, but heard nothing...nothing but Stan's angry footsteps crunching across the backyard, straight for her.

"You little smart-ass bitch!" growled Stan, grabbing her roughly by the arm. "You answer your elders when

124

spoken to, understand? Now get your sassy butt inside that trailer before..."

She startled him by turning and giving him the dirtiest, most mean-eyed look she could muster. "Let go of me, Stan," she said, "or so help me I'll yell 'rape' to the high heavens."

Her stepfather was a little taken aback by her boldness, but not enough to relinquish his bruising hold. He stared at her for a long moment and a broad grin split his five o'clock shadow. "You know, don't you? You've known of my intentions all along. Well, you oughta know me well enough to know that there's no way out of it. You know I always get what I want, no two ways about it. And, by God, I'll have what I've set out to get tonight!" He pulled her bodily off the hood of the Plymouth and began to drag her toward the open trailer door.

Knowing that she had no other choice, Becky Mae began to scream just as loud and with as much force as she possibly could. "Shut up, you hear me?" said Stan. "Shut the hell up!" He loosened his hold long enough to give her a couple of backhand slaps across the face. She continued her screaming as she dropped to the ground and curled up to ward off the raining blows of his work-hardened fists. Her nose bled freely and her eyes began to swell shut as Stan's calloused knuckles fell time and time again.

"You can make it hard or you can make it easy," he warned, pulling a heavy leather belt from the loops of his trousers. "It's up to you. Shut your trap and crawl into that trailer and maybe I won't mess you up too bad tonight. But if you keep up that hollering, you might not make it to morning alive." When she continued her loud rebellion, Stan shook his head and, with a grin, raised the belt for the first downward stroke.

Then a howling from the west echoed over the desert like the roar of an impending doom.

"What in Sam Hill?" asked Sam in puzzlement. Becky Mae brought her head from beneath her crossed arms and, with battered, tearful eyes, stared toward the broken horizon. An imposing wall of dust the shade of burnt umber boiled toward them with a violent turbulence that obscured entire buttes and swept through the shallows of drywashes like an earthen tide.

Stan discarded his belt and, grabbing Becky Mae's arm and a fistful of her hair, began to back toward the trailer door. "Hell of a duststorm coming up, sweetheart," he snickered. "We'd better get on inside. Don't worry, though. We'll find something to keep ourselves occupied while we weather the storm."

Angrily, she batted ineffectively at him with her clenched fists, bringing howls of laughter rather than grunts of pain. They were almost ten feet from the open door, when something totally unexpected happened. Unexpected for Stan perhaps, but not for Becky Mae. She had been hoping fervently for something to take place, something that would deliver her from the horrible fate Stan had in store for her.

The dust at the foot of the back steps began to boil. It rose skyward on spiraling currents of air, until a dust devil seven feet high blocked Stan's pathway. Its color was not the soft beige that Becky Mae remembered from before, but an angry red. The twister bobbed and weaved like a boxer awaiting its opponent. Stan took a couple of steps to the side to go around it, but it shifted swiftly, stopping his progress. Then a fetid wind like the winds of Hell itself washed over the man and his captive, roaring, demanding in bellowing currents of air...*Let her go!*

Stan Jessup stood there and gaped, wondering if he actually heard what he thought he had. Then he knew for certain when the dust devil barreled forward with a vengeance, firing grit with such force that it lodged in the pores of his skin. *I said... LET...HER...GO!*

The mechanic's natural bravado got the best of him. "The hell you say!" he growled, swaggering forward with Becky Mae in tow.

Before he knew it, it was upon him. A pain lanced through his wrist, as if every bone there had been shattered. Becky Mae escaped his grasp. She tumbled to the side and crouched against the gathering fury of the sandstorm. Stan, like the fool he was, swung blindly at the thing that had hold of him, but his blows flailed through open air, hitting nothing. He moaned in terror as the dust devil lifted him within its swirling cone, the tiny rocks and cactus needles in the currents ripping at his clothing and flesh, drawing blood. He spun end over end, screaming madly as the wraith manhandled him, twisting and battering him until his entire body was racked with agony.

Then, when he thought he would surely be torn asunder, he was discarded like a rag doll. He was expelled from the cyclone with such force that he sailed through the open door of the trailer, across the cramped kitchenette, and landed headfirst into the cedarwood cabinet. He was out cold the second his skull split the hardened wood and bent the steel piping of the sink beyond.

Becky Mae lay trembling for a long moment and, when she thought it safe enough to lift her head, discovered that the dust storm had passed. Only the hovering dust devil, now its regular size and color, waited nearby. Her victorious suitor, her knight in shiny armor, so to speak.

She approached it with a smile on her blood-streaked face, her hands fidgeting nervously. "Thank you," she sobbed happily. "Oh, thank you so very much." She giggled as soft currents caressed her face, brushing away her tears. Then Stan came back to mind and she looked toward the open doorway of the trailer. He lay slumped across the peeling linoleum floor, pretty roughed up, but still alive. That meant that she had not yet escaped.

He would wake up eventually and, madder than before, insist on having his way with her. She would never be able to escape the lustful fury of Stan Jessup.

That was *unless*...

She started forward. In turn, the dust devil approached her in its smooth, shimmying gait. They stood there for a hesitant moment, regarding each other like two, long-lost lovers. Then, closing her eyes, Becky Mae stepped into the heart of the funnel and let herself go.

■■■

Stan Jessup came to an hour later and found three men standing over him. One was a uniformed police officer, while the other two were plain-clothes detectives.

"Are you Stanley Jessup?" one asked him.

"Yeah. Who the hell are you?"

"El Paso Police Department, Mr. Jessup," they said, flashing their credentials. "Will you accompany us outside, please?"

With some effort, Stan picked himself up from the floor. He was a real mess. His clothes were torn and his face and arms were lacerated and scratched. "She sure put up a hell of a fight, even if it didn't do her any good," the uniformed cop noted with some satisfaction. Stan couldn't figure out what he was driving at, until he reached the open door of the battered house trailer.

Several people stood in the backyard. There was Mrs. Ketchum and her son, two Fire Department paramedics, and, lying sprawled and misshapened on the sandy earth, was Becky Mae. His stepdaughter's clothes were nearly torn away, her slender limbs cocked at odd angles from her body. Her face was a mask of contradiction, wearing an expression torn between intense agony and blissful rapture. A light powdering of dust coated the orbs of her open eyes.

"He did it!" Connie Ketchum jagged an accusing finger at the bewildered Stan. "He killed her! Lordy Mercy, I could hear the poor child screaming her head off over here, just before the dust storm blew in."

"Do you deny that, Mr. Jessup?" Detective Joe Harding asked, hoping for an easy confession.

Stan stared in pale-faced shock at the heap of broken bones and damaged flesh that he had intended on sleeping with that night. The flame of desire he had been

128

carrying for so long went cold and, in its place, lingered a sick sensation in the pit of his stomach. "Huh? What are you getting at?"

"Our abuse center has received a few complaints concerning you, Mr. Jessup," the other detective, Terry Moore, told him. "Seems that your stepdaughter has been coming to school looking like she's been in a dogfight. Now, it isn't our place to go telling a man how to discipline his children, but this has gone beyond discipline, hasn't it, Mr. Jessup? This is downright cold-blooded murder."

A cold fear lanced through Stan Jessup's lanky frame as he looked from the three policemen to the twisted body of Becky Mae. *Why didn't that thing kill me?* he had been wondering since his awakening. *Why did it let me live?*

Now he knew.

"Look, Mom!" piped Tony Ketchum, pointing out across the desert. "Will you look at that!"

They all looked. Not more than a hundred yards away hovered a lonely dust devil, bouncing back and forth between clumps of mesquite and prickly pear. But, no, as they continued to watch, the twister split and suddenly became *two*. The twin sand spouts separated, then joined, like two wistful lovers in union.

I love youuuuu, the wind seemed to whisper and a fleeting, high-pitched whistle, like the voice of a teenage girl, returned the sentiment.

They stood and watched the two dust devils as they drifted slowly across the border, blending into the dusky horizon, then vanishing. Everyone beside the trailer grew strangely silent, except for Detective Moore, who finished reading Stanley Jessup his rights.

THE BOXCAR

I always thought the depiction of most vampires in literature as being wealthy and affluent was a complete fallacy. Most books have them dwelling in crumbling European castles or stately manors. But what about all the bloodsuckers who are just regular folks...the salt of the earth, so to speak? What about the ones who don't wear tuxedos and expensive silk capes—the ones who don't have two nickels to rub together?

That could have very well been the case during the Great Depression, when men rode the rails and wandered aimlessly across the land. But, if so, where would such creatures find refuge when the dark of night gave way to the cleansing rays of dawn?

HELLO, the camp!" I yelled down into that dark, backwoods hollow beside the railroad tracks. We could see the faint glow of a campfire and shadowy structures of a few tin and tarpaper shacks, but no one answered. Only the chirping of crickets and the mournful wail of a southbound train on its way to Memphis echoed through the chill autumn night.

"Maybe there ain't nobody down there," said Mickey. His stomach growled ferociously and mine sang in grumbling harmony. Me and Mickey had been riding the rails together since the beginning of this Great Depression and, although there were a number of years between us—he being a lad of fifteen years and I on into my forties—we had become the best of traveling buddies.

"Well, I reckon there's only one way to find out," I replied. "Let's go down and have a look-see for ourselves."

We slung our bindles over our shoulders and descended the steep grade to the woods below. We were bone-tired and hungry, having made the long haul from Louisville to Nashville without benefit of a free ride. It was about midnight when we happened across that hobo camp. We were hoping to sack out beside a warm fire, perhaps trade some items from our few personal possessions for coffee and a plate of beans.

As we skirted a choking thicket of blackberry bramble and honeysuckle, we found that the camp was indeed occupied. Half a dozen men, most as rail-thin and down on their luck as we were, sat around a crackling fire. A couple were engaged in idle conversation, while others whittled silently, feeding the flames of the campfire with their wood shavings. They all stopped stone-still when we emerged from the briar patch and approached them.

"Howdy," I said to them. "We called down for an invite, but maybe ya'll didn't hear."

A big, bearded fellow in a battered felt fedora eyed us suspiciously. "Yeah, we heard you well enough."

I stepped forward and offered a friendly smile. "Well, me and my partner here, we were wondering if we might—"

My appeal for food and shelter was interrupted when a scrubby fellow who had been whittling stood up, his eyes mean and dangerous. "Now you two just stay right where you are." I looked down and saw that he held a

length of tent stake in his hand. The end had been whittled down to a wickedly sharp point.

"We're not aiming to bother nobody, mister," Mickey spoke up. "We're just looking for a little nourishment, that's all."

One of the bums at the fire expelled a harsh peal of
laughter. "Sure...I bet you are."

"Go on and get outta here, the both of you," growled
the fellow with the pointy stick. He made a threatening
move toward us, driving us back in the direction of the
thicket. "Get on down the tracks to where you belong."

"We're a-going," I told them, more than a little
peeved by their lack of hospitality. "A damned shame,
though, folks treating their own kind in such a sorry
manner, what with times as hard as they are these days."

Some of the men at the fire hung their heads in
shame, while the others only stared at us with that same
look of hard suspicion. "Please...just move on," said the
big fellow.

Me and Mickey made the grade in silence and continued on down the tracks. "To heck with their stupid old
camp," the boy said after a while. "Didn't wanna stay there
anyhow. The whole place stank to the high heavens."

Thinking back, I knew he was right. There had been
a rather pungent smell about that hobo camp. It was a
thick, cloying odor, familiar, yet unidentifiable at the
time. And, although I didn't mention it to Mickey, I knew
that the hobos' indifferent attitude toward us hadn't been
out of pure meanness, but out of downright fear. It was
almost as if they'd been expecting someone else to come
visiting. Our sudden appearance had set them on edge,
prompting the harsh words and unfriendliness that had
let us know we were far from welcome there.

We moved on, the full moon overhead paving our
way with nocturnal light. The next freight yard was
some twenty or thirty miles away with nothing but
woods and thicket in between. So it was a stroke of luck

133

that we turned a bend in the tracks and discovered our shelter for the night.

It was an old, abandoned boxcar. The wheels had been removed for salvage and the long, wooden hull parked off to the side near a grove of spruce and pine. We waded through knee-high weeds to the dark structure. It was weathered by sun and rain. The only paint that remained was the faint logo of a long-extinct railroad company upon the side walls.

"Well, what do you think?" I asked young Mickey.

The freckle-faced boy wrinkled his nose and shrugged. "I reckon it'll have to do for tonight."

We had some trouble pushing the door back on its tracks, but soon we stepped inside, batting cobwebs from our path. The first thing that struck us was the peculiar feeling of soft earth beneath our feet, rather than the customary hardwood boards. The rich scent of freshly-turned soil hung heavily in the boxcar, like prime farm-land after a drenching downpour.

We found us a spot in a far corner and settled there for the night. I lit a candle stub so as to cast a pale light upon our meager supper. It wasn't much for two hungry travelers: just a little beef jerky I had stashed in my pack, along with a swallow or two of stale water from Mickey's canteen. After we'd eaten, silence engulfed us—an awkward silence —and I felt the boy's concerned gaze on my face. Finally I could ignore it no longer. "Why in tarnation are you gawking at me, boy?"

Mickey lowered his eyes in embarrassment. "I don't know, Frank...you just seem so pale and peaked lately. And you get plumb tuckered out after just a couple hours walking. How are you feeling these days? Are you sick?"

"Don't you go worrying your head over me, young fella. I'm doing just fine." I lied convincingly, but the boy was observant. The truth was, I *had* been feeling rather poorly the last few weeks, tiring out at the least physical exertion and possessing half the appetite I normally had.

134

I kept telling myself I was just getting old, but secretly knew it must be something more.

Our conversation died down and we were gradually lulled to sleep by the sound of crickets and toads in the forest beyond.

That night I had the strangest chain of dreams I'd ever had in my life.

■■■

I dreamt that I awoke the following day to find Mickey and myself trapped inside the old boxcar. It was morning; we could tell by the warmth of the sun against the walls and the singing of birds outside.

We started in the general direction of the sliding door, but it was pitch dark inside, sunlight finding nary a crack or crevice in the car's sturdy boarding. We stumbled once or twice upon obstructions that hadn't been there the night before and finally reached the door. I struggled with it, but it simply wouldn't budge. It seemed to be fused shut. I called to Mickey to lend me a hand, but for some reason he merely laughed at me. Eventually I tired myself out and gave up.

We returned to our bindles, again having to step and climb over things littering the floor. I lit a candle. The flickering wick revealed what we had been traipsing over in the darkness. There had to be twelve bodies lying around the earthen floor of that boxcar. The pale and bloodless bodies of a dozen corpses.

I grew frightened and near panic, but Mickey calmed me down. "They're only sleeping," he assured me with a toothy grin that seemed almost ominous.

Somehow, his simple words comforted me. Utterly exhausted, I lay back down and fell asleep.

■■■

The next dream began with another awakening. It was night this time and the boxcar door was wide open. The cool October breeze blew in to rouse me. I found myself surrounded by those who had lain dead only hours before. They were all derelicts and hobos, mostly men, but some were women and children. They stared at me wildly, their eyes burning feverishly as if they were in the heated throes of some diseased delirium. There seemed to be an expression akin to wanton hunger in those hollow-eyed stares, but also something else. Restraint. That kept them in check, like pale statues clad in second-hand rags.

I noticed that my young pal, Mickey, stood among them. The boy looked strangely similar to the others now. His once robust complexion had been replaced with a waxy pallor like melted tallow. "You must help us, Frank," he said. "You must do something that is not in our power...something only *you* can perform."

I wanted to protest and demand to know exactly what the hell was going on, but I could only stand there and listen to what they had to say. After my instructions had been made clear, I simply nodded my head in agreement, no questions asked.

■■■

The dream shifted again.

It was still night and I was standing in the thicket on the edge of that hobo camp in the hollow. Carefully, and without noise, I crept among the make-shift shanties, performing the task that had been commanded of me. I removed the crude crosses, the cloves of garlic that hung draped above the doorways, and toted away the buckets of creek water that had been blessed by a traveling preacher-man.

I spirited away all those things, clearing the camp, leaving only sleeping men. They continued their snoring and their unsuspecting slumber, totally oblivious to the danger that now descended from the tracks above.

I stood there in the thicket and listened as the horrified screams reached their gruesome climax, then dwindled. They were replaced by awful slurping and sucking sounds. The pungent scent of raw garlic had moved southward on the breeze. In its place hung another...a nasty odor like that of hot copper.

"Much obliged for the help," called Mickey from the door of a shanty, his eyes as bright as a cat's, lips glistening crimson. Then, with a wink, he disappeared back into the shack. The hellish sounds continued as I curled up in the midst of that dense thicket and, once again, fell asleep.

■■■

That marked the end to that disturbing chain of nightmares, for a swift kick in the ribs heralded my true awakening. It was broad daylight when I opened my eyes and stared up at an overweight county sheriff.

"Wake up, buddy," he said gruffly. "Time to get up and move on."

I stretched and yawned. Much to my amazement, I found myself not in the old boxcar, but in the campside thicket. My bindle lay on the ground beside me. Confused, I rose to my feet and stared at the ramshackle huts and their ragged canvas overhangs. They looked to be completely deserted, as if no one had ever lived there at all.

"There were others..." I said as I tucked my pack beneath my arm.

The lawman nodded. "Someone reported a bunch of tramps down here, but it looks like they've all headed down the tracks. I suggest you do the same, if you don't want to spend the next ninety days in the county workhouse."

I took that sheriff's advice and, bewildered, started on my way.

After a quarter-mile hike down the railroad tracks, I came to the boxcar.

"Mickey!" I called several times, but received no answer. Had the boy moved on, leaving me behind? It was hard to figure, since we'd been traveling the country together for so very long.

I tugged at the door of that abandoned boxcar, but was unable to open it. I placed my ear to the wall and heard nothing.

∎∎∎

Since that night, much has taken place.

I've moved on down to Louisiana and back again, hopping freights when they're going my way and when the yard bulls aren't around to catch me in the act. Still, Mickey's puzzling departure continues to bug me. That grisly string of dreams preys on my mind also. Sometimes it's mighty hard to convince myself that they actually *were* dreams.

Oh, and I found out why I've been so pale and listless lately. A few weeks ago, I visited my brother in Birmingham. Unlike me, he is a family man who made it through hard times rather well. He suggested I go see a doctor friend of his, which I did. The sawbones' verdict was halfway what I expected it to be.

For, you see, I'm dying. Seems that I have some sort of blood disease, something called leukemia. Now ain't that a bitch?

My dear brother insisted that I check into a hospital, but I declined. I've decided to spend my last days riding the rails. Who knows where I'll end up...perhaps lying face down in a dusty ditch somewhere or in a busy train yard, trying to jump my last freight.

However it turns out, I don't really mind. When my end does come, at least I'll have the satisfaction of knowing that mine will be a *real* death, deep and everlasting...and not one that is measured by the rising and the setting of the sun.

THE DARK TRIBE

When I was a boy, I loved to dig. The mystery of things hidden beneath the ground drove that childhood interest. I reckon having the soil of the earth beneath your fingernails holds a natural appeal for most boys...and can even carry on into adulthood, if farming or excavation becomes one's life work.

Mostly we would find possum teeth or Indian money, maybe an old arrowhead every now and then. But what if we had discovered a skeleton? Not just a random bone, but an entire human skeleton? There would have been no greater find for a boy of ten or twelve.

Josh and Andy happened across such a wonderful treasure. But, as they discovered, old bones hold their share of dark secrets...and some more so than others.

HEY, Josh...over here. I think I found something."
   Josh Martin bumped his forehead on the dusty stud of the crawlspace ceiling for the third time that after-

noon. He shook his head, trying to clear away the darting pinpricks of light, then joined his best friend at the far end of the four-foot cavity between bare earth and the reinforced floor of the Martin house.

They had gotten the idea of the excavation from a PBS special about dinosaurs the night before. Or, rather, it had been Andy Judson's idea. Josh had been kind of reluctant about digging around for ancient dinosaur bones, especially since the proposed site was located directly beneath his own house. But Andy always had that annoying way of talking him into things he really didn't want to do. And he usually ended up paying dearly for their little escapades, too, by getting grounded or receiving a sound whipping from his dad.

So far, they hadn't discovered a single dinosaur bone, not even a crummy fossil. He should have listened to his father, who was a professor of archaeology at nearby Duke University. He had told him that there was little chance of anyone finding dinosaur bones in that part of North Carolina. Josh had passed that information on to Andy, but his friend was thoroughly convinced that their native soil did contain the petrified remains of lumbering Triceratops and Tyrannosaurus Rex...and that they had roamed the earth on which Josh's two-story house now stood.

Andy's sudden announcement of a discovery after three hours of digging gave Josh renewed hope. Maybe they weren't getting into trouble for nothing after all.

"What'd you find?" he asked. Then his breath caught in his throat as he peeked over his friend's shoulder and found himself staring full into the face of a skull.

"Man, somebody's done gone and buried a body under your house," Andy said, his chubby face flush with excitement. "Have any of your old man's students turned up missing lately? Maybe some chesty co-ed he had the hots for?"

"Very funny," Josh said. "And keep your voice down, will you? If my mom hears us down here, she'll pitch a fit."

Andy reached down to grab the skull by the dirt-caked hollows of its eye sockets and wrench it from its ancient grave, but Josh stopped him. "No, that ain't the way to do it. This is an important historical find. We have to be professional, like real archaeologists. Here, let me show you."

He retrieved a garden trowel and some other things from where he had been digging at the far end of the crawlspace. The summer sunlight threw diamond patterns through the latticework of the front porch foundation as he set to work, mimicking the actions of the scientists they had seen on the dinosaur show. First he cleared away the excess dirt, inch-by-inch, careful not to disturb the position of the exposed cranium. Then he meticulously brushed away particles of dust and earth with a small paintbrush he had procured from Dad's workbench in the garage.

Soon, the skull was completely uncovered. It was old...incredibly old. It was smooth and pitted, oddly enough not the ivory color that denuded bone normally was. Instead, it had a peculiar charcoal gray hue. The lower jaw was there too, and all the teeth were present and accounted for. In contrast to the color of the skull, they were dark and almost pearly black in color. The skull grinned ghoulishly up at the two ten-year-old boys, giving them the creeps.

They continued with their work, painstakingly careful not to do any damage. By the time evening had rolled around and Mom was calling out the back door for Josh to wash up for supper, they had an entire skeleton lying in an open grave before them. It was completely intact, not a single gray bone out of place or missing.

"Who do you think he was?" asked Andy.

Josh shrugged. "I don't know. An Indian, probably. Maybe an old Cherokee. Dad says there were a lot of them around these parts before they had to leave and walk something called the Trail of Tears."

"Looks like this guy missed out on the marathon."

141

They were about to leave the dank, earthy confines of the crawlspace, when the lingering rays of the setting sun washed through the latticework and glinted on something hidden deep inside the skeleton's collapsed ribcage. Upon further inspection, they found it to be an arrowhead wedged tightly in the vertebrae of the spinal column, between the shoulder blades.

It was no ordinary arrowhead...not like those Josh had seen made of sandstone or chiseled flint. No, this one seemed to almost be transparent and of a sparkling blue color. It looked as if it might be crafted from molten glass or maybe even from some precious jewel, like a sapphire.

Andy, of course, had his hand out, ready to pluck it from the bone.

Josh caught his wrist in time. "Are you terminally dumb or something? I told you before, this is real important stuff we've found here. We shouldn't move anything...not until I get Dad to take a look at it."

"You're the one who's short on brain cells, pal," Andy told him. "You're not actually thinking of letting your old man take all the credit, are you? That's what he'll do, you know. He's a big-shot college professor, while we're only a couple of stupid kids. Figure it out for yourself."

Josh knew he was probably right. "What should we do, then?"

"Let's stick with the digging for a couple of days. Maybe we can find more old bones, maybe some pottery or a neat tomahawk or two. Then we'll drag your dad into the limelight...but only after we make sure that we get most of the credit. Okay?"

"Okay," Josh agreed, and they shook on it. Then Mom called for him again—a little crankier this time— and they scurried from beneath the house and went to their respective supper tables, covered from head to toe in dank soil and spider webs.

■■■

As the month of June came to an end and the Fourth of July approached, Josh and Andy continued their work in the crawlspace of the Martin house. In a span of two weeks they had uncovered five more skeletons, bringing the final count to a grand total of six. All were ancient and amazingly intact, and all possessed the same puzzling gray color.

Also, all six possessed the same strange, blue arrowheads wedged within their fleshless bodies. Some were caught between ribs, while others were stuck between the discs of spines or the tight crevices of leering skulls.

"Really weird about these arrowheads," Andy said for the umpteenth time. "Can't we just pry one of them out? It'd make a neat good luck charm, along with my rabbit foot and lucky buckeye."

Josh was unswayed on the professionalism of crawlspace archaeology however. "Not yet. First we'll get Dad and some of the other eggheads at the university to take a look at all this. Then maybe we can each have one of these arrowheads to keep."

Andy grumbled in agreement and, again, they left at the call of suppertime.

Later that night, after he had accompanied his folks to the grocery store in quest of wieners and chips for the big Fourth of July cookout the Martins were having the following evening, Josh caught his father alone in his study.

"Are there any Indian burial mounds around here?" he asked, trying to be as casual as possible.

"Sure," said Dad. "There must be hundreds of them around these parts. But they are all considered to be sacred ground, like a regular cemetery. In fact, it's against the law to dig up a mound. The Cherokee people worked long and hard to have their ancient grounds protected by federal law. A man can be sent to prison for desecrating the grave of an Indian."

Josh swallowed hard and said nothing.

The professor smiled and eyed his son, figuring maybe he was game for a good ghost story, now that they were on the subject of Indian history.

"You know, there was one tribe of Indians here in North Carolina that I don't think anyone would mind you digging up. In fact, we at the university have been trying to locate their particular burial ground for years, without success. They were called *Necropato* or "The Dark Tribe" by the other Indians who settled here in the Carolinas back before the white man showed up.

"According to Cherokee lore, the Dark Tribe was not even human, but a race of foul demons in Indian form. The Necropato were said to have been a savage tribe who raided neighboring villages, killing the Cherokee warriors in the most unspeakable ways and stealing their women-folk to serve as unwilling brides. Every once in a while an abducted squaw would escape and return, white-haired and insane, to tell the Cherokee elders of the godless hor-rors the Necropato had inflicted upon them. They told of human sacrifice, cannibalism, and the horrid offspring they had been forced to bear for the evil warriors.

"Finally, the Cherokee medicine man prayed to the Great Spirit, who, in a dream, directed him to a large, blue stone in a creek. The shaman searched for the crystal stone for many days and eventually found it in the place of his dream. The Great Spirit told him that it possessed the power to vanquish certain evils from the face of the earth. He fashioned arrowheads from the blue stone and gave them to the bravest warriors of the tribe, who then headed into the dark forest of the Necropato to engage in battle. A great fight was said to have been waged between good and evil that night and, in the end, the Cherokee emerged victorious. The bodies of the cursed Necropato were buried in graves long forgotten, the cause of their destruction still lodged deep within their bodies—a pre-caution to insure that their great evil would never rise to fight another day."

"Uh, that was...interesting, Dad," was all that Josh said before excusing himself.

The spooky tale had given him goosebumps. That night he lay awake in bed, afraid to go to sleep on the chance that he might dream of the Necropato and their savage atrocities. Finally, he got up and, taking a flashlight from the kitchen drawer, went outside into the humid July night. He stood outside the entrance of the crawlspace, before he finally got up the nerve to squeeze inside.

He went from one skeleton to the next, flashing pale light upon their naked bones. Something about them seemed different, something he couldn't quite put his finger on. Maybe they just looked different in the darkness than they did in daylight.

On his way back out, he stopped beside the one nearest the crawlspace door and studied its grinning skull in the battery-powered glow. Yes, there was something different! The surface of the gray bones held no stain of age to them, as if the flesh of the long-dead warrior had rotted away only hours before, instead of hundreds of years ago. He laid his hand upon a lanky femur bone. His fingers recoiled in disgust. The bone was damp and oddly warm to the touch.

Probably just the humidity, he assured himself before heading back to the safety of his bedroom. But when he got there, he found no comfort. He lay awake half the night, certain that he could hear the sound of ragged breathing echoing from the cracks of the floorboards beneath his bed.

■■■

The next day was full of fun and activity.

The Martins' backyard bustled with laughter and good spirits. Little kids climbed on swingsets and the old-timers pitched horseshoes. Soon, afternoon darkened into evening. Dad set up the grill and began to cook up burgers and hotdogs, while Mom and some of the neighborhood ladies passed out paper plates, napkins, and plastic forks for the big meal. Later, there would be sparklers and fireworks to look forward to.

After they had eaten, Josh and Andy decided to sneak into the crawlspace and check out their archaeological find. Night had already fallen and they knew it would be dark in the crawlspace, so Josh fetched the flashlight. When none of the grownups were looking, they squeezed through the little trapdoor and stared across the raw earth that stretched beneath the foundation of the house.

In fact, that was all the two boys could do...stare in sudden, sinking confusion.

The skeletons were gone. Only the shadowy pits of their shallow graves remained.

"Cripes!" said Andy. "Where are they?"

Josh said nothing at first. A horrible thought crossed his mind, a thought that stretched the boundaries of what his youthful mind could normally comprehend. Then it hit him. He knew now what had been different about the skeletons last night...or rather what had been *missing*. He turned to Andy, who crouched in puzzlement beside him, and fixed him with an accusing glare. Then he told him the story of the Necropato.

After he finished, he locked eyes with his best friend. "Did you do it?" he demanded of the pale and frightened boy. "Huh? You better fess up right now or I swear I'll pound you so hard..."

"Yes," confessed Andy. "I came back yesterday evening, after you went to supper."

Josh's eyes were grim. "Where *are* they?"

Andy fumbled through the pockets of his grass-stained jeans. His pudgy fist extended and opened. In the sweaty palm lay six crystal blue arrowheads.

Josh was about to launch himself at Andy in a fit of anger, when something stopped him. Something outside. Something they could not see, but could hear quite clearly through the cinderblock foundation of the old house.

Screams lanced through the clear night air. There were two types of screaming. One was the shrill screaming reminiscent of old western movies: savage war cries that heralded the coming of torture and death to many an unfortunate wagon train. The other screaming was that typical of the horror movies he and Andy sometimes rented from the video store. The panicked shrieks of helpless victims as they fled from insectile aliens or chainsaw-slinging maniacs.

Then the screaming stopped and, in its place, came a much more hideous sound. The awful rending and tearing of human flesh, as well as the splatter and slow drip of warm, red blood saturating the summer clover and the dusty earth beneath the swings. And there was another, more distinctive noise: a great ripping and sucking sound like strips of Velcro being slowly pulled apart.

Josh and Andy crouched there in the shadows. They listened...afraid to move, afraid to even breathe. Then they heard the soft padding of bare feet circling the house, coming ever closer. They sensed movement at the crawlspace door. Josh turned the flashlight toward the intruder and suddenly wished he had not as a towering form loomed into view.

"Boy, is your old man gonna be PO'd!" said Andy.

Josh figured that he already was.

For as the dark warrior began to squeeze through the opening, long-bladed kitchen knife in hand, he smiled with familiar lips and stared at them from the ragged pits of stolen eyeholes.

And he was wearing Dad's skin.

OLD HACKER

I reckon the act of smoking or chewing tobacco is a rite of passage for some adolescent boys...kind of like sneaking that dog-eared copy of Playboy *out of your daddy's underwear drawer when you were twelve. It gives them a taste of the forbidden and empowers them in the face of parental dominance. Personally, I never indulged in sneaking a smoke behind the outhouse, mostly because I saw how it made my buddies sicker than a grass-eating dog.*

But, hey, boys will be boys. Unfortunately, sometimes kids don't realize the implications of their actions. Sometimes a simple childhood indiscretion can end up haunting you for a lifetime.

EVER since I was a barefoot young'un in these Tennessee hills, I regarded the old man with downright disgust. Or, rather, that particularly nauseating habit of his.

His name was Jess Hedgecomb and he lived out in the West Piney Woods near Hortonburg. Folks said he was something of a hermit; just a lanky, old geezer who lived all by his lonesome in a two-room shack by Silver Creek and roamed the forest, trapping and hunting to make his meager living. He was harmless enough, I reckon. He had a sad way about him, but he was friendly enough in conversation and was known to flip a shiny nickel to any kid who happened to be standing at the candy counter when he sauntered into Dawes Market for his weekly groceries. Yeah, he was a harmless, well-meaning old man, I'll have to admit.

But he still had that godawful habit.

My papa called him Old Hacker, more out of amusement than anything else. See, whenever the old gent was standing around shooting the bull with the regulars on the porch of the general store, he would get this strange look on his face just before he was gonna clear his throat. The racket he made was kind of funny and kind of scary at the same time, especially for a young'un like me. Then, with a turn of his head, Old Hacker would send a great, gray-green glob of phlegm into the dirt road—or a spittoon, if one was handy.

Like I said, it was a nasty habit, one I wrinkled my nose at every time I laid witness to it. However, as I grew older, I began to notice something that gradually changed my revulsion into a strange fascination.

■■■

It began during the summer of my seventeenth year. I was working for Mr. Dawes part-time, sweeping up the store, stocking shelves, and pumping gas out front whenever a customer pulled up.

One sweltering July afternoon, I was helping load cement sacks into the back of Sam McNally's pickup when I suddenly heard that ugly sound. Old Hacker let loose with a glob of mucus that landed no more than a yard from the truck's left rear tire. I shook my head in disgust, glanced down at the ugly mess, and nearly fell clean off the store porch.

That streamer of green spittle was a-twisting and a-wiggling in the clay dust like it was a danged mudpuppy! I looked over at Sam, wanting to call his attention to it, but thought better of it. When I glanced back down, the thing was gone. Not dried up by the scalding summer sun, though—I mean it was plumb, lickety-split *gone*.

It happened again a couple of weeks later. I was pumping unleaded into some out-of-towner's big Buick. Old Hacker was sitting on the porch, playing barrel-top checkers with Mr. Dawes. I just stood there, watching the old man, waiting for him to cough up a hefty lunger. Directly, he did just that, sending a glob to the side, so that it hit the white-washed porch post.

Half in horror, half in awe, I watched as it inched its way up the post like some slimy green worm. When it reached the rain gutter, it stretched out and barely caught hold. I held my breath, sure that it was gonna drop to the ground with a splat. But, finally, it found its footing and disappeared over the slope of the corrugated tin roof.

Almost afraid to, I looked back to the checker game. Much to Dawes' surprise, Old Hacker skipped the remaining three of his reds, winning the game. Then the old-timer turned and stared straight at me, flashing me a knowing wink. It spooked me so badly that I pumped two gallons over the amount the stranger wanted and had to pay for the mistake out of my own pocket.

That weekend I hiked out to the West Piney. I had my .22 rifle and my hound dog, Bones, with me. But taking potshots at blue jays wasn't my only intention for walking the woods that day. I had half a mind to drop by Jess Hedgecomb's place. So I did.

Old Hacker was reared back in a caneback rocker, his feet propped up on the porch railing and his nose buried in a dog-eared copy of the *Farmer's Almanac*.

"Mornin'," I called out. I had a nervous feeling in my belly, the kind you get while waiting in the dentist's office, listening to his drill at work.

"Mornin' to you," acknowledged the old man. "You're Harry Dean's eldest boy, ain't you?"

"Yes, sir," I replied.

He stuck the almanac in the side pocket of his over-alls and removed his store-bought reading glasses. "Well, come on and pull up a chair, young man." He grinned, looking his eighty years and then some. "I don't get a whole lot of company way out here in the sticks."

"Yes, sir," I said politely. I sat down in a rocker identical to the one Mr. Hedgecomb occupied.

We sat there in silence for a good long time. Then Old Hacker looked over at me, his eyes sparkling. "Just dropped by for a neighborly visit...that right, son?"

I reached down to scratch behind Bones' droopy ears. "That's right."

"Naw, I don't think so," he chuckled. "I seen you watching me over at Dawes Market. I figure it was more curiosity than good manners that brought you out here this fine morn."

Then he leaned forward in his chair and started that noisy hacking cough that I had grown to loathe so much. When he finally spat into the dry dust of the front yard, we both sat there and watched. Bones bared his teeth and growled as the gray-green glob slowly made a bee-line down the pathway, toward the thicket.

"They always travel west," Old Hacker said, as if discussing the migration of birds. "No matter where I am in the county, whenever I cough up one of the little devils, they always head west—straight for the piney woods."

I held onto Bones' collar and watched the high grass part as the living lunger disappeared into deep forest. "Why is that?" I asked.

"Oh, I know why," Jess Hedgecomb told me. "But maybe you shouldn't want to. Maybe you shouldn't want to know anything about me or my...affliction."

Looking straight into that old man's haggard eyes, I said "Yes, I do." I knew that I really didn't, that I would probably be better off if I took my leave that instant and never returned. But it was kind of like standing in line for the freak show at the county fair. You have the creepy feeling that what you're about to see will be horrible, but you still want to see it all the same.

The strange tale that Jess Hedgecomb told me that day was much worse than any freak show I could ever hope to attend, real or imagined.

"I was born the son of a tobacco farmer," he began innocently enough. "So were my boyhood buddies, Lester Wills and Charlie Gooch. We worked the fields with our fathers. We planted, harvested, and hung the leaves in the barn for curing. But we were absolutely forbidden to partake of the stuff. 'I catch you smoking before you come of age and I'll tan your hide right good,' my papa would warn me. Of course, none of us listened. We'd do what most kids our age did: smoke corn silk or sneak old butts outta the ashtrays down at the train depot.

"I'd say we were about twelve years old that summer we found our own little goldmine out in the dark hollows of West Piney Woods. We were walking home from skinny-dipping in Silver Creek, when we came upon a heavy patch of wild tobacco growing pretty as you please. What a stroke of luck, we thought. Now we could harvest our own little crop without anyone knowing about it. Lester and Charlie smuggled boards and tin from home and we built us a small curing barn about the size of a doghouse. We stripped the leaves off the stalk, hung them up in that little shed, and smoked them with charcoal I filched from my papa's barn. We'd only cure them leaves for a couple of days before we couldn't stand it no longer. Sometimes the leaves would still be half green when we rolled them into cigars and set the match to them.

"Well, towards the month of September, we were down by that patch of wild tobacco. We were shooting the breeze and cutting up, when Lester tore apart one of those leaves, like kids will do on a whim of the moment. And, Lordy Mercy, there was something *alive* in it! The juice that dripped out of the veins of that shredded leaf

153

just twitched and squirmed like crazy. Lester threw the leaf down and we watched that tobacco sap crawl like tiny snakes through the thicket...straight for that wild tobacco patch. Me and the boys hightailed it outta that section of West Piney and never went back. But the damage was done. We'd already smoked a summer's worth of that horrid stuff into our lungs."

Mr. Hedgecomb paused, a pained expression on his ancient face, then continued, "I've been to many a doctor in my time, trying to find one who could rid me of this confounded stuff I carry around inside. They all look at me like I'm batty and tell me maybe I should see a psychiatrist. But I ain't crazy. I know the damned things are inside of me. When I lie in my bed at night, I can feel the little buggers stirring around, boiling in my lungs, trying to find a way out. They never find it on their own. I have to cough up the slimy bastards little by little, but there never seems to be an end to it. I truly believe that I'll be cursed with this awful infestation until my dying day. Then maybe we'll *both* be able to find the release we've been searching for all these years."

Me and that old man sat there in stone cold silence for a long time afterwards. I was wondering if his tale was true and, at the same time, knowing it was true. Old Hacker looked like he was having second thoughts, like maybe he shouldn't have bared his soul like he had. "I reckon you'll be wanting to get the hell outta here now," Hedgecomb uttered bitterly. "Well, I can't say I blame you. It ain't none of your concern anyhow."

I looked over at Jess Hedgecomb and, in those rheumy old eyes of his, I saw a loneliness so dark and empty that it made my heart ache. I knew then the true reason why Jess, Lester, and Charlie had been lifelong bachelors. It wasn't because they were queer for each other, like some folks in town thought. No, they never married for fear that a single kiss might have infected their spouses with that awful thing living inside their bodies. For nearly seventy years they had endured the horror and had endured it alone.

I just settled back in that rocking chair and propped my feet up on the railing. "Naw, I reckon I'll sit a spell longer," I told him.

Old Hacker smiled. Not that sad, little half-grin that I had seen all my life, but an honest-to-goodness, heartfelt smile.

■■■

We grew to be close friends during the months that followed.

Every day after school, I would do the old man's chores for him, then spend the evening playing checkers and talking. My parents thought it was a fine thing, a young fellow like me taking interest in a lonely old man like that. I do believe those last eight months of Jess Hedgecomb's life were the happiest, simply because he had someone there in that drafty cabin to pass the time with.

But the happy days didn't last for long and, by wintertime, both Old Hacker's health and his outlook on life hit rock bottom.

I must admit, there were times during his long bout with pneumonia when I felt like leaving that place for good. But I didn't. There were times when his congestion and coughing spells became so frequent that the old coffee can beside his bed nearly overflowed with living phlegm...times when writhing, green lungers crawled the bedroom floor until finally finding escape through the cracks in the boards. But I didn't lose my nerve. I stayed. I sat right there in the chair beside his bed, doing whatever I could for him. I just didn't have the heart to abandon him...not at a time like that.

It was a snowy day in early February when I found the old man dead.

I walked into his dark room, a cold dread heavy in the pit of my gut. The pneumonia had taken its toll, drowning him in his own bodily fluids. His skin was icy to the touch. I was just about to pull the blanket up over his head, when his chest hitched violently. Stepping back, I watched in horror as his chest rose and fell, his throat emitting a wet wheezing sound. The old man was dead, yet he was breathing. I could hear the mucus within his lungs churning and sloshing of its own accord.

Then his ribs began to snap...one by one.

I fled from that dark house, but lingered on the front porch, torn between going and staying. From within the house I could hear a terrible racket, the ugly sound of splintering bone and ripping flesh. I stood on that porch for what seemed an eternity, my hands clutching the frozen railing, my attention focused on the tranquil snowscape of the West Piney Woods. Then I was aware of a shuffling, liquid sound behind me...the sound of ragged breathing from the open doorway. *I made a mistake,* I tried to convince myself.

The old man's not really dead.

I turned around and screamed.

On the bare boards of the front porch, trailing a gory residue of fresh blood and slime, was Jess Hedgecomb's *lungs.* They heaved and deflated like a pair of gruesome bellows, pulling themselves across the porch with a life of their own. Then they paused, as if my screaming had drawn their attention.

The gory windpipe, weaving like the head of a serpent, turned my way and regarded me blindly, the hollow of the gullet staring like a deep, eyeless socket. I pulled my own eyes away, hearing the wet *clump, clump, clump* of the thing making its way down the porch steps.

When I finally did gather the nerve to look, it was gone, leaving an ugly trail of crimson slime across the virgin snow. I could hear it thrashing through the dead tangle of thicket, huffing and puffing, could see plumes of frosty breath rise as it headed into the wooded hollow.

As far as I know, the thing never returned to the dilapidated shack beside Silver Creek again...and neither did I.

■■■

I mostly keep to myself these days, preferring not to involve myself in other people's affairs. Every now and then, I can't help it, though, especially where the old man's childhood buddies are concerned. Lately there's been a lot of talk going around about them and the grisly death of Jess Hedgecomb. Whenever some busybody asks me about those last days with Old Hacker, I politely tell them to mind their own damn business.

Lester Wills died the other day over in McMinnville. There was a big ruckus in the newspaper about it. Seems that a wild animal got into the nursing home somehow and tore out poor Lester's throat and lungs right there on his deathbed. Of course, I know that ain't what happened...and so does Charlie Gooch, the last remaining of the three. Charlie ain't looking so hot these days, either. Every time I see him in town, his face is pale and worried. And when he has one of his bad coughing spells, I turn my head, afraid to look.

Sometimes when I'm out squirrel hunting in the West Piney Woods, I can hear something crawling through the honeysuckle. Something just a-puffing and a-wheezing as it makes its way through the shadowy hollows along Silver Creek. Sometimes it sounds as though there might be more than one.

My twelve-gauge is hanging in the window rack of my pickup truck, cleaned and loaded with double-aught buckshot. I hang around the general store and the courthouse in the evenings, waiting, listening for word that old Charlie has finally kicked the bucket.

And, when I do, I'll take my gun and a pack of hounds, and I'll go hunting.

THE WINDS WITHIN

This was the first of two stories I wrote featuring the Atlanta detective team of Ken Lowery and Ed Taylor. Unlike other homicide detectives, this pair always seemed to come across particularly gruesome and macabre aspects to the murders they investigated. I always considered the Lowery-Taylor tales to be sort of a "Southern-fried X-Files."

IDLE hands are the devil's workshop, so goes the saying.

Particularly in my case.

During the day, they perform the menial tasks of the normal psyche. But at night, the cold comes. It snakes its way into my head, coating my brain with ice. My mind is trapped beneath the frigid surface, screaming, demanding relief. It is then that my hands grow uninhibited and become engines of mischief and destruction.

As the hour grows late and the temperature plunges, they take on a life of their own. They move through the frosty darkness like fleshen moths drawn to a flame. Searching for warmth.

And the winds within howl.

■■■

"Dammit!" grumbled Lieutenant Ken Lowery as the beeper on his belt went off. He washed down a mouthful of raspberry danish with strong black coffee, then reached down and snapped off the monotonous alarm of the portable pager. "I knew it was going to be a pain in the neck when the department passed these things out. Makes me feel like I'm a doctor instead of a cop."

Lowery's partner, Sergeant Ed Taylor, sat across from him in the coffee shop booth. He nibbled on a cream-filled donut, looking tanned and rested from his recent vacation to Florida. "I hope it's not anything serious," said Taylor. "I don't think I could stomach bullet holes and brains my first day back on the job. Not after I've spent the last week in Disney World, rubbing elbows with Mickey Mouse and Goofy."

Lowery stood up and stared at the man with mock pity. "Oh, the tragic and unfair woes of a homicide detective."

"Okay, okay," chuckled Taylor. "Just make the call, will you?"

The police lieutenant went to the front counter and asked to use the business phone. He talked to the police dispatcher for a moment, then returned to the booth, looking more than a little pale.

"What's up?" asked Taylor. "Did they give us a bad one?"

Lowery nodded. "You know that case I was telling you about earlier? The one I was assigned to while you were on vacation?"

"The mutilation murder?"

"One and the same. Except that it's *two* and the same now."

Taylor felt his veneer of tranquility begin to melt away. The lingering effects of the Magic Kingdom faded in dreadful anticipation of blood and body bags. "Another one? Where?"

"The same apartment building," said Lowery. "1145 Courtland Street."

"Well, I'm finished," said Taylor. He crammed the last bite of donut into his mouth. "Let's go."

"Welcome back to the real world, pal," said Lowery as they climbed into their unmarked Chrysler and headed for the south side of the city.

■■■

The apartment building on 1145 Courtland Street was one of Atlanta's older buildings, built around the turn of the century. It was unremarkable in many ways. It was five stories tall, constructed of red brick and concrete, and its lower walls were marred with four-letter graffiti and adolescent depictions of exaggerated genitalia. The one thing about the structure that did stand out were the twin fire escapes of rusty wrought-iron that zigzagged their way along the northern and southern walls from top to bottom. The outdated additions gave it the appearance of a New York tenement house, rather than anything traditionally Southern.

There were a couple of patrol cars parked out front, as well as the coroner's maroon station wagon. "Looks like the gang is all here," observed Lowery. He parked the car and the two got out. "The dispatcher said this one was on the ground floor. The first murder was on the fourth floor. The victim was an arc-welder by the name of Joe Killian. And, believe me, it was a hell of a mess."

"I'll check out the case photos when we get back to the office," Taylor said. He followed his partner up the steps and past a few curious tenants in the drab hallway. The apartment building was nothing more than a low-rent dive; a place where people down on luck—but not enough to resort to the housing projects or homeless shelters—paid by the week to keep off of the cold streets. And it was plenty cold that month. It was only mid-December, but already the temperature had dipped below freezing several times.

They located the scene of the crime in one of the rear ground floor apartments. The detectives nodded to the patrolman at the door—who looked as if he had just puked up that morning's breakfast—and then stepped into the cramped apartment. Tom Blakely from the forensic department was dusting for prints in the living room, which was furnished with only a threadbare couch, a La-Z-Boy recliner, and a 25-inch Magnavox.

"The ME is in the bedroom with the stiff," Blakely told them, not bothering to look up from his work.

Lowery and Taylor walked into the back room. The coroner, Stuart Walsh, was standing next to the bloodstained bed, staring down at the body of the victim, while Jennifer Burke, the department's crime photographer, was snapping the shutter with no apparent emotion on her pretty face.

"Morning, gentlemen," said Walsh with a Georgia drawl. He eyed Taylor's tanned but uneasy face. "So, how was the weather down in Orlando, Ed?"

"Warm and sunny," the sergeant said absently. He felt the donuts and coffee boil in his stomach. "Who do we have here?"

"The landlord of this establishment," said the medical examiner. "Mr. Phil Jarrett. White male, fifty-seven years of age."

"Who found him?"

"According to the officer in the hallway, a tenant stopped by to pay his rent early this morning. He knocked repeatedly, but got no answer, and found the door securely locked. He then went around the side of the building, stepped onto the fire escape, and peeked in the bedroom window over yonder. That's when he discovered Mr. Jarrett in his present state.

Lowery stared at the body of the middle-aged man. "Just like the other guy?"

"Yep. Exactly the same. The same organs were taken after the throat was slashed from ear to ear, just like Killian."

"Organs?" asked Taylor.

The coroner bent down and, with a rubber-gloved hand, showed the detective the extent of the damage. "Pretty nasty, huh?"

"I'll say," said Taylor. He turned away for a moment. He felt nauseous at the sight of mutilation, even though he had been on Homicide detail for nearly ten years. "Why would someone do something like that?"

Walsh shrugged. "I reckon that's what we're here for." The coroner turned to Lieutenant Lowery. "Did you ever find any leads after the Killian body was found?" he asked.

"Nope," said the detective. "Haven't had much of a chance. The Killian murder was only last Friday, you know. I interviewed the landlord here. He didn't have anything useful to say. Looks like that's still the case."

Ed Taylor regained his composure and studied the body again. It was clad only in a V-necked undershirt and a pair of Fruit-of-the-Loom boxer shorts, both saturated with gore. He stared at the ugly wounds, then glanced at his partner. "Did you interview any of the tenants, Ken?"

"Not yet," said Lowery. "But that would be the best place to start." The detective looked over at the lady photographer, who had finished taking the crime photos. "Could you have some prints for us later today, Jenny?"

Burke lit a cigarette and blew smoke through her nostrils. "I'll have some glossy 8x10s on your desk by noon," she promised, then glanced around the grungy bedroom with disgust. "This guy was a real scum-sucker. Look at what he put on his walls."

The detectives had been so interested in Jarrett's corpse that they had neglected to notice the obscene collage that papered the walls of the landlord's bedroom. Pictures from hundreds of hardcore magazines had been clipped and pasted to the sheetrock. A collection of big-breasted and spread-eagled women of all sizes and races graced the walls from floor to ceiling, as well as a number of young boys and girls who were far under the legal age.

"Yeah," agreed Lowery. He spotted a naked child that bore an uncomfortable resemblance to his own six-year-old daughter. "Looks like the pervert deserved what he got. Kind of makes it a shame to book this bastard's killer. We ought to pin a freaking medal on his chest instead."

"We've got to find the guilty party first," said Taylor. "And we're not going to do that standing around here chewing the fat."

"Then let's get to work." Lieutenant Lowery clapped Walsh on the shoulder. "Send us your report when you get through with the post mortem, okay, Doc?"

"Will do," said the coroner. "And good luck with the investigation."

"Thanks," said Taylor. He glanced at the mutilated body of Phil Jarrett and shook his head. "Hell of a contrast to Snow White and the Seven Dwarfs."

"Like I said before," Lowery told him, "welcome home."

■■■

"Pardon me, ma'am, but we'd like to ask you a few questions concerning your former landlord, Mr. Jarrett," Lowery said. He flipped open his wallet and displayed his shield.

The occupant of Apartment 2-B glared at them through the crack of the door for a moment, eyeing them with a mixture of suspicion and contempt. Then the door slammed, followed by the rattle of a chain being disengaged. "Come on in," said the woman. "But let's hurry this up, okay? I've gotta be at work in fifteen minutes."

Lowery and Taylor stepped inside, first studying the tenant, Melba Cox, and then her apartment. The woman herself was husky and unattractive, sporting a butch haircut and a hard definition to her muscles that hinted of regular weight training. The furnishings of her apartment reflected her masculine frame of mind. There was no sign of femininity in the décor. An imitation leather couch and chairs sat around the front room, and the walls were covered with Harley-Davidson posters. The coffee table was littered with stray cigarette butts, empty beer cans, and militant feminist literature. Lowery and Taylor exchanged a knowing glance. Cox was either a devout women's libber or a dyed-in-the-wool lesbian. A combination of both, more than likely.

"Really nothing much to say about the guy, is there?" asked the woman. "He's dead, ain't he?"

"Yes, ma'am," said Taylor. "We just wanted to know if you have any idea who would kill Mr. Jarrett? Did he have any enemies?"

"Oh, he had plenty of enemies," declared Cox. "Me included. Jarrett was a real prick. Always hiking the rent, never fixing a damned thing around here, and always making lewd remarks to the women in the building. He tried to put the make on me once. I just about castrated the sonofabitch with a swift kick south of the belt buckle."

"What about the other victim? Killian?"

Melba Cox frowned. "Didn't know him very well, but he was a sexist pig, just like Jarrett was. Just like all men are."

"Have you seen or heard anything out of the ordinary lately?" Taylor asked. "Arguments between Jarrett and a tenant, maybe? Any suspicious characters hanging around the building?"

"Nope. I try to keep my nose out of other people's business, and hope that they'll do the same." She glanced at a Budweiser clock that hung over the sofa, then scowled at the two detectives. "I gotta go now. Unless the Atlanta PD wants to reimburse me for docked pay, that is."

"We've got to be going ourselves," said Lowery as they stepped into the hallway. He handed her one of his cards. "We would appreciate it if you would give us a call if you happen to think of anything else that might help us."

Melba Cox glared at the card for a second, then stuffed it into the hip pocket of her jeans. "Don't hold your breath," she grumbled, then headed down the stairs, dressed in an insulated jacket and heavy, steel-toed work boots, and toting a large metal lunchbox.

"Wonderful woman," said Taylor.

"Yeah," replied Lowery. "She'd make a great den mother for the Hell's Angels." His lean face turned thoughtful. "She might just be the kind of bull dyke who would hold a grudge against a guy like Jarrett, too. And maybe even do something about it."

■■■

"Won't you gentlemen come in?" asked Dwight Rollins, the tenant of Apartment 3-D. "Don't mind old Conrad there. He won't bite you."

Lowery and Taylor looked at each other, then entered the third floor apartment. The first thing that struck them about Rollins was that he was blind. The elderly, silver-haired man was dressed casually in slacks and wool sweater, giving him the appearance of a retired college professor. But the effect was altered by the black-lensed glasses and white cane. The dog that lay on the floor was the typical seeing-eye dog: a black and tan German Sheperd.

"We didn't mean to disturb you, Mr. Rollins," said Lowery, "but we wanted to ask you a few questions concerning the recent deaths of Phil Jarrett and Joe Killian."

Rollins felt his way across the room and sat in an armchair. "Terrible thing that happened to those fellows, just terrible. Not that I'm surprised. This certainly isn't one of Atlanta's most crime-free neighborhoods, you know. Some young hoodlum broke into my bedroom six months ago. The bastard slugged me with a blackjack while I was asleep and stole my tape player and all my audio books. Now why would someone stoop so low as to steal from a blind man?"

"There are a lot of bad apples out there, sir," said Taylor. "Some would mug their own grandmother for a hit of crack. About Jarrett and Killian...what sort of impression did you have of them?"

"Killian was nice enough. He was a welder. I could tell that by the smell of scorched metal that hung around him all the time. I never said much to the gentleman, though. Just an occasional 'hello' in the hallway." The old man frowned sourly at the thought of his landlord. "Jarrett was a hard man to deal with sometimes. He could be downright dishonest. He tried to cheat me out of rent money several times, telling me that a ten was a five, or a twenty was a ten. I'd never let him hornswoggle me, though. The bank where I cash my disability checks always Braille marks the bills for me. Of course, I really couldn't say much about Jarrett's treachery. A blind man has a hard enough time making it on his own, without making an enemy of the one who provides a roof over his head."

"Have you seen—?" Embarrassed, Lowery corrected himself. "Have you *heard* anything out of the ordinary lately? Strangers? Maybe an argument between Jarrett and one of the other tenants?"

"There's always some bad blood in a place like this, but nothing any worse than usual." The old man's face grew somber. "I have had the feeling that somebody's been prowling around the building, though. I've heard strange footsteps in the hallway outside. Several times I've felt like someone was standing on the other side of my door, just staring at it, as if trying to see me through the wood." He reached down to where he knew the dog lay and scratched the animal behind the ears. "You've sensed it, too, haven't you, Conrad?"

The German Sheperd answered with a nervous whine and rested its head on its paws.

"Well, we won't keep you any longer, Mr. Rollins," said Taylor. He caught himself before he could hand the man one of his cards, giving Rollins the number vocally instead. "Please give us a call if you think of anything else that could help."

"I surely will," said Dwight Rollins. "Do you think the murderer lives here in the building?"

"We can't say for sure, sir. It's a possibility, though."

"Lord, what's this world coming to?" muttered Rollins. "Well, at least I've got good locks on my door. Somebody would have to be a hell of a Houdini to get past three deadbolts."

The two detectives said nothing in reply. They thought it best not to upset the old man by telling him that, strangely enough, the apartment doors of both Jarrett and Killian had been securely locked from the inside, both before and after the times of their murders.

■■■

"Who the hell is it?" growled a sleepy voice from Apartment 4-A.

"Atlanta Police Department, sir," called Lowery through the door. "We were wondering if we could talk to you for a few minutes?"

"Is this real important?" asked the tenant, Mike Porter. "If you're selling tickets to the freaking policeman's ball, I'm gonna be mighty pissed off!"

"There's been another murder in the building, Mr. Porter," said Taylor. "We'd like to talk to you about it."

The click of deadbolts and the rattle of chains sounded from the other side, then the door opened. A muscular fellow with dirty blond hair and an ugly scar down one side of his face peered out at them. "Somebody else got fragged?" he asked groggily. "Who was it this time?"

"The landlord," said Lowery. "Mr. Jarrett."

"Well, I'll be damned," grunted Porter. He yawned and motioned for them to come inside. "You fellas will have to excuse me, but I work the graveyard shift. I catch my shut-eye in the daytime."

"We just need to know a few things," Taylor told him. "Like what your impression of the two victims was and if you've noticed anything peculiar around the building lately."

"Well, old Jarrett was a first-class asshole. That's about all I can tell you about him. The other fella, Killian, was an okay guy. Had a few beers and swapped a few war stories with the man. He was a die-hard Marine, just like yours truly."

Taylor walked over to a bulletin board that was set on the wall between the living room and the kitchenette. A number of items were pinned to the cork surface: a couple of purple hearts, an infantry insignia patch, and a few black and white photos of combat soldiers. "You were in Vietnam?" he asked.

"Yes sir," Porter said proudly. He shuffled to the refrigerator and took a Miller tall-boy from a lower shelf. "The Central Highlands from 1968 to '69. Just when things were starting to get interesting over there." He plopped down on a puke green couch and popped the top on his beer can.

"What about things here in the building?" asked Lowery. "Any fights or arguments between the tenants or with the landlord? Maybe someone hanging around that you didn't recognize?"

"It hasn't been any crazier than usual. I'm not surprised that it's happening, what with all the crack dealers and gangs in this part of town." Porter grinned broadly. "They just better not screw around old Sergeant Rock here." He stuck his hand between the cushions of the couch and withdrew a Ka-Bar combat knife. "If they do, I'll gut 'em from gullet to crotch."

The two detectives left their number and exited the apartment. As they headed up the stairs to the fifth floor,

Taylor turned to his partner. "Did you notice anything strange back there in Porter's apartment?"

"Other than that wicked knife and the crazy look in the grunt's eyes?" replied Lowery. "Not really. Did you?"

Taylor nodded. "Those pictures on the bulletin board. One of them showed Porter wearing something other than his dog tags."

"And what was that?"

"A necklace...made out of human ears."

"Interesting," said Lowery, recalling the mutilation of the two victims. "Very interesting."

■■■

"What do ya'll want?" glared the tenant of Apartment 5-C. The skinny black woman balanced a squalling baby on her hip as she stared at the two detectives standing in the hallway.

"We'd like to talk to you about the recent murders here in the building, ma'am," Lowery said. "May we come in for a moment?"

"Yeah, I guess so," she said. "Just watch that you don't go stepping on a young'un."

Lowery and Taylor walked in and were surprised to see four other kids, ranging from eighteen months to five years old, playing on the dirty carpeting of the living room floor. Three looked to be as dark-skinned as their mother, while one was obviously the odd sock of the bunch, from the lightness of its complexion and the color of its hair.

When they asked Yolanda Armstrong about the landlord, she scowled in contempt. "That bastard got just what he deserved, if you ask me. He was white trash, that's what he was. Wasn't about to take responsibility for things that were rightly his own."

"Pardon me?" asked Taylor, trying to clarify what she was talking about.

"The one beside the TV there, that's his. I came up short on the rent a couple of summers ago and Jarrett took it out in trade. Tried to get him to wear a rubber, but he was all liquored up and horny."

Lowery's face reddened slightly in embarrassment. "Uh, no need to go into your personal life, ma'am. All we need to know is if you've noticed anything strange going on in the building lately. Strangers in the hallway, or arguments you might have happened to overhear."

"Lordy Mercy!" exclaimed the woman. "If I was to pay attention to every bit of trouble that's gone on in this building, I would've gone plumb crazy by now. Half the people in this place are junkies and drunks, and the other half are losers and lunatics. You'd just as well take your pick of the litter. Anybody in this here building could've killed both those men."

"Including yourself?" asked Taylor.

"Don't you go accusing me!" warned Yolanda Armstrong shaking a bony finger in his face. "True, I've been wronged more than most. But I'm too damned busy trying to put food in my babies' mouths to go getting even with every man who treated me badly. I just take my lumps and hope they don't come knocking on my door again."

After the two detectives left, they called on the rest of the tenants who were there at that time of day, then headed back downstairs. It was nearly twelve-thirty when they climbed into their car and headed for a rib joint on Peachtree Street. "So, what do you think?" asked Taylor. "Think we have a suspect somewhere in that bunch?"

"Maybe," said Lowery. "Or our killer might be a neighborhood boy. A pusher or a pimp that Jarrett and Killian might have wronged in the past."

"Or we could have something a little more sinister on our hands. Maybe a serial killer."

"Let's not go jumping to conclusions just yet," Lowery told his partner. "This is just a couple of murders in a sleazy apartment building in South Atlanta, not some Thomas Harris novel. We'll grab a bite to eat, then head back to the office and check out the crime photos and Walsh's autopsy report. Later this evening we'll go back and interview the tenants we missed the first time around."

"Sounds good to me," said Taylor. "I just hope we come up with something concrete pretty soon. I have a bad feeling that this could turn into a full-scale slaughter before its over and done with."

"Yeah," agreed Lowery. "I'm afraid you might be right about that."

■■■

The warmth has gone and the chill of the winter twilight invades me once again, freezing the madness into my brain. My hands shudder and shake. They clench and unclench, yearning for the spurt of hot blood and the soft pliancy of moist tissue between their fingertips. The damnable winds must be stopped! They must be driven away. And only death can provide that blessed relief.

But I must be careful. The first was easy enough, and so was the second, but only because no one expected it to happen again so soon. The next time might very well be the last. But it simply must be done. There is no denying that. Even if there are suspicious eyes and alert ears on guard throughout the building, I must let my hands do the work that they are so adept at. I must allow them to hunt out the warmth necessary to thaw my frozen sanity.

Oh, that infernal howling! The howling of those hellish winds!

■■■

Lowery and Taylor were going over the coroner's report and the 8x10s of the two victims, when a call came in from Doctor Walsh. Lowery answered and listened to the medical examiner for a moment. Then he hung up the phone and grabbed his coat from the back of the chair.

172

"Do you still have those binoculars in your desk drawer, Ed?" he asked hurriedly.

Taylor recognized the gleam of excitement in his partner's eyes. "Sure," he said. "What's up? Did Walsh come up with something important?"

"Yep. He found some incriminating evidence on both of the bodies."

"What did he find?" pressed Taylor. He retrieved the binoculars from his desk and grabbed his own coat.

"I'll fill you in on the way," said Lowery with a grim smile. "Let's just say that I think our killer is going to strike again, sooner than we think. And I have a pretty good idea who it is."

■■■

The blanketed form was so sound asleep that it didn't hear the metallic taps of light footsteps on the fire escape. Neither did it hear the rasp of the bedroom window sliding upward, giving entrance to a dark figure with the glint of honed steel in hand.

The snoring tenant knew nothing of the intruder, until she felt the weight of the body pressing on her chest and the edge of a knife blade against the column of her throat. She lay perfectly still, afraid to move, waiting for the fatal slash to come. But the action was delayed. Instead, she felt a hand creep along her flesh, the fingers clenching and unclenching, searching through the darkness. Suddenly, she recalled the rumors that had been going around the building that day. Rumors of the organs that had been forcefully taken from Phil Jarrett and Joe Killian.

Then, suddenly, the room was full of noise and commotion. She heard footsteps coming from the direction of the open window, as well as the sound of cursing. Abruptly, the weight of her attacker was pulled off of her, along with the sharpness of the deadly blade.

Melba Cox reached over and turned on the lamp beside her bed.

The two detectives who had visited her earlier that morning were standing in the room. The one named Taylor was beside the window, holding a snubnose .38 in his hand. The other, Lowery, was pressing the attacker face-first down on the hardwood boards of the bedroom floor. As Melba climbed shakily out of bed, she watched as the detective cuffed the killer's hands.

"Are you alright, ma'am?" asked Taylor, holstering his gun and walking over to her. She saw that he had a pair of binoculars hanging around his neck.

"I think so," she muttered. She pressed a hand to her throat, but found no blood there.

Then the face of the sobbing intruder twisted into view and the woman got a glimpse of who her assailant had been. "You!" she gasped. "I would've never figured you to be the one!"

The wail of sirens echoed from uptown, heading swiftly along Courtland Street. A frigid wind whistled through the iron railing of the fire escape and whipped through the open window. The blustery chill caused Melba Cox and the two policemen to shiver, but it made the captured murderer howl in intense agony, as if the icy breeze was cutting past flesh and bone, and flaying the tortured soul underneath.

■■■

It was two o'clock in the morning when Ken Lowery and Ed Taylor stood in the main hallway of their precinct, drinking hot coffee in silence. They dreaded the thought of entering the interrogation room and confronting the murderer and mutilator of Jarrett and Killian. The suspect had stopped the cries of torment when brought into the warmth of the police station. That was probably what had spooked the homicide detectives the most. Those awful screams blaming the winter winds for the madness that had taken the lives of two human beings.

"Well, I guess we'd better get it over with," said Lowery, crumpling his Styrofoam cup and tossing it into a wastebasket.

"I reckon so," said Taylor. He thought of the suspect and shuddered. He secretly wished he had taken two weeks of his vacation time instead of only one. Then he would have been fast asleep in an Orlando hotel room, rather than confronting a psychopath in the early hours of the morning.

They opened the door and stepped inside. The suspect was sitting at a barren table at the center of the room. Fingers that had once performed horrible mutilation by brute strength alone, now rested peacefully on the Formica surface. There was an expression of calm on the suspect's face. The cold December winds had been sealed away by the insulated walls of the police station, returning the killer to a sense of serenity. It was a serenity that was oddly frightening in comparison to the tormented screams that had filled the car during the brief ride back to the precinct.

"You can go now, officer," Taylor told the patrolman who had been keeping an eye on the suspect.

"Thanks," said the cop, looking relieved. "This one really gives me the creeps."

After the officer had left, Lieutenant Lowery and Sergeant Taylor took seats on the opposite side of the table and quietly stared at the suspect for a moment.

"What put you onto me?" the killer asked. "How did I slip up?"

"The coroner found some strange hair samples on the bodies of Jarrett and Killian," Lowery told him. "Dog hair. And you were the only one in the building who was allowed to keep an animal."

Dwight Rollins smiled and nodded. "Unknowingly betrayed by my best friend," he said, then bent down and patted the German Sheperd on the head. "I don't blame you, though, Conrad. I should have brushed off my clothes before I went out."

The dog whimpered and licked at its master's shoes. Lowery and Taylor had brought the dog along, hoping that it would pacify the old man. But only the warmth of the interrogation room had quelled the imaginary storm that raged in the blind man's mind.

"Can we ask why, Mr. Rollins?" questioned Lowery. "Why did you do such a terrible thing?"

Rollins calmly reached up and removed his dark glasses. "*This* is why."

"Good Lord," gasped Taylor, grimacing at the sight of the man's eyeless sockets.

"It happened when I was a child," explained Rollins. "I was running like youngsters do, not really watching where I was going. I tripped and fell face down into a rake that was buried in the autumn leaves. The tines skewered both my eyes and blinded me for life. I used to have glass eyes, you know, during happier and more prosperous days. But hard times fell upon me and I had to pawn them to buy groceries. I had no idea what a horrible mistake that was."

"And why was that?" asked Lowery. He tried to lower his gaze, but the gaping black pits in the man's face commanded his attention, filling him with a morbid fascination.

"I could have never foreseen the horror of the winds," he said. "They've tormented me during these first days of winter. They squeezed past my glasses and swirled through my empty eye sockets, turning them into cold caves. And do you know what lurked in the damp darkness of those caves, gentlemen? Demons. Winter demons that encased my brain in ice and drove me toward insanity. I would have become a raving lunatic, if it hadn't been for my hands." He brought his wrinkled hands to his lips and kissed them tenderly. "They saved me. They found the means to seal away the winds...if only for a short time."

Taylor felt goosebumps prickle the flesh of his arms. "You mean the stolen organs? The eyes of Jarrett and Killian?"

"Yes. They blocked out the winds. But they didn't last for very long. They would soon lose their warmth and feel like cold jelly in my head." A mischievous grin crossed Rollins' cadaverous face, giving him the unnerving appearance of a leering skull. "You know, I was wearing them when you gentlemen came to call."

"Wearing them?" asked Lowery with unease. "You don't mean—"

"Yes," replied Rollins. "Jarrett's eyes. I was wearing them when you came to my apartment yesterday morning." The old man put his glasses back on. "And you didn't even know it."

An awkward silence hung in the room for a moment, then Taylor spoke. "You'll be transferred to the psychiatric section of the city jail across town. A couple of officers will take you there later this morning. You'll remain in custody until your arraignment, after which you'll likely be sent to the state mental hospital. There you'll be evaluated to see if you're psychologically fit to stand trial."

"Very well," said Rollins passively. "But I do hope that the cell they put me in is well heated."

"We'll make sure that it is," promised Lieutenant Lowery. "I'm afraid that you won't be able to take your dog with you, though. It's against police policy, even given your handicap. But we'll see to it that Conrad gets sent to a good home. Maybe we can find some blind kid who needs a trained guide dog."

"That would be nice," said Rollins. "But couldn't he just ride to the jail with me? That wouldn't hurt, would it?"

"No," allowed Lowery. "I suppose we could bend the rules just this once."

"God bless you," said the old man. He leaned down and hugged his dog lovingly.

After calling for an officer to watch the confessed murderer and leaving instructions for those who would transport Rollins to the main jail, Ken Lowery and Ed Taylor left the station, hoping to get a few hours sleep that morning. As they walked through the precinct parking lot, a stiff winter breeze engulfed them, ruffling their clothing and making them squint against the blast of icy air.

Before reaching their cars, each man put himself in the shoes of Dwight Rollins. They wondered how they might have reacted if the cold winds had swirled inside their own heads, and if they might not have grown just as mad as the elderly blind man under the same circumstances.

■■■

It is cold here in the police van. The officers who are driving me to my incarceration claim that the heater is broken and tell me to quit complaining, so I do. I sit here silently, enduring the creeping pangs of winter, hoping that I can make it to the jailhouse before a fine blanket of frost infects the convolutions of my aged brain and once again drives me toward madness.

A mile. Two miles. How far away is the comforting warmth of my designated cell? It is dark here in the back of the van. Dark and as cold as a tomb. My hands jitter, rattling the handcuffs around my wrists. I try to restrain them as they resume their wandering. Through the shadows they search for the warmth that I must have.

My friend. My dearest friend in the world...I am so very sorry. But it shall be over soon enough, I promise you that. You must remain faithful, my dear Conrad. You must serve me in death, just as you have in life.

You must help me block out the winds. Those horrible winds within.

OH, SORDID SHAME!

Some folks have a bad case of root rot in their family tree. Sometimes it is a genetic abnormality that is passed down from generation to generation. Recently, it was discovered that the McCoy family—of the infamous Hatfield and McCoy Feud—suffers from an inherited disorder that causes horrible fits of blind rage, which may partially explain the longevity of that historical conflict.

Sometimes—genetically or otherwise—there are those who simply can't hold their temper. Long before the McCoy condition was brought to light, I wrote this story of a similar family who lived in the Old South of the mid-1800s. A family whose dark and awful shame was passed down throughout the years.

BY the very nature and eloquence of this writing, few would believe that I was once a man enslaved.

That fact alone may cause some men to dismiss the validity of my story entirely, their suspicion of the Negro race conquering their potential for open-mindedness. But the tale that this testament holds is truth. I swear by God that it is. Surely it might have remained untold for all time—and perhaps best so. But a dying man must purge his troubled soul. Therefore, I take pen in hand and cleanse my own of the stain of that horrid incident some sixty years ago.

I first came to know the name of Bellamere in the mid-1800s. Since my birth, I had been bound body, mind, and soul to the possession of another man...in fact, several over a twenty-five year period. When gold had once again exchanged hands and I was bought by the family of Bellamere, I was a husband and father. Fortunately, the elder Bellamere was a man of compassion and not one to break up the family unit, putting so much faith and stock in his own. So, without ceremony, the three of us, my wife Camilla, my son Jeremiah, and I, were delivered to the Bellamere estate. We arrived with the obvious fears and expectations, figuring to be cast into yet another dismal world of cotton fields, slave shacks, and cruel overseers.

However, much to our surprise, life with the Bellamere family was nearly idyllic. Unlike our more unfortunate counterparts of dark descent, our servitude was pleasant and without conflict. There were no chains, no bullwhips, and never once did we hear the word "nigger" cross our master's lips. Since the Bellameres' wealth was one of inheritance rather than the livelihood produced by cotton or sugar cane, the extent of the plantation and its grounds were simply there for the family's comfort and leisure. I was dressed in the finest of garments, taught the most impeccable of manners, and transformed from an ignorant field hand into a poised and proper butler. Camilla attended to the cooking and housework, while Jeremiah, then a small boy, took care of the stables.

Another benefit of serving the Bellameres was their uncustomary interest in our education, or rather lack of it. Sebastian Bellamere and his wife, Catherine, possessed an immense library of both ancient and current volumes.

All manner of books and periodicals were made available to us. While my former masters had deliberately kept my family and I in intellectual darkness—a common practice in the South during that period, generated more out of fear than hatred—the Bellamere clan seemed to encourage our pursuit of knowledge. The Bellamere's only daughter, Emily, had hopes of becoming a schoolteacher someday and we were her first pupils. We became well versed in the classics, reading Dickens, Shelley, and Keats, and studying the histories and philosophies of the world. I would not be penning this testament this very evening if Miss Emily's tutorial guidance had not left such a lasting impression.

And we were offered companionship as well. Camilla shared activities with Lady Catherine and Miss Emily, while I often went quail hunting with Master Sebastian and his eldest son, Collin. And the Bellamere's youngest child, Martin, was my son's bosom buddy. He and Jeremiah made the whole of the Bellamere estate their private playground, climbing trees, skinny-dipping in the fish pond, and playing their favorite game, marbles, in the earthen circle drawn for that purpose beneath one of the garden's great, spreading magnolia trees.

So what went wrong? Why were we not allowed to live out the remainder of our lives in such a paradise, void of prejudice and strife? I have asked myself that question often over the years. Perhaps if I had paid closer attention, I could have foreseen the catastrophe to come. Perhaps if I had not been so blinded by my loyalty to the Bellameres, I might have been able to do something to alter the course of events that led to the downfall of that most inoffensive and genteel of Southern families.

The history of the Bellameres was very much a mystery to me, as it was to most everyone in that part of Mississippi. From their accent and customs, it was obvious that they were originally of foreign lineage, most likely British. It was also known that the family had left their native country under the shadow of some great scandal.

Sometimes, when partaking of strong drink, Sebastian would slip and mention "exile" and some terrible "shame" that had forever tarnished the family name. He never elaborated on precisely what that shame was, only that it had taken place during wartime. My suspicion was that cowardice was the black mark of which he spoke, since Sebastian and his family were of an overly reclusive and gentle nature. They had very little to do with the neighboring planters and whatever business was done in Vicksburg was performed by myself. Collin and Emily had no interest in people their own age and never attended any of the dances or social functions prevalent during those days of antebellum grace. And young Martin shunned the neighboring children, finding companionship only in the company of my own son.

The only other clue I had to the family's mysterious background was something I discovered in the Bellamere library. It was a journal belonging to one Woodrow Bellamere, grandfather to my master Sebastian. Woodrow had been a man of medicine, a scientist in the purest sense of the word. He had been most interested in the workings of the human mind and the chemical imbalances that caused negative behavior, such as paranoia, anxiety, and, as in the case of his own heritage, fear and timidity. It was known that the doctor had developed a serum to purge future generations of such weaknesses. A few of the passages even hinted that Woodrow might have tested the concoction on himself. But from what I had witnessed of the Bellamere legacy, Woodrow's pursuit for genetic strength and stability had proven a dismal failure.

However, I did not allow their eccentricities to affect me. I respected the privacy they demanded and attended to my appointed duties. Camilla and Jeremiah did the same. For a while, things went pleasantly. Then a couple of incidents took place that were both puzzling and frightening to someone familiar with the mild nature of such people.

The first concerned Sebastian Bellamere himself. He and his wife rarely exchanged hostile words; rather, they

182

seemed most loving and considerate of one another. Yet, one evening, their customary civility gave way to a heated argument. It concerned Catherine's desire to enroll Emily in a finishing school in Vicksburg and Sebastian's absolute refusal to allow the girl to venture from the solitude of the Bellamere household. The more Catherine pressed the matter, the angrier Sebastian became. His agitation was disturbing, for it was an emotion I had never seen grip the man before. I watched from the open door of the parlor as Sebastian's face grew deathly pale. And there was something else. His eyes—the whites of his eyes had grown blood red. Not bloodshot like those of a drunken man, but pure blood red, only the pupils showing in contrast to the surrounding crimson orbs.

Sebastian took a trembling step toward the lady, his hand aloft and balled into a fist. I am certain he would have struck her if I had not stepped into the room and drawn his attention. The man turned and regarded me with a fury that could only be described as murderous. At first, I thought he might take his anger out on me, but instead he stormed past, heading downstairs to the wine cellar. I followed at his urgent request and, soon, he and I were alone in the basement. There was an empty storage room at the rear of the dusty bottle racks, one with a sturdy oaken door and iron lock. He instructed me to lock him within the windowless cell and not come to release him until early the next morning.

My protests only seemed to feed the fuel of his madness even more, so I complied and did as I was told. The following morning I returned to find him crouched in a corner, his clothes disheveled, but his mind having regained its normal state of serenity.

The second event of this nature had to do with young Martin. He was only five years old at the time and, even then, small and frail for his age. While he and Jeremiah were out cavorting near a neighboring plantation one day, they strayed upon a broad cow pasture. Halfway across, a great black bull appeared from a wooded thicket and gave chase. Both children reached the safety of the bordering fence, but the frantic run had played havoc with poor Martin's nerves. By the time they returned home, the boy was overcome with fear and trembling. He was put to bed immediately. He developed a high fever the following day, but it did not seem to be from any form of sickness. Rather, it appeared that Martin was in the throes of some bizarre temper tantrum, as if his initial fear had bled away into a creeping rage.

Later that night, while the household slept, young Martin left his bed. Lady Catherine discovered the absence and alerted her husband. On horseback, Sebastian, Collin, and I searched the expanse of the estate, but found nothing. Then instinct nagged at me and I suggested we ride to the pasture where the bull had chased the two boys. As the dawn came, we reached the field and found the child lying in the dewy clover, his nightshirt torn and stained with blood. As father and brother carried the sleeping boy home, I lingered, wondering what had become of the mean-spirited bull. A short time later, I found out. The bull was sprawled in the wooded hollow, cold and dead. Its belly had been torn open and its entrails scattered throughout the brambled thicket.

Nothing else of such a morbid and inexplicable nature happened again for a very long time. Life with the Bellamere family continued as smoothly as it had before, leaving only uneasy reflections of the strange incidents to linger in the dark corners of my mind.

Then came the conflict between abolitionists and slave owners. The Southern states seceded from the Union, the Confederacy was born, and the great Civil War tore the fabric of normal existence asunder.

Men of all ages and social distinction enlisted to fight the Yankee hordes that were sure to march across the Mason-Dixon line and put a halt to the ways of the Old South. The Bellamere men, however, did not. They remained neutral and refrained from the wearing of the gray. They were content to make the Bellamere estate their private haven from war, intending to spend their time as usual: reading their books, hunting quail and fox, and living quietly and inconspicuously far from the roar of the cannons and the death screams of gut-shot soldiers.

They were ridiculed for their decision at first. Men rode onto the plantation in the dead of night and goaded them with curses and stones, calling the Bellameres "yellow-bellied cowards" and "Yankee sympathizers." During each episode of violent taunting, Sebastian and Collin were locked in the wine cellar, their eyes flaring like red-hot coals with each chiding word.

Eventually, more and more marched off to fight the war in Virginia and Tennessee, and less and less found time to torment the family who wanted no part in the conflict.

By the second year, the plantations and cotton mills around Vicksburg had grown quiet and deserted from disuse, and the Bellameres found themselves left alone, just as they wished to be.

And that was the way it remained...until a fateful night in the summer of 1863.

There had been much activity that day; the sound of marching troops and wagons on every road around the city and the roar of cannon fire from the wide channel of the Mississippi River. By nightfall, a division of Union cavalry was galloping up the road from Vicksburg to lay waste to any plantation loyal to the Stars and Bars. When the procession of flaring torches could be seen from the windows of the main house, Sebastian Bellamere gave precise instructions as to what would be done. Rather than fight for their home and honor, he and Collin would retire to the security of the cellar as usual. The rest of the Bellameres, along with my family and I, would hide in the upstairs parlor with orders to stay put no matter what transpired.

I did exactly as I was told. By the time the males had been locked in and the women and children were secure in the mansion's upper level, I watched from the upstairs window as a group of cavalrymen invaded the Bellamere property, leaving the rest of the division to conquer other pockets of resistance.

No one will resist you here, I thought as the soldiers dismounted and marched boldly to the mansion's front door. *There is no one here but a few frightened women and children...and a couple of craven cowards hiding in the cellar.*

But I was wrong about that. Very wrong.

A Union colonel kicked at the door with his dusty boot. "Open up this door, you traitorous rebels, or so help me I'll burn this house to the ground with you in it!"

There was the sound of breaking glass, the steely rasp of drawn sabers, and the sound of wild laughter as soldiers—some drunk on confiscated spirits—began to ready themselves for the destruction of the massive structure of whitewashed wood and alabaster stone.

I looked to Lady Catherine. She looked frightened, but strangely enough, not because of the gathering of military men below. She held Emily and Martin in her arms, but the gesture did not have appearance of a mother's loving protection. Instead, she seemed to be holding them in *restraint*.

The crackle of splintering wood echoed from somewhere downstairs. I was sure that the soldiers had breached the security of the locked and bolted front door. But, upon listening further, I discovered that the noise was too muffled to be coming from the ground floor. No, it seemed to issue from some lower level. From the shadowy depths of the wine cellar.

Then came the most horrifying wail of pure rage that I had ever heard in my life. It was fury torn between the mortal soul of man and the raw bloodlust of the most primal of beasts. It barreled up out of the pit of the mansion's black bowels, demanding to be vented, filling all who heard it with a fear so strong that it was as paralyzing as the venom of some exotic and deadly snake.

I turned and saw Emily and Martin then. Their faces were as pale as lard, their expressions contorted into a rictus of intense mental anguish. And their eyes...their eyes were the same shade of brilliant crimson as that which their father had exhibited that night so many years ago.

"I can't hold them any longer!" gasped Catherine, her slender arms surrendering the two struggling children. Emily and Martin ran for the door, their faces like those of demons, their hands curled into pale, fleshed claws. I moved to stop them, but the woman's voice cried out, "Let them go! Let them go or they will tear you apart!"

I stepped aside and they hit the door with such force that the lock was torn loose from its moorings. With enraged wails that more resembled the fitful snarling of beasts than that of innocent children, they disappeared down the staircase to join in the conflict below.

And what a conflict it was. There came another crack and splinter of wood, again from the inside. There was the sound of the main door being torn from its hinges and tossed aside. And there were screams. Lord in heaven help me, I can still hear those awful screams of fear and torment shrilling through the night air, climbing higher and higher, pushing the limits of the human vocal cords, then faltering into choking silence. Only a few gunshots rang out and there was the clatter of hooves on the flagstones as a few of the horses escaped into the summer darkness. After the screams of dying men faded, all that could be heard was the maddening sound of flesh being ripped apart. That and the wailing chorus of earthbound banshees performing atrocities in the outer courtyard.

After a time, the horrible noises ended. "Wait here," Catherine Bellamere said, then, despite my protests, went downstairs alone. My family and I waited in the upstairs parlor, straining our ears. All that we could hear was the lady's gentle, soothing voice and the sound of soft sobbing.

Minutes later, Catherine reappeared. Her gown was stained crimson with blood. Quietly, she avoided our questions and went to an iron safe in her husband's study. She opened the safe and withdrew a small bag of gold

OH SORDID SHAME

coins and a folded document. "Come with me," she said and the four of us went down to the ground floor of the Bellamere house.

The marble floor was splattered with streaks of fresh blood, leading from the darkness of the courtyard beyond. "Stay here for a moment," Catherine requested. Her voice was rock steady, despite the carnage around her. As she slipped through the door of the downstairs sitting room, I caught a fleeting glimpse of huddled forms in the golden glow of a kerosene lamp. They were the forms of monsters, hideous fiends clad in blood-dyed rags. As the door swung shut, I watched as one of them looked my way, its eyes running the gamut from crimson to pink to eggshell white.

It was a demon I knew. A demon that possessed a familiar face, as well as a familiar voice. "Oh, what shame," it moaned tearfully. "What sordid shame!"

A moment later, Lady Catherine exited the den. She handed me the gold sack and the folded paper. "Here is money and your freedom. Take a buggy and two strong horses from the stable and go. Never return to this house again, and for God's sake, never utter a word of what took place here this night."

Confused, we did as she said. We left the house and stood for a long and horrified instant in the courtyard beyond the alabaster columns of the Bellamere mansion. In the pale glow of moonlight we laid eyes on the massacre that the Bellameres' secret shame had brought about. Soldiers and horses lay everywhere, torn and broken, like huge toys mangled by some vicious giant-child and cast aside. Fresh blood glistened in the nocturnal light, as well as the stark whiteness of denuded bone. When I quickly led my family past the awful scene of human devastation, I noticed that some of the bodies appeared to have been partially devoured.

As we made our way through the garden for the stable, the titter of childish laughter erupted from beneath the spreading magnolia tree. "Jeremiah," called young Martin from the shadows. "Come play with me."

My son took a step toward the tree, but I pulled him back. Moonlight shone upon the dirt circle where the Bellamere child crouched. His marble game was different that night from the countless times I had witnessed before. For, instead of the colorful balls of glass, onyx, and agate, Martin shot the circle with huge black orbs that seemed slick and slimy in appearance. It took me a moment before I realized that what he played with were the gouged eyes of a cavalry soldier's horse.

We hitched two of the stable's finest steeds to a wagon and left that horrible place, escaping the Federal soldiers by way of a desolate backroad. Although I have never spoken of that horrible night before this writing, I have thought about it many times. I have revisited the Bellamere mansion many times in my dreams, have heard the bestial screams of bloodlust and smelled the coppery scent of violent death in my nostrils. And I always wake with a scream trapped firmly behind my lips. Sometimes that scream escapes, like steam escaping from a boiler, saving my mind from the mounting pressure of certain insanity.

I am an old man now. I have lived past the conquering of the West, past the turn of the century, and now into the time of the Great War. I have watched the world progress before my aged eyes, have seen people live and die, including my own family. And I have watched for word regarding a particular surname. That search has ended with a story from a recent newspaper, a report about a soldier by the name of Bellamere who was court-marshaled for crimes unspeakable, even by the conventions of war. I cannot help but wonder if that poor soldier is a distant offspring of the family I once knew and if he is damned with the same seed of shame that his ancestors were.

I lay here now, bedridden and ill, my frail hands unfolding a document yellowed and crumbling with age. It is the declaration of freedom given to me some sixty years ago…my own private Emancipation Proclamation.

As I stare at the hastily scrawled signature at the bottom of the page, my heart grows heavy with uneasiness. For the name of Sebastian Bellamere is signed not in simple ink, but in the blood of a dozen slaughtered souls.

THE CEREBRAL PASSION

Because of my religious beliefs, I don't hold to the theory of evolution. But I do believe that it can take place in horror fiction. Not a gradual evolution over hundreds of thousands of years, but an abrupt and horrifying transformation of the normal into the abnormal. One day everything is fine and dandy, and then, out of the blue, everything changes...for the worse.

Even during such an abominable transformation of circumstance, love sometimes endures. And whatever you have become, man or monster, desperately clings to that fragile lifeline of human emotion.

THE headaches only worsened as the week drew on. In a span of four days, Henry Beck had graduated from regular aspirin to extra-strength Tylenol to a painkiller Estelle had left over from her gall bladder surgery last spring. However, nothing seemed to help.

"Go see Doc Rhodes," his wife urged, not naggingly, but out of genuine concern. "It could be something serious."

Henry just shrugged off her suggestion. He had always been a stubborn man who preferred sticking to his common sense rather than relying on the advice of others. Besides, he needed no doctor to tell him what caused the awful migraines that plagued him from sunrise till midafternoon each day. He had a good idea precisely what brought them about.

Henry had been harvesting his tobacco crop the week before last with the help of Fred and Jimbo Hayes, a couple of neighboring boys from down the road a piece. The work had been hard and hot, the temperature in the mid-nineties that late August day. The boys had a truckload of cut leaves and were toting them to the graywood barn to be split, hung on poles, and smoke cured, when Henry found himself alone in the dusty field with a powerful thirst.

He had gone to the old stone well at the edge of the pasture, the well that his great-grandfather had dug over a hundred and twenty years before. It had been covered in disuse for many years, but Estelle's Frigidaire with the Mason jar of ice water on the center shelf seemed so very far away at the moment, that he turned the wooden lid aside and lowered the ancient bucket into its depths. The water looked a little brackish, but it was cool, so he took a long swallow. It went down like bad medicine, strangely slick like mucus, the foul taste of algae, sulfur, and something else Henry couldn't quite place causing him to sputter and gag. With a curse, he had returned the cover to the well and then forgotten the whole sorry episode.

As the days wore on and the pain intensified, he began to wonder if the well had been poisoned. If that were the case, then he would have been stricken with nausea and stomach cramps. Neither had appeared, only the headaches. That and the tenderness along the sides of his neck from the collarbone to just behind the ears. And there was that weird way the headaches abruptly ended around two or three o'clock in the afternoon. Afterward, Henry always felt refreshed and strangely energized, as if he were half of his seventy years. Instead of dragging in, bone-weary and sullen, from a hard day's work, he found himself coming in from the fields, whistling and grinning, feeling like a million bucks.

Estelle Beck also noticed the change. For years she had witnessed a gradual breakdown in their relationship, a barrier of disinterest forming between them that she had both dreaded and sadly resigned herself to. But recently Henry had come in from his work an entirely different man. He would bring her wildflowers from the pasture and give her a big smile and a peck on the cheek, a rare show of affection for a man as grim as her Henry. Why, the last evening he had even picked her up, his calloused hands hooked beneath her arms, and waltzed her cheerfully across the kitchen floor.

Toward the end of the week, Estelle began to gradually lose her sense of impending doom and that nagging sense that they were no more than two strangers with only a yellowed marriage license to link them.

■■■

The knots appeared Friday morning.

Small and doughy, they rose atop the hard ridges of his collarbones and just behind the lobes of his ears. The tenderness had turned into soreness, but again the pain only lasted as long as the headaches.

Henry began to feel a great calm overtake him that Friday evening, a peace of mind that he had not experienced since his youth. It was as if the horrible migraines had a cleansing effect, as if they drained his brain of mental impurities. He could think clearer than before. His senses seemed sharpened to a point he had never known. The evening sunset that appeared upon the Tennessee hillscape seemed to possess colors he had never noticed before. The honeysuckle and magnolia blooms seemed more sweet to the smell, while his wife's cooking was definitely more delicious to his heightened taste buds. It was as if his mind had been rejuvenated; as if the blinders had suddenly been lifted after years of drab, narrow-minded living.

And his newfound well-being wasn't confined merely to his head. His physical strength and endurance seemed to increase, and not only in relation to the work he did in the fields. That night Estelle had come to bed and found him ready for her. She had been both surprised and secretly delighted. Due to a back injury, Henry had been hopelessly impotent for nearly seven years. But now he had no such problem. Aroused, he had moved to her side of the bed, gently caressing her, peppering her face and neck with small kisses that made her heart leap with joy. With a passion unequaled since they were newlyweds, Henry and Estelle made love. Slow and natural, devoid of the awkwardness that had always strained their love-making before, it seemed to last for hours, then end with a flashpoint of ecstasy that Estelle had never experienced in fifty years of marriage.

They fell asleep in each other's arms, Henry snoozing with the dreamless ease of an infant. His wife lay awake a while longer, an odd mixture of elation and deep-seated dread swimming in her thoughts until slumber finally came.

■■■

The next morning she was alarmed to find that the bumps on Henry's neck had grown in size. They also had an ugly bruised color to them. Estelle once again voiced her concern.

"Probably nothing more than swollen glands," grumbled her spouse as he chugged the last of Estelle's painkillers with his morning coffee. She wasn't convinced of that at all, but did not press the matter, afraid that the wall between them might thicken where it finally seemed to be crumbling.

Despite Henry's blinding headache, they drove to the nearby town of Coleman as they always did on Saturday morning. They did their shopping, ate lunch at the corner café, then visited Estelle's sister for an hour or so. As they drove down the main street for home, the courthouse clock struck the hour of three. Henry's brow, which had been creased with pain, suddenly smoothed and he turned to his wife with a big smile. "What do you say we go to the fair?" he proposed with the enthusiasm of a ten-year-old.

Estelle stared at him as though he had spoken in a foreign tongue. She could hardly believe that it was her husband talking. Henry Beck, although never bitter or cynical, had always been a solemn, no-nonsense man. Oh, he had been fun when they were first courting, always ready with a joke, always making her laugh. But three straight years of drought and failed crops after their wedding had dampened the man's spirit and hardened his outlook on life. And now here he was eagerly wanting to take in the Bedloe County Fair. She was beginning to seriously wonder if severe headaches were a warning sign of Alzheimer's disease.

Fifteen minutes later, they were there on the crowded midway, surrounded by the music of the calliope and the sugary scent of cotton candy. Like children, they gorged themselves on sweets and rode all the good rides—the rollercoaster, the dodge'em cars, the Tunnel of Love—both totally unaware of the strange looks they were receiving from their friends and neighbors. While on the Ferris wheel, the gears had jammed, leaving them suspended at the very top. They had kissed long and soulfully in the privacy of mid-air, loosening their embrace only when the grind of machinery once again pulled them earthward.

During the drive home, in the darkness of the truck cab, their hands had met, their fingers entwining. Their eyes had locked in the faint light of the dash, conveying that mutual signal which was far too intimate for spoken words. This time they hadn't waited for the seclusion of home. Pulling off the road into a grove of crabapple trees, Henry and Estelle expressed their love in the bed of the pickup, as shameless as two feverish teenagers, beneath a velvety blanket of autumn stars.

∎∎∎

Later that night, Henry Beck awoke to find himself standing in the open pasture. Standing beside the old, stone well.

Confusion gripped him momentarily, making him feel faint. He had fallen asleep under the patchwork quilt of their big brass bed with Estelle slumbering silently beside him. Now he was standing in knee-high thicket, his right hand resting upon the roughly-hewn lid of the well. He was bewildered to find himself drenched with sweat, as if fresh from some horrid nightmare, the cool September breeze plastering his damp nightshirt to his lean body. The fleshy knots throbbed along his neck as big as goose eggs.

He stared up at the sky. From the set of the moon, Henry figured it to be past three in the morning. Why was he out there? Did he sleepwalk or had something drawn him there to the well? The thought was not entirely implausible to him. For some reason, the ancient well had come to mind several times in the past few days. Not disturbing thoughts of the fetid waters within, but strangely comforting thoughts. Images of cool, black liquid and smooth stone walls, of something down there in the darkened pit, something of great presence and longevity. A longevity that, after countless ages, was slowly ebbing, moving toward nonexistence.

Tomorrow...

The word echoed in his mind as if he himself had spoken it aloud. What was it about tomorrow? Tomorrow he would board up the well securely or fill it completely with a ton of earth and rock? No, the very thought of doing such a thing seemed to sicken him. It was like considering the desecration of something holy, although he could not for the life him figure out why. It was only an old well full of stagnant water. Nothing more.

Or was it? His mind thought differently. He slid back the wooden lid and peered down the curving walls. Moonlight flickered on the pool at the bottom and, for a moment, he thought he saw movement. He sighed and felt a great peace engulf him, barreling up at him from out of that dank pit like a tangible force. He experienced an emotion he could only describe as *belonging*; a bizarre kinship that he had never actually felt with members of his own family.

Then something seemed to whisper up from the black waters, the unintelligible meanderings of a weakened and dying race. But, strangely enough, the gist of understanding tickled at his subconscious...promising things dark and unfathomable.

Henry pulled the lid back into place and started back across the dusty furrows that had once blossomed with leafy green Burley. His bluetick hound, Old Sam, met him at the edge of the field. He crouched and scratched the dog absently behind the ears. "Am I going crazy, boy?" he asked hoarsely. "Or am I just a damned old fool?"

The dog had no answers for him. He sniffed at his master's bare ankles as they walked through Estelle's flower garden for the house. Henry looked back only once. The well was a squat lump of stone and mortar on the edge of the dark thicket, sitting where it always had. The old man felt a great loneliness wash over him. Tears began to well in his ancient eyes and suddenly he found himself sobbing without control.

Tomorrow...

■■■

Sunday went as it usually did. After church, Henry and Estelle had come home, ate dinner, and then went about their own weekend activities. Estelle did her needlepoint, while Henry piddled around in his workshop in the barn. He was in the process of finishing a handmade highchair for his newest grandchild, who would be making its appearance in late November. The Becks had two children, both grown with families of their own. It was their daughter Elizabeth who was expecting, for the third time in five years.

Normalcy reigned over the rural tobacco farm until three o'clock. Then existence, as he had known it, abruptly changed for Henry Beck.

He glanced down at his pocket watch, pleased to see the hands nearing the third hour. Relief would come now, as it did every day at that time. The awful headache would peter out and he would feel reborn again, the aches and pains of his advancing years traded in for a refreshed sense of physical and mental renewal.

He eagerly anticipated the strike of three, but this time it brought about an entirely different effect. The pain in his head did not diminish. Rather it increased tenfold, spearing through the very core of his skull, coursing through the lean column of his neck like liquid fire.

"Oh, dear God, what's happening?" he gasped, slumping to his knees in the dust and manure of the barn floor. His hands went to his neck, which was now rigid, the muscles taut, stretched to their limit. His fingers played across the knots and found them huge and pulsating. They flexed beneath the thin membrane of skin as if something were there, suddenly awake and restless. Something *alive*, yet part of him.

Dear Lord in heaven, what's wrong with me? The searing agony in his neck continued to intensify. It almost felt as though his head was attempting to pull itself from his body. But that was utter nonsense, wasn't it? He knew at once that it was not as the tendons in his neck began to snap, one by one. At the same instant, the arteries tore open, flooding his esophagus with a gorge of fresh blood.

He opened his mouth to scream for Estelle, but to no avail. The cartilage of his larynx pulled apart, the vocal cords popping like strands of rotten twine. He fell upon his back, crushing the inflamed nodule behind his left ear. Hot blood bathed the side of his face as it ruptured. There was blood everywhere. It coursed in swift rivulets down the front of his blue chambray shirt.

The agony reached a crescendo that Henry could no longer endure. He felt himself slipping into merciful unconsciousness. But before that blessed oblivion came, something unfolded from that burst knot behind his ear. Like a gory spider it passed before his eyes, flexing and unflexing. It looked as though it was—no, it couldn't have been—but it *was*, a tiny, perfectly formed *hand*.

■■■

It opened its eyes.

The murky shadows of the barn's interior seemed to have lost their depth, the sparse light intensifying to brilliance near overbearance. The optical nerves adjusted swiftly however. It stared at the body that lay on the earthen floor several feet away. The liver-spotted hands were gnarled from the final throes of boundless agony, the trunk of the neck ragged and frayed like the end of an old rope, the tendons and bloodless arteries exposed.

The transition had gone well. Yes, there had been pain, but wasn't there always discomfort in every form of change? From the expulsion of an infant from the womb to the passage of the soul at the point of death, there was always a violent rending involved. There had been a period of horror at first, a few seconds of confused fear when the host had failed to understand the nature of what was taking place. But there was no fear now. Only understanding and total acceptance.

The Henry-thing struggled from its prone position, the newly formed limbs jerking erratically. The swollen knots had sprouted skinny, malformed appendages, an alien life form's blind interpretation of the human form. Silently, it strained to a stance, trying hard to keep its balance. It took a few staggering steps, each movement increasing in coordination. Yes, it was much better this way, without the cumbersome weight of the farmer's body. Existence would be much simpler with the physical condition reduced to a minimum. The cerebral state would reign as it should—as it had reigned for years in the dank liquid world of the well.

A low growling came from the barn door. The Henry-thing turned on under-developed legs and faced Old Sam. The dog bared its teeth at the scent of fresh blood and this *thing* that stood before him. There was some nagging familiarity about this strange, creature, a mixture of emotion that Old Sam couldn't quite comprehend.

The thing took a couple of faltering steps forward, its jaws working silently. *Go on, boy,* echoed words with no sound. *Get outta here!*

The hound reacted in absolute terror at the realization that the words in his head were his master's voice and that the thing in question possessed his master's blood smeared face. Old Sam's mind snapped. He ran like hell across the open field and into the woods beyond. A power company worker would discover the poor dog a few days later, three counties away, having literally run itself to death.

A pang of remorse flared in the Henry-thing for a second, then faded. A sound caught its attention, drawing it like a magnet through the barn doors and into the warm sunlight of the yard beyond. The sound of singing drifted from the backdoor screen of the white farmhouse. It was a sweet sound that stirred something in the underlying psyche that had once been Henry Beck. For a moment it stood trembling in indecision. Then, tentatively, it crept to the rear of the house.

Through the wire mesh of the screen door it stared at the woman who stood washing dishes at the kitchen sink. Estelle, singing an old-time hymn, her voice as light and musical as that of a songbird. Estelle, the woman Henry Beck had fallen in love with the first time he had seen her sitting alone at the grange hall square dance in the autumn of 1938. Estelle, the woman who, for so many years, had shared his laughter and tears, who had endured the hard times along with the good.

It stood there uncertain, the confusing emotion welling up like a dam on the point of bursting. It wanted to call out to make its feeling known. But as Estelle began to turn toward the door, a great fear washed into its mind. *Can't let her see me...not like this!*

Estelle Beck walked idly to the back door and looked toward the barn. Henry's work had grown quiet in the last few minutes. She had a sudden whim to take him some coffee and a wedge of pecan pie and maybe take a look at the chair he was making for the new grandbaby. She had stepped outside with the snack in hand, when she noticed the tracks in the dust of the back stoop. They were tiny, peculiar looking tracks the likes of which she had never seen before. About the size of a raccoon print, but strangely *human* in shape.

"Henry!" Estelle called with a half-smile on her face. "Henry, come out here and take a gander at these queer little tracks." After receiving no response from her husband, she went out to the barn to see what was keeping him.

■■■

It fled deep into the wooded hollow, through the tangle of briers and bramble, to the cool, babbling brook of Green Creek. In its ears rang the awful sound of a woman's hysterical screams, brimming with terror and grief. It was a sound that wracked the Henry-thing's very existence with a hurt that went far beyond mental boundaries. A sound that bit down deep into the tender meat of its soul.

It collapsed into the cool rush of the backwoods branch, letting the water wash away the congealed blood that covered it. The veins and arteries underneath had sealed upon its metamorphosis. A single quart of life's fluid coursed through the disembodied head, the pulse of its temple circulating the blood in absence of a working heart.

Eventually the screams gave way to the wailing of sirens and then the sound of men with guns walking through the woods. The creature spent that night hidden beneath a mulberry bush, shivering against the cold. The awful ache of betrayed love thrummed through every nerve ending. It fell asleep, its thoughts torn between the woman Estelle and those who had been forever left behind in the depths of the ancient well.

In its troubled dreams, the dying words of its own kind drifted on the dark currents of its slumber. They steeled its floundering resolve and told it exactly what must be done to survive.

■■■

Estelle sat numbly in the front porch swing. She watched the last car pull from the gravel drive and head up the main road toward town. The Reverend Ford, who had said comforting words over Henry's closed casket, had been the last to leave. Her son and daughter had made their hasty exit right after the burial, making excuses that Estelle did not question in the shadow of her grief. She reckoned she couldn't blame them for wanting to shut out the horrible events of the past few days. She would have done the same herself, but the recurring nightmare of Henry's headless body kept replaying unmercifully, turning her into a nervous wreck.

What was it she had overheard the sheriff tell the reverend earlier that day? That Henry's head had not been cut off, but rather *pulled* off by some great force? A cold shudder ran through the woman's body and she got up to go inside, straightening her black dress and removing the dark net of the mourning veil.

She was about to open the door, when something drew her attention to the flower garden across the drive. Something was singing—singing in Henry's voice.

In a daze, Estelle found herself in the garden, standing there amid marigolds and iris, steadying herself beside the concrete birdbath. It was an old Jimmie Rogers song, one that Henry had sang to her numerous times during their courting. Her husband had always had a fine singing voice, a deep baritone that rumbled a head above the rest in the pews at church. But now the tone seemed different. It was almost as if Estelle wasn't actually hearing the voice, but rather *thinking* that she did.

Abruptly, the singing ended. She felt a presence behind her, an overwhelming sensation of someone standing there.

"Henry?" she whispered.

I love you, Estelle.

The widow's heart beat like a triphammer and she took a deep breath. *There are such things as ghosts*, she thought and turned around.

Estelle Beck screamed until she collapsed into the wilting greenery of her flower garden, the eerie image of Henry's smiling face wedged in the bough of a silver maple tree following her into blessed oblivion.

■■■

The tranquilizers that Doc Rhodes prescribed for her after the fainting spell helped Estelle sleep better that night. But it did not stop the dreaming.

She dreamt that Henry was there with her, in the brass-framed bed they had shared since their wedding night. She had been sleeping and he had come to her. *I love you, Estelle,* he whispered, his hot breath in her ear.

203

I love you, too, she gasped, relishing the closeness of him. *I love you so very much.*

Then they had kissed, a deep endless kiss. Their tongues entwined with a relentless passion they had lost with their youth, yet had now regained. Their saliva mingled. An unpleasant taste lingered in Estelle's mouth. It was the taste of stagnation and sulfur and a vile rankness she could not quite place. But she had not pulled away, wanting to hang onto Henry as long as she could, even if it was all in her mind.

The dream ended when she brought her arms up to run her hands along her lover's muscular back and found nothing there.

■■■

The headaches worsened as the week drew on, as did the soreness behind her ears, and every night there was the sound of singing in the garden.

THINNING
THE HERD

When I was a kid watching all those great Universal monster movies on TV, I often fantasized about my favorite monsters battling it out. You know, Frankenstein's monster slugging it out with the Mummy, or the Wolfman going toe-to-toe with the Creature from the Black Lagoon.

In my boyish imagination, I sometimes wondered how it would have been if those old movie monsters had somehow taken over the earth. In such a world, would vampires and werewolves be allies...or enemies?

CHANEY waited until the first, pale hint of dawn seeped over the flat Texas horizon. Then, making sure everything was set, he descended the rusty ladder of the old water tower and made his way to the barn across the street.

He was the thirteenth in line. When his time came, he stepped up to the landlord's desk and appraised the man. He was human—that was easy to see. Fat, lazy, willing to bow to those who had taken command of the new frontier. His name was Hector. He had a patch over one eye, a prosthetic leg that needed oiling, and a monkey named Garfunkel who perched like a growth on the landlord's shoulder and picked lice from his master's oily scalp.

Hector eyed the gaunt man in the black canvas duster with suspicion. "Don't think I've ever seen you around here before."

Chaney's impatience showed as he reached into his coat for his money pouch. "You gonna flap your lips or rent me a bed for the day?" Gold coins jingled within the small leather bag like the restless bones of a ghostly child.

"How do I know you are what you say you are? There are plenty of bounty hunters about these days. Doesn't pay to rent out to strangers, especially when you cater to the type of clientele I do."

"Your clientele is going to fry out here if you don't hurry up and give the man his bed," growled a customer at the end of the line.

But Hector was not to be rushed. "I'll need proof."

Chaney smirked. "What do you want? An ID? How about my American Express card?"

The landlord reached into the desk drawer and withdrew a small, golden crucifix. "Grab hold of this."

Chaney averted his eyes, as did the others in line. "Is that necessary?"

"It is if you want a bed."

The stranger nodded and extended a pale hand. He closed his fist around the cross. A sizzling of flesh sounded as contact was made and a wisp of blue smoke curled from between Chaney's fingers. "Satisfied?" he asked in disgust.

"Quite." Hector pushed the register toward him and collected the gold piece Chaney had laid upon the counter. The one-eyed landlord noticed that Chaney carried a black satchel in one hand. "What's that?" he asked.

Chaney flashed a toothy grin. "A noonday snack." He shook the black bag, eliciting the muffled cry of an infant from within.

By the time the first rays of the sun had broken, they were all checked in. The barn's interior was pitch dark, letting nary a crack or crevice of scorching sunlight into their temporary abode. Chaney found a bed on the ground floor, he removed his long coat, hanging it on a peg over his bunk, and set the satchel close at hand.

He lifted the lid of his sleeping chamber and scowled. Just a simple, pine wood casket. No silk liner, no burnished finish, and no ornate handles on the sides; just a no frills bunk in a no frills hotel. He wasn't complaining, though. It would suit his purpose well enough.

"Lights out!" called Hector, laughing uproariously at a joke that had lost its humor years ago. The tenants ignored his mirth and set about preparing for a good day's rest. Chaney followed suit, taking a packet of graveyard earth from his coat pocket and spreading it liberally in the bottom of his rented coffin.

When every lid had been closed, Hector stepped outside the barn, shutting the double doors behind him. He took a seat on a bench out front, laid a pump shotgun across his knees, and started reading an old Anne Rice novel he had bought from a traveling peddler.

The morning drew on, the sun rising, baking the Texas wilderness with its unrelenting heat. The little town moved as slow as winter molasses. Its inhabitants went about their normal business, or as near normal as could be expected after the much-heralded End of the World.

The courthouse clock struck twelve o'clock before Chaney finally made his move. It was safe now; his neighboring tenants were fast asleep. Quietly, he lifted the lid of his casket and sat up. "Snack time," he said to himself and reached for the satchel.

He opened it. The first thing he removed was the rubber baby doll. He laid it on the barn floor, smiling as it uttered a soft "Mama!" before falling silent again. Chaney then took a .44 AutoMag from the bag and began to make his rounds.

He didn't bother to pull the old "stake-through-the-heart" trick. To do so would be noisy and messy and net him only a small fraction of the undead he had come there to finish off. Instead, he used the most state-of-the-art anti-vampire devices. He placed Claymore mines at strategic points throughout the barn's interior. But they were not ordinary Claymores. He had replaced the load of ball bearings with tiny steel crucifixes and splinters of ash wood.

After the mines had been placed and the timers set, Chaney knew it was time to take his leave. He walked to the barn doors and, cocking his pistol, stepped out into the hot, noonday sun.

Hector was snoozing on the job, of course. The landlord's head was resting on his flabby chest, snoring rather loudly from the nose. Chaney stood before the man and loudly cleared his throat.

The fat man came awake. Startled, he stared up at Chaney. "Hey," he breathed. "You ain't no vampire."

"No, I ain't," agreed Chaney.

"But I saw your hand burn when you touched the cross!"

Chaney lifted his scarred left palm to his mouth and peeled away a thin layer of chemically-treated latex with his teeth. "Special effects," he said.

"Well, I'll be damned."

Chaney brought the muzzle of his .44 to the man's forehead. "That you shall be...traitor." Then he painted the barn wall a brilliant red with the contents of the man's disintegrating skull.

The bogus vampire walked to where his primer-gray van was parked near the water tower. He got in, started the engine, and cruised slowly down the empty street of the town. He checked his watch, counting the seconds. "Five...four...three...two...one..."

The Claymores went off first. Their metal shells split under a charge of C-4, sending thousands of tiny crosses and toothpick-sized stakes in every imaginable direction. The projectiles penetrated the caskets, as well as their sleeping occupants. Then they traveled onward, piercing the walls of the makeshift hotel. The old structure, already weakened by time and weather, could take no further abuse. It collapsed in a dusty heap, burying fifty dying tenants beneath its crushing weight.

Chaney watched in his side view mirror for the *coup de grâce*. It came a moment later. A glob of wired plastic explosive belched flame, splitting the steel reservoir of the water tower in half. A cascade of water crashed down upon the collapsed barn, drenching the jagged timbers and whatever lay beneath it. The significance of that crowning touch was that the water was holy. Chaney had blessed it, using a prayer he had bought from a convent across the Mexican border, before he had set the timer and joined the others in line.

"Filthy bloodsuckers!" said Chaney as he headed for the open desert. He pushed a tape into the cassette player and rocked and rolled down the long abandoned highway toward the sweltering blur of the distant horizon.

■■■

"You sure you don't want something to drink?" the bartender asked Stoker, who sat alone at a corner table.

"No," replied the bearded man. "I'm fine."

"You sure? Beer, whiskey? Some wine, maybe?"

Stoker stifled a grin. "No, thank you."

The hefty bartender shrugged and went about his business. The tavern, named Apocalypse After Dark, was empty except for Stoker and the barkeep. A wild-eyed fellow had been playing the slot machine an hour before, but the geek had left after his tokens were depleted. *Ghoul,* Stoker had thought to himself. *Probably rummaging through the death pyres right now, looking for warm leftovers.*

But Stoker had no interest in cannibals that night. At least not the kind that sneak around in shame, feeding off disposal plants and graveyards.

He sat there for another hour before he heard the sound that he had been waiting for. The sound of motorcycles roaring in from the west.

Headlights slashed across the front window of the saloon. Engines gunned, then sputtered into silence. Stoker tensed, wishing he had ordered that drink now. His hand went beneath the table, caressing the object he wore slung beneath his bomber jacket.

He watched them through the front window as they dismounted their Harley Davidsons like leather-clad cowboys swinging from the saddles of chromed horses. There were an even dozen of them; eight men and four women. Another woman, naked, sat perched on the back of the leader's chopper. She was chained to the sissy bar, a dog collar around her slender throat keeping her from escaping.

"Poor angel," whispered Stoker. He was going to enjoy this immensely.

The batwing doors burst open and in they came. Bikers: big, hairy, ugly and ear-piercingly loud. They wore studded leather with plenty of polished chains, zippers, and embroidered swastikas. On the back of their cycle jackets were their colors. A snarling wolf's head with flaming eyes and the words BLITZ WOLVEN.

"A round for me and the gang before we do our night's work," bellowed the leader, a bear of a man with matted red hair and beard. His name was Lycan. Stoker knew that from asking around. The names of the others were not important.

The bartender obediently filled their orders. Lycan took a big swig from his beer, foam hanging on his whiskers like the slaver of a rabid dog. He turned around and leaned against the bar rail, instantly seeing the man who sat alone in the shadowy corner. "How's it going, pal?" Lycan asked neighborly.

Stoker said nothing. He merely smiled and nodded in acknowledgement.

"How about a drink for my silent friend over yonder," the biker said. "You can put it on my tab."

The bartender glanced at the man in the corner, then back at Lycan. "Told me he didn't want nothing."

"What's the matter, stranger?" asked a skinny fellow with safety pins through each nostril. "You too good to drink with the likes of us?"

"I have a low tolerance for alcohol," Stoker said. "It makes me quite ill."

"Leave the dude alone," said Lycan. "Different strokes for different folks, I always say."

The skinny guy gave Stoker a look of contempt, then turned back to the bar.

"It takes all kinds to make a world," replied Stoker. "Especially a brave new world such as this."

"Amen to that," laughed Lycan. He downed his beer and called for another.

"Blitz Wolven? Does that have a hidden meaning? Are you werewolves or Nazis?"

Lycan's good-natured mood began to falter. He eyed the loner with sudden suspicion.

"Maybe a little of both. So what's it to you?"

Stoker shrugged. "Just curious, that's all."

"Curiosity killed the cat," said an anorexic chick with a purple Mohawk. "Or bat or rat...depending on what supernatural persuasion you are these days."

"I'll keep that in mind, dear lady."

"Well, enough of this gabbing, you freaks," said Lycan. "Time to get down to business." They left the bar and walked to the far end of the tavern where a number of hooks jutted from the cheap paneling. Stoker watched with interest as they began to disrobe, hanging their riding leathers along the wall.

"What is this?" he asked. "The floor show?"

"You know, buddy," said Lycan, his muscular form beginning to contort and sprout coarse hair. "You're whetting my appetite something fierce. In fact, you might just be our opening course for tonight."

THINNING THE HERD

Stoker sat there, regarding them coolly. "I'm afraid not, old boy. I've got business of my own to attend to."

They were halfway through the change now. Faces distorted and bulged, sprouting toothy snouts and pointed ears. "Oh, and what would that be?" asked Lycan, almost beyond the ability to converse verbally. He stretched his long, hairy arms, scraping the ceiling with razor claws.

Stoker stood up, stepped away from the table, and brought an Uzi submachine gun from under his jacket. "I'll leave that to your brutish imaginations," he said, and opened fire.

The one with the pins in his nose began to howl, brandishing his immortality like some garish tattoo. Then he stopped his bestial laughter when he realized the bullets that were entering his body were not cast of ordinary lead. He screamed as a pattern of penetrating silver stitched across his broad chest, sending him back against the wall. He collapsed, smoking and shriveling, until he was only a heap of naked, gunshot humanity.

"Bastard!" snarled the female werewolf with the violet Mohawk. She surged forward, teeth gnashing, breasts bobbing and swaying like furry pendulums.

Stoker unleashed a three-round burst, obliterating the monster's head. It staggered shakily across the barroom, hands reaching up and feeling for a head, but only finding a smoking neck stump in its place. The werewolf finally slumped against the jukebox with such force that it began blasting out an old Warren Zevon tune with a boom of bass and tickling of ivory.

"How appropriate," said Stoker. He swept the barroom at a wide angle, holding the Uzi level with the ten remaining werewolves. One by one, they were speared by the substance they loathed most. The beasts dropped to the saloon's sawdust floor, writhing and twitching in agony, before growing still.

Lycan leaped the bar, ducking for cover as Stoker swung the machine gun in his direction. Slugs chewed up the woodwork, but nothing more. After a few more

212

seconds of continuous fire, the Uzi's magazine gave out. Stocker shucked the clip and reached inside his jacket for a fresh one.

That was when Lycan, fully transformed now, sprang over the splintered bartop and tore across the tavern for his intended victim, smashing tables and chairs in his path. "You ain't gonna make it!" rasped Lycan. It came out more as a garbled snarl than an actual threat.

"Quite the contrary," Stoker said calmly. He drew a serrated combat knife from his boot and thrust it upward just as Lycan came within reach. The sterling silver blade sank to the hilt beneath the werewolf's breastbone.

Lycan staggered backward, staring dumbly at the smoking knife in his midsection. He looked at Stoker with bewildered eyes, then fell over stone cold dead, the impact of silver-shock shorting out his bestial brain cells.

Stoker walked over and withdrew the dagger from the wolf's body, wiping the blade on the fur of Lycan's vanishing coat. He slipped the weapon back into its sheath and looked toward the bartender, who was peeking over the edge of the bar. "How much do I owe you for damages?"

"No charge," the man said, pale-faced but happy. "I've been trying to keep this mangy riff-raff outta my joint for years."

Stoker left Apocalypse After Dark and stood outside for a long moment, enjoying the crisp night air and the pale circle of the full moon overhead. Then he noticed Lycan's pet sitting on the back of the Harley. He walked over to the girl and smiled at her softly. He cupped her chin in his hand. "Poor angel," he said soothingly, then blessed her with a kiss.

"What a glorious night, don't you think, my dear?" he asked as he swung aboard the big chopper and stamped on the starter, sending it roaring into life. The woman was silent, but she snuggled closer, wrapping her arms around his waist, and laying her weary head upon his shoulders.

Together they winged their way into the dead of night.

■■■

Chaney parked his van between a black Trans-Am and a rusty Toyota pickup. He left his vehicle and mounted the steps of the Netherworld Café, a local hangout for the natural and unnatural alike.

He walked in and started down the aisle for the rear of the restaurant. A wispy ghost of a waitress took orders, while a couple of zombie fry-cooks slung hash behind the counter. Chaney waved to a few old acquaintances, then headed for the last booth on the right. Stoker was sitting there, poised and princely as usual. There was a girl, too, wearing Stoker's bomber jacket and nothing else.

Chaney sat down and ordered the usual. Stoker did the same. They regarded each other in silence for a moment, then Chaney spoke up. "Well, is it done?"

"It is," nodded Stoker. "And what about you?"

"I kept my end of the bargain."

"Good," said Stoker. "Then it's settled. I get the blood."

"And I the flesh," replied Chaney.

They shook on their mutual partnership then, Chaney's hirsute hand emblazoned with the distinctive mark of the pentagram, while Stoker's possessed the cold and pale bloodlessness of the undead.

BLOOD SUEDE SHOES

I love rock and roll. Even after all these years, I still listen to classic rock from the '60s and '70s (it all sort of fell flat on its face in the '80's, in my opinion). I even listen to it while I'm writing. Total silence equals a blank page to a Southern rocker like myself.

This tale takes place in a different era of rock and roll—the rockabilly period of the 1950s. That nostalgic time that gave us the likes of Elvis Presley, Jerry Lee Lewis, Carl Perkins—and a rowdy, young fella by the name of Rockabilly Reb...

RUBY Paquette was walking home from the big show in Baton Rouge, when the headlights of a car cut through the moonless night. The lights blazed like the luminous eyes of a demon cat, casting a pale glow upon the two-lane highway and the swampy thicket to either side. She turned and regarded the approaching vehicle, squinting against the glare. The car sounded like a predator, too; its big eight-cylinder engine seemed to rumble and roar with an appetite for something more than oil and gasoline.

The crimson '58 Cadillac began to slow when the headlights revealed her short, dumpy form walking along the gravel shoulder. Ruby turned her back to the headlights and kept going. She stared straight ahead, following her own expanding shadow and the white-washed borderline beside the highway. As the automobile slowed to a creep and prepared to pull alongside her, Ruby chanced a quick glance over her shoulder. The illusion of a ravenous feline was compounded by the Caddy's front grillwork. It leered at her with a mouthful of polished chrome fangs.

"Hey, sugar!" called a man's voice from the convertible. "Can I give you a ride somewhere? Kinda late for a beauty like you to be out all by your lonesome."

Beauty? Ruby bristled at the word, especially when it was directed at her. She was no beauty and she knew it. She was just a homely Cajun girl; an overweight, acne-ravaged teenager with limp black hair and jelly-jar eyeglasses. How could the driver of the expensive car have made such a stupid mistake? True, he probably hadn't seen her face yet, but he didn't really need to. One glimpse of her squat, elephantine body waddling down the road should have told him that she was certainly no beauty.

"No, thanks," she called back to him. "I don't have far to go." She was aware that the Caddy was almost at a standstill now, inching its way beside her. She twisted her face toward the tangle of swamp beyond the road. *Please, God, just let him drive on,* she thought to herself. *I don't want him to see how much of a dog I really am.*

"Aw, come on, darlin'," urged the driver. He was right alongside her now. "Let ol' Reb give you a ride home."

It was the dawning familiarity of the voice, as well as the mention of his name, that made Ruby's stomach clench with excitement. She looked around and, yes, it *was* him. It was Rockabilly Reb in the flesh!

"You know who I am, don't you, sugar?" grinned
Reb, flashing that pearly smile that was becoming increasingly famous in the South and beyond.

"Yeah," said Ruby in bewilderment. "You're Rockabilly Reb. I saw you at the Louisiana Hayride tonight."

"And I saw you, too."

Reb winked at her—actually winked at *her*—Rumpy
Ruby, as her peers at high school were cruelly fond of
calling her.

"Third row, fifth girl to the left...right?" Reb asked.

"Right." Ruby blushed, feeling the heat of embarrassment blossom in her full cheeks. She stopped walking and
stood, wondering if her encounter was actually a dream.
She crossed her thick arms and pinched herself through
her sweater. No, it was really happening. She was actually
talking, face-to-face, with a genuine rockabilly singer.

"Well, how about it, sugar? Gonna let me play the
Good Samaritan tonight and give you a lift home? I was
heading in that direction anyway." Reb's immaculate
smile hadn't faltered in the least. It seemed to be a part of
his natural charm.

Ruby looked ahead toward the three miles of swamp
that stretched between Baton Rouge and her bayou
home, then back to the idling Cadillac and the offer of
getting there in style and comfort. What was she going
to say—"No, thanks, but I'd rather walk?" This was
the bad boy of rock and roll—the potential heir to the
heartthrob throne left empty after Elvis Presley had been
unexpectedly drafted into the army earlier that year. Her
mother was forever drumming the rule of never riding
with strangers into her mind, but to pass up such a
golden opportunity would be pure madness. It wasn't
every day that a chubby wallflower got the chance to
cruise with a certified superstar.

"Okay," she said. Ruby opened the passenger door
of the car and climbed inside. The seats were smooth,
crimson leather, as was the rest of the interior. From the
rearview mirror dangled a set of fuzzy dice, jet-black

RONALD KELLY

with bright red spots like tiny eyes peeking through the dark fur. She settled onto the seat next to the driver, feeling the coolness of the upholstery against the back of her thighs. That, along with the thrumming vibration of the Caddy's big engine, sparked a naughty sensation deep down inside her—the same sensation of arousal that she got at night, when she lay awake in her bed and thought about Will Knox, the high school quarterback, and the time she had passed the boys' locker room and caught a fleeting glimpse of him, completely naked, just before the door shut.

"Ready to go?" asked Rockabilly Reb.

"Sure," said Ruby. "There's a turnoff about a mile down the road. I live a couple of miles back in the swamp there."

Reb nodded and sent the big convertible roaring down the highway. The singer flashed a glance at his young passenger. "So, you're a bobby-soxer, are you?"

Ruby's face turned beet red. She looked down at her clothes: navy blue sweater and skirt, monogrammed white blouse, white ankle socks, and sneakers. She knew the outfit looked silly, especially on a fat cow like her. "No," she blurted self-consciously, "I just dress like this when I go to a show."

Reb flashed another smile that turned her heart to jelly. "So you're just a rock and roll beauty, eh?"

Again, that twinge of bitter anger. "Why do you keep calling me that? I'm not pretty at all. Are you making fun of me or something?"

The singer shook his head. "Why, I'd never do a thing like that, darlin'. I wouldn't hurt one of my fans for anything in the world. True, you may not be a Marilyn Monroe or a Jayne Mansfield, but you do have your own inner beauty. You know how a candy bar looks like a dog turd when you tear off the wrapper? It doesn't look very appetizing at all, does it? But when you bite into it, it's just as delicious as can be. That's how some girls are. They ain't

218

so pretty on the outside, but underneath they're honest-to-goodness beauties."

Reb's simple explanation put Ruby at ease. She pushed her shyness aside for a moment and studied the man sitting next to her. He looked a little different than he did up on that stage surrounded by klieg lights and a blaring sound system. Up there he looked like a wild Adonis, clad in sparkling red, white, and blue. But here in the car, Reb seemed less glamorous and more than a little exhausted. His bleached-blond hair looked frizzled and lank, like corn silk that had withered beneath a hot August sun. His lean face seemed pale and lined with the weariness of long, sleepless miles on the road. Even his trademark costume had seen better days. Up close, the rhinestone coat with a rebel flag emblazoned on the back seemed dull and lackluster. And his red suede shoes—the opposite of Carl Perkins' famed blue ones—looked scuffed and rusty, like blood that had congealed and dried to an ugly brown crust.

Thunder rumbled in the dense clouds overhead and a few drops of rain began to hit them. "Looks like we're in for a real downpour," Reb said. He pushed a button on the Caddy's dash and the top began to unfold behind the backseat and rise slowly over them. By the time Reb fastened the clips to the top of the windshield, the bottom fell out. Great sheets of water crashed earthward, drenching southern Louisiana with their wet fury.

Reb turned off where Ruby told him to, but they had gone only a quarter of a mile into the black tangle of the swamp when the rain cut their visibility down to nothing. "I reckon we'd better park for a while and wait out the storm. Wouldn't want to make a wrong turn and end up in the swamp as some hungry gator's midnight snack."

"I reckon not." Ruby sat there, her bashfulness pushing her to the limits of the seat and pressing her against the passenger door.

"How about a little music to pass the time?" Reb turned on the AM radio. Chuck Berry's "Johnny B.

Goode" was winding down and next up was Rockabilly Reb's newest single, "Rock and Roll Anatomy Lesson."

■■■

"A little bit of heart, a little bit of soul,
A little bit of mind, and a whole lotta rock and roll..."

■■■

"What a coincidence!" Reb laughed.

Ruby sat listening to the monotonous drumming of rain on the roof and the haunting melody of Reb's electric guitar. After the song ended and the Everly Brothers' "Bird Dog" began, Ruby eyed the grinning rocker with wonderment. "I can't believe that I'm really here...sitting right next to you."

"Well, you are, Ruby." Reb's smile glowed dashboard green in the darkness.

The girl returned his smile, then frowned just as quickly. "How did you know my name was Ruby? I didn't tell you it was."

Reb shrugged. "I don't know. You just look like a Ruby, that's all." Smoothly, he changed the subject. "So, how did you like the show tonight?"

"It was great!" Ruby thought back to the three-hour Louisiana Hayride that had featured big names like gravel-voiced Johnny Cash, piano-playing Fats Domino, and, of course, Rockabilly Reb. "You were the best, though." She smiled demurely. "I think you're even better than Elvis."

Reb chuckled. "Well, that's mighty high praise, darlin'. But I reckon I must have disappointed some folks on those last couple of songs I did. My voice was kinda going out on me and my guitar-picking was a bit off."

Ruby recalled the last two numbers: "High School Honey" and "Bayou Boogie." Reb's voice had been unusually flat and his normally hot guitar licks seemed strangely off-key. She had attributed it to the rigors of being on the road too long, driving from gig to gig without time to rest up.

"Want me to sing you a song, Ruby?"

The bespectacled girl felt her heart leap with joy. "Sure!" Again, she couldn't quite believe that she was here, stranded in a violent downpour with her idol. And now he was going to sing to her!

Rockabilly Reb reached into the backseat and found his guitar. It was a sunburst Les Paul Special—a custom-made model for the left-handed player. He slipped the sparkling rhinestone strap around his neck. The sickly green glow of the dashboard light played upon the taut strings of the instrument and the glittering spangles of his gaudy jacket, illuminating the interior of the car with an eerie light.

"Sorry I can't hook up my amplifier, but we'll just have to make do the best we can. So, what would you like to hear? What's your favorite Rockabilly Reb song?"

Ruby smiled. "Forever Baby," she said without hesitation.

Reb grinned. "That's my favorite one, too. Here goes..." He began to strum on the unplugged guitar, producing a series of metallic cords that could scarcely be heard above the rainstorm.

■■■

"Ruby, Ruby, be my forever baby...
Ruby, Ruby, be my forever lady...
Ruby, baby, tell me you'll be mine."

■■■

The teenager was a little startled. He was using her own name in place of the customary one. Sitting there listening to him, Ruby couldn't quite remember whose name originally had embellished the lyrics. Sometimes it sounded like Lucy, sometimes like Judy or Trudy. Every time she heard the song on the radio or on the jukebox in the soda shop in town, it seemed as though Reb sang about a different girl. But that was impossible. The record company wouldn't allow him to cut alternate versions of the same hit, using a different name each time.

After he was finished, he sat back and grinned that country-boy grin of his. "I know, I was a little off-key, but it's been a long night and I'm kinda tired."

"It was perfect," Ruby said. "You know, I always wondered how you got your start. I hadn't even heard of you until the first of the year, and now here you are a big star and all."

"It wasn't an easy row to hoe, I'll tell you that." Reb lost his smile for the first time since he'd picked her up. "Started out as a guy who was long on good looks, but mighty short on talent."

"I can't believe that," she said in disbelief.

"Well, it's the God's honest truth, sugar-pie. I saw all those fellas out there making records and money by the fistfuls, and I figured to get in on the action. And I thought I had a good chance, too, but there were others who thought otherwise. I went up there to Sun Records once, and you know what old Sam Phillips told me? He said, 'You got the look, boy, and you got the moves, but ain't got a lick of natural-born talent. You can't pick a guitar, can't tickle the ivories, and can't sing a note without sounding like a year-old calf with its privates hung up in a barbwire fence.' I must admit, it was pretty darned discouraging, that trip to Memphis."

"But he was wrong, wasn't he?"

"No, Ruby, dear, that man was right on the mark. I had no talent at all, except for looking pretty and grinning like a happy jackass. I figured I'd have to just face the fact that I wasn't gonna make it in the music business. Then, when I was drowning my sorrows in a honky-tonk on Union Street, I made the acquaintance of my present manager, Colonel Darker."

"You mean Colonel *Parker*, don't you? Elvis's manager?"

"No, Darker is the complete opposite. He's an oily little rat of a fella, but he has a good head for business. He sat down at the bar and asked me what was wrong. I told him, and he made me the strangest offer I ever heard. Said he'd make me a bona fide rock and roll star if I'd sign my soul over to him. I thought it was pretty darned funny at the time. I mean, I'd heard of such corny lines before, but only on spooky radio shows and in those EC comics before they were banned. Well, since I was half drunk and didn't figure I'd need that no-account soul of mine anyway, I agreed. I signed the contract on the spot, and then he took me out to the parking lot. He gave me the keys to this apple-red Cadillac, as well as the costume you see me wearing and the guitar I'm holding here. He also told me what I'd have to do to get the talent to be a star. At first, I didn't want to have no part of it, but soon my hunger for money and fame got the best of me."

Ruby felt her skin crawl with a sudden shiver. "What... what did you have to do?" Something deep down inside her wanted to know, while another part didn't.

Rockabilly Reb smiled, and this time it possessed a disturbing quality; a quality that had been there all along, only hidden. "Tell me something, Ruby," he said in a voice that was barely a whisper. "Do you believe what all those hellfire preachers say about rock and roll? Do you believe that it's unwholesome and unclean? That it's the Devil's music?"

"No, of course not," stammered Ruby. "That's just silly talk by a bunch of holy rollers. Rock and roll is just plain fun, that's all."

"I'm afraid you're wrong about that, dumpling. Rock and roll *can* be safe and fun, but it can also be dark and dangerous. The grown-ups, they can sense something is basically dangerous about the music, but they can't quite put their finger on it. Most of the time the music is sung by decent, God-fearing boys like Elvis and Roy Orbison and Carl Perkins, to name a few. I don't know about Jerry Lee. That old boy has a mean streak a country mile long."

Ruby said nothing. She just pressed her back against the passenger door and listened to him ramble on. Inconspicuously, her chubby hand fumbled for the door handle, but, strangely enough, she couldn't find it. The inner panel of the door was smooth...and warm to the touch.

"I'm one of the first of the truly dangerous ones," he told her. His pale blue eyes blazed with the madness of desperation. "My talent wasn't a gift from God, but from Satan himself. Colonel Darker likes rock and roll because it reminds him of hell. All those girls screaming and hollering, well, that's just how the Bible describes purgatory—weeping and wailing and gnashing of teeth.

"The Colonel, he's given me fortune and fame...as well as power. And when someone gets in the way of my success, I get riled up. I went up north recently and auditioned for a winter tour that's coming up with Buddy Holly, Ritchie Valens and the Big Bopper. But they turned me down. Said I was too much of a vulgar hillbilly to appeal to midwestern teenagers. Well, they'll learn their mistake soon enough. Me and the Colonel are gonna cook up a little surprise. Those boys are gonna climb to the top, only to fall...and fall mighty damned hard, too."

Ruby believed every word he said. She watched in growing horror as Reb's eyes lost their natural blueness and took on a muted crimson hue, like a smoldering coal wavering between living fire and dying ash. Behind her back, her hand continued to search for the door handle, but still she was unsuccessful in finding it.

"You know where I get my talent?" asked the rocker. "The human soul. But not from my own... no, the Colonel has my own damned soul under lock and key. That was stipulated in the contract. Instead, I must have the soul of an innocent, the truly beautiful essence of an unsoiled virgin to give me the power I need to rock and roll."

It was at that moment that Ruby noticed that the head of the electric guitar was not like that of other instruments. It was wickedly pointed at the end and honed to razor sharpness. Reb gripped the neck of the guitar and began to lower it, directing it toward the center of her broad chest. She screamed and tried to push up on the movable roof of the Caddy. Her hands recoiled in repulsion. The underside of the roof was sticky with warm, wet slime.

"Let me sing you a song," Rockabilly Reb rasped.

Then the blade of the guitar was inside her, slicing through her blouse and the elastic of her bra, then past soft flesh and the hardness of her breastbone. As her heart exploded, Ruby heard the song Rockabilly Reb had sung to her only moments before. But this time it came with a savage ferocity that originated from a realm commanded by the notorious Colonel Darker.

"RUBY, RUBY, BE MY FOREVER BABY...RUBY, RUBY, BE MY FOREVER LADY...RUBY, BABY, TELL ME YOU'LL BE MINE!"

"No!" she screamed. She watched in mounting panic as her life's blood flooded the floorboards of the car in great, sluggish pools. It was instantly absorbed by Reb's red suede shoes, which pulsed with a life of their own, bulging with dark veins as they drank in the crimson fluid. Reb's costume took on a new brilliance, sparkling with an unholy inner fire. His face lost its pallor. His skin grew tanned and robust. The head of lifeless hair grew fuller and lighter in hue, until it blazed like white-hot steel.

"TELL ME!" shrieked the singer. "TELL ME, RUBY! TELL ME YOU'LL BE MINE!"

Ruby could feel the guitar strings strumming within her body, sending sonic notes of utter agony throughout her tubby frame. She opened her mouth to scream in protest, but she no longer possessed a tongue to vent her awful terror. The vibrations from the hellish instrument racked her spine and blossomed with deadly force into the chamber of her skull. There was a moment of incredible pressure and then her ears and mouth gave explosive birth to her brain. She felt her eyes shoot from their sockets with such force that the lenses of her glasses shattered.

Rockabilly Reb's demonic song grew in intensity and her empty skull became the guitar's makeshift amplifier. Waves of trebled sound flowed from the orifices of her head, turning the inside of the Cadillac into a concert hall for the damned. Then, as the ballad came to an end, she felt her soul being siphoned from her body, channeled through the strings, into the wooden body of the Les Paul.

As unconsciousness took her into its dark and comforting folds, Ruby knew that there was no longer any use in struggling. She mouthed a single word in answer to Reb's evil chorus...a silent *yes*. And, although she could neither see nor hear, she knew that the rocker's voice was rising in a howl of triumph and his grin stretched wide with a renewed power born of a spirit that was not his own.

■■■

Colonel Darker was right. It *was* like hell.

The screams, the writhing bodies, the pressing heat of the spotlights and the crowd—it filled the high school auditorium like a crazed purgatory confined within four walls. And she and Rockabilly Reb were at center stage, engulfed in the dancing flames of youthful passion.

She sensed the Colonel standing in the wings, watching the show. She loathed the man as much as she loathed her treacherous lover. She could sense his eyes upon the crowd, enjoying the thrashing of young bodies and the shrill shrieks of females torn between teenage infatuation and womanly lust. She had been among them once, but that seemed like an eternity ago. She had not been beautiful like most of these squealing girls. She had been burdened with an ugly and cumbersome body, but at least it had been one of flesh and bone, and not one constructed of gleaming steel and polished wood, like the one she now possessed.

Rockabilly Reb finished the song and stood before the microphone, letting the screams of wild adoration engulf him. He glanced at his manager and gave the man a wink. Colonel Darker nodded and, with a wolfish grin, merged with the backstage shadows.

"Thank you very much," said Reb, sending the crowd into a renewed frenzy with a flash of his smile. "Here's one of my biggest hits and one of your favorites."

He began to sing,

■■■

"Ruby, Ruby, be my forever baby…
Ruby, Ruby, be my forever lady…
Ruby, baby, tell me you'll be mine."

It was her song and she had grown to despise it. During the past few weeks it had thrummed through her new body, bringing pangs of disgust and despair rather than the rapture of undying passion. The promise of eternal love was a lie. Others had shared the song before her and there would be others afterward. It was only hers until the essence of her captured soul faded like a faltering flame.

As Rockabilly Reb's nimble fingers caressed her taut strings, bringing forth the hot licks of demon rock and roll, she could restrain herself no longer. She screamed out in tortured anguish, hoping that at least one of the teenyboppers in the crowd would hear the cry and recognize it as a warning.

But her torment fell on deaf ears. It emerged as the piercing squeal of feedback, then was swallowed up by the blare of the music.

And the damned rocked on.

PYROPHEX-FOURTEEN

The current state of the earth's ecology is questionable at best. We've all heard the warning cries on the evening news concerning the depletion of the ozone, global warming, and the wholesale polluting of air, earth, and water.

For the most part, the hills and hollows of my native Tennessee have been minimally impacted by man's inhumanity toward his earthly home. The streams are still fresh and flowing, the earth still prime for crops, and the forests are teeming with wildlife. But it wouldn't take much at all to change that. It would only take a fool (or a corporation of fools) to dump some type of chemical agent into the nearby fishing hole and start a downhill spiral that would be impossible to contain.

You might consider this a cautionary tale of sorts: a story of evil men and an equally evil substance.

JASPER Horne knew something was wrong when he heard the cows screaming.

He was halfway through his breakfast of bacon, eggs and scorched toast when he heard their agonized bellows coming from the north pasture. At first he couldn't figure out what had happened. He had done his milking around five o'clock that morning and herded them into the open field at six. It was now only half past seven and his twelve Jersey heifers sounded as if they were simultaneously being skinned alive.

Jasper left his meal and, grabbing a twelve-gauge shotgun from behind the kitchen door, left the house. He checked the double-aught loads, then ran across the barnyard and climbed over the barbwire fence. It was a chilly October morning and a light fog clung low to the ground. Through the mist he could see the two-toned forms of the Jerseys next to the Clearwater stream that ran east-to-west on the Horne property. As he made his way across the brown grass and approached the creekbed, Jasper could see that only a few cows were still standing. Most were on their sides, howling like hoarse banshees, while others staggered about drunkenly.

Good God Almighty! thought Jasper. *What's happening here?*

A moment later, he reached the pasture stream. He watched in terror as his livestock stumbled around in a blind panic. Their eyes were wild with pain and their throats emitted thunderous cries, the likes of which Jasper Horne had never heard during sixty years of Tennessee farming.

The tableau that he witnessed that morning was hideous. One cow after another dropped to the ground and was caught in the grip of a terrible seizure. Their tortured screams ended abruptly with an ugly sizzling noise and they lay upon the withered autumn grass, twitching and shuddering in a palsy of intense agony. Then the sizzling became widespread and the inner structures of the Jerseys seemed to collapse, as if their internal organs and skeletal systems were dissolving. A strange, yellowish vapor drifted from the bodily orifices of the milk cows, quickly mingling with the crisp morning air. Then the black and white skins of the heifers slowly folded inward with a hissing sigh, leaving flattened bags of cowhide lying limply along the shallow banks of the rural stream.

Numbly, Jasper approached the creek. He walked up to one of the dead cows and almost prodded it with the toe of his workboot, but thought better of it. He couldn't understand what had happened to his prime milking herd. They had been at the peak of health an hour and a half ago, but now they were all gone, having suffered some horrible mass death. Jasper thought of the stream and crouched next to the trickling current. He nearly had his fingertips in the water when he noticed the nasty yellow tint of it. And it had a peculiar smell to it, too, like a combination of urine and formaldehyde.

The farmer withdrew his hand quickly, afraid to explore the stream any further. He stood up and puzzled over the dozen cow-shaped silhouettes that lay around the pasture spring. Then he headed back to the house to make a couple of phone calls.

■■■

"I don't know what to tell you, Jasper," said Bud Fulton. "I can't make heads or tails of what happened here." The Bedloe County veterinarian knelt beside one of the dead animals and poked it with a branch from a nearby sourgum tree. The deflated hide unleashed a noxious fart, then settled even further until the loose skin—now entirely black and gummy in texture—was scarcely an inch in thickness.

"Whatever did it wasn't natural, that's for sure," said Jasper glumly.

The local sheriff, Sam Biggs, lifted his hat and scratched his balding head. "That goes without saying," he said, frowning at the closest victim, which resembled a cow-shaped pool of wet road tar more than anything else. "Do you think it could have been some kind of odd disease or something like that, Doc?"

"I don't believe so," said Bud. "The state agricultural bureau would have contacted me about something as deadly as this. No, I agree with Jasper. I think it must have been something in the stream. The cows must have ingested some sort of chemical that literally dissolved them from the inside out."

"Looks like it rotted away everything: muscle, tissue and bone," said Jasper. "What could do something like that?"

"Some type of corrosive acid, maybe," replied the vet. He squatted next to the stream and studied the yellowish color of the water for a moment. Then he stuck the tip of the sourgum branch into the creek. A wisp of bright yellow smoke drifted off the surface of the water and, when Bud withdrew the stick, the first four inches of it were gone.

"Well, I'll be damned!" said Sheriff Biggs. "That water just gobbled it right up, didn't it?" He took a wary step back from the stream.

Bud nodded absently and tossed the entire stick into the creek. They watched as it dissolved completely and the ashy dregs washed further downstream. "I'm going to take a sample of this with me," said the vet.

The doctor opened his medical bag and took out a small glass jar that he used for collecting urine and sperm samples from the area livestock. He lowered the mouth of the container to the surface of the stream, but dropped it the moment the glass began to smolder and liquefy. "What the hell have we got here?" he wondered aloud as the vial melted and mingled with the jaundiced currents, becoming as free and flowing as the water itself.

The three exchanged uneasy glances. Jasper Horne reached into the side pocket of his overalls and withdrew a small, engraved tin that he kept his smokeless tobacco in. He opened it, shook the snuff out of it, and handed it to the veterinarian. "Here, try this."

Bud Fulton stuck the edge of the circular container into the creek and, finding that the chemical had no effect on the metal, dipped a quantity of the tainted water out and closed the lid. He then took a roll of medical tape, wrapped it securely around the sides of the tobacco tin, and carefully placed it in his bag. "I'll need another water sample," he told Jasper. "From your well."

Jasper's eyes widened behind his spectacles. "Lordy Mercy! You mean to say that confounded stuff might've gotten into my water supply?" He paled at the thought of taking an innocent drink from the kitchen tap and ending up like one of his unfortunate heifers.

"Could be, if this chemical has seeped into an underground stream," said Bud. "I'm going to make a special trip to Nashville today and see what the boys at the state lab can come up with. If I were you, Jasper, I wouldn't use a drop of water from that well until I get the test results."

"I'll run into town later on and buy me some bottled water," agreed Jasper. "But where could this stuff have come from?" The elderly farmer racked his brain for a moment, then looked toward the east with sudden suspicion in his eyes. "Sheriff, you don't think—?"

Sam Biggs had already come to the same conclusion. "The county landfill. This stream runs right by it."

"Dammit!" cussed Jasper. "I knew that it would come to something like this when they voted to put that confounded dump near my place! Always feared that this creek would get polluted and poison my animals, and now it's done gone and happened!"

"Now, just calm down, Jasper," said the sheriff. "If you want, we can drive over to the landfill and talk to the fellow in charge. Maybe we can find out something. But you've got to promise to behave yourself and not go flying off the handle."

"I won't give you cause to worry," said Jasper, although anger still flared in his rheumy eyes. "Are you
coming with us, Doc?"

"No, I think I'll go on and take these water samples
to Nashville," said Bud. "I'm kind of anxious to find out
what those state chemists have to say. I'm afraid there
might be more at stake here than a few cows. The con-
tamination could be more widespread than we know."

■■■

"What are you saying, Mr. Horne?" asked Alan
Becket, the caretaker of the Bedloe County landfill.
"That I deliberately let somebody dump chemical waste
in this place?"

Jasper Horne jutted his jaw defiantly. "Well, *did* you?
I've heard that some folks look the other way for a few
bucks. Maybe you've got some customers from Nashville
who grease your palm for dumping God-knows-what in
one of those big ditches over yonder."

Sheriff Biggs laid a hand on the farmer's shoulder.
"Now, you can't go making accusations before all the
facts are known, Jasper. Alan has lived here in Bedloe
County all his life. We've known him since he was knee-
high to a grasshopper. That's why we gave him the job
in the first place: because he can be trusted to do the
right thing."

"But what about that stuff in my stream?" asked the
old man. "If it didn't come from here, then where the hell
did it come from?"

"I don't know," admitted Sam Biggs. He turned to
the caretaker. "Can you think of anything out of the ordinary that might've been dumped here, Alan? Maybe some
drums with strange markings, or no markings at all?"

"No, sir," declared Becket. "I'm careful about what I
let folks dump in here. I check everything when it comes
through the gate. And if someone had come around

wanting to get rid of some chemicals on the sly, I'd have called you on the spot, Sheriff."

Biggs nodded. "I figured as much, Alan, and I'm sorry I doubted you." The lawman stared off across the dusty hundred-acre landfill. A couple of bulldozers could be seen in the distance, shoveling mounds of garbage into deep furrows. "You don't mind if we take a look around, do you? Just to satisfy our curiosity?"

"Go ahead if you want," said the caretaker. "I doubt if you'll find anything, though."

Sheriff Biggs and Jasper Horne took a leisurely stroll around the dusty expanse of the county landfill. They returned to the caretaker's shack a half hour later, having found nothing of interest. "I told you I run things legitimately around here, Sheriff," Alan said as he came out of the office.

"Still could be something out there," grumbled Jasper, not so convinced. "A man can't look underground, you know."

"We can't go blaming Alan for what happened to your cows," Biggs told the farmer. "That creek runs under the state highway at one point. Somebody from out of town might have dumped that chemical off the bridge. We can ride out and take a quick look."

"You can if you want," said Jasper. "I've pert near wasted half a day already. I've got some chores to do around the farm and then I've gotta run into town for some supplies." He cast a parting glance at the barren acreage of the landfill. Although he didn't mention it openly, Jasper could swear that the lay of the land was different somehow, that it had changed since the last time he had brought his garbage in. The land looked *wrong* somehow. It seemed *lower*, as if the earth has sunk in places.

Alan Becket accepted the sheriff's thanks for his cooperation, then watched as the two men climbed back into the Bedloe County patrol car and headed along the two-lane stretch of Highway 70.

235

After the car had vanished from sight, a worried look crossed the caretaker's face and he stared at the raw earth of the landfill. But where there was only confusion and suspicion in the farmer's aged eyes, an expression of dawning realization shone in the younger man's face. He watched the bulldozers work for a moment, then went inside his office. Alan sat behind his desk and, taking his wallet out of his hip pocket, fished a business card out of it.

The information on the card was simple and cryptic. There were only two lines of print. The first read TY-ROPHEX-14, while the second gave a single toll-free phone number.

Alan Becket stared at the card for a moment, then picked up the phone on his desk and dialed the number, not knowing exactly what he was going to say when he reached his contact on the other end of the line.

■ ■ ■

It was about six o'clock that evening when Jasper Horne left the county seat of Coleman and returned to his farm. After catching up on his chores that afternoon, Jasper had driven his rattletrap Ford pickup to town to pick up a few groceries and several gallon jugs of distilled water. He felt nervous and cagey during the drive home. He had stopped by the veterinary clinic, but Bud's wife—who was also his assistant—told him that the animal doctor hadn't returned from Nashville yet and hadn't called in any important news. He had checked with Sheriff Biggs too, but the constable assured him that he hadn't learned anything either. He had also told Jasper that he and his deputies had been unable to find any trace of illegal dumping near the highway bridge.

However, that didn't ease Jasper's mind any. He could picture himself forgetting the grisly events of that day, maybe stepping sleepily into the shower tomorrow morning and melting away beneath a yellowish cascade of deadly well water. He forced the disturbing image from his mind and drove on down the highway.

He was approaching the driveway of his property, when he noticed that a South Central Bell van was parked smack-dab in the middle of the gravel turn-off. Jasper craned his neck and spotted a single repairman standing next to a telephone pole a few yards away, looking as though he had just shimmied down after working on the lines.

Jasper tooted his horn impatiently and glared through his bug-speckled windshield. The man lifted a friendly hand and nodded, walking around to the rear of the van to put his tools away. The old farmer drummed his fingers on the steering wheel and glanced in his rearview mirror to see if there were any vehicles behind him. There weren't. The rural road was deserted in both directions.

When Jasper turned his eyes back to the road ahead, he was startled to see that the telephone repairman was standing directly in front of his truck, no more than twelve feet away. The tall, dark-haired man with the gray coveralls and the sunglasses smiled humorlessly at him and lifted something into view. At first, Jasper was certain that the object was a jackhammer. It had the appearance and bulk of one. But on second glance, he knew that it was a much stranger contraption that the man held. It had the twin handles of a jackhammer, but the lower part of the tool resembled some oversized gun more than anything else. There was a loading breech halfway down and, beneath that, a long barrel with a muzzle so large that a grown man could have stuck his fist inside it.

"What in tarnation—?" began Jasper. Then his question lapsed into shocked silence as the repairman aimed the massive barrel squarely at the truck and fired once.

Jasper ducked as the windshield imploded. The projectile smashed through the safety glass and lost its force upon entering the truck cab, bouncing off one of the padded cradles of the gun rack in the rear window. Jasper looked up just as the cylindrical object of titanium steel landed on the seat next to him. He stared at it for a moment, not knowing what to make of the repairman's attack or the thing he had fired into the truck. Then the old man's confusion turned into panic as the projectile popped into two halves and began to emit a billowing cloud of yellow smoke. He knew what it was the moment he smelled the cloying scent. It was the same rancid odor he had gotten a whiff of that morning at the creek.

Jasper Horne wanted to open the truck door and escape, but it was already too late. He was engulfed by the dense vapor and was suddenly swallowed in a smothering cocoon of unbearable agony. That sizzling noise sounded in his ears, but this time it came from his own body. He felt his clothing fall away like blackened cinders and his skin begin to dissolve, followed by the stringy muscle and hard bone underneath. He recalled the screams of his Jersey cows, and soon surpassed their howls of pain...at least until he no longer had a throat with which to vent his terror.

■■■

The following morning, Bud Fulton received an urgent call from Sheriff Biggs, wanting him to come to Jasper Horne's place as soon as possible.

Bud didn't expect to find what he did when he arrived. A county patrol car and a Lincoln sedan with federal plates were parked on the shoulder of the highway. Only a few yards from Jasper's driveway was a blackened hull that looked as if it might have once been a Ford pickup truck. It contained no glass in its windows and no tires on the rims of its wheels. A knot of cold dread sat heavily in the vet's stomach as he parked his jeep behind the police car and climbed out. Slowly, he walked over to where three men stood a safe distance from the body of the vehicle. One was Sam Biggs, while the other two were well-groomed strangers wearing tailored suits and tan raincoats.

The sheriff introduced them. "Bud, these gentlemen are Agents Richard Forsyth and Lou Deckard from the FBI." Forsyth was a heavy-set man in his mid-forties, while Deckard was a lean black man with round eyeglasses.

Bud shook hands with the two, then turned his eyes back to the truck. "What happened here?" he asked Biggs. "Damn, this is old Jasper's truck, isn't it? Did it burn up on him?"

"No," said Deckard. "The truck body hasn't been scorched. The black you seen on the metal is oxidation. Something ravaged both the exterior and interior of this vehicle, but it wasn't fire. No, it was nothing as simple as that."

The veterinarian stared at the federal agent, then at the sheriff. "It was that damned chemical, wasn't it, Sam? But how did it get in Jasper's truck?" He peered through the glassless windows of the truck, but saw no sign of a body inside. "Where the hell is Jasper? Don't tell me he's—"

"I'm afraid so," replied the sheriff, looking pale and shaken. "Take a look inside, but be careful not to touch anything. Agent Deckard is a chemist and he thinks the black residue on the truck might still be dangerous."

Cautiously, Bud stepped forward and peeked into the cab of the truck. Like the rubber of the tires and the glass of the headlights and windows, the vinyl of the dashboard and the cushions of the truck seat had strangely dissolved, leaving only oxidized metal. Amid the black coils of the naked springs lay a pile of gummy sludge that resembled the remains of the dead cows. In the center of the refuse were a number of shiny objects, all metal: a couple of gold teeth, a pocket watch, the buttons off a pair of Liberty overalls, and the steel frames of a pair of eyeglasses, minus the lenses.

Bud stumbled backward, knowing that the bits of tarnished metal were all that was left of his friend and fishing buddy, Jasper Horne.

"We appreciate you bringing this to our attention, Mr. Fulton," said Agent Forsyth. "I know you must have been frustrated yesterday when the state lab refused to give you the test results of the samples you brought in, but we thought it best to have Agent Deckard analyze them before we released any information to local law enforcement or civilians in the area. We had to be certain that they matched up with the other samples we have in our possession."

The veterinarian looked at the FBI agent. "Do you mean to tell me that this has happened before?"

"Yes," said Deckard. "Three times in the past six months. We've done our best to keep it under wraps and out of the news media. You see, this is a very delicate investigation we have going. And the chemical involved is a very dangerous and unpredictable substance."

"Do you know what it is?" Bud asked him.

"It is a very sophisticated and potent type of acid. More precisely, it is a super enzyme. From the tests we've run on the previous samples, it is not biological in nature, but completely synthetic. It can digest almost anything: organic matter, paper, plastic, wood, and glass. The only thing that it has no destructive effect on is metal and stone. We believe that it was produced under very strict and secretive conditions. In fact, its development might well have been federally funded."

"You mean the government might be responsible for this awful chemical?" asked Bud incredulously.

Agent Forsyth looked a little uncomfortable. "We haven't been able to trace its origin as of yet. That's what Agent Decker and I are here to find out. You must understand, Mr. Fulton, the United States government funds thousands of medical, agricultural, and military projects every year. It is possible that one of these projects accidentally or intentionally developed this particular enzyme and that it somehow got into the wrong hands, or has been unscrupulously implemented by its manufacturer."

"Do you have any leads in the case?" asked the sheriff.

"We have several that are promising," said Deckard. "The previous incidents concerning this chemical took place in Nebraska, Texas, and Maryland. There seems to be only one solid connection between those incidents and the ones here in Tennessee."

"And what is that?"

"Municipal and rural landfills. There has always been one within a few miles of the reported incidents."

Sam Biggs and Bud Fulton exchanged knowing glances. "So old Jasper was on the right track after all," said the vet. "Do you think Alan Becket might have something to do with this?"

The sheriff shook his head. "I don't know. I was sure that Alan was a straight-shooter, but maybe he isn't as kosher as we thought."

"I suggest we pick up this Becket fellow for questioning," said Forsyth. "He might just have the information necessary to wrap up this case."

The four climbed into their vehicles and headed east for the county landfill. None of them noticed that a van was following them at an inconspicuous distance. A telephone company van driven by a tall man wearing dark sunglasses.

■■■

It was seven o'clock that night when Alan Becket finally decided to come clean and tell them what they wanted to know.

Sam Biggs brought Becket from the cell he had been confined to most of the day and led him to the sheriff's office on the ground floor of the Bedloe County courthouse. Alan took a seat, eyeing the men in the room with the nervous air of a caged animal. Agent Forsyth was perched on the corner of a desk, looking weary and impatient, while Agent Deckard and Bud Fulton leaned against a far wall. Despite his veterinary business, Bud had decided to stick around and see how the investigation turned out. Jasper Horne had been a close friend of Bud's and he wanted to see that justice was done, as far as the elderly farmer's death—or murder—was concerned.

"So, are you ready to level with us, Mr. Becket?" asked Forsyth.

"Yes, I am," said the man. "I've been thinking it over and I think it would be in my best interest to tell you everything. But, believe me, I had no idea that what I did was illegal or unethical. And I certainly didn't think that it would end up killing anyone."

"Why don't you tell it from the beginning," urged the FBI man. "And take your time."

With a scared look in his eyes, Alan Becket took a deep breath and began to talk. "It happened a couple of months ago. A man came to the landfill office. He claimed to be a salesman for a chemical firm called Tyrophex-14. At first, I thought it was a pretty peculiar name for a corporation, but after he made his sales pitch, it didn't seem so odd after all. He said that his company manufactured a chemical called Tyrophex-14, and that the chemical digested non-biodegradable waste...you know, like plastic and glass. It also sped up the decomposition process of paper, fabric and wood. He said that one treatment per month in six calculated spots in the landfill would keep the volume of garbage to a minimal level. You see, after a month's worth of garbage was buried, a representative would arrive with a weird-looking contraption and inject this chemical, this Tyrophex-14, six feet into the earth. The capsule that held the chemical unleashed a gaseous cloud of the stuff, which wormed its way through the air pockets of the buried garbage and digested it.

"Let me tell you, it was a strange process. Minutes after the chemical was injected, the trash underneath seemed to simply disappear. The earth would sink, leaving empty ditches that were ready to be refilled and covered once again. In my eyes, it was a miraculous procedure and the cost was surprisingly affordable. I signed a one-year contract with the guy, sincerely thinking that I was doing it for the benefit of the community. I mean, just think of it. A perpetual landfill that digests its own garbage; a dumping ground that will never reach its projected capacity. I thought it was some sort of incredible environmental breakthrough, one that would do away with the need to find new landfill sites. The old ones could be used over and over again."

"But this miracle of modern science didn't turn out to be such a blessing after all, did it?" asked Forsyth. "At least not for Jasper Horne, and nine other human victims that we know of."

"I'm sorry," said Becket. "I know I should have checked it out, or at least okayed it with the county commission before I signed that contract. It was just that I didn't see any need to. The monthly treatments were only a few hundred dollars, and the county allots me twice that amount for supplies and maintenance."

"How do you get in touch with this corporation?" asked Forsyth. "Did they leave an address or name of the sales representative?"

"No, just a card with a phone number on it. It's in my wallet."

Agent Forsyth exchanged a triumphant glance with his partner Deckard, then turned to the county constable. "Sheriff, could you please get me Mr. Becket's wallet? I'll call the phone number into the bureau office in Nashville and have them trace it. It shouldn't be long before we know exactly who has been distributing this synthetic enzyme across the country."

Sheriff Biggs was about to open the side drawer of his desk and get Becket's personal property, when the upper pane of the office's single window shattered. "Get down!" yelled Forsyth, drawing his gun and hugging the floor. The others followed suit—all except Alan Becket. The caretaker of the county landfill merely sat frozen in his chair as a cylindrical projectile of shiny steel spun though the hole in the window and landed squarely in his lap.

"Oh God, *no!*" he screamed, recognizing the capsule for what it was. He grabbed it and was about to toss it away, when the pod snapped in half, engulfing him in a dense cloud of corrosive gas.

"Everybody out!" called Sheriff Biggs. "This way!" The other three obeyed, crawling across the room in the general direction of the office door. They could hear the crash of broken glass as two more projectiles were shot through the window. When they reached the temporary safety of the outer hallway, they rose to their feet and looked back into the room. They watched in horror as the screaming, thrashing form of Alan Becket dissolved before their eyes, along with the wooden furnishings and paperwork of the sheriff's office.

Two hissing pops signaled the activation of the second and third projectiles. "Let's get out of here!" said Deckard.

By the time they reached the front door of the courthouse, they could hear the creaking and crackling of the wall supports dissolving away and collapsing beneath the weight of the upper floor. They glanced back only once before escaping to the open space of the town square, and the sight they witnessed was truly a horrifying one. A rolling cloud of the yellow gas was snaking its way down the hallway, leaving a trail of structural damage in its wake.

"The one who shot that stuff through the window!" Bud suddenly said. "Where is he?"

He was answered by the brittle report of a gunshot. He and Sam Biggs turned to see Agents Forsyth and Deckard rushing to a dark form that lay beneath an oak tree. They joined the FBI men just as they were holstering their guns and cuffing the man's hands behind his back. The tall, dark-haired man in the gray coveralls had been hit once in the calf of his right leg. Next to him lay the injection tool that the late Alan Becket had described. No one went near the thing or picked it up, afraid that they might accidentally trigger another lethal dose of Tyrophex-14.

A moment later a thunderous crash sounded behind them and they turned. The Bedloe County courthouse had completely collapsed, its lower supports chemically eradicated by the spreading cloud of vaporous enzyme. All that was left were bricks and blackened file cabinets. As for the destructive mist that had wreaked the havoc, it drifted skyward and dissipated in the cool night air, soon becoming diluted and harmless.

■■■

"Well, we finally got the story," called the voice of Richard Forsyth. "And believe me, it turned out to be a lot worse than we first suspected."

Sam Biggs and Bud Fulton looked up from their coffee cups as the two FBI agents entered the lounge of the federal building. It was almost midnight and the pair had been at it for hours, interrogating the man who had been responsible for the deaths of Jasper Horne and Alan Becket. From the weary but satisfied expressions on their faces, the county sheriff and the rural vet could tell that they had finally cracked the killer's shell and gotten the information they wanted.

Forsyth and Deckard got themselves some coffee and sat down at the table. "First of all, the suspect's name is Vincent Carvell," said Forsyth. "He's a white-collar hit man; a trouble-shooter that hires out to major corporations and takes care of their dirty business. And it seems that his latest client paid him very generously to help keep Tyrophex-14 a big secret."

"Exactly who was his client?" asked Bud.

"A major corporation whose name you would instantly recognize. We would reveal it, but unfortunately we can't, due to security risks," said Forsyth apologetically. "You see, this corporation manufactures some very well-known products. In fact, it is responsible for thirty

245

percent of this country's pharmaceutical and household goods. What the public doesn't know is that its research and development department also does some government work on the side. Mostly classified projects for the military." The older agent sipped his coffee and looked to Deckard, passing the ball to him.

"Although we can't give you specific details," continued Deckard, "we can give you the gist of what Tyrophex-14 is all about. You see, this corporation was doing some work for the Defense Department. Their scientists were attempting to develop an enzymatic gas to be implemented by the armed forces. It was originally intended to be used for chemical warfare in the event that similar weapons were used against our own troops. But the Defense Department pulled the plug on the project when the corporation's scientists perfected a gas that dissolved any type of matter, organic or otherwise, with the exception of metal and stone. Tests showed that it was very unstable and difficult to control, so the project was quickly terminated and hushed up."

"But what the Defense Department didn't know," said Forsyth, "was that this corporation had already produced quite a large quantity of this destructive chemical, which had been labeled Tyrophex-14. They did a battery of tests, unbeknownst to the federal government, to see if it had any practical commercial use. And, obviously, they believed they had found it. Maybe their intentions were good at first. Maybe they actually believed that they had discovered a solution to the earth's garbage problem. But, ultimately, they failed to seek the proper approval and chose to market it covertly. That was when the unstable properties of Tyrophex-14 got out of control...and began to kill innocent people."

"And they hired this hit man to hush things up?" asked Sheriff Biggs. "He killed Jasper Horne and Alan Becket, just to cover this corporation's tracks?"

"Yes, and he would have killed us too, if we hadn't escaped from the courthouse. Carvell figured he could

246

erase the threat of discovery if the investigators and the evidence vanished in a cloud of Tyrophex-14."

The thought of having come so close to death cast an uneasy silence over the four men. They thought of the blackened hull of Jasper's pickup truck and the rubble of the Bedloe County courthouse, and thanked God that they hadn't fallen victim to that corrosive monstrosity that had been conjured from the union of raw elements and complex chemical equations.

■■■

A couple of nights after the collapse of the county courthouse, Bud Fulton sat alone in his den, stretched out in his recliner and sipping on a beer. The room was dark and the nightly news was playing on the television, but he wasn't really paying very much attention to what transpired on the screen. Instead, he thought of the phone call he had received at the clinic that day. It had been Sheriff Biggs, filling him in on the results of the FBI's midnight raid on the shadowy corporation responsible for manufacturing the deadly chemical gas known as Tyrophex-14.

Sam had told him that the raid had taken place discreetly and that it would remain a secret matter, solely between the federal government and their unscrupulous employee. The FBI had failed to say what sort of steps would be taken to see that the project was buried and that experimentation in that particular area was never explored again. But Agent Forsyth had volunteered one last bit of information, albeit disturbing, to repay Biggs and Fulton for keeping silent on the delicate matter.

Forsyth had said that the records of the corporation had listed twenty 50,000 gallon tanks as being the extent of the chemical's manufactured volume. But when the federal agents had checked the actual inventory, only seventeen of the tanks had been found on the company grounds.

Bud drove the sordid business from his mind and tried to concentrate on the work he had to do tomorrow. He was scheduled to give a few rabies and distemper shots in the morning, after which he would head to the Pittman farm to dehorn a couple of bad tempered bulls. Somehow, the simple practices of rural veterinarian seemed downright tame compared to what he had been through the night before last.

Bud finished his beer while watching the local weather and sportscast. He was reaching for the remote control, intending to turn off the set and go to bed, when a news anchor appeared on the screen again with a special bulletin. Bud leaned forward and watched as the picture cut away to a live report.

A female reporter stood next to a train that had derailed a few miles north of Memphis, Tennessee. Firemen milled behind her and the wreckage was illuminated by the spinning blue and red lights of the emergency vehicles that had been called to the scene. The reporter began to talk, informing the viewers of the details of the train derailment. But Bud Fulton's attention wasn't on the woman or the story that she had to sell.

Instead, his eyes shifted to the huge tanker car that lay overturned directly behind her. He prayed that he was mistaken, but his doubts faded when the TV camera moved in closer, bringing the details of the cylindrical car into focus.

Bud's heart began to pound as he noticed a wisp of yellow vapor drift, almost unnoticed, from a rip in one of the tanker's riveted seams. And on the side of the ruptured car, were stenciled a series of simple letters and numbers. To those on the scene, and in the city beyond, they meant absolutely nothing. But to Bud Fulton they were like the bold signature of Death itself.

And its name that night was Tyrophex-14.

SCREAM QUEEN

Sometimes there is a fine line between fandom and obsession. It's okay to appreciate a person's talent or expertise in a certain area—be it literature, music, or the performing arts—but when that interest turns into an unhealthy compulsion, that's when things start getting out of control. Every now and then, the obsessed individual pushes the envelope too far. They end up straying beyond the constraints of the red carpet and actually knocking on the subject's front door. And that can sometimes be more dangerous for the eager fanboy than for the target of his infatuation.

THE images on the screen were black and white, grainy with too many dropouts. The sound was bad, harsh and scratchy. The music was even worse. Too melodramatic. The scene was set somewhere up in the California mountains: a lot of boulders, dry grass, and scrubby underbrush.

Ted Culman lay on the full-size bed, naked, his eyes glued to the nineteen-inch TV. The landscape was unremarkable—the backdrop for countless low-budget movies made in the fifties and sixties. The only distinguishing factor about the old flick appeared a moment later, rounding a boulder and walking up a dusty mountain trail.

Ted sunk into the pillows at his back, as if settling into the cockpit of a jet fighter. He was in control now. The hand that rested on his belly crept toward his groin. Soon it was fisted around him, stroking. He was already aroused.

The woman who appeared on the screen was a real beauty. Average in height, but noticeably buxom, her breasts swelling behind the cloth of her checked blouse. She was platinum blond, much in the style of Marilyn Monroe or Jayne Mansfield. Her lovely face was partly obscured by too much lipstick and partly by a pair of white-framed sunglasses, circa 1956. Ted studied the woman's lower region: flaring hips encased in skintight white slacks, long shapely legs, and tiny feet slipped inside simple sandals.

The woman on the screen made her way up the lonesome pathway, her hips swaying like a pendulum, her delicate jaw working on a gob of Wrigley's spearmint gum. Ted's hand quickened as a muffled roar sounded from off-screen and caused the woman to whirl in her tracks. An atrocious-looking swamp monster—all dangling latex and bulbous tennis ball eyes—leapt down clumsily from a neighboring boulder, its thick arms extended in menace.

That was when Ted closed his eyes and let his imagination take over. As his hand went on autopilot, Ted imagined himself to be the shuffling creature. But there was no menace in his monstrous eyes, only desire—a desire shared by the woman he confronted. In a matter of seconds, his claws had torn past her blouse and bra, tossing tatters of cloth and elastic away until her breasts were exposed. The nipples stood out, pink and hard. She reached out for him and soon they were on the sandy earth. His claws went to work again, hooking past tight cloth, rending it easily. She lay beneath him, completely nude now. They embraced hungrily, a melding of human and alien flesh. Ted felt his bestial member jut from his loins, searching, aching passionately. The woman writhed hungrily against him, then he was there, surrounded by warm wetness.

Ted felt himself quickly reaching the brink. He opened his eyes. The blonde's lovely face filled the screen, just as he had anticipated. Her sunglasses had been knocked askew and one eye stared straight into the camera. Then those luscious lips parted and a shrill scream powered up from out of her throat. But in Ted's ears it was not the shriek of terror that it was intended to be. Instead, it was a cry of unbridled ecstasy.

Pleasure shot through him, exploding at the base of his spine, causing his hips to buck slightly. Then, a second later, it was all over. The scene had changed. Ted was watching a pipe-smoking scientist explaining a screenwriter's theory of evolution, while Ted's penis shriveled in the palm of his hand.

Ted paused the VCR with the remote control, while his other hand shucked a tissue from its box and sopped up the juices of his passion. After the strength had returned to his legs, he hopped off the motel bed and walked into the bathroom. He tossed the damp wad of tissue into the toilet, then cranked up the shower and stepped in.

As he bathed, he smiled to himself, recalling the scream of the monster's blond victim. No one could break the decibel level like Fawn Hale. Oh, many had tried, but none had managed to surpass...at least not in Ted's opinion.

Fawn was well-known and appreciated by aficionados of horror and science-fiction cinema, particularly the cheaply made features of the fifties and sixties. Fawn was considered by the majority to have been the premier scream queen of that era, very much the way Bettie Page had become a cult favorite in the realm of nostalgic pin-ups. There had been dozens of others, some even more beautiful and bustier than Fawn. But none had possessed the lungs she had. For sheer expression of horror and vocal power, the actress had no equal. Ted remembered the first time he had heard Fawn scream. He had attended an all-night Halloween fright fest at a run-down theater off campus. Fawn's shriek had overloaded a couple of the theater's main speakers. They had popped with a burst of ozone, incapable of accommodating the high frequency of Fawn's famous cry.

Just thinking about it made Ted horny again, but he ignored the impulse and finished his shower. He had someplace to go that morning, someplace very important. It was so important, in fact, that he had driven nearly two thousand miles just to get there.

Ted toweled off and then dressed. He left his suitcase behind, but unhooked the VCR and took it with him. He didn't want to risk the chance of the maid ripping it off when she came to clean his room. He also took the cardboard jacket of the tape that was still in the video player. The movie was creatively titled *Curse of the Swamp Monster* and sported a black-and-white shot of the beast in all its low-budget glory.

He stepped outside and locked the door behind him. Ted looked around for a second. The Days Inn he had checked into the night before was off an exit on Interstate 24 in the heart of Tennessee. There was only one reason why a California grad student would waste his spring break and make a cross-country journey to the land of the Grand Ole Opry and Jack Daniels, and that reason could be summed up in two words.

Fawn Hale.

Ted walked to his car—a restored '69 Mustang convertible—and opened the trunk. He set the VCR next to a cardboard box full of videotapes. All were the kind of schlock horror flicks Ted thrived on—the outrageously bad classics of Edward D. Wood and Herschell Gordon Lewis. And two out of three of them featured Fawn Hale and her bloodcurdling scream somewhere between the title and the ending credits.

Before he closed the trunk, he picked up a copy of *Filmfax* that lay on top of the box. It was an article in the movie magazine that had been responsible for his journey south. The story chronicled the history of a dozen popular scream queens and, in the portion devoted to Fawn, had laid the key to a mystery that had bugged Ted for several years. After Hale had retired from films in 1968, she had left Hollywood and seemingly vanished off the face of the earth. But, according to the article, Fawn had returned to her hometown of Cumberland Springs in central Tennessee.

That single tidbit of information had been a revelation for Ted. Fawn had almost become an obsession to him, creeping into his sexual fantasies lately. His dorm room was papered with posters and glossy photos of the B-movie blonde, while Ted's dreams were filled with bizarre images of Fawn being seduced by the monsters she had shared the screen with. It wasn't long before Ted began to imagine himself inside those garish suits of latex and fur, conjuring screams of pleasure from the actress, rather than ones of horror.

After reading the article, Ted simply couldn't put it out of his mind. The closer spring break grew, the more maddening the knowledge of Fawn's whereabouts seemed to be. Finally the thought of driving to Tennessee crossed his mind, lodging there like a splinter. It was during the day of his last class that Ted had made his decision. He took seven hundred dollars out of the bank, packed up his suitcase and VCR, and hit the road. He knew it was foolish and against his better judgment, but he had still gone. Now, three days later, he was only a short distance from his destination.

Ted closed the trunk, taking the magazine with him. He climbed into the Mustang's bucket seat and sat there for a long moment. Across the main highway—which boasted several other motels, an Amoco station, and a McDonald's—was a post bearing two signs. The upper one pointed west and read MANCHESTER—15 MILES. The one underneath pointed east and proclaimed CUMBERLAND SPRINGS—7 MILES.

Well, what're you waiting for, Culman? he thought, feeling a little nervous. *You came this far. Seven miles more and you'll be able to get this out of your system for good.*

He took a deep breath to calm himself, then put the Mustang in gear and pulled out onto the highway.

■■■

The town of Cumberland Springs could scarcely be considered one at all. It consisted of only a church, a post office, and an old-timey general store with a couple of ancient gas pumps out front. A few white clapboard houses were scattered around the main buildings, but that was about the extent of the little hamlet.

Ted stopped at the general store, which was called Roone's Mercantile, and bought himself a honey bun and a Dr. Pepper for breakfast. After he had paid for the food, he regarded the man behind the register. Oscar Roone was a lanky man of sixty with bushy eyebrows and a perpetual scowl on his weathered face. Ted debated asking the man for directions, then decided that it wouldn't hurt.

"Excuse me, but could you tell me how to get to the Hale place?"

The old man glared at the overweight boy with the shaggy brown hair and glasses.

"Why in Sam Hill would you wanna go way out there?" he asked.

Ted was at a loss for an answer at first. He shrugged. "I just have some business there, that's all." Nosy old bastard.

Roone looked like he'd bitten into a green persimmon. He opened his mouth to say something, then changed his mind. "You go on down the highway here about a half mile, till you pass the Knowles farm. You'll know the place. The barn's got 'See Rock City' painted on its roof. Well, you take the next turnoff, a dirt stretch called

Glenhollow Road, and head on that way for three or four miles. The Hale place is the first house on the right."

"Thanks," said Ted. He gathered up his purchases and made his way past the tightly-packed aisles of canned and dry goods, eager to be out of the shadowy store and back into the sunshine. He glanced back only once and saw the old man staring at him peculiarly. As if he wanted to ask Ted something...or maybe tell him something.

He quickly gobbled down the honey bun and chased it with the soda. Then he started his car and headed farther eastward, trying to keep Roone's directions fresh in his mind. He found the Knowles farm without any trouble and turned down the dirt road, even though there was no visible sign marking it as being Glenhollow.

Ted drove down the rural road, his hands clenching and unclenching the steering wheel. The day was beautiful and the dense woods to either side of him were green and cool. Birds sang in abundance from overhead and the air was rich with the scent of honeysuckle, but those things failed to soothe his frazzled nerves. He felt none of the control he had felt earlier that morning, when he had masturbated to the monster movie.

It seemed like an eternity, but he finally reached the first house on the right side of Glenhollow Road. Ted parked the Mustang next to a drainage ditch, a hundred feet from the structure. It was a simple, two-story farmhouse that looked as if it hadn't been treated to a good roofing or paint job for ten or twelve years. Tall oaks surrounded the house, and the yard was knee-high with weeds. Standing at the side of the road was a single mailbox with the name HALE painted on the side, nothing more.

It was at that moment that Ted Culman wondered exactly what he was doing there. Exactly what had he had in mind when he left California? Had he come to simply tell her how much he appreciated her movies and ask for her autograph? Or was there more to it than that? Ted thought about the fantasies he had been indulging in lately, but they concerned the Fawn Hale of the past. The woman had been nearing her forties when she retired. She would be in her sixties now, drawing Social Security and soaking her teeth in a glass by her bed.

The thought made Ted feel a little nauseous. He had the sudden urge to make a U-turn in the country road, retrieve his suitcase from the motel, and head home. But he knew if he did that, he would always wonder about Fawn and the meeting he had aborted out of sheer panic. He took a deep breath and, climbing out of the car, started up the driveway to the Hale residence.

As he crossed the unmowed yard, he began to wonder if anyone even lived there anymore. The front porch was littered with dead leaves, and many of the house's windows were broken, most notably those of the upper floor. The steps creaked beneath his feet as he approached the front door, and beyond the storm door he could only make out darkness. From the other side of the screen drifted a scent of mustiness and decay, the odor of a house that had not been aired out in a very long time.

Nervously, he raised his fist and knocked on the doorjamb.

At first he didn't think anyone was going to answer. Then a form emerged from out of the gloom. "Can I help you?" asked a feminine voice with a soft southern drawl.

Ted stared at the woman on the other side of the door and, at first, the mesh of the screen caused an unnerving illusion. For an instant it was like looking at a freeze-frame of a grainy black-and-white film. A frame of a buxom blonde, minus the sunglasses and fifties clothing. The resemblance was uncanny, almost frightening.

"Fawn?" blurted Ted, even though he knew that the woman couldn't possibly be the one he had come to see. She was too young; a little older than him, maybe twenty-six or seven. And her hair wasn't platinum, but a more natural shade of strawberry blond. But the eyes were identical to Fawn's, and that mouth! There certainly was no mistake that it had been derived from the same voluptuous gene pool.

The girl smiled. "No, but I'm her daughter, Lori," she said. She stared at him for a moment, waiting. "Uh, can I do something for you?"

"My name's Ted Culman," he said, still stunned by how much she looked like Fawn. "I'm a big fan of your mother. I wonder if I could talk to her for a minute, if it wouldn't be too much trouble?"

The smile faltered on Lori's face and she looked a little sad. "I'm sorry, but that's impossible."

"Please," said Ted, sensing that something was wrong. "Just a couple minutes and I—"

"You don't understand," said Lori Hale. She hesitated for a moment, her eyes full of pain. "My mother...she's dead. She passed away about a year ago."

Ted felt as if someone had sucker-punched him in the gut. "Oh no," he muttered. "But...how?"

"Cancer," she told him.

Ted took a step back, his face pale. For a moment he felt as if he might pass out.

He heard the girl unhook the screen door and open it. "Are you all right?" she asked, concerned.

"I...I don't know," he said truthfully. Even though Fawn Hale had died in practically every movie she had been featured in, Ted had a difficult time accepting the fact that she was actually dead in real life. "Could I sit down somewhere for a minute?"

"Sure," said Lori. "Come on inside."

Ted accepted her invitation and was soon sitting on a threadbare couch in a dusty parlor. The room was decorated with antique furniture, and the walls alternated between old family photographs and glossy 8x10 stills of Fawn in her prime, most of them showing off more her teeth and tonsils more than anything else.

When some of the color had returned to Ted's face, the young woman seemed to relax a little. "Are you sure you're okay?" she asked again.

"Yeah," replied Ted. "I was just surprised, that's all."

"And disappointed, too," said Lori. "I see it in your face. Just how far did you come to see my mother?"

"San Diego," he said.

"California? No wonder you're so upset." She started toward an adjoining hallway. "I'll go to the kitchen and fetch us something to drink. I just fixed a pitcher of iced tea. How does that sound?"

Ted's throat felt parched. "Great," he replied.

A minute later, Lori returned with a tall glass of iced tea in each hand. When she entered the room, Ted couldn't help but admire the girl's figure, clad only in a halter top and a pair of denim cutoffs. She possessed practically the same body that her mother had in her youth: perfectly formed breasts, graceful hips, and long, muscular legs.

Lori seemed to sense his attention, but didn't seem to mind. She sat down next to Ted and slipped a cold glass in his hand. "There you go," she said. She watched as he gulped several swallows of tea. "So you were a fan of Mama's?"

"Yes," said Ted. The tea was a little strong for his taste, but it seemed to calm him down. "I have about every film she ever made on video."

"Really?" asked Lori, impressed. "Even *Demon Conquerors from Mars?*"

Ted laughed. He knew the film she was talking about. It was a dreadful science-fiction flick made on a shoe-string budget of two thousand dollars and featured some really horrendous special effects, such as a sinister robot constructed from an oil drum, and a magnified iguana attacking a shoddy model of a small town. If there was one shining point about the movie, it was the appearance of Fawn as an unsuspecting diner waitress who falls victim to the Martians and their oversized lizard.

"I do have that one," he said.

"That was one of my favorites," said Lori. She smiled. "You know, I do appreciate you coming. Mama would've appreciated it, too."

"I'm just sorry I couldn't have met her," he said. Ted thought of the way he had exploited the actress in his own sleazy fantasies and suddenly felt ashamed.

"She would have enjoyed talking to you," Lori told him. "She liked talking about her career." A strange expression surfaced in the woman's eyes. "Well, most of it, that is."

Ted drank his tea, a question suddenly coming to mind. He wondered whether he should ask it or not, then figured it was safe to do so. "Exactly why did your mother retire, Lori? I've read about everything I could dig up on her, but I've never been able to find out the reason."

Lori avoided his gaze at first. "There was a scandal."

"Scandal?"

"Yes," she went on. "It happened during her last picture, *Night of the Jungle Zombies*. They had finished up a day's shooting on location near Los Padres National Park. It was after dark and Mama was walking through the forest back to her trailer. Before she got there, someone jumped out of the shadows and attacked her." Lori paused for a moment.

"She was raped."

Ted couldn't believe what he was hearing. "Did she know who it was?"

"Yes, although she never told anyone," said Lori. "It was a bit player in the picture. A guy by the name of Trevor Hall."

"Trevor Hall," repeated Ted. The name sounded familiar, but Ted had difficulty matching it with a face. There had been hundreds of bit players in the industry back then, some only lasting a picture or two.

Lori stared at Ted for a long moment, watchful. Then she continued. "After the attack, Mama found out that she was pregnant," said Lori. "She decided to leave Hollywood and come home, to this house that once belonged to my grandparents. She had dreams of going back to California and taking up where she left off, but she never did. I was born and that was the end of it."

"Oh, I see," said Ted. He raised the tea glass to his lips, but it seemed strangely heavy in his hand. "You know, it wasn't your fault," he assured her. "It was that Hall jerk who screwed it up for her."

Anger suddenly flared in Lori's eyes. "My father was never as bad as folks made out," she snapped. "He was just...misunderstood."

Ted was surprised. He couldn't understand the outburst, especially considering what the man had done to her mother. Ted couldn't figure out why he was beginning to feel so exhausted, either. He guessed the long drive was catching up to him.

Almost as quickly as her anger had surfaced, it was gone. She smiled, eyeing him in that odd, attentive way of hers. "You haven't told me about yourself, Ted," she said. "What do you do for a living?"

Ted's head began to swim. His eyelids felt heavier than lead, as if they could hardly stay open. "Uh, what did you say?" he asked.

"I asked what you do for a living," she repeated. Her smile was fixed, unwavering.

Ted had to think for a moment before he could answer. "Nothing yet," he said. His words seemed to flow as slowly as molasses. "I'm still in college." He looked over at Lori. Two of her wavered before his eyes. "What do you do?" he asked softly.

"I make movies," she said.

Before he knew it, Ted could no longer sit up. He slumped forward and rolled off the sofa, onto the parlor's hardwood floor. He looked up at Lori, expecting to see a look of alarm on her pretty face. But it wasn't there. Instead, there was a peculiar look of satisfaction.

"I make movies," she repeated, as if making sure that he had heard. "Just like my mother." Her smile broadened a little, curling wickedly. "And my father."

Then her face turned into a blur and faded to black.

■■■

Ted was in the midst of a dream. One of the dreams that starred Fawn Hale.

He was on a big round bed that seemed to take up the entire room. He was naked, except for his glasses. Even then, his vision was a little hazy, like a camera fitted with a soft-focus filter.

The mattress sagged a little as someone joined him. It was Fawn Hale, also naked, her platinum hair gleaming in the harsh glare of a klieg light. She wore the sunglasses she had worn in *Curse of the Swamp Monster*, the ones with the white frames. The lenses were pitch black. Impenetrable.

Without a word, she crept across the bed toward him with the predatory grace of a cat. He moaned when she reached him and her flesh touched his. A tiny grin crossed her lips as she moved over his midsection and mounted his hips. Ted stared up at those wondrous breasts. They stared back at him, transfixing him, like the eyes of a Svengali.

Fawn purred deep down in her throat, then lowered herself. Ted groaned. They joined effortlessly.

The platinum-haired beauty seemed to ride him forever, her head thrown back, her huge breasts bouncing in time to the rhythm. Ted found himself to be powerless. He simply lay there and let the actress have her way with him.

Eventually Fawn could contain herself no longer. Her thighs tightened around his waist and her pace began to quicken. Ted felt himself begin to climax, too. The mounting pleasure in his groin seemed to clear his head a little and the sluggish, weighty feeling began to lift.

That was when he saw the black object at the far end of the bed. It was video camera on a tripod. Aimed straight at him and Fawn.

Ted remembered something Lori had told him. *I make movies.*

Suddenly, he knew that he wasn't dreaming.

And there was something else. Something that he had failed to recall before. Trevor Hall. He knew who he was now. Hall had not been a bit player, but a stuntman. A hulking stuntman big enough to play a convincing monster. And he had played them, too: werewolves, robots, swamp monsters. But that was not all that Ted remembered about Hall.

The stuntman had been a serial killer. In the early 'seventies he had been convicted of brutally raping and murdering several dozen women over the span of two decades. The evidence had been what had bought him a seat in the electric chair: an entire library of sixteen-millimeter reels Hall had filmed himself. Snuff films of those he had violated and slaughtered.

Ted stared up at the woman on top of him. He reached up slowly, his arms as heavy as concrete. He removed the white-framed shades. Lori's eyes sparkled down at him. They looked as crazy as the photos Ted had seen of her father. Gleaming with a fiendish satisfaction that was a mixture of ecstasy and bloodlust.

He reached out for the platinum wig, but it was beyond his grasp. Lori leaned in closer, smiling. Her shoulder flexed as she brought her right hand from behind her back.

"Scream for me," she whispered.

Ted felt the coldness of steel against his throat. He opened his mouth, perhaps to reason with her. But just staring into those lovely eyes and seeing the legacy of darkness that danced beyond them, Ted knew that any attempt would be futile.

As the edge of the knife stung his flesh, he braced himself and, regretfully, gave her what she wanted.

■■■

The images on the screen were color. Sharply defined, perfectly lit. The sound was minimal. The creaking of bed springs and the low murmurs of passion. There was no music. No soundtrack was necessary.

Lori Hale lay on the round bed, naked, her eyes glued to the television at the far side of the room. She watched as the image of a platinum-haired beauty straddled the hips of an overweight boy with brown hair and glasses.

She watched the scene unfold, slowly snaking her hand past the flat of her stomach to the cleft just beyond. Soon her fingers were at work, stroking.

The video—one of many—continued at a leisurely pace, finely orchestrated and leading toward a familiar finale. Lori watched as the woman reached beneath the edge of the circular mattress and withdrew a long-bladed butcher knife.

As the scene reached its climax, Lori found herself reaching her own. Her fingers worked furiously as she awaited the command she had given more times than she could remember.

Waves of ecstasy gripped Lori, washing through her, giving way to abandonment. Gritting her teeth, she clutched the bedcovers and felt the stiffness of dried blood in the fabric of the sheets.

Then she closed her eyes tightly and listened for the sound of the scream...

DEVIL'S CREEK

Several years ago, not far from where I grew up, folks were encountering some grisly discoveries in the forests and even off the hiking trails of one of the state parks. A few of the local dogs had been decapitated and their heads burnt as some sort of sacrificial offering. There was a lot of talk of devil worshippers and, for a little Southern town smack dab in the center of the Bible Belt, such talk can be mighty disturbing.

Even more disturbing was the fact that locals were believed to be responsible for the gruesome rituals. It could have been a friend or a neighbor...even one of their own kin. Eventually, the offerings stopped and the whole sorry business was forgotten. In a way, it was probably for the best. If some prominent member of the community had been linked to the practice of black magic and Satanism, the repercussions could have been devastating for such a God-fearing town.

THE baying of Old Boone rang throughout the August darkness. It started deep down in the hound's throat, escaping his gullet hoarsely and filling the backwoods hollows. A short silence followed, then another fit of triumphant howling was unleashed, heralding the end of that night's lengthy pursuit.

Clinton Harpe grinned as he headed south though the black tangle of the Tennessee forest. The hound was closing in for the kill; he could tell by the frantic pitch of the dog's voice. It wouldn't be long before Old Boone treed the coon that had eluded them both for the better part of two hours. In his mind's eye, Clinton could see the bluetick hound, lithe and lathered, stalking the shadowy woods like a pale ghost. The dog's nose would be close to the ground and filled with the scent of its prey, its bright eyes peering into the darkness, eager for the first glimpse of furry movement shimmying its way up the trunk of a black oak or sourgum tree.

The hunter kept his ears keen. With the double-barreled shotgun tucked safely beneath his armpit, he scrambled down a slope of fragrant honeysuckle and hit the wet channel of Devil's Creek running. Moonlight filtered through the heavy foliage of the surrounding trees, glistening on the surface of the brook, turning the rushing water into rippling currents of quicksilver.

Clinton wondered where he was at the moment, for that night's coon hunt had taken him on a long and winding trek through the southern reaches of Bedloe County. It had been a while since he had traveled the heavy woods along Devil's Creek. It was a land that possessed a dark past, a God-forsaken stretch of wilderness in the truest sense. Most folks preferred not to venture into its rambling labyrinth of blackberry bramble and dense woodland in broad daylight, let alone in the nocturnal hours following sundown.

If Clinton Harpe hadn't been so caught up in the chase, he might have thought better than to plunge headlong into the dark forest, alone and without the company of others. But the fever of the hunt was within Clinton's blood, the same as with Old Boone. He could no more halt his mad scramble through the darkness than the dog could put the brakes on his own instinctive nature.

Clinton thought of the history of Devil's Creek as he moved onward. There had once been a small settlement of gypsy farmers a half mile further on, a tight-knit community of drab houses and barns built along the clearwater stream. As a group, they worked and associated solely with their own kind, living in what might be considered a commune of sorts. They were a swarthy race of people, dark of hair and eyes, as well as of character. Unlike their European counterparts, these gypsies were a brooding lot, as silent and somber as a granite tombstone. They did not sing or dance with the gaiety of those brilliantly-clothed vagabonds that most folks identified with the gypsy myth. When they came to the rural town of Coleman for their monthly supplies, they had walked the streets with an air of disdain and contempt, speaking only when necessary, then heading back to their farming community on the fertile banks of Devil's Creek.

They were a religious people, although their devotion was completely opposite of what most folks' spirituality consisted of. They belonged to an organization known as the Church of the Alternate Father. It didn't take an educated man to figure out exactly who that alternate father was...Beelzebub, Lucifer, the Prince of Darkness. One only had to catch a glimpse of their place of worship to know that they were in league with the Devil. The steepled churchhouse was painted jet-black instead of pure dove white like most, and the high, peaked windows were darkly shuttered, bearing the blasphemous symbol of an inverted cross on each. It was said that on nights when the moon was round and high, the sound of chanting could be heard inside the shuttered building, soon followed by the aroma of burning flesh and the cries and moans of carnal acts being committed within. Every once in a while, a hunter's dog would end up dead or a Cole-

267

man farmer would find a prized hog or cow slaughtered in its pen or pasture. In each case, only the head of the animal would be missing. The rest of the body was left, whole and intact.

Then, one night in 1938, the Church of the Alternate Father caught fire, along with most of the other buildings along Devil's Creek. A good portion of the gypsy population died in the blaze, while the survivors scattered to the four winds afterward. Although it was never said out loud, most suspected that the fire had been set by folks whose tolerance of the blatant midnight rituals and wanton atrocities had finally reached its limit.

The legend did not sway Clinton in his quest for raccoon hide and meat, however. He continued on, splashing through the center of the creekbed, partly out of urgency, partly out of need to cool himself off. The summer night was sweltering and humid, despite the lateness of the hour. Clinton removed his hat, dipped it into the cold current, then dumped the contents over his head, nary a step of his long-legged stride faltering as he did so.

He was nearing the gathering of dilapidated, burnt-out buildings, when he became aware that Old Boone was no longer barking. Had he lost the coon? Whether he had or not, the dog would have still been howling to the high heavens. Clinton slowed his pace as he reached the edge of the forest, and it was a good thing that he did, too. He stopped stone still, hidden within the concealment of a heavy pine grove, and watched through the prickly boughs at what took place in the clearing beyond.

Dark figures gathered around the ramshackle hull of the long-abandoned church. It was difficult to make out their features, for the moonlight was all that illuminated them. They seemed to be dressed in hooded robes, similar to those worn by the Ku Klux Klan, though completely black in color. The shape and size of the mysterious forms varied. Some were men, while others appeared to be women and children. All were silent as they filed, one by one, through the open doorway of the fire-gutted structure.

A chill ran down the spine of Clinton Harpe, for he was sure that he was witnessing the ghosts of those who had worshipped there some twenty years ago. But such thoughts of haunting spirits vanished when he saw a group of men standing beneath a nearby tree. Old Boone was with them, jumping playfully, sniffing around as though he were among friends. "Good dog," said a big fellow, crouching down. He hugged the hound close to him and scratched behind the bluetick's floppy ears.

Clinton's apprehension eased up at the sight of the man's friendliness and he nearly stepped from the shadows to retrieve his misguided hound. But before he could, he watched in horror as the man grabbed the dog roughly by the ears, yanking the animal's head back and bringing a yelp of startled surprise. Moonlight flashed on honed steel as the blade of a knife appeared, slashing horizontally across Old Boone's throat, slicing deeply, drawing a fountain of dark crimson.

Shock gripped Clinton in its numbing grasp, followed by the heat of mounting anger. He was about to raise his twelve-gauge and confront the sadistic dog-killer, when he noticed that several of the robed men carried rifles and shotguns. He restrained his urge to step into view and watched the big man saw back and forth with the knife, slashing through the tender muscle of Old Boone's neck, as well as the hardness of raw, white bone. Soon, the blade had completed its grisly work and the dog's body fell away from its head. It dropped to its side on the summer grass, paws and tail twitching as the last of its lifeblood ebbed from the fatal wound.

Clinton felt a gorge of bile rising into his throat. He swallowed hard and fought off the nausea that threatened to overcome him. He watched as one of the men, tall and lanky beneath his hooded robe, turned and glanced his way. "Thought I heard something over yonder," he said in little more than a whisper. His eyes glittered within the dark eyeholes, as he cocked the lever of a Winchester rifle and took a curious step toward the edge of the woods.

As quietly as possible, Clinton retreated into the darkness of the thicket. The last thing he saw before he turned tail and ran, was the big man heading for the old church house, holding the severed head of Old Boone by its ears.

■■■

The next morning, Clinton rode out to Devil's Creek with Sheriff Boyce Griffin. They took the main highway out of Coleman, then headed down a turn-off that was little more than two rutted tracks of bare earth with weeds growing high in-between. It looked as though no one had traveled that lonely road in years, let alone the night before.

Clinton honestly believed that Boyce was making the trip simply to put his mind at ease. The sheriff was a good, level-headed man, an outsider who had moved into Bedloe County a few years ago and earned the respect of the local citizenry. He had been a deputy on the county force for a while, then was elected into the position of Sheriff when the previous constable, Taylor White, had died of a heart attack in 1952. Since then, he had proven himself to be a fair man and no one thereabouts had ever found cause to complain about the performance of his job.

They arrived at the charred ruins of the Devil's Creek settlement around nine o'clock.

It was a beautiful day and the cleansing rays of the summer sun shone upon the burnt buildings and the surrounding land, easing the severity of the sinister events of the night before. Boyce parked his Ford patrol car next to the abandoned church. Then they got out and walked around a bit.

"Where'd you say this fella killed your dog?" asked the sheriff, prying specks of ham and eggs from between his teeth with a café toothpick.

"Over yonder, beneath that tree." Clinton headed in that direction and Boyce followed.

When they reached the spot, there was nothing to be found. Hide nor hair of the bluetick's body remained, not even a trace of blood on the grass. "This was where it happened," swore Clinton. "This was where that bastard done in Old Boone."

Boyce shrugged his beefy shoulders. "Well, no sign of the dog that I can see." The sheriff eyed the lanky farmer with a trace of suspicion. "You sure you didn't tie one on down at the Bloody Bucket last night and dream the whole thing up?"

Clinton was irritated by the insinuation. "I've had nary a drop since last weekend. I didn't imagine what happened here last night, Boyce, and you know it." Clinton knew for a fact that a strange rash of missing animals had hit Bedloe County recently: mostly lost dogs, but also a few stolen hogs and calves.

"I ain't ready to believe all this bull I keep hearing about devil worshippers in Bedloe County," Boyce told him flat out. "I know that it happened here once on Devil's Creek, but that was pert near twenty years ago. And from what I've heard tell, all those gypsies either died in the blaze or left the county with their tails betwixt their legs."

"Mind if we check out that church?" asked Clinton.

The lawman shrugged. "I ain't got nothing better to do."

They approached the black hull of the building that had once provided services for the Church of the Alternate Father. All four walls were intact, but the doors and windows had burned away, leaving narrow openings in the scorched building. They stepped inside the rickety structure and strolled amid the ash and debris. Most of the original pews stood upright, as well as the pulpit at the front of the building. The charred rafters of the great pitched roof stood starkly against the pale blue of the morning sky like the exposed bones of an enormous ribcage.

Once, on a morning very much like this, men had-picked through the smoldering ruins of the church and removed the burnt bodies of those who had died while worshipping their profane master. Most were men who had been present the night before, men who had carried hatred in their hearts, as well as torches and gasoline cans in their hands. Clinton's father, Wallace Harpe, had been among them, although he and a few others had only stood and watched, while the others ran through the little village, playing avenging angel and arsonist with the same self-righteous zeal.

"Don't look like anybody's been in this old church in a month of Sundays," said Boyce, smiling faintly at his pun. "How many folks did you say you saw come in here?"

"Had to be at least two dozen," said Clinton. He walked up the center aisle and halted before the podium. "Hey...come and take a look at this here."

The sheriff joined him at the dark altar. A single object sat on top. It was the fire-blackened skull of an animal...a dog, from the size and shape of it. There was no meat or hair left on it. Only scorched bone remained. Clinton picked it up and held it in his hand.

"Still warm," he said, passing it to Boyce Griffin.

Boyce took it and gave it a thorough examination. "That don't prove anything, Clinton. The sun could've heated it up. Looks to me like the thing's been sitting there for a mighty long time."

"You just ain't gonna believe a word I said, are you?"

"Well, hell, Clinton, what do you expect?" said the sheriff, a mite peeved at having been dragged out there on a wild goose chase. "Just look around you. This place is a damned ghost town. Nobody's set foot in this part of Devil's Creek in years. I can't rightly launch an investigation when there's no evidence that a crime has been committed."

"What about the killing of a man's dog?" asked Clinton.

Boyce shook his head and began to walk back to the doorway of the old church.

"A shame if something did happen to Old Boone, but killing an animal ain't grounds for a murder charge. And, if it was, who would we convict of it? You can't slap handcuffs on a ghost, you know?"

"Is that what you think?" snapped Clinton with anger in his eyes. "That it was some figment of my imagination?"

"I keep thinking about all those times you've slept off a drinking binge at the county jail, Clinton. Now why don't you just admit that you had a snoot full and get off this crazy business about animal sacrifices and hooded Satan worshippers."

"I wasn't drunk," proclaimed Clinton. "Not by a long shot."

He heard the sheriff's sigh of frustration and the crunch of his footsteps across the ashen floor of the churchhouse. Clinton held the warm black skull in his hands and stared into the empty eye sockets. *Is that you, Old Boone?* he wondered. *Is this all that's left of you now?*

The skull simply stared back mutely, giving him no answers. Clinton set the hunk of scorched bone back atop the pulpit, then reluctantly joined Boyce outside. During the ride back to Coleman, the hoarse baying of a bluetick hound echoed in the back of Clinton's mind, as well as the panicked yelp drawn by the cold flat of honed steel against canine flesh.

■■■

That night, Clinton Harpe sat on the back porch of his farmhouse, listening to the radio and staring into the darkness. A Hank Williams song drifted from inside the kitchen, "Lovesick Blues" from the sound of the tune. Clinton's mind wasn't much on lyrics that evening. He looked up at the full moon overhead, as high and bright as the one last night, and thought of Old Boone, the finest coon-hunting dog in all of Tennessee. He also thought of a night twenty years ago. A night full of confusing incidents...and unexpected visitors.

He had been eight years old that night in the autumn of 1938. He remembered his father grabbing his hat and coat and leaving with a number of local men who drove pickup trucks and dark sedans. He had recognized a few faces from the window of his bedroom: Woody Sadler, who owned the general store at the forks, as well as others like Buster Cole and Dusty Ballard. Among those who had gone but not had a hand in the torching, was Clayburn Biggs, whose son Johnny had been brutally murdered with two boys in an old tobacco barn several years before.

He recalled watching them head toward the southern half of Bedloe County and then climbing back into bed. He had slept fitfully, dreaming of dark forms gathered in some great structure, ominous forms that danced and chanted in a tongue he had never heard before. He awoke to the sound of his father coming in the back way. There had been a bout of angry discussion between his parents, then things had died down a bit. Curiously, he opened the door of his room, which joined the kitchen, and saw that the room was dark and empty...except for two small forms that huddled in front of the potbelly stove.

Clinton had entered the kitchen and walked closer. It was two children, a brother and sister, clutching a woolen blanket around their naked bodies. As he studied them from the doorway, he saw that they shared the same raven-black hair and dark liquid eyes. And they had one more thing in common. Along the flesh of their inner arms were etched a number of strange symbols. Tattoos of five-pointed stars in circles and crude beasts with spiraling horns and cloven hooves lined their bare flesh, looking vaguely sinister in the flickering light of the cast-iron stove.

The children had merely stared at Clinton, regarding him with the glazed expression of things associated more with death than with life. Those hollow-eyed stares had put a chill in his youthful soul and driven him back to the safety of his room. When he awoke in the morning, the siblings were gone. Both his father and mother denied they had ever been there, claiming that he had dreamt the entire episode.

For many years, Clinton thought that perhaps they had been a part of some disturbing childhood nightmare. But shortly after the death of his father, Woody Sadler had told him the truth about that night. It seemed that during the confusion and chaos of the Devil's Creek fire, two small children were discovered cringing in the shelter of a stone springhouse near the edge of the branch. Wallace Harpe and the others had spirited them away without the knowledge of their fellow vigilantes, not knowing what might happen if the others got hold of them. Clinton's father had brought them home with him and, early the following morning, had driven them to an orphanage in Nashville, where he had left them in the care of those who knew how to handle abandoned children.

It hadn't been a dream then, and it certainly hadn't been a dream last night, with the loss of Old Boone. Disturbing images kept surfacing in Clinton's mind. Images of the hound's head gracing the black altar, eyes glassy with death and tongue lolling from the side of its gaping mouth. Then a touch of a torch set the severed head aflame, consuming hair and hide and flesh, boiling away membrane and blood, turning the loving eyes into simmering pits of jelly. Soon, the dark forms would breathe in the heady scent of burning flesh and, as the last of the meat gave way to charred bone, they would end their chanting and disrobe. Then the church of Satan would echo with the cries of pain and pleasure, and the blackened pews would rock with the violent abandon of mass fornication.

Clinton drove the thoughts from his mind and spat tobacco juice off the edge of the back porch, onto the bare patch of earth where Old Boone once lay in the sun and dreamt of coons and rabbits and bitches in heat. *You're just plain batty for thinking of such*, he thought.

But, for some reason, he couldn't convince himself that the perverse images were false. On the contrary: his most outlandish imaginings seemed to fall short of the true horrors that must have taken place following his escape from Devil's Creek.

He left his place on the porch and walked back into the kitchen. His wife, Phyllis, was washing the supper dishes at the sink. She gave him a gentle smile, for she knew he was still upset about the loss of Old Boone. He returned the smile. Clinton had met Phyllis while he was working at a textile mill in Nashville. She had been a welcomed change from the loose women he usually encountered in the bars and honky-tonks. Phyllis had been a shy and prudent girl, and still was. Their affection had only been shared in darkened rooms and he had never once seen her naked throughout their entire marriage. When his father died, they had taken over the responsibility of the farm and made a life for themselves. Except for pulling an occasional drunk, Clinton had done his best to make a good home for his wife of seven years.

The sole product of their physical union sat at the kitchen table, playing with paper dollies. Six-year-old Nellie Sue beamed up at him, her smile drawing him like a magnet. He lifted her from her chair and gave her a big hug. When he returned her to her seat, he looked down at her with both pride and sadness. She was a lovely young'un, all freckled face and bright blue eyes. Her curly locks were honey blond, taking after his own hair rather than the dark hue of her mother.

But one flaw marred her radiant beauty. A great strawberry-red birthmark covered the left side of her face, from temple to chin. Sometimes it made Clinton's heart ache to see the disfiguring patch of skin on her smiling face and hear the cruel remarks of the children when they went shopping in town. He was sure that Nellie Sue wasn't the first child in Coleman to be ridiculed for being different, but it still pained him to see her suffer because of some stupid fluke of nature.

"I'm gonna take a walk," he told Phyllis, giving her an affectionate peck on the back of the neck. "Wanna clear my head a bit." He saw her turn and give him an inquisitive look. "And don't worry. I ain't going down to the Bloody Bucket. I've chores to do early in the morning."

"Don't be too long," she said, then left the sink and herded their daughter off to bed. Clinton stepped out on the back porch, letting the screen door slam behind him. He stood and hoped for a cool breeze to stir, but like last night, the air hung around him like a warm and sticky blanket. He stared into the darkness, listening to the sounds of crickets and toads.

Finally, he made up his mind. He cut across the cornfield and entered the woods that bordered his property, then headed southward.

■■■

He must have walked for a couple of hours, picking his way through the dense growth of the forest, then taking the winding route of the creekbed toward his destination. All the while, thoughts of Old Boone festered in his brain, driving him onward. Let Boyce Griffin think what he wanted to. He knew that the slaying of Old Boone had been for real, as well as those who had been responsible. He needed to prove that to himself, if to no one else.

Clinton reached the edge of the forest around midnight. He peered from the shelter of the trees, searching for black-robed men with guns, but he saw no one. He was beginning to wonder if maybe Boyce had been right after all, when he heard the faint sound of chanting echo from the ashen hull of the old church. He held his breath and listened to the sing-song melody of the strange words that flowed from the open windows. A fire blazed somewhere within; he could see the yellow glow flickering from inside.

Carefully, making sure that he would not be seen, Clinton darted from one patch of shadow to another, working his way toward the side of the black structure. When he had reached the scorched wall, he stood there, breathing shallowly and gathering the nerve to take a look inside. Finally, he chanced a glance through one of the arched windows.

Row upon row of dark, hooded forms sat in the charred pews of the old church. Others who did not have seats stood against the inner walls, arms folded, watching solemnly from the pits of their black cowls. Clinton turned his gaze on a large form standing before the pulpit. From the size and bulk of the high priest, Clinton recognized him as being the one who had killed Old Boone. The man's hood had been replaced by the fire-burnished skull of a huge bull. Broad horns swept gracefully from the sides of the bony head, while human eyes gleamed from the shadows of the gaping eye sockets.

The dark priest knelt beside a pale form that lay naked before him. From where Clinton stood, he could only tell that it was the form of a small child. The sight of the brute's hands hovering a few inches above smooth, unblemished skin sent a thrill of panic through Clinton. He wished now that he had brought his gun along. If he had, perhaps he could have stopped what was about to take place. But his hands were empty and he could only watch in growing horror as a long dagger appeared in the fist of the high priest. Firelight glittered on polished steel as the blade rose, slowly and deftly, then plunged.

Clinton closed his eyes and moaned softly. He felt as though he might pass out as the ugly sounds of slaughter echoed in his ears. When he finally found the strength to return his eyes to the grisly ceremony, he saw that the child's head had been placed atop the altar. Blood trickled in dark rivulets down the front of the pulpit, mingling with the flaky ashes and giving the podium a slimy sheen in the muted firelight.

He ducked below the row of side windows and made his way to the front door to get a better view. Clinton could do nothing now, but perhaps he could see something that might later identify those who performed the horrid ritual. He was sure that Boyce Griffin would take him seriously when he found out that an innocent child had been sacrificed, rather than mere dogs and livestock.

When he reached the open doorway, he found that the head of the child had already been ignited. Flames engulfed the tiny face, licking along the smooth skin and the delicate curls of cornsilk hair. It was then that a cold dread crept like a snake through the bowels of Clinton Harpe. For as he pulled away from the concealment of the outer darkness and began to walk down the center aisle, he found himself looking into features that were as familiar to him as his own.

A great wail of anguish tore from his throat as the fire took hold, turning the golden blond hair into flying cinders and the brilliant blue eyes into shriveled gray blisters. And as the freckled flesh blackened and shrank away from the bone, a thicker patch of tissue remained a second longer, blazing brightly against the charred meat. A long splash of strawberry-redness stretching tautly between temple and chin.

Then the odor of the sacrifice drifted throughout the dark church, curling its way up the nostrils of the hooded followers and driving them into a frenzy. Screams of abandonment joined Clinton's screams of terror as the hellish congregation tore their garments asunder, exposing themselves. In an orgy of mad passion they clutched at one another, biting, clawing, rutting like wild animals. Clinton found himself standing, utterly forgotten, amid a pale sea of heaving bodies. The stench of burnt flesh was soon accompanied by the acidic taint of human sweat and sex.

Clinton Harpe turned and fled. He left the dark church and plunged into the dark tangle of the deep forest. Like a lunatic, he tore through the woods along the moonlit channel of Devil's Creek. The sound of his screams rang through the Tennessee hills and hollows, as well as the cries of evil rapture vented by the Church of the Alternate Father. Like Old Boone, he shot through the darkness of night, chasing an elusive target known as sanity. He could sense it ahead, dodging and darting, swiftly slipping from his grasp.

■■■

Hours later, Clinton found himself sprinting through the corn stalks of his back field, heading for the farmhouse at a dead run. He tripped, fell, got back up and continued on. The house was dark, nary a light in the place. He struggled to understand why, then realized that it must be two or three o'clock in the morning. No lights would be burning at such an ungodly hour.

He crossed the back porch and flung open the screen door. As he raced through the kitchen and down the hallway, toward the bedroom of his daughter, he found himself wishing for the power to scream as he had in the wilderness of Devil's Creek. But he could not. All he could do was wheeze breathlessly as his feet pounded the hardwood floor and his hands groped through the darkness for the proper door.

Clinton found the brass knob and nearly tore the door from its hinges. *It was all a terrible nightmare,* he fought to convince himself, like a lawyer trying to defend a hopelessly guilty man. *She'll be here, tucked safely in her bed and sleeping.*

Then the palms of his hands reached out for the bed and, instead of finding the warmth of his daughter's slumbering body, they found only the cool emptiness of clean white sheets. "Oh, Lord God!" he wailed at the top of his lungs. "Why did they take her? Oh, Lord in heaven, why *her?*"

But as Phyllis appeared next to him, eyes wide with fear and hands clutching at his thrashing form, he knew why they had taken his beloved Nellie Sue. It was because of *him* that she had fallen prey. It was because of his discovery of their evil coven and his interference with their most sacred and secretive ritual.

280

"What's wrong?" shrilled Phyllis in his ears. "What's happened?"

But he could not bring himself to answer her. He could not bring himself to do anything at all...except surrender to the dizzy pull of darkness that drew him into the depths of comforting oblivion.

∎∎∎

When Clinton Harpe awoke it was still dark.

He stared up from where he lay across his daughter's empty bed and looked up into the faces of Phyllis and Sheriff Boyce Griffin. At first, he was confused by their presence. Then the night's horrors reclaimed his thoughts and he lurched to his feet, grabbing at the front of Boyce's khaki uniform shirt.

"Oh, God, Boyce, I was right!" he groaned. "I was right about what I saw last night! And I paid for it...with my child!"

"Calm down, Clinton," urged the lawman, putting his hands on the farmer's lanky shoulders. "Just calm yourself down and tell me what this is all about."

Clinton sat on the bed and began to tell the sheriff about that night's horrifying events. By the time he was finished, he was nearly in hysterics again. He searched for compassion and reassurance from those around him, but his tears distorted their faces and he could not tell whether they truly believed him or not.

For a long time they simply stood and stared at him. Then Boyce gently took him by the arm and helped him to his feet. "Do you feel up to taking a ride out there?" asked the sheriff grimly.

"Yes," gulped Clinton, wiping away his tears. "Yes, I'll go out there with you. We've gotta make those bastards pay for what they did tonight."

It wasn't long before Clinton found himself sitting in the back seat of the patrol car. Oddly enough, Phyllis

chose to accompany them to the scene of the heinous sacrifice. She rode silently up front with the sheriff.

As they headed along the state highway toward the
southern end of Bedloe County, Clinton sat there numbly,
breathing raggedly and staring straight ahead. Soon, his
mind began to grow clearer and his distress over Nellie
Sue was replaced by a more immediate sense of alarm.

In the green glow of the dashboard light, Clinton began to notice startling similarities between the two who
rode up front. Similarities like the way they both wore
long sleeves, even in the broiling heat of summer, and the
fact that he had never seen the bare flesh of their arms
exposed in the light of day.

And there was one other thing. For the first time,
Clinton realized how very much Phyllis and Boyce resembled one another. They had the same jet-black hair,
the same dark eyes, the same swarthy complexion. They
could have easily passed for brother and sister.

Clinton Harpe leaned his head back on the cushioned
seat and screwed his eyes tightly shut, knowing that there
was no escape as the patrol car headed down the deserted
dirt road toward Devil's Creek. He lifted a trembling
hand to his throat and felt the fragility of the flesh and
muscle, as well as the pounding pulse of the blood-engorged arteries within.

And he found himself thinking of the flash of moonlit
steel and the dark altar of that unholy backwoods church.

IMPRESSIONS IN OAK

Everyone's got something in their past that they'd just as soon keep in the dark.

Sometimes it's little things: a word blurted in anger or a blow thrown in the heat of the moment. Then there are other shames of a larger nature: teenage theft or vandalism, lurid behavior due to alcohol and drugs, or crimes committed.

Some folks succeed in putting their indiscretions behind them. Others are still tortured by past wrongs, years or even decades later. Every now and then, just when you think it's hidden away forever, a face from the past comes back to haunt you.

BULLSHIT!" said Todd Hampton with a wave of dismissal.

"It's true," declared Darrell Yates. "I saw it with my own eyes!"

Todd took a long draw of draft beer from his mug, then wiped the foam of the head from his beard. "Aw, why don't you just give it a rest, Darrell. You know that crap about the face on the tree is just an old wives' tale and that's all."

The lanky truck driver glared at his buddy, who sat at the far end of the tavern's long bar. "I'm just telling you what I saw, Todd. It was her, big as day, staring at me from the trunk of that big black oak on the Old Logging Road. The girl went to high school with me. I'd recognize her anywhere."

Todd laughed out loud. "And I reckon you could tell the color of her hair, too, ain't that right?"

"Now that you mention it, yeah," said Darrell. He poured two fingers of Jim Beam into a shot glass and downed it as if it were buttermilk. "Auburn red it was, just like I remember back in school."

"Like I said before," scoffed Todd with shake of his head. "Pure, Grade-A bullshit!"

Darrell's lean face turned as solemn as stone. "Are you calling me a liar?"

"Hell, no!" said Todd. "But liquor can cloud a man's mind sometimes. You know that as well as I do. When you've enough whiskey in your system, you could end up seeing pert near anything."

"I was stone-cold sober!" claimed Darrell. "I saw it, I tell you! I swear I did."

"Saw *what*, Darrell?" asked a voice from the far side of the barroom. "What did you see?"

Todd and Darrell turned toward the front door and instantly grew silent. Danny Ray Fulton had entered the honky-tonk during their bantering debate and they hadn't even noticed. Darrell stiffened up and stared at the bottom of his empty shotglass, afraid to look up. Todd, on the other hand, glanced over at the tall, broad-shouldered man. Danny Ray was one of the many unchanging aspects of Hawkshaw County. The big man with the oily shock of black hair and the brooding eyes looked the same as he had for the past fifteen years. His daily schedule was as predictable as his physical appearance. He worked all day laying asphalt for the state, then spent what little free time he had at the Roadhouse Saloon, drowning his troubles in hard liquor and mournful country tunes on the jukebox. Everyone at the Roadhouse understood why Danny Ray drank so much.

They would, too, if they were married to a bed-hopping whore like Lizzie Fulton, and had to put up with a squawking brood of five snot-nosed kids, half of them not even the product of his own loins.

All eyes in the tavern—except for Darrell's—were on Danny Ray as he slammed the door behind him and crossed the room to the bar. His muddy brown eyes, which held that customary expression torn somewhere between angry contempt and hang-dog misery, centered on the lanky truck driver as he chose a stool and sat down.

"I asked you a question, Yates," he said flatly. "Exactly what did you see out on the Old Logging Road?"

"Nothing," mumbled Darrell. "I didn't see nothing."

Danny Ray knew the man was lying and also knew the reason why. "You've been talking that crap again, haven't you? That bullshit about Betsy Lou."

He glanced over at Todd Hampton for confirmation, but Todd was keeping out of it. His eyes were centered on his work-callused hands and the day's worth of dirt that had accumulated beneath the fingernails.

"What about it, Stu?" Danny Ray asked the bartender. The middle-aged man with the bald head and the collection óf faded tattoos on his brawny arms stood behind the bar, thumbing through an issue of *Hustler*.

Stu Kilpatrick, who had never liked Darrell or his habit of idle boasting, grinned with tobacco-stained teeth and nodded his head.

Danny Ray's rage cranked up a couple of notches. "What did I tell you about spreading those damn rumors, Darrell? That tree up yonder is just a tree and nothing else."

The liquor in Darrell's stomach momentarily quelled his fear of the brawny road worker and he glared boldly into Danny Ray's eyes. "How the hell would you know?

You ain't been up there lately, have you? The last time you were up there on the Old Logging Road was the night it happened...the night you killed Betsy Lou Brown."

Danny Ray lost his temper then. His big, work-hardened fist lashed out, catching Darrell across the bridge of his nose. With a yelp, Darrell fell back off his barstool, blood running freely from his nostrils. He hit the floor hard on his ass with enough force to make his teeth rattle.

Before Danny Ray could make his way around the corner of the bar and do more damage to Darrell Yates, Todd Hampton jumped up and grabbed hold of the man's arm. Danny Ray whirled, his fist cocked back, but he refrained from acting when he saw the warning look in Todd's eyes. Danny Ray was a big man, but Todd was bigger by fifty pounds and had a reputation in Hawkshaw County as a man not to be messed with.

"I'd suggest you just calm down, Danny Ray," said Todd. He gradually released his hold on the man's arm. "Ol' Darrell, he's just liquored up and talking trash. He didn't mean nothing by it."

"Then he oughta keep his mouth shut," grumbled Danny Ray.

"Yeah, you're right," agreed Todd. "He should. Listen, Danny Ray, everybody in the county knows what happened that night and they know you weren't responsible. That curve out on the Old Logging Road is a real sonuvabitch. Anyone could have made the same mistake."

From the dark expression in Danny Ray's eyes it was plain to see that the man didn't want to talk about it. He turned to the bartender and laid money on the counter. "Just give me a bottle of Wild Turkey, Stu, and I'll be on my way."

Stu set the bottle of liquor on the bar, then counted out Danny Ray's change. "I don't mind you sticking around," he told him. "You're welcome here any time, just as long as you don't cause trouble."

"Naw, I think I'll just go on home," said Danny Ray. He directed a withering glare at Darrell Yates, who still sat on the floor, holding a hand to his bloody nose. "I might just get the urge to turn rowdy again. And that might be dangerous for one of your customers."

Danny Ray grabbed up the Wild Turkey and stalked toward the front door. Before he stepped out into the humid night of the Tennessee summer, he regarded Yates once again.

"Remember what I said, Darrell. Keep your mouth shut about that damn tree."

When Danny Ray had left, Darrell picked himself up and reclaimed his place on the barstool. "Crazy asshole!" he cussed. "He's got a short fuse, that's for sure."

"Shut up, Darrell," said Todd. "Danny Ray's a good man. It's just that some fellas can only be pushed so far. And, if you ask me, Danny Ray's been pushed way too far already. A helluva lot farther than most men could handle."

■■■

Lizzie was at it again. Danny Ray knew it when he saw Fred Larson's Chevy Blazer pulling out of his driveway. Fred was a cocky bastard. He even grinned and waved at Danny Ray as he drove past.

The compulsion to turn his own Ford pickup around, run Fred off the road, and beat him half to death crossed Danny Ray's mind, but he fought down the urge. He had acted on similar whims before and they had only netted him public disgrace and short terms in the county jail. Danny Ray let his truck idle in the road for a long moment, his knuckles white with anger as he clutched the steering wheel tightly. He waited for the violent impulse to pass and, a few seconds later, it finally burned itself out.

Danny Ray turned into the gravel drive and drove to the shabby single-wide trailer that he had bought, used, after he and Lizzie had gotten married. He parked his truck, seeming to be in no hurry to enter the place he called home. He broke the seal on the bottle of Wild Turkey, unscrewed the cap, and took a long, burning swig of the amber liquor. He sat there for a while, staring at the lighted square of his bedroom window. Behind the drawn curtains, the silhouette of Lizzie flitted back and forth, first rearranging the linens of their bed, then spraying the stale air of the room with Glade, attempting to mask the tell-tale scent of sweat and sex with the overpowering odor of potpourri.

Danny Ray waited until the bedroom light winked out. He took a couple more swallows of whiskey, then left the cab of the truck. He crossed the unmowed yard, mounted the junk-cluttered porch, then let himself in through the front door.

The living room was dark, except for the glow of the 25-inch Magnavox in the far corner. Danny Ray's five youngsters—ranging from ages two to nine—lay on the filthy carpet, snacking on pretzels and cherry Kool-Aid while they watched a late night talk show. It was already an hour and a half past their bedtime, but their mother didn't seem to care. She was stretched out on the couch in her housecoat and fuzzy pink slippers, sipping a Coors Light while she watched TV with the kids.

Danny Ray stood in the doorway for a long moment, totally ignored by the members of his family. Then he marched across the room, took the remote control from where it lay on the coffee table, and cut the television off with a press of a button. The action brought a mutual moan of disappointment from the children, but they grew silent when they saw the stormy look in his eyes and the bottle in his hand.

"To bed," he told them flatly. "Now."

No protests were uttered as the five jumped up from the floor and headed down the hallway to the two bedrooms they shared. When Danny Ray heard the last door slam shut, he turned to Lizzie, scarcely able to contain his rage.

Lizzie took a sip from her beer and stared back at him curiously. "Does that go for me, too?" she asked sarcastically.

"No, you've already been to bed once tonight, haven't you?" he asked her.

"What do you mean?" replied Lizzie. She smirked as she took another swallow of beer.

Danny Ray stepped quickly to the couch and slapped the can from her hand. It spun across the room, landing in a threadbare armchair and splattering its cushions with beer. Lizzie flinched at the blow at first, then gathered her nerve and laughed in his face.

"You whore!" growled Danny Ray. He loomed over his snickering wife, his hand raised overhead, on the verge of striking again. "Sleeping with every man who'll buy you a six-pack or a carton of cigarettes...and in front of your own children, too."

Lizzie's laughter was hard-edged with cruelty. "That's right. And why the hell not? You sure ain't gonna satisfy me like I want to be. Dammit, Danny Ray, you can't even get it up half the time."

"Shut up!" said Danny Ray. His fist quivered, aching to plunge down into the center of her sneering face.

"I ain't gonna do it! Not this time!" Lizzie's jaw jutted in defiance. "You know as well as I do what your problem is. Or, rather, *who* it is."

"Don't say something you might regret, Lizzie," warned Danny Ray.

"Well, it's true, ain't it?" said his wife bitterly. "You're still in love with her. Still in love with a woman who's been dead for going on fifteen years."

Danny Ray suddenly felt his rage turn into deep despair. "Don't say that. It ain't right you should say such a mean-spirited thing."

"Don't make me out to be the wicked witch!" yelled Lizzie. "I tried to make this marriage work when we first got hitched. I really was crazy about you back then and that's no lie. But trying to compete with *her* for your love just got to be too damn much for me to handle. If she were a living, breathing woman, maybe I'd have a chance. But how can I fight a corpse? Why don't you tell me that, Danny Ray?"

"You're wrong, Lizzie," he told her dully.

"No, I ain't," replied his cheating wife. "I'm right on the money." She left her spot on the couch and turned toward the hallway. "I've had it up to here with you, Danny Ray. If you love Betsy Lou Brown so much, why don't you go on over to the graveyard and pay her a visit? Take that shovel out of the tool shed and dig her confounded carcass up. Maybe there's enough left of her for you to screw around with."

A few moments ago, such a remark would have incited Danny Ray toward violence. Killing violence. But his rage had dissipated. A great sadness settled atop his broad shoulders like an unbearable weight as he watched his slutty wife shuffle off toward their bedroom at the rear of the trailer. He wanted to hurt her at that moment, wanted to make her beg for forgiveness for what she had said about Betsy Lou. But he just couldn't seem to muster the energy necessary to do that.

Instead, he turned and left the trailer. Danny Ray climbed back into his pickup truck and started the engine. He took another swig of Wild Turkey, then backed the vehicle down the driveway to the main highway. Once the truck's tires hit asphalt, Danny Ray shifted into gear and stamped the gas pedal. Soon, he was heading north, toward the county line and a lonely stretch of rarely-used back road that he honestly thought he would never have to travel again during his lifetime.

■■■

Just about everyone in Hawkshaw County knew what had happened on the Old Logging Road back in the summer of '78.

They knew about the car crash, how Danny Ray Fulton had misjudged the sharpness of a single curve and drove smack-dab into the center of that big black oak that the road made a sudden hairpin turn around. They also knew what had happened to Danny Ray's girlfriend, Betsy Lou Brown. How the force of the collision had propelled her head-first through the windshield and into the unyielding trunk of the tree.

The folks of Hawkshaw County also knew the old wives' tale concerning the tree on the Old Logging Road. Several people had sworn that they had traveled the curve of the dirt road late at night and, in the glow of their headlights, witnessed a strange sight. They claimed to have seen the distinct impression of Betsy Lou's lovely face on the western side of the big tree, forever etched there by a split-second of deadly impact. Other folks embellished the story a bit, swearing that even the color of the dead girl's hair and eyes could be seen on the face on the tree.

That was where Danny Ray was headed that night. He wanted to see for himself whether or not the rumor about the face on the tree was true. He hadn't been back to the curve on the Old Logging Road since the night of that awful crash, but tonight he felt the need to witness the phenomenon on his own, if it did, indeed, exist.

Danny Ray reduced his speed as he approached the fatal hairpin turn on the rural road. He squinted against the darkness. There was no moonlight to speak of that night and, even with the help of the truck's high beams, it was difficult to see where he was going. The pitch darkness of the Tennessee woods seemed to absorb all light and instantly turn it into blacker shades of shadow.

Finally, he reached the notorious curve. Danny Ray pulled his truck to the side of the road, then cut the engine as well as the headlights. The night closed in around him, almost claustrophobically so. Danny Ray listened to the abundance of night sounds that echoed through the dense thicket: the singing of crickets, the rustle of small animals picking through the underbrush in search of food, and the occasional cooing of a lonesome dove.

I want doves, she'd said once. *I want doves at my wedding.*

Danny Ray took another swallow from the bottle of Wild Turkey. He hoped that the liquor would fortify his nerve and give him the strength to proceed. But his paranoia was at a fever pitch that night, as well as that weighty feeling of oppressive guilt, the feeling he had never quite been able to shake, even after all those years.

He was on the verge of making a U-turn in the road and hightailing it back to town, when he gathered the courage and decided to go through with it this time. He set the whiskey bottle on top of the dashboard, took a flashlight from beneath the seat, and climbed out of the truck. Then he walked slowly, but deliberately, toward the tree that had caused him so much pain and grief that summer night fifteen years ago.

He waited until he was almost to the tree before he switched on his light. When he did, he played the beam across the textured column of the ancient oak. The eastern side of the tree was unscarred. It was the opposite side that had taken the full brunt of the head-on collision.

Danny Ray stood there for a moment, breathing in the muggy night air, afraid to witness what lay on the far side of the old tree. He closed his eyes and recalled that night. He remembered the scent of Betsy Lou's perfume, the deep thrum of his Trans-Am's big eight-cylinder engine, even the song that blared from the car stereo...Lynyrd Skynyrd's "Gimme Three Steps."

He took a deep breath, braced himself, and then made his way to the other side of the tree. The first thing he noticed in the glow of the flashlight was the deep scoring at the base of the trunk. It was the spot where the nose of his Trans-Am had impacted with hard wood. He then let the light play upward. He found what he was looking for midway up the trunk.

"Good God Almighty!" he whispered. "It's true. It really is."

Danny Ray reached out and lay his hand upon the oval indentation, then drew his fingers away and studied the pattern that had been permanently etched into the trunk of the oak. It was her face. The face of Betsy Lou.

He would have known that face anywhere. The petite nose, the wide-set eyes, the luscious lips, full and pouty. It was a face Danny Ray had fallen hopelessly in love with during his junior and senior years in high school. It was the face of the girl he had intended to marry and raise a family with, as well as share all his secret hopes and dreams for the future.

It was also a face that he had hated angrily, if only for a single fateful moment.

As Danny Ray stared at the death-mask of his beloved Betsy Lou, memories began to nag at him. He began to remember things...things he had fought to suppress for years and, for a while, had been successful in doing so. For a long time those memories had been kept at bay, buried deep down in the dark side of his soul. But, now, they began to resurface, swiftly and without warning, assaulting his conscience with their painful clarity.

He remembered the argument. He remembered the biting accusations, the slamming of the car door, and the swish of Betsy Lou's plaid skirt in the glow of the headlights. He remembered the pressure of his foot on the gas pedal and the speed of the Trans-Am surging forward...as well the impact of steel against fragile flesh and bone.

A potentially hot date that night had turned terribly sour. They had been on their way to their regular make-out spot on the Old Logging Road, when Betsy Lou had confronted him about going out with another girl the previous weekend. Danny Ray had denied it, of course, but Betsy Lou hadn't bought his innocent act. She demanded that he stop the car and let her out. He did and she immediately began her angry march back down the road toward the main highway.

And what had Danny Ray done? Had he jumped out of the car and apologized for cheating on her? No. He had sat, fuming, in his car for a long moment, then lost his temper entirely. Shifting the Trans-Am into gear, he turned the car around and roared down the road after her. They were on the far side of the hairpin turn. It loomed immediately up ahead.

An instant later, he saw her in his headlights. And, in that instant, he reacted childishly...if cold-blooded murder could be described in such simple terms.

He had caught a glimpse of her walking away from him and all the little things about Betsy Lou that grated on his nerves—her stubborn streak and petty fits of pouting—had struck him the wrong way, fueling his anger. He stamped the accelerator to the floorboard and gave the steering wheel a quick jerk to the left.

Regret and the return of rationality came only with the jarring impact of the car against her body. The force of the collision threw Betsy thirty feet forward and she landed, headlong, into the oak tree he now stood before. Danny Ray recalled the ugly sound of her lovely face smashing into the center of the tree trunk, as well as the ugly crimson splatter of blood and brains against the bark. He remembered the way her limp body had folded and sank to the ground in an unmoving heap.

The next few moments had been crucial ones. First there had been panic and overwhelming remorse. Then there had been fear of discovery and cold calculation.

Danny Ray had parked his car, climbed out, and dragged Betsy Lou's mangled body from beneath the tree. He had set his dead girlfriend in the passenger seat with the seat belt unfastened. Then he had climbed in, buckled his own belt, and backed up a hundred feet or so. Danny Ray had taken a deep breath, then floored the gas. As he rushed toward the oak tree at forty miles per hour or so, he knew that what he was attempting might be suicide. But he knew he had no choice. If he didn't try to cover his tracks, he would end up dying anyway...on Death Row at the state penitentiary.

The impact had been devastating...but had done the job. As the front end of the Pontiac folded inward into the engine block, the body of Betsy Lou had been thrown forward. She had crashed through the windshield and ended up, torn and crumpled, on the jagged folds of the car hood. Danny Ray had barely survived himself, despite the restraints of his seat belt. When the county police arrived, they found him unconscious. He had suffered a bad concussion, a broken arm, and a shattered left leg. Everyone said that he was one lucky bastard to have survived such a terrible wreck.

Believe it or not, it had worked. The local authorities had taken the apparent car crash at face value. The county sheriff had been too stupid to investigate further and the county coroner had been too lazy to perform a thorough autopsy on poor Betsy Lou. Danny Ray had covered his tracks well and pulled the stunt off, escaping the consequences of his deadly actions scott-free.

Or had he? Danny Ray thought about the years following the car crash. The low-paying, dead-end job, his cheating wife, the brood of troublesome kids, his constant battle with alcohol and trying to stay out of jail...hadn't they all served as some form of punishment for him? Hadn't they separated him from his goals and dreams, and turned him into the bitter, miserable man that he was today?

Danny Ray stared at the face on the tree again. His heart ached at the expression that was permanently tattooed there. An expression of shock and terror. And the hurt of betrayal. That most of all.

"I love you," moaned Danny Ray tearfully. "I still love you." But even as he said it, he knew that it was much too late for that. Just like it was too late to ask for forgiveness. The word "sorry" had little meaning to someone who had been dead and buried for a decade and a half.

Danny Ray placed his face close to the one on the tree. He pressed his lips against hers, recalling the soft warmth of Betsy Lou's supple mouth. He longed for that enlivening sensation, but all he felt was the cold, coarse hardness of tree bark. He realized that the tree was no substitute for his lost love. It was only a lasting memorial to that final horrifying moment of her young life.

Violent sobs racked the husky form of Danny Ray as he turned away from the tree on the Old Logging Road and walked back to his truck. As he stumbled through the darkness, he considered going to the sheriff and confessing to the crime he had committed. But he decided not to. Conviction and incarceration could not match the sentence he was now serving. In his heart, Danny Ray Fulton knew that he deserved to suffer for what he had taken from Betsy Lou...and suffer he would.

He climbed into his truck and headed back toward town. Toward his pointless work, his dishonest wife, and the maddening draw of the liquor bottle. Toward the worst form of punishment he could imagine...a lackluster life full of broken dreams.

As Danny Ray drove away, the face on the tree remained where it had for fifteen years, and where it would be for countless years more. The lovely eyes of Betsy Lou glistened with a mixture of tree sap and the salty tears of her remorseful lover, as if she, too, were mourning what had been lost that distant night on the dark stretch of the Old Logging Road.

BOOKMARKS

When I "found religion"—as the country folk say—in 1996, I felt downright guilty about having written this story, which cast Christians in a bad light. But, with time, I've realized that there could be some truth and possibility to it. Fanatical religious groups possess a perverse sort of power. They can lead a nationwide boycott or protest a military funeral and the media flock to them in droves like thirsty hounds to the water bowl. Perhaps it's farfetched that one such group might inject itself into the political mainstream and take absolute control...or perhaps not.

Maybe the good Lord inspired me to pen this cautionary tale, if only to expose "false prophets and teachers," as the Bible calls them.

JENNIFER huddled against her father's body, seeking warmth and comfort. There was little of either there in the camp. She faintly remembered her room, bright and cheerful, filled with colorful toys and decorated with posters of Sesame Street and Disney characters. It was during periods like this—when she was hungry, exhausted, and on the verge of slumber—that the six-year-old could remember the good times the best. In the daylight hours, with the drab and dirty tents, with the men in white jumpsuits standing on the wall with guns, Jennifer had a difficult time remembering the past. All she experienced then was misery and resignation, as if she had been born there in the filthy hovel they now called home.

Drowsiness began to overcome her and, gradually, she remembered things as they had been a year ago. The big two-story house in a Memphis suburb. Her father in his study, sitting in front of his computer. Her mother baking raisin oatmeal cookies and taking care of the new baby. But that had changed abruptly in the dead of night, with rough hands dragging Jennifer from her bed and strips of tape sealing away her screams of terror. The next thing Jennifer knew, she and her family were in the compound, surrounded by people dressed in dirty pajamas and nightgowns like themselves. Some of the people cried, while others merely sat there and stared into space.

She thought that maybe their imprisonment had something to do with Daddy and his job. Daddy didn't go to work like other daddies did. He stayed at home and wrote books. Books that had scary names and pictures on the covers that gave Jennifer nightmares if she looked at them too long.

She remembered the people that made Daddy mad: the ones who marched in front of their house, carrying signs and yelling Bible verses. They said that their book was a Good Book and that Daddy wrote Bad Books. They said Daddy worshipped the Devil and that he would burn in the Bad Place. The people had frightened Jennifer. She had cried and Daddy had told her that it wasn't true. He told her that what he wrote was just make-believe, like Curious George or the Cat in the Hat.

Then things got worse. Daddy started crying, too, and drinking the Nasty Tasting Stuff because the stores in town didn't sell his books anymore. He looked real sad and didn't play with Jennifer or Baby Joey like he once

298

did. He didn't talk to Mommy very much, didn't hug or kiss her like he used to. He just sat there, drinking the Nasty Tasting Stuff and watching the congressional hearings and the new President talking about "reviving moral values" and things like that.

Jennifer opened her sleepy eyes and stared at her mother, who lay curled up on her side at the other end of the tent. Mommy hadn't said anything for a long time. Not since Baby Joey went away. Her little brother had coughed and cried for days. Then he stopped, turning as still and cold as a rubber baby doll. The big, fat woman they called Preacher Lady came and took Joey away. She told Mommy that Joey was in the Bad Place and that God wouldn't let him into the Good Place with the angels because of what Daddy wrote. Mommy had screamed and cried for a while, then she curled up and hadn't said a word since.

Jennifer cuddled in Daddy's lap, ignoring the stinky way he smelled, and hoped that she would dream of Barbie dolls, Dr. Seuss, and chocolate pudding. As she dozed off, her tiny fingers traced the picture on Daddy's chest—a tattoo he called it. Out in the muddy yard, the speakers sang "Amazing Grace." It almost drowned out the sound of weeping, the sound of sickness and despair...but not quite.

■■■

Samuel Markham waited until his daughter was asleep, then tenderly took her in his arms and carried her to the neighboring tent. Florence Delaney was awake and waiting for him. "Take good care of her," he said, laying her on a palate of filthy newspaper.

"I will," promised the former librarian. She ran her fingers through Jennifer's dirty blond hair, then looked at the gaunt man dressed in tattered pajamas. "I don't think you should go. It's a terrible risk to take."

"I know, but I have to," said Sam. "For all of us. I have to see how bad it is...if it's as widespread as I think." He reached out and took the woman's frail hand, a hand that had once proudly stamped library cards and sorted a million books. "Anyway, what's the worst that could happen if I get caught? They'd just ship me back here. It's not like they're going to kill me or anything."

"Don't be so sure," said Florence. "Would you have ever thought of them pulling something like this?"

Sam's face darkened. "No, I guess not." Then, planting a parting kiss on Jennifer's forehead, he slipped out of the tent and took to the shadows.

Only half of the guards were on sentry duty during the graveyard shift. Sam crouched in the darkness beside a ramshackle barn and waited until the oscillating searchlights swung the other way. Then he sprinted to the old henhouse and the wall of timber and barbed wire beyond. From what Sam could tell, the camp had once been a farm. He wondered where the owners of the property were and whether it had been bought from them or taken by force.

He found the depression that he had been working on for three nights solid and began to rake the loose earth and dead leaves away. He cast a fleeting glance at the corner towers and saw the white clad men holding their M-16s and Uzis. Fortunately, their attention was dulled by the lateness of the hour. Carefully, Sam squeezed under the fence and ducked into the thick, dark woods to the north. The singing of crickets and the peeping of water toads masked his footsteps as he headed through the dark thicket. He breathed deeply and smelled the scent of the muddy Mississippi nearby. It was a smell he had not experienced for twelve long months.

He reached the main highway a half hour later, but kept to the underbrush, reluctant to reveal himself to the headlights of passing cars. Around three o'clock in the morning, he came to a peach orchard and tried to gorge himself on the sweet fruit. But his stomach rebelled and he became violently sick. Normal food seemed much too exotic to his digestive system. He was more accustomed to a diet of rat meat and raw insects now.

■■■

The first gray light of dawn found Sam Markham on the outskirts of Memphis. He reached his own neighborhood around five o'clock. Except for a couple of things, his house seemed the same as it had the night of his family's abduction. However, there was someone else's name on the mailbox and a strange car parked in the drive.

Sam made his way inconspicuously to the back door of the house, then remembered that he had no keys. He went to Brenda's flower garden, which was now overgrown with weeds, and then reached up into the cedar birdfeeder that had been built in his own workshop. He felt around in the gritty layer of birdseed, hoping that it was still hidden there. Soon, his fingers found the emergency key that was stashed there. A better hiding place than under the welcome mat or on top of the door sill, he remembered telling his wife, and he had been right.

Quietly, he unlocked the back door and stepped into the kitchen. The place was a mess: dirty dishes in the sink and soda cans and food wrappers littering the breakfast table. He took a cast iron skillet from where Brenda's kitchen utensils hung and silently climbed the stairs. Once on the second floor, Sam checked the rooms. They were all unoccupied, except for the master bedroom. A man stretched out in the king-sized bed that Sam and Brenda had once slept and made love in. He was young, blond, and muscular. Sam glanced at a chair next to the bed. A snow white jumpsuit and beret were draped there, as if waiting for the ringing of the alarm clock. On the cedar chest at the foot of the bed lay an AK-47 and a gunbelt with a magnum revolver in its holster.

Suddenly, a great rage overcame Sam. The bastard was one of *them!* He walked over to the bed, raised the iron skillet overhead, and with all his might, hit the sleeping stranger in the head. The man's eyelids fluttered and he unleashed a low grunt as the edge of the frying pan cleaved his skull in half. Sam didn't stop there. He struck again and again, until his anger had been depleted. He stared in disgust at the skillet, which was caked with blood, hair, and brain matter, then flung the makeshift weapon across the room.

He sat on the carpeted floor of his bedroom until eight o'clock, then decided that it was time to get ready. He stripped off his filthy rags, showered, shaved, and then returned to the bedroom. He studied himself in the full-length mirror on the closet door and grimaced. Even scrubbed clean, he looked terrible. He had lost nearly forty pounds since his imprisonment. He looked like a walking skeleton.

He dressed in the white jumpsuit and was zipping it up, when the tattoo on his chest drew his attention. He studied it in the mirror, recalling its origin. It had happened during the first World Horror Convention in Nashville. He had been a fledgling horror writer then, only a few short stories and a novel to his credit. He and some other writers had gotten drunk and stumbled into a tattoo parlor on lower Broadway. They had all agreed on the same design...a winged serpent entwined around a flaming cross. It had seemed pretty damned funny at the time, but now the memory pained him like a cancer. That had been nearly twenty years and twelve bestsellers ago.

After dressing, Sam took the guns and went downstairs to raid the refrigerator. He saw nothing there that he could stomach, except for a steak in the meat drawer. He ate it raw and bloody, pretending that it was fresh rat meat rather than choice sirloin. Then he walked down the hallway to his study. It was almost like he had left it. The stereo system was still there, as well as his computer and the La-Z-Boy recliner that he did his reading in. His collection of rock & roll CDs was gone, as well as every book in every bookcase that lined the four walls. He was stunned. His Dark Harvest and Ziesing hardcovers were gone, along with his limited editions of King, Barker, McCammon, and Lansdale. Even his own books, both paperbacks and hardbacks alike, had been cleaned out.

Sam went to the TV in the family room and turned it on. Most of the cable stations were scrambled. Those that weren't showed religious programming. Tearful preachers pounded pulpits and demanded donations for the Unified Church of America, a faction of organized religion that Sam was all too familiar with. He had endured the non-stop teachings of that religious conglomerate during his time in the prison camp. It was a disturbing hybrid of several religions, distorting the belief of God into something fanatical and perverse. He turned on CNN. The anchorman reported on the President's recent press conference. Sam shuddered as he watched. The death penalty for homosexuality and abortion. The Cold War back into full swing again. Then the bland face of the President came on the screen and Sam remembered when the Mississippi minister had been something of a joke in the media, with his sponsor boycotts and his demands for wholesome, family programming.

Feeling a little sick, Sam turned off the TV. A lot had taken place in twenty years. For one thing, no one was laughing now.

■■■

Sam took the car of the man he had murdered and drove toward the heart of the city. He drove north up Elvis Presley Boulevard and passed Graceland. The home of the King had been altered. The great iron gates with the musical notes and silhouette of a guitar-picking Elvis were gone. In their place were gates decorated with praying hands and crosses.

He turned onto Union Avenue and headed for downtown Memphis. He was surprised by how immaculate the place was. No litter, no unsightly billboards, half as many cars and buses as usual, and not a homeless person in sight. The extent of the city's cleanliness was almost obscene. *Is it like this everywhere?* he wondered. *All over the country?* He noticed the people on the sidewalks. They were dressed in their best Sunday clothes, smiling unnerving, plastic grins. He wondered how they could manage to maintain such a look of complete happiness and contentment, then noticed the abundance of surveillance cameras at every street corner.

He parked his car in a lot next to an old book bindery that still seemed to be in operation. He sat there for a while and stared across the street at the great columned front of the Memphis Public Library. He hated the thought of walking into that building, but he knew he had to...for himself, and especially for Florence, who had worked there for nearly thirty years. He had to see how extreme things had actually become.

Sam left the car, slipping the strap of the assault rifle over his shoulder and plastering a dopey, good-natured grin across his face. Then he walked across the street and up the stone steps to the library. Above the double doors were words in polished bronze relief. He remembered that it had once said READ A GOOD BOOK TODAY. It had been changed to READ THE GOOD BOOK TODAY.

The library was nearly deserted at that time of morning. An elderly woman with silver-blue hair and a golden cross on her black dress smiled as he walked up and he did his best to return the gesture with as much sincerity as possible. "May I help you find something, officer?" she asked sweetly.

"No thanks," he told her. "Just browsing."

The librarian gave him a strange look as he started down the aisles of books, then seemed to pay him no more attention. At first, things looked the same as they had a year ago. But as he noticed the titles on the spines, horror began to grip him. The reference books, encyclopedias...everything had been replaced. In their place was the *Encyclopedia Biblical* and *Bakker's Guide to the Holy Scriptures.* Sam made his way to the periodical section. Religious magazines and newspapers replaced *Time, Newsweek,* and *The Wall Street Journal.* A crisp edition of a daily newspaper called *The Unified Word* lay on a reading table. It was so thick that it rivaled the *New York Times* in volume.

Secretly, Sam wondered if it might have been published on the same press that the Times had once been printed on.

Swiftly, he headed for the second floor and the fiction section. A scream of anguish almost escaped him when he found row upon row of empty shelves. They were all gone; the classics of Shakespeare, Dickens, Faulkner and Hemingway had been stripped from their rightful places and disposed of. Like a madman, he ran down the aisles, his eyes growing tearful at the absence of Poe, Lovecraft, Tolkien and Bradbury. Even with its emptiness, the place grew oppressive with the sheer magnitude of the horrible crime that had been committed there. Panicked, Sam ran for the emergency stairs and headed for the roof.

Once there, he staggered to the ledge and breathed deeply. He stared up into the sky. A Goodyear blimp hovered overhead, the word REPENT flashing across its side. He directed his eyes toward the Mississippi River and saw a parade of huge barges heading downriver from the north. He couldn't believe his eyes, but they seemed to be heaped twenty feet high with books.

"How?" he wailed, not caring who heard him. "How could this have happened? It's only been a year. One damned year!"

Then, suddenly, he heard the sound of footsteps behind him. He turned and saw the librarian standing there with three armed officers dressed in angelic white and carrying sub-machine guns. "There he is!" she said. "That is the man!"

"Surrender!" demanded one of the men. He cocked the bolt of his Uzi and aimed it at Sam. "Throw down your weapons and put your hands behind your head."

At first, Sam considered slipping the AK-47 from his shoulder and resisting them. But even if he survived the inevitable firefight, would he want to? Would he want to live in a society with one frame of mind? A society that denied its citizens individualism and freedom of speech? Could he live in a country where religion ruled and those considered unworthy were packed away in concentration camps or worse?

He didn't even need to give it a second thought.

"I give up!" he called out, tossing the rifle down and unbuckling his gunbelt. "You can take me away. You can take me back home." All he wanted at that moment was to be with his family again.

The three officers converged on him and grabbed him roughly. One hand grabbed the front of his jump-suit and tore it open. His bare chest was exposed...as well as the tattoo.

"He has been marked!" screamed the librarian, leveling a finger of righteous accusation. "He's been cursed with the Mark of Cain!"

He was quickly handcuffed and shoved across the roof to the stairwell. "Mark of Cain!" chanted the three men, their faces frozen in grisly smiles. "Mark of Cain!"

Suddenly, Sam Markham knew that he wouldn't be going back to the camp and that he would never see his wife and daughter again. He screamed long and loud as they herded him from the library and across the street to his fate.

To the book bindery.

■■■

Jennifer huddled in the corner of Florence Delaney's tent. Florence was on work detail that afternoon and the girl was alone. Jennifer's unresponsive mother was gone.

Some men had come several days ago, loaded her on a stretcher, and taken her to the big building on the far side of the compound. Florence called it the barracks and said it was the place where the men who guarded the camp slept at night. Jennifer couldn't figure out why they would take her there. She couldn't talk or make oatmeal raisin cookies anymore. All she could do was lie there.

It had been a week since her father had left in the middle of the night without saying good-bye. Jennifer still felt hurt and confused. She couldn't understand why her father would run away and leave them there. It just didn't seem fair.

"Read and repent!" called a woman's stern voice from the compound outside. "Repent, lest you be condemned to eternal damnation."

Trembling, Jennifer crouched in the dank shadows. She stared at the open flap, until a hulking shadow blocked out the sunlight. It was the Preacher Lady, the warden of the camp. Preacher Lady was over three hundred pounds, wore horn-rimmed glasses, and carried a purse large enough for Jennifer to fit into. That afternoon she was carrying a bulky shopping bag in the crook of one flabby arm.

Preacher Lady stared at her from the door of the tent. "Read and repent, child," she said, reaching into the shopping bag. "Read the teachings of the Good Book or be forever damned."

The girl watched as the bag tipped, showing its contents. Inside were small copies of the Unified Testament, bound in soft leather. Each was unique in its own way. Some were pale and freckled, while some bore tiny scars or moles. Others were dark brown, caramel, or golden yellow in hue. Preacher Lady took one from the bag, tossed it at her filthy feet, and then moved on to the next tent.

Jennifer stared at the testament for a long moment, then picked it up. Its cover was as pale as her own sickly complexion. And, in the center, there was a mark that was familiar to Jennifer, one that she had marveled at many times before.

Huddling deeper into the shadows of the ragged tent, she pressed her face to the cover of the Good Book. As her tears glistened upon the faded design of a winged serpent upon a fiery cross, she imagined that she could feel the warmth of her father's skin and hear the distant beating of his heart.

ROMICIDE

This is the second story I wrote featuring the Atlanta homicide team of Lowery and Taylor, two detectives who always seemed to find something grim and gruesome in their case files. This one explores the phenomenon of spontaneous human combustion, a subject I always found intriguing, whether it was actually true or not.

A word of warning—the computer jargon in this story may seem a bit dated after all this time, but it was written when cyberspace was under construction and the Internet was in its infancy, and eight megabytes of RAM was the norm. Can you imagine that?

THEY were due for a bad one.

The '96 Olympics had come and gone, leaving everyone on the force expecting the floodgates to open. During the festivities, it seemed as though the entire city of Atlanta had been on its best behavior. With the exception of the Centennial Park bombing, crime as a whole had reached an unnerving low. Of course, vice had been busy with streetwalkers and pickpockets, but muggings and violent crime had seemingly dropped from the books. The eyes of the world had focused on Atlanta and, if only for a while, it was as if the local low-life population had kicked back in front of the TV with a cold beer, watching the show with everyone else.

But that was over now. The Atlanta PD's homicide division had its hands full once again.

It was a night in mid-September when Lowery and Taylor got the call. They pulled their white Chrysler off Peachtree Street and into a well-to-do apartment complex called Tara Court. They drove past the main office—which resembled a miniature version of Scarlett O'Hara's famous mansion—then cruised down the winding avenues of the complex itself. Half of the buildings were standard flat-type apartments, three stories tall, while the others consisted of townhouses, all decorated in the same *Gone With The Wind* motif.

"Pretty original, isn't it?" said Sergeant Ed Taylor.

"Tacky is more like it," replied Lieutenant Ken Lowery. "I mean, look at the names of the streets. Rhett Butler Avenue, Ashley Wilkes Drive, Aunt Pitty-Pat Lane. It's a little overdone, if you ask me."

His partner shrugged and spotted the telltale flash of blue and red emergency lights coming from Mammy Boulevard up ahead. "Maybe. But this *is* Atlanta. And it *is* better than a *Wizard of Oz* theme, you've got to admit that."

"I suppose so," agreed Lowery. He could imagine such a complex with an office that resembled the Emerald City and apartments that were patterned after Munchkinland.

They parked in a space outside a line of townhouses. Each had its own distinctive form of Southern architecture. Two patrol cars and a metro fire engine were already there, as well as Stuart White's maroon station wagon. Four out of five times, the city coroner beat them to the scene of the crime, which was kind of funny considering that Stu Walsh was nearly seventy years old.

"That's it over there," said Lowery, pointing to a townhouse with white brick and immaculate Roman columns framing its doorway. "Apartment 503."

The two homicide detectives left the car and crossed the sidewalk to the townhouse. A border of yellow police tape had been erected around 503, but there were no curious bystanders lingering beyond it, like at most crime scenes. But then this was a complex that catered mostly to young professional types who were apparently more discreet with their rubber-necking than most spectators. On further inspection, they could make out the silhouettes of the neighboring residents in the lighted windows of their apartments, wondering what type of sordid occurrence had taken place in their clean, crime-free complex.

A police officer stood beside the open door of Apartment 503, talking to a firefighter. "Officer Mangrum," Lowery said in greeting.

The young patrolman seemed grateful that he had been remembered. "How are you doing, Lieutenant?" He nodded to the other detective. "Sergeant?"

"We're doing fine, Mangrum," said Lowery. "So what do we have here?"

The officer frowned. "We're not exactly sure, sir. It's pretty weird."

Lowery looked at Taylor. "Then I reckon we'd better take a look at it ourselves."

"My partner, Robinson, is upstairs with Dr. Walsh. It's the bedroom to your right."

"Thanks." The two entered the cramped, but stylish foyer of the townhouse. As they passed through the doorway, they noticed that the front door had been pried open. The wood around the deadbolt was splintered. They mounted the narrow stairway. As they approached the upper floor, they immediately detected a cloying odor. An odor that was nearly sickening in nature.

"Smells like burnt barbecue," said Taylor.

"More like a burnt body to me," his partner said. "Remember that case over in the projects? When that woman set fire to her drunk of a husband after he'd raped their ten-year-old daughter? Smells kind of like that bastard did, after she got through with him."

Taylor nodded. "You're right. But this smells even *worse*."

When they reached the head of the stairs, Lowery called out. "Stu?"

"In here, Ken," replied the coroner's gravelly voice.

Lowery and Taylor stepped into the bedroom, which was really no bedroom at all. It looked to have been used more as an office than anything else. Stark black-and-white Ansel Adams prints decorated the walls. Beneath them were several file cabinets and a large Ricoh copier, the type that high-volume offices use. Against one wall were a stereo system and two speakers, as well as a rack of classical CDs. At the wall directly opposite was a large computer work center, complete with an IBM system with a Pentium microprocessor and a state-of-the-art laser printer.

But the surroundings of the upstairs room paled in comparison to the central focal point, which was directly in front of the computer desk. It was a dark, scorched patch that stretched across the neutral gray carpeting. The two couldn't see it very well at first. Stu Walsh was crouched on the floor, obscuring their view.

"What have we got here, Stu?" Lowery asked.

"The damnedest thing I've ever seen," said the coroner.

When Walsh stood up and stepped aside, they saw exactly what was on the carpet. At first, their minds balked at what they were looking at. It seemed utterly impossible. Then, slowly, it began to dawn on them that what lay before them was for real.

The carpet wasn't scorched after all. Rather, an outline of powdery black ash covered the floor. An outline that was undeniably *human* in form.

But that wasn't all there was to it. Within the outline was a blackened pair of eyeglasses with melted plastic lenses, several human teeth, some with fillings, and a steel surgical pin where the outline of one leg was. A computer chair lay on its side next to the outline. The seat and back cushions were charred down to the foam padding, but little of the chrome framework had been scorched.

Lowery and Taylor may have thought the whole thing was some elaborate practical joke someone had pulled, except for one factor. At the end of the outline's left arm was part of an actual human limb. The hand and forearm of a man lay there. It was clad in the sleeve of a white sweatshirt, only the upper end of which was scorched. From where they stood, they could see that the stub of arm seemed to have been burnt off, rather than severed. And the stump appeared to have been cauterized by some intense and inexplicable heat.

"Good Lord," said Taylor. "What is it?"

"Well, it may sound crazy," said Stu Walsh. "But I believe it's the remains of a young man."

Lowery looked doubtful. "You mean the one who lived here?" He turned to Officer Robinson. "What was his name?"

Robinson stepped forward, looking pale and shaken. "Phillip Bomar. He'd lived here for three years." He handed the lieutenant a black leather wallet. "I found this on the nightstand in the master bedroom."

Lowery opened the wallet and studied a Georgia state driver's license. From the information there, he gathered that Phillip Bomar had been twenty-six years old and was five feet, nine inches tall. The photograph showed a lean, young man with longish brown hair and pale green eyes. He wore eyeglasses identical to the scorched frames that lay within the parameter of the outline's ashen head.

"I don't understand," he said. "You're saying that *this* is Bomar?'

"I'm saying that it's *probably* Bomar," said Walsh. "I can't say for sure just yet."

"The hand's wearing a college ring," said Taylor. "Looks like it's from the University of Georgia."

Stu Walsh pointed to a framed diploma on the wall. "Bomar attended UG. But that doesn't prove for certain that it's him."

"But what the hell happened to him? Did some psycho take a flame-thrower to him?"

"That's very unlikely," the coroner explained. "If that were the case, there would be traces of chemicals and fuel here. There isn't. And the entire apartment would have gone up in flames. As you can see, it didn't."

Lowery took a step closer to the computer desk, careful not to tread on the bizarre outline of black ashes. He suddenly noticed that some incredible heat had been generated directly where the outline lay. The gray-white plastic housing of the computer monitor and microprocessor had buckled and melted, and the monitor screen was cloudy and cracked. The keyboard had melted so badly that all the keys were practically fused together.

Taylor looked down at the mouse, which sat on a charred rubber pad beside the keyboard. Clots of gummy soot spotted the oval instrument. "What's this black stuff?" he asked Walsh.

"Burnt flesh," he replied grimly. "Looks like the guy was holding onto it when it happened."

"That's the big question," said Lowery, shaking his head. "Exactly what *did* happen?"

The coroner looked as though he was reluctant to answer. He sighed, then went ahead. "Have either of you ever heard of spontaneous human combustion?"

Taylor laughed, but it was a nervous laugh. "Sure, but that's just a load of bull, isn't it? Things like that don't really happen."

"There have been documented cases," Walsh told him.

"Yeah, but this isn't the freaking *X-Files*," Lowery said. "And we're not Mulder and Scully." He searched the coroner's face. "Don't you have any other explanation? One that's not so unbelievable?"

"I'll let you know after I complete my examination of the remains back at the lab." It was obvious that no conventional autopsy could be performed. "But, as of right now, spontaneous combustion seems to be the apparent cause of death."

Lowery and Taylor stared at the ashy outline for a long moment. "Okay," said the lieutenant. "Let's get all the evidence we can while the scene is secure. Get Blakely over here with a forensic team. I want him to go over everything in this room with a fine-tooth comb. And I want plenty of pictures. Call Jenny Burke and have her snap a couple rolls, of the body—if you can call it that—as well as the contents of this room. If I have to turn in a report to the chief that says this Phillip Bomar went up in flames for no reason at all, I want plenty of evidence and photos to back it up."

Lowery left the upstairs room and called Robinson into the outer hallway. The police officer gave him a quick rundown of what had transpired. A smoke detector in Apartment 503 had gone off, alerting Bomar's next door neighbor, who called 911. The firemen had pried the front door open—whose deadbolt had been locked from the inside—then proceeded upstairs. There was a light mist of smoke, along with the heavy scent of scorched plastic and burnt flesh. When the firefighters discovered the strange outline on the carpet they called in the Atlanta PD.

Feeling drained and more than a little confused, the two detectives left Apartment 503. They climbed into their car, but simply sat there in front of the townhouse for a while.

"I'm not even sure if this is a homicide, Ed," said Lowery. "It seems more like an unexplained death to me."

"I think there's foul play involved somewhere down the line," Taylor told him. "I don't know why yet..."

Lowery nodded solemnly. "You and me both. It's creepy, isn't it?"

"I'll say," agreed his partner. "Even creepier than those murders Dwight Rollins pulled a few years back."

Lowery shuddered. He vividly recalled the crazy, old blind man who had murdered several people in his apartment building—as well as his own seeing-eye dog. And for what reason? Because it was the dead of winter and he needed their warm eyes to fill empty sockets that his pawned glass eyes had left behind.

"I never thought we'd see one that beat the Rollins case," he said, starting up the car. "But I guess I was wrong."

■■■

The next morning Lowery and Taylor came in to find a message waiting for them. It was from a Doctor James Arendale. All the doctor said was that his call concerned Phillip Bomar. He had left his office address and requested that they see him as soon as possible.

When they arrived at Arendale's downtown office, they were surprised to find the words "clinical psychologist" beneath his name on the door. They had just assumed that he was a physician of the body, rather than one of the mind.

Arendale was a tall, lean man with graying brown hair and a neatly-trimmed beard. He shook their hands, then motioned to two chairs located before his desk. "Please, have a seat."

When they each had one, Doctor Arendale paused, then began to speak. "I am surrendering the restrictions of patient confidentiality on the request of Phillip Bomar's parents. They felt it might assist you in your investigation if I were to clarify exactly who and what poor Phillip was."

"So Phillip Bomar was a patient of yours?" asked Lowery.

"Yes," for nearly twenty-two of his twenty-six years."

"Was he mentally unstable?" asked Taylor.

"In a sense, yes. But in another sense...well, this is sort of difficult to explain. If I don't phrase this very carefully, it might actually sound crazy and impossible to you."

"In light of what we saw last night," said Lowery, "I don't think we'd consider anything crazy and impossible."

The psychologist was silent for a moment, privately choosing his words. "Phillip suffered from a very rare mental/physical condition. He was a stigmachondriac."

"A *what?*" asked Taylor. "I don't believe I've ever heard that term before."

"That's because it is one of my own making," said Arendale with a half-smile. He regarded the two homicide detectives opposite him. "Do you know what the phenomenon of *stigmata* is?"

"Sure," said Lowery. "That's when someone's body plays tricks on them due to some devout belief, mostly of a religious nature. Like someone bleeding from the hands and feet in imitation of Christ's crucifixion."

"Correct," agreed Arendale. "But there are some cases of non-religious stigmata as well. People exhibiting an inflamed handprint in remembrance of a childhood beating, or women exhibiting all the physical characteristics of pregnancy, simply because they believe it to be so."

"And Phillip Bomar was like that?"

"To the extreme. Since the age of four, Phillip exhibited numerous episodes of stigmata. His mind and body were always at a constant war with one another. He could watch TV, see a child being beaten on a show, then dream about the incident and wake up with identical bruises. Once he had a nightmare of falling off a cliff and woke up screaming with a broken leg. He had to have a surgical pin implanted in his knee for that episode."

"His parents were suspected of child abuse at first, but then I was called in. I kept him under clinical observation for a period of time. It was horrifying and, yes,

I admit, professionally intriguing, to watch burns and abrasions appear on a body that had been assaulted only in the mind."

"Was that the extent of Phillip's phenomena?" asked Lowery. "Bruises and broken bones?"

"No," said Arendale. "He could just as easily be tricked into thinking that he was suffering an illness, even a fatal one. Once a team of doctors even believed that he was suffering from advanced leukemia. But once I convinced Phillip otherwise, the symptoms of the cancer disappeared completely. And then there was the matter of the gunshot."

"Gunshot?"

The doctor explained. "When he was a teenager, he and several of his friends went to see a movie, one of the Dirty Harry films I believe it was. When they left the theater and were walking down the sidewalk, a passing car backfired. The noise frightened Phillip. His mind kicked in, convincing him that a gun had been fired. He fell to the ground, bleeding from a large hole in his shoulder. When he was wheeled into surgery, they sutured a wound the exact size that a .44 magnum round would make. You see, his mind was convinced that he had been shot, and so his body reacted to the suggestion. He nearly died from that one."

Lieutenant Lowery sat there quietly for a moment. "So what you're saying is that Phillip was probably killed by his own mind and body?"

"Yes," said Arendale. "If, in fact, it *was* Phillip Bomar's remains you found."

Taylor nodded grimly. "It was. We got a positive ID from the coroner this morning. The fingerprints on the surviving hand matched Bomar's prints precisely."

"That's what I was afraid of," said Arendale. He sank back in his leather chair. "Tell me, exactly how did Phillip die? I haven't been able to find out so far."

Lowery didn't think it would do any harm to tell him. "He was totally incinerated by some unknown catalyst. Do you believe it could have been self-generated?"

"Yes, I'm certain that it could have."

"Tell me this," he continued. "Could it have been suicide?"

Dr. Arendale shook his head. "No, that is out of the question. Phillip had problems, but he had a great zest and love for living. That was the main reason he survived such a chain of severe occurrences. Also, he had done much to insulate himself against experiencing his stigmatic tendencies."

"What do you mean 'insulate' himself?" asked Taylor.

"Did you notice anything strange when you were in his apartment last night? Phillip did not own a television set. He purposely limited his exposure to TV programs, as well as newscasts. The violence he saw on television was potentially dangerous to him. He stopped going to movie theaters for the same reason. And he purified his musical tastes as well. You may have noticed that he listened only to classical music. Music with absolutely *no* lyrics. If he had listened to rock or rap music, the lyrics alone could have actually killed him."

"Damn," said Taylor beneath his breath. "Then the poor kid was like a walking time bomb. But only to himself."

"I couldn't have said it any better," Arendale told him. "But Phillip took great pains to isolate himself from such influences. He was a computer genius and he worked at home, processing data for various corporations. He made quite a comfortable living at it, too. Incidentally, his only interests were listening to classical music and playing non-confrontational computer games. He didn't even read books, afraid of what the printed word might conjure inside his psyche."

"Did he have friends? A girlfriend perhaps?"

"No. Unfortunately, Phillip was something of a recluse. He had no social life whatsoever. He was afraid of loving another human being. He actually feared that rejection might cause something within him that could not be mended with steel pins or stitches."

"So what you're saying, doctor, is that Phillip's death was due to no fault of his own."

"That's what I'm saying, Lieutenant." The psychologist stared at Lowery and his partner somberly. "I believe in my heart that Phillip was murdered. Murdered by someone who knew precisely what he was. And, with that knowledge, used his own condition against him. Yes, someone murdered him, just as sure as if they'd shot him with a gun or stabbed him with a knife."

■■■

On their way back to the office, the two discussed their meeting with James Arendale.

"Was he just being melodramatic?" asked Taylor. "Or was he on the money?"

"I think he's on the right track," said Lowery. "I'm actually beginning to believe that someone turned Phillip Bomar against himself and caused him to spontaneously combust."

"Maybe Blakely has something for us in Forensics," said Taylor.

He did. When they walked into the lab, Tom Blakely looked excited, the way he always did when he had discovered some particularly damning piece of evidence. "Just the guys I've been waiting for," he said with a big grin on his face.

"Looks like you found something," said Lowery.

"Several things in fact," said Blakely. "From the crime scene, we've gathered that Bomar was sitting in front of his computer, right?"

"Right."

"Well, I was curious as to exactly *what* he was doing at the moment of his death," said the forensics expert. "So I took the liberty of bringing his computer system to the lab. And look what I found in the CD-ROM drive after I pried the drawer loose."

He handed them a CD-ROM in a protective evidence bag. Taylor read the title on the silver disk: *You Are There...Famous Disasters!*

"So exactly what is it?"

"Well, as you know, I'm something of a computer buff myself," said Blakely. "This is an interactive CD-ROM in which the participant experiences actual historical disasters, both natural and man-made."

Lowery looked at Taylor, thinking the same thing. "Interesting. So what sort of disasters are on this disk?"

"Tornados, earthquakes, mostly stuff like that," he told them. "But then there are others, like the crash of the Hindenburg and the atomic blast at Hiroshima."

"Sounds like either one of them could have done the trick," said Taylor.

"No, I believe it was another program entirely that killed Mr. Bomar," said Blakely. He walked toward a computer in an adjoining office. "Step this way, gentlemen."

"Talk about melodramatic," said Lowery beneath his breath.

They watched as Blakely inserted the CD-ROM into the drive. "I've already programmed this into the system, so it's ready to go." A menu appeared on the monitor screen, displaying the choices available. Blakely used the mouse to click on the one he desired, then took them through the program. They found themselves following a line of several people dressed in pale blue coveralls with NASA patches sewn to the upper sleeves."

"I think I know where this is leading," said Taylor in amazement.

"In this particular program, you're playing the part of a particular person who was supposed to be the first civilian teacher in space," said Blakely. He followed the group with the aid of his mouse. Soon they had entered a chamber whose walls and roof were covered with electronic consoles. DO YOU WISH TO PROCEED? asked a box that appeared on the screen. Blakely clicked on YES and found himself strapped into a seat with the others similarly seated around him.

Lowery and Taylor waited breathlessly as the countdown came, followed by the lift-off. A clock in the corner of the screen counted off the seconds until the expected disaster took place. Then it happened. A burst of bright light flashed at the far end of the chamber, followed by a roaring rush of pure fire as the inhabitants were fully engulfed.

"Okay, we've seen enough," said Ken Lowery. He felt as though someone had just sucker-punched him in the stomach.

"It was the explosion of the space shuttle *Challenger*," said Taylor. "That was what incinerated Phillip Bomar?"

"I'd stake my reputation on it," said the forensics expert.

"Well, that tells us *how*," said Lowery. "That just leaves *who* and *why*."

Blakely looked pleased with himself. "I believe I've figured that out for you, too."

"You're really earning your paycheck on this one, Tom," said the police lieutenant. "What have you got?"

He handed them a five-page printout. "I found this on Bomar's hard drive. It seems that he made a record of people he communicated with through the Internet on a regular basis. Just hold onto that and I'll show you something else."

They waited while he brought out a brown padded mailing envelope. "I found this in Bomar's wastebasket. I believe the killer sent him the CD-ROM in this envelope."

Taylor read the return address. 'Rom Exchange.' What's that?"

"It's a computer software exchange network," said Blakely. "I've used it before. You can rent CD-ROM games from this company in Seattle. They have their own website on the net."

"So does this murderer work for this Rom Exchange?"

"No. I think they forged a mailing label and sent Bomar this CD-ROM on the chance that he might use it." Again, that look of smug satisfaction. "I peeled the mailing label away and found another one underneath. The name and address had been scratched out, but it didn't take much work to lift the impressions from the envelope underneath."

Lowery looked at the name and address that had been lifted from the mailing envelope, then looked at the Internet record. It was there, several dozen times in the past month.

The last entry was four days ago.

Susan Graham, 577 Oceanview Drive, Jacksonville, Florida.

"But what I want to know is how come Bomar even put the disk in his system and checked it out?" asked Taylor. "He must've known how dangerous it could be."

"Maybe he was just bored," suggested Lowery. "Or curious. And, like the proverbial cat, his curiosity ended up killing him."

"But not without some help," said Blakely.

■■■

It was the following morning when they made their move, with the assistance of the Jacksonville Police Department.

"It still sounds pretty crazy to me," said Detective Art Stafford as they pulled up in front of 577 Oceanview Drive."

"I don't know, Art," said his partner, Steve Kraft. "We've had some weird cases ourselves. Remember when that teenager disappeared for three weeks and then showed up in the middle of that shopping mall, claiming

323

he'd been abducted by aliens? And the polygraph claimed that he was telling the truth?"

"That kid was a nutcase," said Stafford.

"We're not here to argue whether this case is plausible or not," Lowery said from the backseat of their unmarked car. "We've got arrest and extradition warrants for this Susan Graham and that's what we're here for. So let's get to it."

"Okay," said Stafford. "But I hope you guys aren't making fools of yourselves."

The four men left the car and walked up the concrete sidewalk to a clapboard house painted coral pink. The front yard was decorated with pink flamingoes standing on wire legs and seashells collected from the beach, which was just a stone's throw away.

They opened the screen door and paused for a moment, unbuttoning jackets and unfastening holsters. Then Stafford knocked on the door.

They heard someone stir inside, but no one answered the door.

He knocked louder. "Miss Graham, this is Detective Stafford of the Jacksonville Police. Please open the door...right now."

They half expected some resistance, but they were surprised. They heard the rattle of a chain being disengaged and then the door opened.

Susan Graham didn't look like a murder suspect. Instead, she looked like a sadder, heavier version of Phillip Bomar. Her shoulder-length hair was a lusterless red, she wore tortoise-shell glasses, and her plain face was pimply and utterly devoid of makeup. She wore a Miami Dolphins T-shirt, white shorts, and green flip-flops.

"Come in," she said softly, almost in a whisper. The two Atlanta detectives received the same impression. She was shocked and scared by their appearance on her doorstep, but there was a grim acceptance as well. In a way, she had hoped to get away with her crime scott-free, but in another she knew that she never would.

324

The four policemen stepped into a cramped living room decorated with second-hand furniture and the type of framed prints you can buy at Wal-Mart. The only point of sophistication in the entire room was a desk bearing an expensive Hewlett Packard computer and laser printer. Taste wise, it was as far from Phillip Bomar's upstairs office as you could get. But it still held the same dreary air of isolation.

"Susan Graham," said Lowery. "Were you acquainted with a Phillip Andrew Bomar?"

"Yes," said the young woman with a sigh. "But only through the Internet. I never actually met him in person."

Taylor took the CD-ROM from his jacket pocket. "And did you mail Mr. Bomar this?"

Susan Graham stared at the disk for a long moment. "Yes, I did."

The lieutenant showed her the papers. "Miss Graham, I have a warrant for your arrest on the charge of the willful and premeditated murder of Phillip Bomar."

She stared at them silently, then began to back away. "Okay," she said in resignation. "I did it. I admit that. But before you take me, let me tell you *why* I did what I did."

"Maybe you ought to wait until you talk to an attorney, Miss Graham," suggested Detective Stafford. "This is a serious crime you're being charged with."

"I know how serious it is!" she snapped at him. She stopped her slow retreat and stood in the center of the living room. The computer was to her left, while a doorway leading into the back of the house stood to her right. "Just let me tell you and get it over with, okay?"

Stafford shrugged and looked over at Lowery. "It's your ballgame, pal. If she wants to talk now, that's okay with us."

Taylor took a micro-recorder from his pocket, showed it to the young woman, and turned it on. "Be advised that anything you now say can and will be used against you in a court of law."

They stood and waited, giving her time to gather her thoughts. Then Susan Graham began to talk.

"I met Phillip on the net. We were both lonely and we just sort of lucked upon each other by accident. We found we both had a lot of the same interests and started talking to each other through the computer. I fell in love with him and told him so. But then I guess he got scared. He refused to communicate with me anymore. For a couple of weeks, I left messages on his E-mail, but he wouldn't answer them. I was crushed at first. Then I guess I sort of lost my temper."

"You were aware of his condition?" asked Lowery.

She nodded. "He told me about it a week or two after we started talking."

"And you sent him this CD-ROM out of spite? For dumping you?"

Tears began to bloom in Susan Graham's eyes. Slowly, she began to back toward the doorway. "Phillip was stupid! So damn stupid! He didn't know how lucky he was!"

Taylor shucked his revolver from his holster and held it at his side. "Stay where you are, Miss Graham."

But she ignored him. Step by step, she made her way toward the far end of the living room. "He didn't realize how much we had in common!" she sobbed. "He didn't realize just how much alike we were!"

"Miss Graham—" called the police sergeant, raising his gun.

Suddenly, she turned and ran through the doorway and down a short hallway to a bathroom. By the time they got there, the door had been slammed shut and locked from the inside.

"Open this door, Miss Graham," called Lowery. "Or we'll be forced to break it down."

For a moment, there was only silence. Then a long, mournful scream shrilled from the opposite side of the door.

"Let's do it!' said Taylor. He and Lowery kicked at the door three times before the doorframe splintered around the lock and the door slammed inward with a crash.

The four detectives crowded through the doorway and stopped. They stood frozen in their tracks, staring at the mess on the bathroom floor.

"Oh dear God," said Lowery.

Detective Stafford's eyes grew wide with shock, unable to comprehend what he was looking at.

"What happened?" he demanded to know. *"What the hell happened to her?"*

■■■

At the request of the Jacksonville coroner, they stepped into the lab.

"There are a few points that I need to clarify before I proceed with the autopsy," he said. "This was the condition you found her in upon entering the bathroom?"

Lowery, Taylor, Stafford, and Kraft took a step closer. They stared at the naked body of Susan Graham lying on the stainless steel gurney. "Yes," Lowery said, speaking for them all.

"And it was only a matter of seconds between the time she locked the door and the time you gained entrance?"

"That's right," said Stafford.

The coroner shook his head. "I don't understand. I simply don't understand how this could have taken place in such a short period of time."

Ken Lowery and Ed Taylor stared at the fatal injuries that had taken the life of Susan Graham.

The coroner pointed them out with a rubber-gloved hand.

"Severe lacerations of both wrists, resulting in massive blood loss."

No razor blades or sharp objects had been found in the bathroom.

"Indications of strangulation and rope burns around the throat."

No rope or cord had been discovered, either.

"And this," said the coroner, shaking his head in bewilderment. "A circular wound to the right temple and severe hemorrhaging of the brain. Like a bullet hole, but with no evidence of powder burns around the opening of the wound."

They had searched the bathroom several times. Absolutely no gun had been found.

Silence hung in the room for a long moment. Then Lowery spoke. "She was right then."

"About what?" asked Stafford.

Lowery glanced over at his partner. He could tell by the look in Taylor's eyes that he had come to the same conclusion. "She and Phillip Bomar *were* a lot alike. But in all the wrong ways."

WHOREHOUSE HOLLOW

Back in high school, I was always puzzled by the apathy and lack of drive that seemed to rule some of my classmates. Oh, there were those of us who had big plans and wanted to bust the world wide open following graduation. But there were an equal number who seemed content to simply do as their parents had done...digging ditches or tending the home, forever with a load of clothes in the washer and a passel of young'uns under-foot. (Not that there's anything wrong with either. I was raised to believe that any work, if hard and honest, is honorable work.)

I reckon it was just that utter absence of am-bition that perplexed me so. The most promising students and athletes just seemed to throw it all away. It was as though their zest for life had been siphoned completely out of them.

JUST as they had promised Coach Winters, the Bedloe County Bears delivered the final victory of that football season, as well as the coveted mid-state champion-ship.

Not that such an accomplishment was anything new for the elderly coach or the annually-changing team that he had commanded for nearly twenty years. Under the stern training and no-nonsense guidance of Bud Winters, the Bears had won every single game, both at home and away, as well as the mid-state championship since the autumn of 1973. Exactly how such a feat was accomplished consistently, year after year, was debated by sports fans and neighboring high schools throughout the state of Tennessee.

Even some of the major colleges in the area, such as Vanderbilt and UT in Knoxville, had attempted to analyze the mixture of skill and pure luck that seemed to bless Winters' team of beefy farmboys on a puzzlingly regular basis. In fact, entire theses had been written by a number of graduate students, attempting to theorize exactly what the Bears possessed that no other high school team in the state seemed to. But, in actuality, no one really had a clue.

No one, that was, but the members of the team itself. Those strapping, young men who made up the ranks of the victorious Bears certainly knew what the motivation of their unequalled stamina on the gridiron and their infallible will to win was due to. And that magical motivation could, quite simply, be summed up in two words.

Whorehouse Hollow.

Unbeknownst to those who spent their free time debating the phenomenon of the Bedloe County Bears—from blue collar workers in sleazy honky-tonks to state senators at their posh and manicured country clubs—there was one factor and one factor only that made the team an unbeatable winner each and every season. And that factor was plain and simple horniness.

When fall training began on the football field of Bedloe County High every September, the inevitable pep talk was given. Coach Winters drummed the importance

330

of team spirit, organization, and brute force into those young minds. The talk was taken patiently as always, the new members of that season's team squirming on the risers of the wooden bleachers until that anticipated promise was made by the crabby, cigar-puffing coach. Then the old man would smile and give them what they had been waiting for. "Do it for me, boys," Coach Winters would say, "Win that mid-state championship for me this year just like all the years before, and at the end of the season, you all will be rewarded. And I reckon you all know what that reward will be, don't you?"

Snickers of dirty laughter and sly looks were always exchanged by the members of that year's incarnations of the Bears. Yes, they all knew what the coach's payment for a successful season of winning was. It had been the same for the past twenty years. A couple cases of Budweiser...as well as a trip to Whorehouse Hollow.

For a team of teenaged boys with a field of wild oats to sow, such an offer of free beer and unlimited sex was enough to drive them toward an ultimate victory. And that current year, like every one before, proved to be no exception.

■■■

Boisterous laughter and shrill rebel yells echoed through the boys' locker room following that final game, as well as words of congratulation and customary pats on the butt. The Bears had done it once again. They had annihilated the Crimshaw County Cougars, 28 to 0, and taken the mid-state championship, no contest.

A season's worth of hard work had finally paid off. Now it was time to relax and enjoy the spoils that victory had netted them. Namely the night of debauchery that Coach Winters had promised them that first day at practice.

Among the eighteen seniors who gathered in the locker room, peeling off their sweaty, grass-stained uniforms and taking their turn in the showers, only one seemed to lack the air of excitement that the others shared. Tony Frazier, star quarterback of the Bears, sat on the bench in front of his locker. He grinned triumphantly and exchanged high-fives with his fellow teammates, but, inwardly, he was having second thoughts about the anticipated fulfillment of the coach's promise.

Tony wasn't like most of the Neanderthals who made up the ranks of the football team. Unlike them, he had a head on his shoulders, as well as high ambitions beyond the realm of the rural Tennessee high school. Tony was a straight-A student. He was bound to graduate with honors and, hopefully, with a football scholarship to one of the big Southern universities as well. Strangely enough, despite the longstanding winning streak that Bedloe County boasted, not one player in a span of twenty years had gone on to play college football. Tony couldn't understand exactly why. It seemed like, when scholarships were being awarded at all the other high schools, the star players of the Bears always turned down the opportunity. The reason? Plain and simple apathy. After the big win, the members of the Bedloe County Bears always seemed to lose their drive. Just like the alumni before them, they graduated from high school and led dismal and lackluster lives. They either married too young, ended up with a passel of unwanted kids, and spent their days working their fingers to the bone at some dead-end job, or ended up drinking themselves to death or landing in prison. Exactly why those gallant warriors of the gridiron succumbed to such paths was as much a mystery as their constant wins of decades past.

Tony Frazier vowed that he wouldn't end up like that. He was going to march across the football field on graduation night, proudly accept that football scholarship from Principal Allen, and then go on to a future as a pro player. He wasn't going to let the apathy that cursed most of the good old boys in Bedloe County infect him. He was a

332

lover of life and expected only the best for himself in the years to come.

As he finished undressing, he noticed his teammates as they entered and exited the stalls of the boys' shower room. Most of them already sported raging hard-ons in anticipation of the night to come. All they had on their minds were a couple cans of Bud and a trip to the most infamous whorehouse in Bedloe County.

Tony had heard the stories, passed down in whispers from upperclassmen the year before. The stories of Whorehouse Hollow and the old two-story mansion located deep in the depths of the woods south of town, and how the madam, Fanny Eldritch, and her twelve beautiful daughters awaited the wants and needs of the county's horny men, willing to do anything for only a few measly dollars. The pleasures that Whorehouse Hollow boasted were legendary. They said that Fanny and her girls knew everything imaginable about getting a man's rocks off, and put that well-honed knowledge to good use. What they could do with their hands and mouths—as well as other bodily orifices—well, it just had to be experienced to be believed.

No wonder the Bedloe County Bears had enjoyed such a solid winning streak. Each and every new team that Coach Winters put together were enticed by the carnal pleasures that Whorehouse Hollow promised at the end of the season. The winning machine that made up the high school football team ran off of one chemical and one chemical alone: pure, 100 percent testosterone.

Tony jumped when he felt a strong hand on his broad shoulder. He looked up to see Coach Winters standing over him. The elderly man grinned paternally down at the quarterback, grinding the butt of his Tampa Nugget cigar between the stubs of his tobacco-stained teeth. "Whatcha doing sitting here, Frazier?" asked the coach. "You'd best get in there and shower. You wanna be fresh and ready for all that hot tail you're gonna find down there in the Hollow."

"Yes, sir," was all that Tony said. He forced a grin and left the bench. As he headed for the scalding spray of the showers, he looked back over his shoulder. Coach Winters continued to grin at him, hands in his pockets, his eyes like tiny black marbles beneath those bushy gray eyebrows. Something about the coach's expression disturbed Tony. It was almost predatory in nature. He had seen it before, both during practice and in the heat of the actual game. The coach was a man who enjoyed winning at any cost, that was plain to see. And when the winning was over, Winters like to gloat. The coach savored making the opposition feel as insignificant as a maggot in horseshit, while he himself felt ten feet tall and invincible.

As Tony found a vacant stall and began to soap himself up beneath the hot spray of the shower, he began to wonder if he could actually go through with that night's secret trip to Whorehouse Hollow. He thought of his steady girlfriend, Pamela Sue Cripps, and began to feel a pang of guilt nag at him. Tony had gone with the pretty blonde since the start of the school year and he really cared for the girl a lot, maybe even loved her. One thing was for sure and that was that Tony saw more in Pamela Sue than any of the other girls he had dated in high school. In fact they had never made love. Their intimacy had never gone further than kissing or petting. She simply didn't feel comfortable going all the way and Tony, respectful of her feelings, had never forced the issue.

Now here he was on the verge of cheating on her with some whore he would encounter in some sleazy one-night stand. It just didn't seem right. It seemed somehow dirty and shameful. But he certainly couldn't make his feelings known to the other guys. They would rag him about his reluctance for the rest of the school year and he simply didn't need that kind of hassle. As he began to lather his lower abdomen and legs, Tony felt himself become suddenly aroused. He closed his eyes and imagined how tonight would turn out. Although guilt cast its shadow his

334

way, Tony was still a red-blooded teenage boy. His hormones kicked in and he fantasized about Fanny Eldritch and her voluptuous daughters. He imagined the paleness of creamy skin in the moonlight, the solidity of firm flesh and muscle against his body, and the warm wetness of lips and tongues teasing him, from head to toe.

Tony looked down at his crotch and saw that he had hardened, just like all the others. He fought hard to drive all thoughts of Pamela Sue from his mind. *Just one night,* he told himself as he stepped from the shower and vigorously toweled off. *Hell, what could it hurt? She'll never know.*

"Let's hurry it up, boys!" called Coach Winters from the locker room. "Fanny and her gals don't like to be kept waiting!"

A cheer of primal lust went up from the ranks of the Bedloe County Bears. And, like it or not, Tony Frazier's was among them.

■■■

A half hour later, they were on their way.

Coach Winters had borrowed one of the Bedloe County school system's big yellow buses to take them to their intended destination. After stopping off at a tavern called the Bloody Bucket and purchasing two cases of Budweiser tallboys, as promised, the coach headed the diesel due south along U.S. Highway 70.

After a few miles, fertile farmland gave way to dense forest. Without warning, Winters jerked the wheel to the left, pulling the bus onto a long stretch of uneven dirt road. "Next stop...Whorehouse Hollow!" he called out.

The eighteen young men—half drunk and horny—whooped and hollered in reply as the bus left the familiarity of the open highway and began to descend deeper and deeper into unknown territory.

Tony nursed his can of beer quietly, choosing not to drink quite as freely as the others. He had almost talked himself into enjoying this brief adventure back in the high school locker room, but now he began to have reservations once again. This time it didn't involve Pamela Sue. Rather, he thought back to the old tall tales and ghost stories that his Grandpa Frazier had told him when he was just a kid. Hackle-raising stories concerning an old house deep down in the south woods where a witch and her brood of daughters lived. The old man had been half senile, so sometimes the details of his tall tales varied a bit. Sometimes he claimed the daughters were vampires, while other times he said they were ghosts who would suck the very life from a man if they got a hold of him. Tony shook the creepy stories from his head, telling himself they had been nothing but hogwash. More than likely the tales had been concocted by the menfolk of Bedloe County, hoping to discourage curious children from exploring the vicinity of Whorehouse Hollow. It wouldn't have done to have little Junior sneaking around the Eldritch house at night and accidentally catch a glimpse of his papa with his pants literally around his ankles.

Another half hour passed. The thick branches of the pinewood forest seemed to interweave over the roof of the bus, shutting out the nocturnal light of the autumn moon. The farther they traveled, the worse the trail became. The road of dusty red clay gradually deteriorated until it was only a couple of deep ruts surrounded by heavy thicket on each side. The group of boys grew uncustomarily silent as the bus made several tricky, hairpin turns and then began to make an almost unnoticeable slope downward into the depths of a large hollow. As the Tennessee hills reared up on either side of them, the basin of the hollow grew steeper and steeper. The forest around them neglected to let up, too. Dead honeysuckle vines, thorny blackberry bramble, and prickly pine boughs scratched noisily against the windows of the school bus. A brawny linebacker named Bubba Stewart laughed somewhere in the back, but it wasn't his usual mule-bray of witless mirth. Instead, it was a nervous laugh, much like that of a boastful child walking through a graveyard that he's secretly frightened to death of.

Then, abruptly, the downward descent ended and the yellow diesel braked to a halt. "We're here," said Coach Winters. His liver-spotted hand reached out and gave the release handle a sharp yank. The bus's folding doors opened with an unnerving squeal.

In single file, the Bedloe County Bears left the belly of the bus. Quietly, they gathered beneath the shelter of an ancient oak tree, eyeing the big house that stood before them.

From the looks of it, it had probably once been one of the finest mansions in the state of Tennessee. It stood two stories tall, not counting its upper attic of four windowed gables, and stretched nearly the entire width of the hollow it sat in. A wraparound porch spanned the ground level and an ornately carved balcony encircled the upper story.

Yes, it would have certainly been a historical showplace, except that time and neglect had paid its toll on the big house. Its paint was peeling clear down to the bare wood, the glass of its windows was cracked and broken, and the roof looked as though it was sagging in places. Also the immaculate grounds that once surrounded the structure were nonexistent now. Thorny thicket and dense kudzu had encroached upon the property. It would have taken a bulldozer to clear away the amount of wild underbrush that surrounded the old Eldritch house.

The boys searched the windows for any sign of light, but none could be detected. Truthfully, the place appeared to be completely deserted.

"Fanny and her girls can only take thirteen at a time, so some of you boys will have to wait your turn," said the coach. He snapped on the beam of a flashlight and picked out the lucky thirteen—Tony included—then led them through the bramble to the porch of the Eldritch house.

They were scarcely assembled before the front door, when it opened on creaking hinges. The soft glow of lantern light shone from within, causing the boys to squint against the sudden brilliance.

"Please, gentlemen," coaxed a husky voice. "Come on in."

Tony turned and saw that Coach Winters had already left them and returned to where the other Bears anxiously awaited their chance. Being the leader of the team on the football field, Tony decided to take the first step inside. What he and the others found within the confines of the Eldritch house was in complete contrast to the decay they had encountered outside.

The floors were of polished marble, the walls decorated with priceless paintings and statuary, and the furniture, while antique, was the finest that money could buy. But that wasn't what impressed the teenagers the most. No, not by a long shot.

Never in their young lives had they encountered so many beautiful women in one place. The Bedloe County cheerleading squad couldn't hold a candle to Fanny Eldritch and her twelve daughters. The matriarch herself certainly didn't look her age, which must have been fifty years of age or older. Her hair was long and raven black, and her smooth, alabaster skin was totally devoid of age lines. Fanny's daughters were just as striking as their mother. Each one was tall and willowy, and each possessed the same length of ebony hair and quality of pure unblemished skin. All thirteen women wore long gowns of white silk, sheer enough to give a hint of the perfect bodies that were hidden underneath.

"Welcome," Fanny told them all. She eyed the young men in their red and white letterman jackets as if they were some sexual banquet to be sampled and savored. "We all know why you're here, so why don't we cut the formalities and get down to business."

"Yes, ma'am!" declared Ricky Nolan, one of the Bears' wide receivers. "We're ready to party!"

Without another word, Fanny and her lovely daughters mingled with the members of the football team, choosing those they would spend the next hour or so with. Tony was surprised when Fanny herself walked up and took him by the hand. "Come with me, Mister Quarterback," she breathed in his ear. "I have something special planned for you."

Tony felt a lump form in his throat as he looked into the dark eyes of the middle-aged woman. The way that she stared at him made him feel light-headed, as if he had ridden some particular heart-pounding carnival ride one time too many. The feeling of mild disorientation bothered Tony a little, but he didn't let it show. He returned Fanny's sly smile and followed as the woman turned and led him up the curving staircase to the upper floor.

When he reached the upstairs landing, he glanced down and saw that Fanny's daughters were doing the same, each woman leading one of his teammates to their own private rooms.

"Don't drag your feet, handsome," whispered Fanny, tightening her hold on Tony's hand. "We have much to do this night."

Tony nodded and followed her down the hallway to the very last door. Fanny opened it, revealing a richly furnished bedroom. Together, they walked to the huge canopied bed.

With little effort, the madam of Whorehouse Hollow pushed Tony to a sitting position on the edge of the bed.

"Just relax," she told him. "Relax and let me do the rest." Then Fanny reached up and, slipping the straps of her silken gown off her white shoulders, let the garment fall down the length of her body until it pooled around her feet.

Tony was captivated by the naked woman who stood before him. He had drooled over plenty of skin magazines during his teenaged years, but none of the air-brushed models on those glossy pages could compare to Fanny Eldritch. The woman, simply put, was utterly perfect. Despite her age, she seemed to possess the body of an eighteen-year-old. Her breasts were high and pert, and her arms, abdomen, and legs were tautly muscled and trim, like that of a prime athlete. As she gracefully stepped out of her gown, Tony found his attention glued to the triangle of raven black hair at the junction of her thighs. He felt himself become aroused at the sight of that secret place, the crotch of his jeans tightening in quick response.

Then, a second later, she was there, scarcely a few inches away. Her warm hands reached out and cupped his face, then brought it up toward her. Tony opened his mouth as their lips meshed, allowing her tongue to entwine with his own. He felt an odd taste fill his mouth; the bite of cinnamon, as well as something else that he couldn't quite identify. It wasn't an unpleasant taste. In fact, as the kiss grew deeper and more passionate, Tony felt himself growing more relaxed, his inhibitions swiftly giving way to abandon.

But, before he could lose complete control, Pamela Sue's innocent face again popped into his mind. Tony pushed the whore away, his breath ragged. "I...I'm sorry, ma'am...but I can't."

Fanny appeared to be amused. "Oh?" she asked. "And why not?"

Tony reddened in embarrassment. "Well, there's this girl. I've been going with her for a while and...well, this just doesn't feel right."

Fanny reached out and stroked Tony's strong face with a long-nailed hand. "It's all right, handsome. You're not cheating on your girlfriend. This is only one night out of an entire lifetime." The woman cocked her head and pointed over her shoulder. "Listen. Hear how well my daughters are treating your friends? Sounds to me like they're having plenty of fun."

Tony listened. The hallways of the old house rang with the sounds of passion and pleasure; the moans and cries of both male and female, the jouncing of bedsprings as a dozen couples rutted like wild animals in heat. The sounds once again tore down Tony's reluctance and he felt the keen thrill of sexual tension course throughout him, raising his adrenaline level to the max.

"I thought so." Fanny laughed. Deftly, she dropped to her knees before the young quarterback, disengaged the zipper of his jeans, and released him from the discomfort that the denim caused.

At first, he felt the warmth of her breath upon his flesh, then the dampness of her mouth. He groaned out loud as she went to work with the measured precision of a machine. Tony cupped her head in his hands, slowing her pace, then quickening it, urging her on.

The pinnacle of climax was reaching its first stage, when Tony Frazier sensed that something was gravely wrong. First of all, the sensation of light-headedness had returned, much stronger than it had been before. He felt fear blossom in the back of his mind, as if he had lost control and was on the verge of losing something very dear and important to him. Then the physical sensation in his loins began to change drastically. The warmth of Fanny's mouth disappeared. In its place was an engulfing coldness like that of a deep freeze. The icy sensation began to engulf his lower body, then climb steadily upward.

Tony wrenched at Fanny's head, intending to disengage her from himself. But she was as stubborn as a leech. She refused to release him. A strange sensation threatened to overcome him at that moment. The feeling that some vital part of his soul was on the verge of tearing loose from its moorings and on the brink of being lost forever.

Tony panicked then and that was the only thing that saved him. He reached over to the nightstand beside the bed, found a heavy statuette of carved jade, and sent it crashing down upon the top of Fanny's head. Fortunately, that did the trick. The woman fell away, stunned, and lay there on the carpeted floor. As Tony tucked himself back into his trousers and zipped his fly, he was shocked by the transformation that Fanny had undergone.

She was no longer the stunning seductress that she had been mere moments ago. Instead, she was a bony hag with a twisted face as ugly as sin. Her white skin was pocked with festering blisters and boils, and, within her gaping mouth, gleamed jagged teeth with points as sharp as razors.

The thing that was Fanny Eldritch grasped at Tony's ankle as he left the bed and hurriedly crossed the room. "Come back here!" she rasped, a mist of frosty breath drifting from the ugly hole of her mouth. "I'm not through with you yet!"

Tony thought differently, however. He pushed open the door and burst into the corridor. As he sprinted down the hallway toward the staircase, he found the doors to the adjoining rooms standing open. Inside, his fellow teammates were being assaulted in the same parasitic fashion that he had almost succumbed to. He caught a quick glimpse of Bubba Stewart lying naked across a bed, one of Fanny Eldritch's daughters straddling his hips. The creature, now just as hideous as her mother, rocked back and forth, as if attempting to pump the very life force from the quivering body of the big linebacker. Bubba's face was blanched and gray, his eyes duller and less responsive than they usually were.

The boy didn't stop to help his buddy. Instead, he hurriedly descended the winding stairs and nearly broke his neck, attempting to make it through the front door. As he stumbled down the porch steps and into the cluttered yard, Coach Winters left the others beneath the tree and started toward him. "Wait up, Frazier!" he called out.

Tony looked into the coach's eyes and saw alarm. But it wasn't alarm over what was taking place inside the old mansion. Rather, it was alarm over Tony's apparent escape. He knew then that Winters would be no ally to him. No, it was clear to see that Winters had orchestrated this entire episode and that he knew precisely what was taking place.

Like a wild man, Tony plunged into the thicket, oblivious to the thorns that ripped at his skin and clothing. He heard the coach's frantic yells behind him, as well as the confused voices of the others. Tony didn't stop. He fought his way through the woods, heading eastward in the direction of the highway. As he climbed the steep grade of Whorehouse Hollow toward freedom, he couldn't help but recall that numbing sensation of total apathy that Fanny Eldritch had almost sentenced him to. Luckily, it seemed that he had escaped just in the nick of time.

■■■

It was well past midnight, when Tony reached Highway 70. He was a nervous wreck by the time he stumbled out of the thicket and onto the lonely stretch of two-lane blacktop. Several times during his mad dash from the backwoods hollow, Tony had been certain that he heard the grinding roar of the diesel bus struggling up the grade toward him. Also, it may have been his imagination, but he was sure that something much more horrifying in nature also dogged his heels. Several times he had glanced over his shoulder and swore that he saw pale-fleshed forms flitting through the dark forest in hot pursuit.

During Tony's frantic exodus from the woods, his mind filled with questions concerning what was taking place that night. He began to wonder if the winning streak that the Bedloe County Bears had enjoyed for two decades was due solely to skill, determination, and the sexual incentive of Whorehouse Hollow. Tony began to wonder if their unparalleled victories had been due to some evil alliance between Coach Winters and Fanny Eldritch. The quarterback recalled some of the plays he had pulled off, seemingly impossible plays, and found himself wondering if perhaps some sort of magic had been responsible. Had Coach Winters made a deal with the witch twenty years ago? Had he promised Fanny and her hellish daughters an annual sacrifice in exchange for a continuous streak of winning seasons? After witnessing what had happened that night, Tony couldn't help but wonder.

Finally, however, his crazed sprint through the underbrush had ended. He escaped the cramped confines of the woods and made it to the open road. He didn't slow down, though. He kept right on running until he reached the first farmstead that he came to.

Tony recognized the big stock barn and the split-level farmhouse that stood a few yards away from it, and thanked God for allowing him to reach such a haven safely.

Tony staggered around the side of the house to a window with frilly pink curtains. He sagged against the wall of white clapboard and tapped on the glass of the windowpane with dirty, bleeding knuckles. A moment later a light came on and the curtains were pulled aside.

"Tony!" cried Pamela Sue in surprise. She raised the sash and stared with alarm at her exhausted boyfriend. "What happened to you?"

The quarterback could say nothing at first. He fought to catch his breath and motioned for her to help him through the open window. Pamela Sue quickly agreed and, soon, Tony was stretched out on her bed. He breathed in deeply, trying hard to clear his head. He looked around at the posters of teen heartthrobs that papered Pamela Sue's bedroom walls, as well as the colorful stuffed animals that the girl collected. The innocent surroundings seemed almost surreal in contrast to those deceptive furnishings inside the Eldritch house. Or perhaps *lair* might have been a better term to describe that hellish structure in the shadowy pit of Whorehouse Hollow.

"Please, Tony," begged Pamela Sue, herself almost in tears. "Tell me what happened tonight."

Tony shook his head violently, the full impact of that night causing him to shudder in remembrance. "I can't," sobbed Tony. "I don't even want to think about it."

Pamela Sue took him in her arms and cradled him as if he were a baby. "Okay," she told him soothingly. "You don't have to say anything. Just try to calm down."

Tony clung tightly to his girlfriend, his face buried in the soft folds of her flannel gown. He half expected Mr. or Mrs. Cripps to burst in to the room, demanding to know what was going on. But fortunately they didn't. They remained in the dark as to Tony's presence in their daughter's bedroom.

After a while, Tony's nervous palsy decreased and he began to relax. He hugged Pamela Sue closer to him and she returned the favor. He breathed in the intoxicating scent of her: baby powder, herbal shampoo, and a hint of her favorite perfume. Tony stared into the girl's worried eyes and saw none of the hesitation that had been there during the nights they had dated. He kissed Pamela Sue deeply and, surprisingly enough, she made the next move, rolling on top of him. His trembling hands snaked past the hem of her gown and stopped at the sheer fabric of her bikini panties.

"I wish..." he stammered, "I wish we could..."

Pamela Sue smiled softly. "We can," she told him. "I feel like it's the right time now."

Tony stared up at her gratefully, then gently peeled the panties away from her hips. At the same time, Pamela Sue unfastened Tony's jeans and slid them down around his legs. Tony thought nothing of safe sex or birth control as he flipped the girl over and began to make love to her. He felt that if he hesitated, even for a moment, he would most surely lose his sanity. All that kept him from freaking out entirely was his love for this beautiful young girl who gave herself freely underneath him.

As the two coupled quietly and tenderly, Tony felt his excitement begin to reach its peak. Pamela Sue seemed to sense his urgency. She wrapped her arms and legs around him, pulling him closer. "I'm ready for you, lover," she whispered in his ear. "I'm ready to take it all."

The girl's choice of words puzzled Tony. "What?" he asked. But his question came too late to prevent what was taking place. The soft warmth that engulfed him abruptly changed to a searing cold as frigid as a January wind and he knew he had been tricked.

"Don't fight it, Tony," said Pamela Sue. Her pale skin seemed to grow soft, merging with his own, locking him into her steely embrace. "Winners always have to pay a price. Believe me, yours is not so bad." When she saw the confusion in his eyes, she explained further. "The coach knew what sort of guy you were. He knew that you wouldn't go through with it, so he enlisted me before-hand, just to make sure that everything went according to tradition."

Thoughts of haunted hollows, witches, and vampires flooded Tony's mind, as well as an obscure term he had learned in Mr. Bailey's mythology class earlier that year. Succubus. A creature who, through the act of sexual intercourse, drains the most vital spark of life from the souls of its victims.

Helplessly, Tony stared down at the girl beneath him. "I...I don't understand."

"I believe you do," explained Pamela Sue, her dark eyes cool and devoid of emotion. "You see, Tony, I lied to you. My last name isn't Cripps. It's Eldritch. And I was born in Whorehouse Hollow."

Then, as Tony felt the climax of ecstasy travel the length of his captive body, bringing a sensation both wondrous and horrendous, he noticed that the roots of Pamela Sue's honey-blond hair were actually jet black in hue.

■■■

A year had passed since that night in Whorehouse Hollow.

Tony Frazier stood at the grill of the Lunch & Munch Cafe, flipping burgers and frying onion rings, just as he had for the past ten months.

Life hadn't turned out like Tony had hoped it would. A month after the end of football season, Tony had strangely lost all interest in school. He had dropped out

346

and, after meeting a white-trash waitress at the local tavern, got the girl pregnant and ended up marrying her. Now Tony was working two jobs, just to pay rent on the rundown trailer they had moved into and trying to keep their heads above water. During his spare time, he occupied a barstool down at the Bloody Bucket, drinking too much and listening to country songs on the jukebox. Mournful songs about hopes and dreams forever lost.

Tony didn't seem to care much, though. His ability to care about how his life had turned out had been wrestled from his grasp months ago. His fellow teammates had suffered similar fates...or worse. Bubba Stewart was in the Tennessee state pen for grand theft auto and Rickey Nolan had driven his pickup truck into the muddy depths of the Harpeth River only a few days ago. Rickey had, at least for himself, put an end to the apathy that seemed to curse the majority of the menfolk in Bedloe County.

Tony didn't realize that it was the anniversary of his emotional gelding until the big yellow school bus pulled up outside the Lunch & Munch. The jangle of the cowbell over the door sounded and he turned to find Coach Winters crossing the dining room to the front counter. He held a brown paper bag in his hand.

"How's it going, Frazier?" greeted the coach, smiling around the stub of his cigar.

"Same as usual," replied Tony with a shrug. He glanced through the plate glass of the cafe and saw the excited faces of that year's team grinning from the windows of the school bus. "Another winning season?" he asked blandly.

"Of course," said Winters. "Are you surprised?"

Tony remembered the promise the coach had made him and his friends scarcely over a year ago. "No," he said. "Can't say that I am."

The coach's tiny eyes glinted beneath his bushy brows. "I heard your wife just had a kid. A baby boy."

Tony nodded. "You heard right."

"Well, it's not much, but I bought him a little present," said Winters. He handed Tony the paper bag. "Could you see that he gets it?"

"Sure," said Tony. Reluctantly, he took the gift. "Thanks."

"I'd like to stick around and talk about old times, but I gotta go," said Coach Winters, heading for the front door. "Can't keep those ladies down in the Hollow waiting, you know."

Tony said nothing. He simply nodded and watched as the elderly man left the restaurant and climbed back onto the bus. Soon, the diesel was on its way, first to the tavern for a couple cases of beer, then farther southward along Highway 70.

When the bus was out of sight, Tony stared down at the sack in his hand, afraid to open it. Finally, he gathered the nerve to do so. For some reason he wasn't at all surprised to see the article of clothing that Coach Winters had bought for Tony's firstborn son.

It was a tiny football jersey. Red and white, with the emblem of the Bedloe County Bears on the front and the word QUARTERBACK stenciled across the back.

DEPRAVITY ROAD

This is one of the few stories I've written that wasn't set in the South, which makes it a rarity of sorts. Fiction-wise, I don't normally stray past the Mason-Dixon Line.

Oddly enough, this tale is set in the heart of the Midwest, but for a good reason...mainly because it touches on an infamous—and particularly gruesome—case of murder and grave-robbery that came to light in the 1950s. One that still haunts the folks of that area to this day.

WE'RE lost."

Fred Barnett didn't want to admit it, not out loud, not in front of *her*. But there was simply no denying it. They had been on that lonely stretch of rural road for quite some time now, driving mile upon mile without seeing any signs of civilization other than a few dilapidated farmhouses and their equally ramshackle outbuildings.

"I told you that an hour ago," huffed Agnes from the passenger side of the '51 Chevrolet. "I shouldn't be surprised, though. Leave it to you to turn a simple ninety-mile road trip into some rambling exodus into the unknown. I swear, Fred, you couldn't find your own butt if you had a compass and a roadmap."

Fred's thin face flushed red with embarrassment. "Please, Agnes...not in front of the kids."

But his wife wouldn't leave it alone. "And why not in front of the kids?" she asked. "They have as much a right as anyone else to know what a total idiot their father is."

As usual, Fred said nothing in rebuttal. He avoided looking at the woman seated next to him, the woman he had once seriously thought of in terms of love, devotion, and, God help him, even lust. He didn't want to see her hefty, thick-limbed frame perched there, punishing the springs of the Chevy's two-toned bench seat. Neither did he want to see the look of smug disapproval on her plump, bovine face. Instead he directed his nervous gaze at the rearview mirror. The children, two boys named Teddy and Roger, sat immersed in their comic books, oblivious to the humiliation their old man was suffering at the razor tongue of their overbearing mother. Or maybe they did hear what was being said and were just ignoring it. They had heard it all many times before. Perhaps burying their noses in pulp pages of ballooned dialogue and brightly inked panels was a way out for them. A method of psychological escape to keep themselves from going totally nuts.

Fred wished he possessed such a haven. But he did not. Since marrying Agnes eight years ago, this shoe salesman had been unable to find one. Every waking hour was spent on the battle line, bitterly swallowing one complaint after another: dissatisfaction over the meager wage Fred was making, putting down the Eisenhower administration (Agnes did not "like Ike"), and griping because the boys were turning out to be a couple of "weird deadbeats" like their father. Of course, Fred simply nodded obediently to every harsh word, uttered a much practiced "Yes, dear," and cowered beneath her contemptuous glare, which was

350

set in her massive face like two, tiny black marbles sunk deep into a tub of lard.

Now he was under the oppressive weight of her wrath once again as he wandered the wintry back roads with no idea where they were. "Got any suggestions?" he asked her, trying desperately hard to keep the sarcasm out of his voice. "You know I've never been to your brother Ben's place before. I've never even been this far north in the state before."

Agnes seemed to settle down a bit, accepting her husband's shortcomings as a burden that must be endured, at least on that Thanksgiving Day of 1954. "Just keep on going and, the next house you see, stop and ask for directions."

"Yes, dear." There was no feeling to his words. They were just a reflex action now, like flinching beneath the fist of a bully.

Fred drove on. Miles of desolate farmland passed on either side of the narrow, dirt road. Some of it was vacant fields already past the time of harvest, some of it dense pine wood and marsh. There was such an air of despair and hopelessness about the area. It was a land that knew no prosperity, no joy, and no fighting chance of being anything but what it was forever destined to be...a bleak and colorless wasteland.

A land as lifeless as the territory of Fred's own floundering spirit.

Agnes sucked on the lemon drops she had bought before leaving Milwaukee and fiddled with the knobs on the radio until a Hank Williams song blared from the speaker. Teddy and Roger giggled and gasped over their comics and slurped from near empty bottles of Nehi Grape bought at a little mom and pop grocery thirty miles back.

And Fred drove...and drove and drove.

Finally, something showed itself amid the snow-speckled fields and rampant forest. A lonely farmhouse stood a hundred yards from the edge of the roadway, along with a scattering of rickety buildings: a barn, chicken coop and outhouse. He didn't slow down at first, though, simply for the reason that the place looked totally abandoned. No vehicles sat in the weedy drive, the windows of the house looked dark and curtained, and what few pieces of farm machinery remained in the yard looked as though they had rusted into uselessness long ago.

But Agnes wasn't so easily convinced. "Stop," she demanded, placing a meaty hand on his slender arm.

"Looks like the place is deserted, dear. I don't think anyone lives there."

"Well, check anyway," she insisted. Her fingers dug into what little muscle he possessed, sending spikes of pain through his upper arm. "I'm tired of wandering around this godforsaken country."

He nodded, said "Yes, dear," and pulled off the road into the driveway of the isolated farmstead.

The boys in the back discarded their comics, craning their necks to see where their sudden detour was taking them. "Neat-O!" said Roger. "A haunted house!"

Yes, thought Fred. That was exactly what it looked like. A house occupied only by ghosts, by the spiritual remnants of the unliving. As he parked a short distance from the building and cut the Chevy's engine, Fred examined it from the warmth and safety of the automobile. It was a typical example of the mid-western farmhouse: two-storied, white clapboarded, its pitched roof and the overhang of the porch covered with a blanket of new November snow. He regarded the windows from his vantage point. A few were boarded over or covered with sheets of curling tarpaper, while others were merely shuttered or sealed off with blinds. The narrow porch was barren. No picturesque rocking chairs or romantic hanging swing adorned it; just naked floorboards and a weathered front door with no screen.

Agnes nudged him in the ribs with a fleshy elbow. "Well, what are you waiting for? Get out and ask."

"I really don't think there's anyone here," he told her, knowing there was no use in arguing about it."

"Humor me," said Agnes in a voice that told him that she very much needed to be humored.

Fred shrugged and, opening the door, stepped into the cold November afternoon.

"Can we go with him, Mom?" asked Teddy. "I gotta pee."

"Me, too." Roger tugged on his coat, as well as his genuine Davy Crockett coonskin cap. "Real bad."

Agnes frowned, partly out of disgust and partly from an overly sour lemon drop. "Okay, go on. But you'd better do your business and do it right. This is definitely the last pit-stop we're making until we get to your Uncle Ben's."

The boys piled out of the back of the car and joined their father, who was stepping through the slushy snow and making a slow trek to the front porch of the house.

"Betcha there's a ghost in there," said Teddy. "A headless man who carries around a bloody axe, looking for another noggin to replace his lost one."

Roger giggled with delight. "Naw, even better...a flesh-eating ghoul who digs up graveyards and breaks into tombs."

Fred looked around at the youngsters as they ran across the yard and hopped up on the porch. "You boys should've stayed in the car."

"We gotta pee."

"All right. There's an outhouse around back. But you boys be careful. Don't go falling into the hole."

The brothers thought that was hilarious. Their laughter rang through the rural silence like a jarring intrusion as they disappeared around the side of the house, sending clods of snow and mud flying beneath their churning feet.

Fred knocked on the top panel of the front door. The sound of his knuckles on the bare wood echoed through the old house. He stood there for a long moment, listening, hearing nothing within. He tried again, putting more force into it this time. Still no answer.

He turned back to the car. Agnes scowled through the Chevy's windshield, motioning for him to try around back.

Fred knew he would get no peace until he did as she said, so he left the empty porch and walked around the right side of the house.

When he made it around back, he noticed that the outhouse door was open, but that there was no one inside. "Maybe they did fall in," he told himself. But his sudden fear faded when he spotted their tracks in the snow, leading both to the privy and then back again to the rear of the old house.

"Teddy, Roger...are you in there?" He went to the screen door and found the inside door open, revealing the shadowy interior of a summer kitchen. Reluctantly, he stepped inside.

It took a moment for his eyes to adjust to the murky surroundings. The summer kitchen was nearly empty. Only a few crates and heaps of trash and old newspaper furnished the cramped room. He walked to a dark corner where a rope was slung over a ceiling beam. At the end of the rope was a crude, wooden crossbar.

Fred crouched and examined the dusty planks of the floor, directly beneath the block-and-tackle. A broad, tacky stain dyed the boards a rusty reddish-brown. Blood. Obviously, the owner of this place was a hunter and used the summer kitchen to dress out his game. The crossbar would have been strong enough to suspend a good-sized deer by its hind feet.

He stood there and stared at the contraption for a long moment. Soon, his imagination played out a grisly scene. He could see Agnes hanging from the crossbar by her heels, naked and submissive...the hunted. And he was a hunter, standing before her, long-bladed knife firmly in hand, ready to butcher her like a hog.

Fred turned his eyes from the crossbar and cleared his head of the disturbing tableau. At first, he was appalled at having conjured such a thought. But then again, he couldn't help but admit a lingering satisfaction. He was sure some psychiatrist would have had an appropriate term for his gruesome, little fantasy, maybe some high-browed explanation about a passive husband's underly-ing hatred for his domineering wife. Not that Fred would have ever thought of actually telling a shrink about his daydreams. In that day and time, revealing such things about one's psyche could land you in a rubber room.

A noise from somewhere inside the house drew Fred's attention and he stepped into the household's work-ing kitchen. Once again he called out "Hello, anybody home?" The rafters creaked overhead, as if someone walked across the upstairs floor. "Teddy? Roger? Are you boys up there?"

He received no reply.

The regular kitchen was even more cluttered than the adjoining room. There were the usual furnishings: a cup-board, an old iron cook stove, and a kitchen table with four straight-back chairs. He had to climb over a heap of refuse in the floor. Junk was everywhere. Burlap bags, cardboard boxes full of yellowed newspaper and old de-tective magazines, and empty tin cans and bottles with remnants of food still clinging to the insides. The kitchen windows were shuttered, allowing only a few slashes of pale gray light through the wooden slats.

He was stepping over a carton of *Startling Detec-tive* and *True Crime* magazines, when muffled laughter echoed from the upper floor. His heart leapt to his throat, for he couldn't determine whether the sound was that of a child or an adult.

Fred lost his balance and bumped against the edge of the table. Among the clutter of empty packages and dirty dishes, was an oddly-shaped soup bowl made of hard pottery or plaster. His agitation at the unexpected noise upset the bowl, causing it to rock on its uneven base and spill the dregs of chicken noodle soup on the tabletop.

He began to notice some strange things then. A couple of books lay next to the soup bowl. One was the Holy Bible, while the other was a volume called *Peckney's Science of Embalming*. And the wicker upholstery of the kitchen chairs seemed to have been refurbished with narrow strips of supple leather. He laid his hand on the interlaced seat of the chair nearest him. It was the finest example of hide tanning he had ever come across.

In fact, it was almost as soft as Agnes' skin...and nearly as repulsive to the touch.

The spell of creepiness conjured by the isolated house broke when the drumming of feet descended the staircase of the outer hallway. Teddy and Roger burst into the kitchen, giggling, their eyes bright with excitement. They grabbed their father's hands and began to drag him to the stairway. "Come with us, Dad," they urged. "You gotta see all the neat stuff that's upstairs!"

Fred didn't want to go upstairs, though. "We're trespassing here, boys," he said with as much parental authority as he could muster. "If the owner came back and found us, we'd be in a lot of trouble."

"Aw, come on, Dad! Please?"

Fred was firm. "No. Now let's get back to the car."

When they got to the car, Agnes was waiting. "Well?"

"Like I said, there was no one home." Fred started up the Chevy and began to back out of the driveway.

The boys' excitement hadn't abated since leaving the house. "You oughta have seen all the great stuff that was stashed upstairs!" piped Teddy with a grin.

"Oh, really?" asked their mother absently, more interested in lemon drops and finding something other than a "hick station" on the radio than anything the children might have to say.

"Yeah! In one bedroom there were masks made out of real human faces hanging on the walls and bleached skulls sticking on the bedposts."

"And that wasn't all!" added Roger. "In the closet there was a woman's skin hanging up like a suit of clothes, with bosoms and everything, and there was a Quaker Oats box full of noses. And in a shoebox there were a bunch of funny-looking things that kinda looked like hairy, little mouths..."

Agnes's face loomed over the edge of the front seat, beet-red and furious. "All right, that's quite enough! Hand them over, right this moment!"

The boys stared at her with a mixture of innocence and fear. "Hand *what* over?"

"You know what I mean! Those blasted comic books!"

Glumly, Teddy and Roger surrendered their copies of *Tales from the Crypt* and *The Vault of Horror*. With an angry flourish, their mother snatched the EC comics from them and tossed them in the floorboard at her feet.

"I've had enough of this garbage! I won't have my children turning into weirdoes or juvenile delinquents!"

"I think you're overreacting, dear," said Fred as he steered the car back onto the road. "I grew up with monsters and ghosts when I was a kid. It's just harmless fun, that's all."

Agnes was unswayed in her opinion however. "Frankenstein and Dracula are one thing. Mutilation, walking corpses, and cannibalism are quite another. Just like that Senate subcommittee says, these confounded horror comics are ruining our children's moral values and leading them down the road to depravity!"

There was nothing more to be said. The children sank into dark despair in the back seat, knowing that no amount of whining or pleading would return their precious comics to them. And Fred wasn't about to push the issue. If he did, Agnes would be sure to blame him for the boys' preoccupation with the macabre and begin one

357

of her endless monologues about his many failures as a husband and father.

Silently, Fred shifted into gear and headed north down the secluded, rural road.

They had only gone a few yards, when a maroon sedan—a '49 Ford from the make and model—turned a curve and headed toward them in the opposite lane.

"There's a car," said Agnes. "Wave it down and see if you can find out where we are."

Fred complied, honking his horn and waving out the side window. The Ford eased to a halt beside the Chevy and the driver rolled down his window. The man was a farmer by the looks of his clothing: denim overalls, a woolen coat, and a plaid deerhunter's cap. He was slightly built, his features average in many ways, except for a drooping left eye and a silly, little grin on his stubbled face.

"Excuse me," said Fred almost apologetically. "But could you tell me how to get to Plainfield?"

The man in the car smiled sheepishly and nodded. "Sure. It's about seven miles straight ahead of you. It's kinda small, but you can't miss it."

"Thanks," replied Fred.

Before the two drivers rolled up their respective windows against the bite of the November cold, their eyes met for an instant. They exchanged something then, something that had more to do with feelings than words spoken aloud. Fred couldn't figure out precisely what it was. Maybe a mutual understanding. Maybe a fleeting link between two kindred spirits who would meet only once during a lifetime, then move on, never to cross paths again.

And there was something else, something mildly disturbing. A sharing of dark emotions such as loneliness and utter despair. Emotions best concealed in the far reaches of the mortal mind...like refuse and filth hidden behind the shuttered windows of a desolate farmhouse.

The friendly motorist gave Fred a twisted grin and drove on. Fred did likewise. He glanced in the rearview mirror and saw the maroon automobile slow in front of the farmstead that the Barnett family had just left. Before turning into the rutted dirt drive, the car passed a weathered mailbox with the name GEIN painted on the side.

"Keep your eyes on the road, for God's sake!" snapped Agnes. "You want to kill us before we even get there?"

"No, dear," replied Fred. There was an unusual edge to his voice that perhaps only he could hear. He regarded his wife's face thoughtfully. It was a deceptive face, one that was soft and fleshy, yet hard and full of cynicism. It was a face of uncompromising strength and scathing ridicule. A face that was the very opposite of his own.

As he turned his attention back to the isolated stretch of Wisconsin roadway, Fred wondered how it would feel to possess such a face and stare at the world through those cold and unforgiving eyes.

BENEATH
BLACK BAYOU

I always wondered how it would be to be thrust into a situation where you were forced to live an existence that was less than human. It has happened before, in the concentration camps of Auschwitz and Treblinka, or the prison camps of Cambodia and Vietnam. Places where one's basic humanity is stripped away, humiliatingly so, until only an animalistic instinct for survival remains.

But what if, after enduring the degradation of such an experience, you denied the chance of returning to normalcy? What if your damaged psyche was so entrenched in the muck and mire of depravity that you shunned the thought of returning to your former state?

REUBEN Traugott set off into the swamp in search of his brother, Lemuel. He took his most water-tight pirogue, a canteen of fresh water, a quarter pound of possum jerky, and a twelve-gauge Mossberg pump. But even as he headed across the dark waters, Rube knew deep down in his soul that he would never find his troublesome sibling alive.

Most who ventured into Black Bayou after nightfall never were.

The bayou held a dozen different dangers, perils that shunned the light of day, yet emerged at twilight to swallow its careless victims whole. There were quicksand pools, poisonous snakes, and wild animals weary of rabbits and weasels, eager for a change of menu. The Cajuns even whispered of the evil La Sanguinaire, a species of demonic spider that trapped wayward swampers in its misty web and fed upon their life's blood.

And then there was Ma Gator. Old Ma was Black Bayou's resident man-eater. It wasn't known if the alligator was indeed a female or not, but the sheer fury of her constant attacks reminded the men in the area of a wrathful woman with an axe to grind. Ma was said to be well over eighteen feet long from toothy snout to scaly tail and close to a thousand pounds in weight. There was no record of precisely how many men had been killed by the gator, but there was speculation that the number had grown to nearly thirty-five since the mid-1950s. Usually the only thing found to mark a Ma Gator attack was the ruin of a canoe or pirogue floating upon the still waters and, occasionally, an arm or leg that had been severed by Ma's massive jaws and forgotten as she dragged the remainder of her catch to the muddy bottom of Black Bayou.

Rube headed out at daybreak, hoping to find some sign of Lem's whereabouts by afternoon, which would allow him enough time to make it back to Point Bleau before darkness fell. His brother had been a damned fool for taking his canoe across the bayou the night before, but then such behavior was to be expected of a man like Lem Traugott. The trapper was a notorious drunkard and wife-beater, and his indiscretions were what drove him from his home twelve hours before. Lem had come in all liquored up and angry over having lost at poker. He had decided to take out some of the misery of his misfortune on his children rather than his long-suffering spouse. But Harriet Traugott had not taken kindly to that. She had grabbed an old scattergun from the corner and peppered Lem's britches with rock salt. Lem had lit out of there like a scalded hog. Cursing to the high heavens, he had untied his canoe and set off across the bayou. Harriet had expected him to show up in time for breakfast the next morning, shame-faced and sore-tailed, but he had not.

So Rube was on the bayou looking for him. The swamper rowed his low, wooden boat slowly through gnarled columns of water-logged Cyprus. Sunlight was sparse, scarcely able to penetrate the upper layer of dense foliage and stringy Spanish moss that hung from the limbs overhead. By noon, Rube had drank half his canteen and nibbled away most of the possum jerky, and still he hadn't discovered hide or hair of old Lem.

It was nearing three in the afternoon and Rube was seriously considering turning back, when he spotted a gleam of sunlight on bare metal a hundred yards ahead. He rowed up next to a sandbar and found the rear half of Lem's canoe beached there. It looked as if it had been cut in half with a chainsaw. But Rube knew exactly what had done it. Only the snaggle-toothed jaws of Ma Gator could have torn the narrow boat so violently asunder.

He made a slow circle of the sandbar, looking for more evidence of poor Lem, but all he found was a splintered oar and his brother's soggy hat with a couple of crawdads walking around the brim. He yelled Lem's name several times, but to no avail. He found himself feeling a little foolish calling to a man who was probably in the process of being digested at that very moment.

"I am sorry, my brother," apologized the Cajun after uttering a silent prayer. "But I must head on back without you. One Traugott for supper is quite enough for dat wicked bitch."

But Ma Gator wasn't so sure.

As Rube steered his pirogue north and started back for Point Bleau, he felt the boat rise below him. It lurched a good two feet into the humid Louisiana air, then hit the water's surface with a resounding splash. Rube forgot the oars and grabbed for his shotgun. He was in the act of jacking a shell into the breech when a great, leathery tail, as thick as a tree trunk and covered with algae and barnacles, rose from the swamp and lashed out. It hit the barrel of the Mossberg, sending the twelve-gauge spinning from his hands and into a dense clump of cattails. Then the tail continued to fall. Like an unyielding pillar of stone it struck the pirogue squarely in its center, parting the sturdy dugout as if it was made of flimsy paper maché.

Abruptly, Rube found himself in the water. He kicked off his knee-high boots and began to swim for the sandbar he had just left. He was halfway there when he felt a heavy tug at his right leg. His heart played a symphony of dread as he felt himself sinking. A crushing pain gripped his lower body as an eighteen-foot demon began to haul him to the very depths of hell.

But, unlike the hell of his upbringing, it was not one of fire and brimstone. This hell was a decidedly liquid one, as cold and black as the womb of a dead woman.

■■■

Rube Traugott awoke...but not in the belly of Ma Gator.

He found himself lying in two inches of rank swamp mud, surrounded by total darkness. He reached up and his hand touched the slimy stone three feet overhead. He was in some sort of cave...an underwater cave from the sound and motion of water lapping at the narrow opening to his left.

Trembling, he ran his hand down his belly toward his lower body and the sharp pulse of agony that had brought him back to consciousness. Relief flooded him as he discovered his right leg intact. It was cocked at a strange angle and broken in a place or two, but was still attached to his hip. But what was he doing here? And why hadn't Ma Gator gorged herself on him during their frantic struggle near the sandbar?

Slowly, Rube's mind cleared and he found that he had a pretty good idea. Gators rarely ate large game at a single meal. While the reptiles gulped down bullfrogs and swamp coons like popcorn, they preferred to take their time with larger critters. It was well known to the Cajun that a gator would sometimes drag a wild boar or small deer down into the depths of the bayou and stash it away in its underwater lair. There it would remain in storage, safe from rival predators, until the gator returned to consume it at leisure.

But there was something particularly odd about Ma Gator's latest catch. It was still very much alive.

Rube sat up and bumped his head on the cave's low ceiling. The man cussed and lay back down, propping himself up by an elbow. He breathed raggedly in the darkness and gagged on the cloying smell of stagnant mud and something else. He had to concentrate for a moment before he realized that the offending odor was that of decay. The creeping decay of something that had not been dead for very long, but was turning sour mighty fast.

The swamper rummaged through his trouser pockets. All he had with him was his lucky buckeye, a black plastic Ace comb, a three-bladed Case pocketknife, and the old Zippo lighter he had carried around with him since the Army. He sat there for a moment, as if waiting for his eyes to adjust to the darkness, but no dice. There was no light to separate shadow from contrast, not even from the narrow mouth of the cave.

Almost reluctantly, he opened the lid of the lighter. He didn't really want to see the cramped conditions of his predicament or the putrid thing that shared it with him. But Rube Traugott was not a man to pussyfoot around when things looked bleak. He placed his thumb on the roller and struck the flint.

The flame licked up, casting a pale glow on the surroundings. The depth of the cave, from mouth to back wall was about thirty feet. Gator dung and old bones lay scattered across the muddy floor. In the corner there was a broad nest constructed of wilted ferns and thick moss. Amid the hollow of the nest were six leathery eggs. The unhatched young'uns of Ma Gator.

Then Rube turned around and the flickering light of the Zippo revealed the source of that godawful stench.

It was the body of his lost brother. Lem lay on his side, arms gnarled into fighting claws of fruitless rebellion, his pale face stretched taut into a rictus of horrible fear. Rube directed his light downward and found that his brother's body ended just below the ribcage. Ma Gator had bitten the poor bastard clean in half.

Rube was overcome with shock and nausea. He doubled over and vomited up that afternoon's jerky, as well as the sorghum molasses and biscuits he had eaten for breakfast. He tossed the Zippo aside and the blue-yellow flame winked out as the lid snapped shut on impact. Merciful darkness embraced him once again. But the smell—oh dear Lord, that confounded smell was still there, stronger than ever.

His brain boiling hot with panic, Rube scrambled for the narrow opening of the cave and squeezed through. Abruptly, he was surrounded by cold, black water. He struggled against the chill blanket of liquid limbo, bubbles of oxygen flooding from his mouth and nostrils. His eyes caught a glimmer of soft light from above and he knew that he was looking at the surface of Black Bayou. He kicked against the muddy bottom, pushing himself upward. An explosion of white-hot agony shot through his shattered leg, sending a wave of sickening dizziness through him. It seemed as though he surged toward the growing light for an eternity. Then his head broke through the barrier and he was back into the world of the living, back into *his* world.

But not for very long.

The first thing he saw when he reached the surface was Ma Gator. She lay on the sandbar, sunning herself in the last crimson rays of the Louisiana sunset. The splash of his emergence drew the reptile's attention. With a snap of horrid bear trap jaws, Ma bellied toward the edge of the sandbar and slid smoothly into the water after him.

Rube had no choice but to return to the dungeon from which he had escaped. He kicked and flailed wildly, diving deeper, ever deeper into the pit of murky darkness. He could feel Ma Gator behind him, getting closer, her huge tail propelling her forward like a leathery torpedo. On his way down, Rube wondered if he would even be able to find the cave again. He struggled with the twisted roots of a sunken cypress for one maddening moment, escaping from its tangle only seconds before the gator's jaws could grab hold.

Then there it was—the narrow mouth of the under-water lair. He pulled himself through and skittered across the mud and excrement to the back wall. His hasty entrance was followed by that of Ma Gator. She poked her huge head through the slit of stone, snapping and bellowing like an angry bull. He could not see the monster coming for him; it was much too dark. For some reason that was much worse than experiencing the horror close up and personal—the thought of not knowing when violent death would come to claim him.

He cringed against the rear wall, squeezing into a thin crevice that ran from ceiling to floor. He held his breath. He could hear the wet sound of Ma Gator crawling through the muck toward him. Rube felt something blunt and alive press against the foot of his injured leg and he knew that it was the reptile's probing nose. He cried out in fear and pain, and pressed himself further into the crevice. As he did so, his hand brushed a long, hard object lying near the nest of eggs. His fingers enclosed the bludgeon. With a snarl of desperation, Rube struck blindly at the stalking gator, catching it across the snout. Ma bellowed with surprise and began to back away. He struck

367

out again and again, driving the gator toward the mouth of the cramped cave. His other hand came into play and grabbed hold. Swinging the object like a baseball bat, he laid a stunning blow between Ma's beady eyes, or the spot where he assumed they were.

It did the trick. The alligator had had enough for now. She slid back through the opening, into the freedom of the open bayou. "Git yourself on away from here, you ugly she-bitch!" sobbed Rube. He collapsed against the floor of the cave and listened to the fading sounds of Ma Gator's retreat.

After a while, he gathered the will to get up. He scrambled around the cave for a time, searching for his discarded lighter. He finally found it. Once again he snapped it on. The fluid-fed wick revealed the true nature of the weapon in his hand. The thing he had chased Ma Gator away with was the denuded leg bone of a full-grown man.

Rube laughed until he cried. "Looky here, dear brother," he cackled, waving the femur above his head. "Now wasn't dat a good one pulled on de old gator, do you not think so?"

Lem Traugott gave no reply. He only laid there and grimaced grotesquely at his living brother. Death had done nothing to improve Lem's sense of humor, which hadn't been much to begin with.

Despite the stink of the decaying body, Rube tenderly propped Lem's upper torso against the back wall and secured the Zippo in the stiffened fingers of one of his hands. He frowned in disapproval at the state of his brother's appearance. He pulled a couple of bloated leeches from Lem's unshaven cheeks and combed the mud-plastered hair carefully into place with the Ace comb. It helped to promote the illusion of life, but not very much. There was still that frozen mask of unspeakable terror seizing his brother's lard-white face. A terror that would remain, transfixed, for as long as the flesh was intact.

■■■

Hours passed. Exhausted, Rube slept, dreaming of him and Lem as children, of the coon hunts they had taken through the marshland and the Huck Finn raft of cut saplings they had constructed and poled all the way down to Baton Rouge.

When he awoke he was hungry. The stench of decay had intensified, but that didn't seem to ruin his appetite. He lit the Zippo again, aware that the flame was growing shorter and dimmer with each use. He had no earthly idea whether it was morning or evening, noonday or night. He had no timepiece to consult with. His father had passed his pocket watch down to the elder Lem upon his deathbed. Whole lot of good it had done his brother, though. The big railroad watch was probably ticking its way through the maze of Ma Gator's bowels by now.

His stomach grumbled, pleading for nourishment. Slyly, he turned his eyes toward the nest in the far corner.

Rube crawled over and took one of the leathery, gray eggs in his hand. His fingers dug into the soft shell and a slimy residue erupted through the punctures. He could feel the small, warm body of a gator embryo loll against his fingertips.

"Eat me, will you, Ma Gator?" grinned Rube. "Maybe so. But a condemned man, he must have his last meal. And while you have a taste for man-meat, I have my own...for gator."

And, with that, he split the shell in half and swallowed the fetus in a single, savory gulp.

■■■

Existence in the gator's lair drew on, changing the shape of Rube Traugott's life, twisting it into something less than that of a human being.

By his estimate—which was distorted and imprecise given the circumstances—he had been holed up there for nearly four days. He had set his broken leg the best he could, using the discarded bones of Ma Gator's victims as splints and strips of cloth from his shirt to bind them with. The limb was crooked and stiff, but the sickening pain had reduced considerably, leaving only dull throbbing.

He found himself sleeping often, like an animal burrowed into hibernation. He had plenty of water to sustain him and outside air filtered from the narrow crack at the rear of the cave. While awake, he kept a fire burning using the Zippo and dry tinder from the nest. Sometimes he sang the old songs and told the corny jokes that he and Lem had traded around campfires during their youth. But his was the only voice that rang through the cramped cave. Lem simply sat there, silent in his slow but steady decomposition.

Sustenance was the biggest problem. He had finished off the last of the gator eggs, as well as any slugs, insects, or leeches he could find in the cave. Despite the severity of his broken leg, he had tried several times to reach freedom. Each attempt, however, had proven futile. Ma Gator was always somewhere around, either laying on the muddy bottom near the entrance or swimming along the bayou surface, always aware of what stirred above and below her. Each time he would regain the safety of the cave, he would find his brother sitting there waiting for his return. And, as his hunger grew from nagging urge to cramping pain, Rube began to regard Lem not as a silent cellmate, but more and more as a side of meat that was rotting needlessly before his feverish eyes.

Once, Ma Gator had come visiting, gathering the nerve to return to the lair after the sound beating she had received at the end of a leg bone. Rube had been napping, when a great splash and a hoarse bellow shocked him from his slumber. He awoke just as Ma's massive jaws shot forward and clamped down. But it wasn't he who suffered the gator's attack, but his brother. The reptile snagged Lem's left arm and began to drag the corpse toward the mouth of the cave. With a scream of angry defiance, Rube reached for his brother's half-body,

370

grabbing it around the neck. Man and gator fought for a solid minute, subjecting the carcass to a grisly tug-o-war. Finally the rope gave out. Lem's arm tore away at the shoulder with a moist rip. Satisfied for the time being, Ma Gator slipped back into the watery darkness, taking the limb with her.

Rube sat there, cradling his rescued brother before the smoldering fire. He held him close and sobbed with the abandon of a frightened youngster. Rube tried desperately to recall memories of him and Lem in the years past, the happy times they had shared along the mossy banks of Black Bayou. But no such recollections surfaced. There was nothing but the encroaching of primitive emotion, eroding away the remaining layers of civilized behavior from his weary mind. Soon, he feared, those dark emotions would grow so powerful that they would drive him toward total madness.

He hugged his brother's body closer, snuggling against it like a child to a battered teddy bear. As his tears began to play out and he drifted to sleep, Rube noticed that the awful stench didn't bother him nearly as much as it had before.

■■■

Rube knew that he must try for freedom once more—before the fine black worms of insanity burrowed too deeply into the tender meat of his brain and gained complete control.

"Farewell, my brother," he said, eyeing the pale form at the rear of the cave with genuine affection. Then he took the folding knife from his pocket and extended the longest and sharpest of the bunch. He would have much rather had a harpoon to defend himself with, but the lock blade would have to do. Taking a deep breath of stagnant air, Rube plunged into the dark waters and began his slow journey to the surface.

Halfway there, he met up with his nemesis. Ma Gator emerged from out of the murky darkness. She swept past and struck him a powerful wallop with a swipe of her tail. He felt ribs crack beneath the force of the blow. The impact and pain drove the reserve of air from his tortured lungs and he felt nasty water begin to snake its way into his nostrils and down his throat.

The gator made a sluggish U-turn and, again, came for him. He knew that there was nothing to do now but kill the monster, or die trying. Motionlessly, he floated there, playing possum, lulling Ma Gator into a false sense of triumph. Then, as the gator's mouth opened to receive its prize, Rube surged up and over the lengthy snout. He found his intended target—the creature's left eye—and, with both hands, drove the blade of the pocketknife downward. The honed blade slid smoothly and without error into the gator's orb. Ma thrashed and snapped, but to no avail. Rube wasn't about to withdraw the knife from the fatal wound. Instead, he pushed harder, bearing down with all his strength, sending the blade past the occipital bone and into the brain.

Ma Gator jerked in a final, rolling spasm, then grew limp and still. Slowly, she began to sink downward toward the murky depths of Black Bayou.

Free! thought Rube Traugott. *Free from the fiend who imprisoned me!*

He began to work his way upward, toward the surface of the bayou and the bright warmth of daylight beyond. There life reigned eternal, full of love, hope, and laughter. Birds sang from leafy branches, hounds bayed and barked joyfully as they chased fox and coon, old men joked and gossiped on the porch of the general store, and young men asked demure ladies to share a dance at the tune of a Cajun fiddle and squeezebox accordion.

Reuben Traugott would go back to his family and fish and trap and live the remainder of his years as a happy and contented man.

But the closer he grew to the shimmering surface, the more that idyllic life seemed impossible, even perversely absurd, in nature. His life beyond Black Bayou had ended in the depths of the gator's lair. It had come to a close with insanity's dark victory and the hideous acts he had performed by the light of a tiny fire.

Rube's heart pounded with panic, his brain swelling with horror as he came within a foot of bursting through. He swam there for a long moment, then began to ease back down into the comforting black depths. As the light of day faded into memory, he drifted to the soft mud bottom, letting the cold currents engulf him, letting the blind catfish and slithering swamp snakes caress his doubts and fears away.

Letting the loving embrace of Black Bayou welcome him home once again.

■■■

Emery DeBossier set off into the swamp in search of the Traugott brothers. He took his john-boat with the big 75-horsepower outboard, his Winchester .30-30, and a Coleman lantern. He had no great expectations of finding Reuben or Lemuel, however. He knew Black Bayou and its reputation well enough to have his doubts.

Unlike most men in Point Bleau, though, Emery was not one who feared the twilight hours. He searched throughout the day and, when dusk passed into night, he didn't seek the safety of the locked door or the comfort of the woodstove. Rather, he ventured further into the far reaches of the dreaded backwater bayou.

It was well after midnight when he made his discovery. Fragments of both brothers' boats laid scattered upon a sandbar, like a graveyard of ships that had chanced a perilous reef and fallen victim to its hidden dangers.

He lit the lantern and steered his john-boat closer to the wreckage.

Suddenly, a gorge of water broke to his right and a long, leathery tail arched through the night air. It hit the glass chimney of the lantern, shattering it. Flaming kerosene splashed across Emery's face and hands. Quickly and without a second thought, he plunged into the cold waters of the bayou, dousing the burning flames before they could do much damage.

The shock of the sudden dive cleared his head, bringing him to the realization that he was in a very dangerous situation. He was about to climb back into the boat, when something grabbed his right foot. He fought the best he could, but he was an old man and not as strong as he had once been. He felt his fingers slipping from the smooth fiberglass hull, betraying him, surrendering him to the thing that grappled with him from below.

The cold black water rushed up to swallow him. He kicked and flailed as the creature pulled him under. His knife! He had nearly forgotten about it! Emery reached for the eight-inch skinner he carried on his right hip. But it wasn't there. It had been—only moments ago. It was as if someone had grasped the staghorn handle and pulled it from the sheath mere seconds before he could get to it.

Deeper into the depths of Black Bayou he sank, the smothering cloud of watery darkness engulfing him. Soon, he could fight it no longer and found himself blacking out.

Emery DeBossier didn't expect to awaken, but he did. He lay there for a while, disoriented and confused. He seemed to be in some sort of cave—a cramped and dank cave underwater. But, strangely enough, it didn't seem like the lair of some marauding reptile. A small fire burned in the corner, casting an eerie glow upon the slimy walls of the cave, upon his shuddering and soaked form, and on the thing that sat nearby.

It was a skeleton. Or, rather, half a skeleton. Its bones were stark white and clean, as if it had hung in some college biology lab instead of moldering in the depths of a dark and muddy cave. Something about it disturbed

Emery to no end. It was *too* clean. No animal could have done that. No animal could have picked the bones of flesh so meticulously and with such cunning precision.

Then, abruptly, the emphasis of Emery's terror shifted. The water at the mouth of the cave began to ripple and churn as his captor arrived. He cringed against the far wall as the great, toothy head poked its way into the cave. Emery could only watch, mortified, as the alligator crammed itself into the limited space. There was something vaguely strange about the way the gator moved, about the way its pebbled skin hung loosely on its body. But the Cajun did not give much thought to such things. All that concerned him at that moment was the dead-meat stench of the creature's breath and the mixture of malice and hunger that gleamed in its single, reptilian eye.

"Ma Gator!" he gasped as the horrid thing shambled closer.

"No," a familiar voice rasped in reply. "But you may call me Pa."

A hand appeared from a slit in the reptile's belly, an undeniably *human* hand, and in its grasp was the old man's missing knife.

It was then that Emery DeBossier looked into the gator's open maw and, from the innermost darkness, saw a grin within a grin.

EXIT 85

When traveling, I sometimes get an uneasy feeling whenever I get off an unfamiliar exit on the interstate. Not the exits with a dozen fast food restaurants and an outlet mall, but those that seem utterly desolate, offering only a rundown gas station and a mom-and-pop diner, if even that.

Often, the folks there act like they really don't want you there in the first place. Or, if they do, it could be for a particularly nasty reason...

BRIAN glanced down at the gas gauge again. The needle was angled downward, dangerously close to the E mark.

He sighed and stared through the windshield. Interstate 75 stretched ahead, the flat black pavement illuminated by the van's headlights and nothing more. There was no moon to speak of that night. The swampy Florida terrain on either side of the interstate was cloaked in darkness. As far as he could tell, there wasn't a single streetlight in sight, or even the lighted window of a distant house. There was only the pale swath of the Windstar's headlights and the bright reflective markers that separated the two northbound lanes of I-75.

Brian tried to keep his annoyance to a minimum and glanced around at the other members of the Reid family. His wife, Jenny, was asleep in the passenger seat, her pretty face turned away from him. In the back, his two children also slept. Five-year-old Kendall was dozing beneath the restraints of his seatbelt, his Mickey Mouse ears cocked haphazardly over his eyes. The baby, Anne, who was barely over a year old, slept peacefully in her car seat, still wearing the Winnie the Pooh bib they had purchased at one of the Magic Kingdom souvenir shops.

He began to regret his decision to leave Florida that evening. Looking back, he knew they should have stayed the night in Orlando and gotten a fresh start the following morning. But after a week at Disney World, they had all pretty much been burnt out and were more than ready to get back home to Illinois.

The one thing Brian Reid hadn't bargained for was the long stretches of desolation between the interstate exits. It hadn't seemed so bad during the drive down, in broad daylight. But in the dead of night, the remote areas seemed to go on endlessly. He had driven for nearly fifteen miles since passing Exit 84, and now he wished he had stopped at the Amoco station there, like Jenny had suggested. Now his gas tank was almost dry and there wasn't a gas station in sight.

Brian reached for the radio and flipped the dial from one station to another, an annoying habit his wife had tried to break him of during their six years of marriage. A minute later he came upon a fuzzy classic rock station. Pink Floyd drifted softly through the van's speaker system as he continued down the road.

He was about to give up hope, when he spotted the reflective green rectangle of an exit sign up ahead. He was nearly upon the sign before he could read what was written on it.

378

EXIT 85—JASPER—SUWANNEE SPRINGS—½ MILE

"Finally," he murmured beneath his breath. He spotted the exit ramp ahead and, switching on his turn signal, veered into the far right lane.

Thirty seconds later, he was off the interstate and crossing an overpass to a gathering of unlit buildings with equally dark signs. He saw the round, star-emblazoned sign of an old Texaco station and headed toward it, keeping his fingers crossed on the steering wheel.

Brian pulled off the road and studied the station as he braked to a halt. There was a pale light in the station office, as well as lights shining through the small, greasy windows of the two auto repair bays. Was someone on duty, or was he just being overly optimistic?

"Aw, come on," he grumbled quietly. "I'm desperate here." He sighed again, then cut the van's engine to conserve what little fuel he had left. Jenny and the kids seemed oblivious to the stop. They continued to sleep soundly.

Brian climbed out of the van and stretched, feeling the bones of his lower spine crackle. He closed the door quietly and looked around. The Texaco station was the only building on the left side of the road. On the opposite side were two other businesses; a greasy spoon café and a convenience store...both closed. Further down the road was a large billboard lit by a couple of spotlights. It read: BOB'S GATOR FARM—LIVE ALLIGATORS & REPTILES—SWAMP CURIOSITIES & SOUVENIRS— FLORIDA ORANGES & SALT WATER TAFFY—3 MILES AHEAD.

He turned back to the gas station. Brian was still uncertain whether the business was open or closed. He walked to the office and tried the door. It was locked. "I guess that answers my question."

He was passing the gas pumps and starting back to the van, when he heard a noise echo from the far side of the station. He turned and caught a glimpse of someone rounding the corner, merging with the darkness beyond.

379

Maybe he wasn't wasting his time after all.

He walked toward the end of the building. The night was muggy and his sport shirt clung damply to his back and beneath his armpits. An unpleasant smell hung in the air, a gassy odor like rotting vegetation.

A moment later, he was peering around the corner. At the rear of the station, a single sixty-watt bulb glowed in the darkness. A cloud of candleflies and mosquitoes swarmed around the dull, yellow light.

"Hello?" he called out. "Is anyone back there?"

At first, he heard only the reedy chirring of crickets in the tall grass. Then a coarse voice answered him. "Come on back," it invited.

Brian stepped around several old car batteries and bent wheel rims as he made his way toward the rear of the building. When he got there, he found the station's back lot to be just as junky as the side was. Crushed heaps of wrecked cars stretched off into the inky darkness and, closer to the station, stood stacks of bald tires and large hunks of busted concrete with rusty lengths of steel reinforcement protruding from them. There were also plenty of aluminum soda cans and beer bottles lying around.

For a moment, he couldn't locate the one who had spoken. "Where are you?" he asked, a little louder than before.

Movement came again, this time from the shadows between two stacks of retreads.

"Over here."

Brian suddenly felt as though he had made a mistake. He watched as the tall, lanky man stepped into the pale glow of the back door light. He was unshaven, with dirty blond hair and an even dirtier Atlanta Braves baseball cap. He was dressed in a ragged white undershirt, faded jeans, and a pair of Reeboks that looked on the verge of falling apart at the seams.

"Uh, do you work here?" Brian asked.

"Hell naw," said the man, eyeing the tourist carefully. "I was just camped out back here when I heard you pull up."

"Well, then, I'm sorry I woke you," apologized Brian.

He was about to leave, when the man reached into the back pocket of his jeans and took out a worn leather wallet. "Come here."

"What?"

"I said come here," the man said. "I got something to show you."

"I really have to go—"

A peculiar expression crossed the man's stubbled face. "I said for you to *come here* and *look.*"

Brian's uneasiness suddenly changed into fear. He wanted to turn and run, but he wasn't sure that was a wise thing to do. The man continued to watch him, as though studying the expression on his face and gauging every little move he made.

"Are you coming?"

"Yeah," said Brian nervously. "Sure."

Cautiously, he walked over to the man. The strong stench of sweat and unwashed clothing was nearly overpowering. But he gave no indication that the man's lack of cleanliness was offensive to him. He sensed he would be making a bad mistake if he did.

The man grinned as he opened the flap and slowly rummaged through the contents of his wallet. Brian spotted a couple of worn dollar bills and some scraps of paper. And something else...a wrinkled Polaroid snapshot nestled in the middle of it all.

"You wanna see something you ain't never seen before?" he asked, his voice a husky whisper. He looked the tourist square in the eyes.

Brian was suddenly aware of the uneven quality of his gaze. The left eye was bloodshot and sickly looking, while the right was almost too normal in appearance. In fact, there wasn't a red vein or imperfection of any kind. It practically *shined* in the yellow light of the back door lamp and when the other eye moved, it remained fixed and steady. It was a second before Brian realized that the man's right orb was made of glass.

"Well, do you wanna see it or not?"

Brian simply swallowed dryly and nodded. He had the feeling that he had better agree...with whatever the man had to say.

The man chuckled softly and withdrew the photo. "Look. Now ain't that pretty?"

Brian felt his breath catch in his chest and, for a moment, he felt as though he was suffocating.

The Polaroid had been taken in the sparse light of a campfire. The naked body of a young man, perhaps sixteen or seventeen years of age, lay on a bed of green moss. Its arms and legs had been hacked off and stacked in a heap to the side.

"That's my doing, you know," rasped the man. Pride gleamed in his one good eye. "Took that picture no more'n a month ago. Not far from here, either."

A mosquito lit on the side of Brian's neck and bit him, but he made no move to shoo the bug away. *You're insane*, Brian wanted to say, but he didn't. He didn't dare.

The man with the filthy blond hair and glass eye scowled and stuck the photograph back in his wallet. "Now don't you git to acting like everyone else I've shown this to."

Brian felt as though he were caught up in a nightmare. He began to back away slowly.

Faster than he would have expected, the man leapt around him, blocking his way. He drew something from a pouch on his belt: a folding pocketknife. He opened it with a flip of his wrist. It was a movement he seemed to be very adept at. A six-inch blade of razor sharpness snapped into view, its steel flat gleaming in the yellowish light.

"Now, you just hold up for a second, hoss," he said with an ugly grin.

"What...what do you want?' Brian managed to say. His heart pounded wildly in his chest.

"Well, if I ain't mistaken, what I *want* is in that van out yonder."

Cold dread bloomed in the pit of Brian's stomach. "My wife?"

"No." The man's grin grew thinner and broader. "The baby."

Brian opened his mouth to reply, but found that he couldn't.

"Looks about the right age to me," the man said. "About a year old, I'd guess."

"Yes," croaked Brian, although he couldn't figure out why he had answered.

The man licked his lips absently. "Ah, just tender enough. Over a slow fire with a little salt and pepper for seasoning. Maybe some wild onion on the side. You take it from me...there ain't nothing better."

Brian suddenly realized what the man was referring to. The very thought chilled him to the depths of his soul.

"Once I get rid of you, I reckon there won't be nothing stopping me," explained the lanky fellow. "The woman'll be dead before she even wakes up. The other young'un might scream a bit...but, hey, let him holler. Nobody's around to hear him anyhow."

He's going to kill me, Brian thought, his mind reeling. *He'll kill Jenny and Kendall, too. And then he's...oh, God...he's going to take Anne and—"*

The man took a slow step toward him. "Now let's hurry this up a bit, okay? It's getting late and I ain't had a bite all—"

Brian hurled himself at the man. He swung blindly at the man's face and felt his fist strike the bristled flat of his jaw. The man stumbled backward, then grinned and lashed out. The blade of the knife missed Brian the first time, but skimmed across his forearm the second. A sharp sting sent Brian into immediate retreat.

"I was gonna make this easy for you, son," the man told him. "But I reckon I'll just have to make it a little more interesting, since you're so all-fired anxious to get in my way."

Again, a burst of terror and rage surged through Brian. With a yell, he launched himself at the man. He caught him by the wrist and slammed it against the gas station wall several times. Finally, his fingers splayed open and the knife went spinning into the darkness.

"You ain't quite what I expected, boy," laughed the man. "But then I reckon I ain't what you expected either." He reached up with his free hand and grabbed hold of Brian's throat. His grubby fingers burrowed into his skin, as though attempting to poke through.

Brian felt his windpipe begin to close and, for a second, couldn't catch his breath. He knew the man was on the verge of killing him. But then he thought of his wife and two children in the Windstar and he knew he had to do something...fast...before he lost consciousness. He kicked out frantically with his left foot and finally managed to trip his assailant.

The man lost his balance and went down. There was a hollow *thunk* as his head struck one of the concrete blocks. Blood trickled from his ears as he moaned and rolled over, struggling to his hands and knees. He reached out blindly with one hand and found a discarded Bud Lite bottle. He curled his fingers around the neck and broke it against the hard ground. Light gleamed wickedly along the jagged brown glass.

"No," Brian whispered. He dropped to his knees, took the man's head in both hands, and drove it face down against the concrete block...forcing it upon one of the steel reinforcement rods.

There was a moment of resistance at first. Then there was a moist *pop* and Brian felt something hit his chest. The man's head slid downward until it could go no further.

Slowly, Brian stood up. The man's arms and legs twitched violently for fifteen seconds, then abruptly grew still. A long sigh of air hissed through his clenched teeth, then only the monotonous tune of crickets filled the night air.

Brian simply stood where he was and watched, half expecting the man to get up. But he didn't. And he never would.

The horror of what had just taken place finally sank in. Brian quickly left that awful place, stumbling through the junk along the side of the gas station and heading for the van.

He prayed that his family would still be asleep when he got there. And they were. All three dozed peacefully, unaware of how very close to death they had come.

Brian climbed into the van and gently closed the door. Then he started the engine and pulled away from the Texaco station.

As he was heading down the exit ramp, back to I-75. Brian knew for the first time in his life how a hit and run driver might feel.

Soon, the van was again heading northward for the Florida state line. He cut off the air conditioner and rolled down the window, letting the wind dry the sweat from his face. It wasn't long before his pulse and breathing had returned to normal.

A minute or so passed before he realized that something was pressing uncomfortably against his chest. He dipped his fingers into the breast pocket of his sport shirt and found something there that shouldn't have been. Something hard and round.

He held it to the pale green glow of the dashboard light. The object between his fingers stared at him, almost accusingly so.

Quickly, he flung the glass eye out the van window. It hit the rushing surface of the blacktop with a brittle crack, then was gone.

Brian felt along the Windstar's console blindly, until he found the packet of pre-moistened wipes that Jenny kept handy for little Anne. He shucked one from the sleeve and wiped his hands, fighting down nausea as he did.

Then he felt a small sting and remembered the cut on his forearm. Almost afraid to look, he turned his arm in the muted light. He expected to find a large gash, but, instead, there was only a thin line of blood, no more than two inches in length. He dabbed at the cut with the towelette, then tossed the damp cloth out the window.

It was so horribly absurd that he nearly laughed out loud. A brutal fight to the death and all he had come away with was an injury the equivalent of a paper cut.

Onward he drove into the Florida darkness, keeping one eye on the gas gauge and praying he would make it to the next exit.

Brian knew his wife would ask about the cut on his arm sooner or later.

He had until sunrise to come up with the right answer.

GRANDMA'S FAVORITE RECIPE

This was the first piece of fiction I wrote after I decided to return to the horror genre. It's both a tale about the hidden darkness in folks' hearts and an introductory story to my novel, Hell Hollow.

The character of Sarah Plummer was a composite of my maternal and paternal grandmothers, God rest their souls. One was kind and generous, as sweet as honeysuckle on a summer breeze, while the other was rambunctious, with a razor tongue and a hint of a wicked gleam in her eye.

MY grandmother was a pillar of the community.
Yeah, I know. You hear that about people all the time. But in this case, it was true.

Sarah Plummer was a kind and loving neighbor, a faithful friend to those around her, and a great woman of faith. She cherished the little farming community of Harmony, Tennessee with all her heart and was very active at the local church. Every Sunday morning, come rain or shine, you would find her there, teaching Sunday school and playing accompaniment on the organ as the choir sang. She always visited the sick at the hospital and the shut-ins at the nursing home, and she mailed out cards daily, saying "Get well soon!" or "Missed you at church Sunday." She visited every yard sale that was held in Harmony and bought at least one item, however insignificant, just to let them know that she had done her part.

And Grandma baked. She was legendary in town for her confectionary masterpieces and her homemade cakes and pies. Her specialty was cookies. Raisin oatmeal, chocolate chip, and, my personal favorite, snickerdoodle. Whenever she got wind that someone was down and ailing, she would take out her ceramic mixing bowls and flour sifter, her cinnamon, nutmeg, and baker's cocoa, and set to work. Grandma did everything entirely from scratch. No store-bought cake mix ever tarnished her kitchen counter. Pure ingredients were always used in just the proper amounts: flour, lard, fine cane sugar, and fresh country eggs from Will Turney's farm a mile outside of town. Then came the additions that really gave Grandma's desserts their sparkle. Big tollhouse chocolate chips, freshly-shred coconut, juicy raisins, pecans and walnuts. When she was through and the pans of earthly delight were cooking in the oven, Grandma's kitchen smelled like how I imagined the sweet aromas of heaven itself might be.

Then, after the cooling, Grandma Plummer would place an even dozen on a plate and cover it with a tent of aluminum foil. Whenever the townfolk saw her walking through town with a silvery parcel in her hands, they smiled. They knew that she would be ringing someone's doorbell soon and wishing them well, with both kind words and a special treat, the likes of which only she could concoct.

Yes, my dear little grandmother was a saintly woman. Or so I thought for a very long time.

■■■

Sarah Plummer had not had an easy way during the ninety-six years of her life.

She had been born to a hard-pan dirt farmer and his wife, a sickly woman who had been weakened by a bout of typhoid fever when she was a child. Grandma's early years had been difficult, hungry ones and, in the year of 1917, she had lost her four brothers and sisters to an influenza outbreak. She had been the only surviving child.

She had married at the age of eighteen to a man named Harold Plummer, who served as postmaster of the Harmony post office for nearly forty years. He had died of a sudden stroke in 1988. Being a housewife for her entire married life, Grandma lived modestly on Grandpa's postal pension in the little, white-clapboard house they had shared on Mulberry Street.

Like Grandma, I too had been dealt my share of hard blows throughout my childhood.

When I was four years old, my father was fatally injured at the sawmill he worked at. He fell into a buzz saw and bled to death before the paramedics arrived. Then a year and a half later, my mother was diagnosed with ovarian cancer. Despite a hysterectomy and numerous chemo treatments, she succumbed to the disease nine months later. I went to live with Grandma Plummer then and thanked the good Lord that she was there to receive me with open arms. She did the best she could to raise me into the man I have now become and I have nothing but gratitude for both the discipline she provided and the love she gave me during those tender years of childhood.

Despite what people thought, my grandmother did possess something of a temper, however. Whenever someone hurt her feelings or she felt slighted or wronged, she would grow absolutely livid. But that never seemed to last very long. She would always take her Bible in hand and, sitting in her rocking chair on the front porch, pray until those anger lines smoothed from her face and that gentle smile returned once again. Then she would get up, go into her kitchen, and bake a peace offering.

■■■

The first time I sensed that something wasn't quite right with Grandma Plummer was shortly after my twelfth birthday. It was a balmy May that year and Grandma's flower garden was brilliant with spring color: marigolds, hyacinth, petunias and moss roses.

There was a neighborhood dog from down the street, however, that had been trying Grandma's patience lately. Buster was the hound's name and he had dug up about every purple and blue iris that Grandma had planted along the driveway. I had pegged him in the hindquarters with a Little League baseball a couple times, but he kept coming back and wreaking more havoc. I suggested that we buy a BB gun—not necessarily to scare the dog off, but because I really, *really* wanted one at that age. But Grandma would hear none of it.

A while later, she walked out the back door with a leftover piece of my birthday cake on a plate. She set it down in the grass and, soon, Buster was there, chowing it down hungrily.

"Why are you feeding the mangy mutt?" I asked her.

"Because even though Buster vexes us with his bad behavior sometimes, he is still one of God's creatures," she explained. "I'm repaying his transgressions with an act of kindness. Turn the other cheek. That's the way the Good Book says it should be."

I wasn't so sure about that. I stood and watched the dog wolf down my last piece of birthday cake. "If you say so," I mumbled, scratching my head.

The next day, Buster was staggering around in the middle of Mulberry Street, snapping and snarling and foaming at the mouth. The neighborhood kids—me included—watched in horror as Sheriff Tom Stratford shot the dog down with his service revolver.

They strung yellow police tape around Buster's stiffening body until a man from the county animal control could

390

come out. He showed up a couple hours later, scooped Buster into a black plastic bag, and hauled him off.

No one in town could figure out how a healthy animal like Buster had contracted rabies so swiftly, with no signs or symptoms to forewarn anyone.

But I had my suspicions.

■■■

That night, after Grandma had gone to bed, I got up and took a flashlight from my nightstand drawer. Then I explored the kitchen pantry.

Something had bugged me the previous afternoon, when Grandma had served that piece of birthday cake to old Buster. It hadn't looked right. The sugary white icing with its red-laced baseballs and hickory brown bats had held a nasty grayish tint to it. And, that evening, when I had gone in for supper, I had spotted a bottle sitting on the kitchen counter. A tall, skinny bottle that held a dark liquid. I just assumed it was vanilla extract from Grandma's baking ingredients. Before I could ask, however, she had taken the bottle and spirited it back to one of the shelves in her pantry.

The little closet smelled of cinnamon and garlic as I swung the pale beam of the light around, searching for that bottle. I found it a few minutes later, sitting on the shelf with her spices and baking supplies. Quietly, I reached to the back of the shelf and brought it forward, where I could get a better look.

It was an old bottle—very old. It was tall and narrow, and sported a single dark cork in the mouth of the stem. A label—yellowed and curled at the edges by age—read:

DR. AUGUSTUS LEECH'S PATENTED ELIXIR—CURES A VARIETY OF PHYSICAL ILLNESSES: GOUT, ARTHRITIS, IRREGULARITY, AND CHILDHOOD AILMENTS.

A cold feeling washed over me at that moment.

391

Augustus Leech. I had heard that name before…a story whispered over a crackling fire at a local summer camp when I was eight years old. A dark, lanky medicine showman with a top hat full of magic tricks, a song and a dance, and a patented elixir that guaranteed to cure all maladies and ailments. He had come to town in the early 1900s and sold his tonic for croup, anemia, and dysentery. And, in the process, poisoned half the children of Harmony.

Legend had it that the menfolk had armed themselves with guns and pitchforks and, like a mob in an old Frankenstein movie, had chased Leech out of town. Deep down into a shadowy place called Hell Hollow…never to be seen again.

Some kids in town had dared to explore the hollow, but I never did. I wasn't a child for taking risks. Not with the share of tragedy fate had given me in my younger years.

I picked up the narrow bottle. The glass seemed oily to the touch. I studied it in the pale glow of the flashlight. It was half full of a dark, syrupy liquid. Curious, I wiggled the cork until it pulled free. The contents smelled both sweet and sickening, like cotton candy and jelly beans mixed with dog vomit and the decay of a bloated possum at the side of the road. I didn't breathe it in very deeply. It made me feel sort of lightheaded.

Is this what Grandma had used to poison poor Buster? Or was poison too kind a word for what had been done? And where had she gotten the elixir? The stuff was absolutely ancient.

In the muted glow of the flashlight, the dark liquid seemed to shift and swirl of its own accord. It almost appeared to change colors somehow, from pitch black to blood red to pond scum green, then black again.

In the darkness of the pantry, something moved. A mouse scavenging for crumbs perhaps. Or perhaps not.

Hurriedly, I corked the bottle and slid it to the back of the shelf where I had found it.

Back in bed, I lay there for a very long time before sleep finally claimed me. And, even then, it was not an easy one.

■■■

The next time Grandma showed her true nature, I was a sophomore in high school.

Our next door neighbors, the Masons, had suffered a very bad year. Bob and Betty Mason's daughter, Judy, had endured a long bout with cancer and had passed away the previous week. I was pretty depressed about her death. I'd had a crush on Judy since sixth grade. I had even asked her out to a school dance the previous year, but she had turned me down. Grandma had watched the whole thing from her kitchen window and I think it made her mad, but she hadn't said anything.

It wasn't long afterward that Judy Mason was diagnosed with leukemia.

I had just stepped off the school bus a few houses down, when I saw Grandma standing at the Mason's door, holding a plate wrapped in aluminum foil in her hands. I couldn't help but smile to myself. The Cookie Patrol was on the roll again.

As I made my way down the sidewalk toward our house, I could hear Grandma talking to Betty Mason at the doorway. "Things will be better," Grandma told her in comforting tones. "All we can do is pray to the good Lord for strength through this difficult time."

Mrs. Mason nodded sadly and smiled. "We appreciate your concern, Miss Sarah. And thank you for the dessert. You know how Bob loves your sweets."

"It's not much," Grandma told her. "But perhaps it'll provide a small bit of comfort to you during your time of need."

Betty Mason thanked her again and closed the door. I was nearly to the gate of the Masons' picket fence, when Grandma turned around. That small, gentle smile crossed her lips, the same smile I'd seen a thousand times at hospital visitations and charity bazaars, and at church as she played her favorite hymns on the organ she mastered so well.

It was her eyes that disturbed me. They held none of the benevolence that the rest of her face showed. They were hard, hate-filled eyes, peering from behind her horn-rimmed glasses like tiny black stones. Then, when she saw me approaching, they changed. They once again became the warm lights of Christian kindness that I was so accustomed to.

"Home a little early, aren't you?" she said. "Well, come on to the kitchen. I've got a fresh apple crumb cake cooling on the counter. I just took it out of the oven."

As I sat in Grandma's kitchen that afternoon, eating my second slice of cake, I couldn't have imagined that Bob and Betty Mason would be dead within a week. The following Thursday, their car had veered unexpectedly across the grass median of the interstate and plowed, head-on, into a tractor-trailer truck. Both had died upon impact.

■■■

On the night following the Masons' funeral, I had the strangest dream. One in which I was not a participant, but a spectator.

I was in an old farmhouse. In one room a baby cried. In the other a frail woman wailed mournfully.

I stood in a doorway between kitchen and bedroom. As the woman vented her grief, two neighboring women were silently at work. Lying across the eating table were the bodies of three children, two boys and a girl. All were dead, being prepared for burial.

A man paced around the room like a bobcat on the prowl. His eyes burned with a rage only a father can feel at the loss of his children.

I turned and looked into the bedroom. A baby—perhaps two or three months old—wept loudly from a handmade cradle. Feeding time had passed, but the infant had been forgotten. And there was another child. A four-year-old girl who sat cross-legged in the center of a big brass bed. The girl didn't seem in the least disturbed by the events that were taking place around her. Her eyes were focused on an object that stood on a cherrywood bureau across the room.

It was a bottle. A tall, skinny bottle with a cork in the top. The label read DR. AUGUSTUS LEECH'S PATENTED ELIXIR.

The little girl smiled. She was quite fond of Augustus Leech, the medicine show man who had driven his horse-drawn wagon into town and stirred things up a bit. She had watched, enthralled, as he performed incredible feats of magic, picked a few tunes on a five-string banjo, and touted his patented elixir as the "Cure-All of the Ages."

And, when her father wasn't looking, he had slipped her a prize. A playing card with a picture of a fairy princess on the face.

She had placed that card beneath her pillow last night and dreamed that she was in an enchanted kingdom full of ogres, dragons, and wizards. A place more real to her than the drab town of Harmony had ever been.

Her baby sister continued to cry. Slowly, the girl left the bed and took the skinny bottle from the bureau. She knelt beside the cradle.

"Hungry?" she asked.

The baby continued to wail.

She uncorked the bottle and unleashed a single drop. The infant rolled the dark liquid around on her tiny, pink tongue for a moment. Then grew silent.

No more middle child, the girl thought. *Only me.*

She smiled a curl of a thin-lipped smile...that girl with my grandmother's eyes.

■■■

I woke up in the darkness, my heart pounding. I climbed out of bed and went downstairs...to the pantry.

The bottle was still there, even after all these years. But it was only a quarter of the way full now.

A cold feeling threatened to overcome me. I began to recall bits and pieces of conflicts during my childhood. Conflicts that didn't involve me directly, but were always between my parents and my grandmother, my grandmother and friends and neighbors. An accusation of infidelity toward my grandfather. A heated argument over meddling interference with my father. A petty grudge between my mother and Grandma that echoed from years before I was born. Hurt feelings and imagined wrongs done to the matriarch of the Plummer family by townfolk and neighbors. But the dust had always settled and peace was always made.

And, afterwards, there had always been sweets from Grandma's kitchen.

Followed by death.

I began to wonder if she was responsible. That maybe she was poisoning folks with that ancient elixir that sat on the pantry shelf. But my mind couldn't comprehend such a thing. The Masons had died in an unfortunate accident, like my father. A ninety-six-year-old woman can't condemn someone to cancer or a fatal car crash by baking them a lemon meringue pie.

I left the kitchen pantry that night, telling myself that I was being foolish, that my kindly grandmother had nothing to do with the misfortunes of the citizens of Harmony. But I could never erase that dream from my thoughts. And that little girl with the wicked grin on her face.

■■■

Several days ago, everything just sort of fell apart for me and Grandma.

It happened on Sunday morning. I was back home from college for the weekend, sitting in a right-hand pew of the sanctuary. Church service was proceeding as it normally did at Harmony Holiness. Jill Thompson, the pianist, and Grandma Plummer at her organ, were playing "Leaning on the Everlasting Arms" flawlessly. Then, before they had finished, Pastor Alfred Wilkes rose to his feet prematurely.

The ladies stopped their playing. The entire congregation froze. Everyone was already on edge, as it was. Bad things had been taking place at the church in the wee hours of the night. Vandalism and desecration.

It had begun two weeks ago. Someone had thrown rocks through three of the stained-glass windows. Then, later, an intruder had stolen the church's 180-year-old King James Bible from a display case in the foyer and set fire to it on the stoop outside.

But the last blasphemous act had been the worst. Someone had defecated on the altar.

Pastor Wilkes' face was long and mournful as his huge hands gripped both sides of the podium. "The Devil has been testing us lately, my friends," he said in that deep baritone of his. "At first I just thought it was some disrespectful kids. But after the second incident, I realized that it was something much more serious. It is not an outsider who has committed these sinful acts, but someone in our own midst."

I couldn't believe what I was hearing. A member of the congregation had done those horrible things? A nervous sensation of cold dread began to form in the pit of my stomach, although I wasn't sure why.

"Following the burning of the Bible, the deacons and I discussed the matter and came to a decision," he told us. A grim smile crossed his face. "It's amazing what you can buy at Radio Shack these days."

He then picked up a manila envelope that was lying atop the podium and unfastened the clasp of the flap. "I really hate to show you this," he said, "but God has compelled me to do so."

Pastor Wilkes then pulled an 8x10 photograph from the envelope and held it at arm's length for all to see. The congregation gasped as one. The nervous ball of dread deep down in my belly suddenly turned into a cold, hard stone.

Pictured there in the dimly-lit sanctuary, with her granny panties and support hose pooled around her ankles, was my grandmother...smearing her feces across the front of the pulpit.

I groaned involuntarily, as though someone had just sucker punched me in the gut. I heard someone clear her throat haughtily from the pew behind me. It was Naomi Saunders, the church busybody. I could feel her hot, self-righteous eyes burning into the back of my neck.

An uneasy silence hung heavily in the sanctuary for a long moment. Then Pastor Wilkes turned and regarded the elderly woman sitting at the church organ. "It grieves me in my heart to do this, Miss Sarah, but I must ask you to leave us now."

I watched as my grandmother primly turned off her organ and, for the very last time, left the spot she had occupied for countless Sunday mornings. With her head held high, she walked down the center aisle, enduring the stares of shock and disgust that etched the faces of the congregation.

As she reached the rear doorway, I shakily stood to my feet. I couldn't believe the pastor had handled my grandmother's comeuppance in such a callous and tactless manner.

Why couldn't he and the deacons have confronted her privately? Standing there, I stared the preacher square in the face. "This isn't right," I told him in front of everyone.

I looked for some sign of satisfaction in his face, but there was none. "No," he said flatly. "It wasn't."

Outside in the parking lot, we sat in the car. "*Why,* Grandma?" I asked her. "Can you give me a reason?"

She was silent.

"Was it because you wanted the church to buy that new organ last month and the budget committee voted it down?"

She said absolutely nothing in her defense. She simply sat there in the passenger seat, head bowed as if in prayer...but eyes wide open.

■■■

I found Grandma dead the following Monday morning.

She lay there peacefully in her bed, wrinkled hands folded across her chest, a tiny curl of a smile upon her thin lips.

The cause of her death was undeniable. Sitting on her nightstand was a tall, skinny bottle. The stained cork sat neatly next to it.

"Aw, Grandma," I sighed as I picked up the bottle. It was completely empty. "You drank it all." It had only been a quarter full the last time I had seen it, but apparently that had been enough.

The next two days were a blur to me. There was so much to attend to. The proper arrangements were made at the local funeral home: the casket, the vault, the times of visitation and, of course, the funeral itself. After the preparations, I went back to that empty little house on Mulberry Street. The place was a wreck. Along with her will to live, Grandma had apparently lost her will to clean. I made the four-poster bed she had died in, then moved on to the rest of the house. There were dirty dishes in the sink and damp towels strewn across the bathroom floor.

The following day, Grandma was stately and dignified in her burnished, rose-hued casket, wearing a dress she had worn at many a Sunday service. The chapel was decorated with a forest of flower arrangements, ceramic angel figurines, and matted pictures of Thomas Kinkade churches that played "Amazing Grace" when you wound a music box on the back.

The funeral was almost unbearably long, populated by the folks of Harmony, as well as the congregation that had ousted her from their midst only a couple of days before. As Pastor Wilkes droned on and on about what a faithful, God-fearing woman she had been, I sat there on the front pew and tried to imagine Grandma in heaven. But I couldn't. It simply wouldn't come to me. Trying to picture her in such a celestial setting was like staring at a blank canvas.

After the graveside service, everyone met back at the church fellowship hall for a lunch of covered dishes and desserts. I wasn't very hungry. I just wanted to accept my share of condolences and get out of there. I had much to deal with that afternoon...mostly the nagging question of exactly why my last living relative had done the terrible things she had.

I found myself standing next to the dessert table with Naomi Saunders. As the woman stuffed her face, she told me about how wonderful a woman Grandma had been and how they were all going to miss her dearly. I pretty much nodded my head solemnly and thought about how very delicious the cookie I was munching was, my second one, in fact.

"These are pretty good," I said. I took another bite and washed it down with sweet tea.

"Snickerdoodles," Naomi said with a smile. "She always said they were your favorite."

I stopped chewing. "Who made these?"

"Your grandmother, apparently," she told me. "We found them on that table when we came to set up this morning."

Dirty dishes in the sink. Coffee cups, supper plates, mixing bowls...

"I guess it was one last, loving gesture...God bless her." Naomi picked up a greeting card from off the table and handed it to me. "This was with it."

Numbly, I took it. The card face read, *"From your Sister in Christ."* When I opened it I found there was no printed caption, only Grandma's unmistakably floral penmanship. I barely took two breaths as I read the inscription.

Farewell, my friends...May we meet again in the glorious hereafter...where the hearth fires shall crackle with warmth and we shall labor together in eternity. I shall see you there. Love, Sarah.

"Sad, but sweet, wasn't it?" said Naomi.

I stared at the handwriting in the card. What had she been talking about? There were no hearth fires in heaven...no fire at all. And paradise was a place of rest, not a realm of endless labor...

I looked down at the half-eaten cookie in my hand, then at the platter on the table. Only three cookies remained where there had been an even two dozen before.

As I left the church, I wanted to puke...but I couldn't. The poison was there to stay.

When I had cleaned the house, I had made the bed... but had neglected to look beneath Grandma's pillow. When I did look, I knew exactly what I would find.

A yellowed playing card with a fairy princess on the face.

Now I understood why I couldn't picture Grandma in heaven. She was in a much more sinister place. A fiery realm full of ogres and dragons...and wizards named Leech.

MIDNIGHT
GRINDING

The first half of this story is absolutely true. There really was a demented farmhand named Green Lee who terrorized the children of a Tennessee farm camp back in the early 1900s. One of those children was my late Grandmama Spicer, who would chill me to the bone with the deranged exploits of Green Lee and his back porch whetstone. I gave myself the creeps when I wrote this story and it still disturbs me every time I read it. It was almost as though it was written by a hand other than my own. Perhaps even the bony claw of Green Lee himself.

WHICH one must I kill first? Oh, sweet Lord in heaven, please tell me...which one must I kill first?"

The first time Rebecca heard the voice of Green Lee it came rasping through the lush leaves of the tobacco rows like the coarse hide of a snake rubbing against dried corn husks. She and her brother, Ben, had been performing the chore that Papa had given them that day: picking off the plump, green worms that nibbled on the summer tobacco, and squashing them beneath the toes of their bare feet. But as they left one dense row and moved on to the next, the old man's whispering plea echoed in the dusty afternoon air, curling through their youthful ears and stopping them dead in their tracks.

Rebecca and Ben backed up a few steps, listening to the sinister words and watching for a sign of the one who uttered them. "Heavenly Father, Lord Almighty on high, please tell me...which one shall it be?"

A rustling of tobacco leaves sounded from a few feet away, drawing the frightened eyes of the two children. And from within that dense patch of greenery crept a gnarled claw of stark white bone.

The youngsters broke from their fearful paralysis. Screaming, they ran along the field rows, feet churning clouds of powdery clay dirt into the hot, still air of mid-July. They soon burst from the high tobacco, their cries rising shrilly as they crossed the barren road to the gathering of shabby tin and tarpaper shacks that made up the itinerant farm camp. They saw their mother sitting on the front porch of one such house, washing a few articles of clothing with a scrubboard and a bucket of sudsy, gray water.

"Lordy Mercy!" said Sarah Benton, looking as drab and threadbare as the clothing she washed. "What's the matter with you young'uns?"

It was a moment before they could summon the breath to tell her. "There's a ghost in the tobacco field," gasped eight-year-old Rebecca. "A ghost with a bony claw!"

"Ya'll hush up now," said their mother. She cast a glance at the house next door and saw their neighbors sitting on the porch, snapping beans and eyeing the two children curiously. "I don't wanna hear such foolishness from the two of you!" The Benton family had only joined the farm camp a few days ago in that sweltering summer of 1908 and it wouldn't do to have the three neighboring families thinking that the Benton children were touched in the head or some such thing.

"But it was there, Mama!" proclaimed little Ben, nearly in tears, "and it said it was gonna kill us!"

Sarah was about to put her bucket and board aside and give the unruly pair a sound thrashing, when her husband, Will, emerged from the tobacco rows with a few of the other farmers. He approached the stone well that stood in the middle of the encampment, where a bucketful of cold water had been drawn, and took a long drink from a gourd dipper.

Rebecca and Ben left their mother and ran to the big, rawboned man. They frantically told their father the story of the voice in the rows and the bony claw that had poked out of the leaves.

Will Benton laughed heartily and put comforting hands on their shoulders. "Aw, don't go fretting yourselves about such. That was just old Green Lee over yonder. He ain't gonna hurt you none."

The children looked to where their father pointed and saw a man standing in the speckled shade of a hickory tree several yards away. The fellow was gaunt and lanky, wearing faded overalls and filthy longhandles underneath. He leaned against the trunk of the tree and grinned at them, his teeth stained with tobacco juice and his eyes holding a disturbing shine of madness. He had a scraggly gray beard and what little hair he possessed laid lank and lifeless along his scalp like sun-shriveled cornsilk. The children looked to his crossed arms and saw that the right hand was strong and whole, hard with the calluses of daily work. But the left one was fleshless—a gnarled claw of stiffened bone, looking like the pale, dry husk of a spider that had curled in upon itself in death.

Rebecca stared at the man, still uneasy in her mind. From the shadows of the big tree his eyes burned with a feverish light and his lips silently mouthed those awful words she had heard him utter in the close-grown rows of the hundred-acre field. Then, with a big wink, the old man turned and walked to his own house no more than a stone's throw from the place where Rebecca and her family lived.

■■■

That night after supper, their father told them the story of Green Lee.

He had once been a good man, a religious man who tilled the earth of the fields during the week and preached the word of God on Sunday morning. He had fought in the Spanish-American War as a young man and, after serving his country, had returned to his native Tennessee and worked as a farmer in the tobacco fields near the rural town of Coleman. He married a sturdy woman named Charlotte Springer, who a year later bore him twin sons. In all, Green Lee was a respected member of the community along Old Newsome Road…or he had been until his unfortunate accident in the spring of 1903.

It had been a scorcher of a day and Green Lee was plowing a forty-acre stretch, when something peculiar happened to him. His wife went out to call him to supper that evening and found him in the center of the half-plowed field, standing over the lifeless body of his finest work mule. When she walked out to see what had happened, she found her husband giggling wildly like a demented child. The mule had been stoned to death, obviously by the farmer himself.

Large hunks of uncovered rock lay scattered around the poor animal and a particularly heavy chunk had been used to shatter the mule's skull.

By the time Charlotte could summon some of the neighboring farmers, Green Lee had collapsed in the evening shadows and lay trembling in a violent palsy of unknown origin. He was immediately put to bed and his body bathed with cool water. The local physician drove out that night in a horse and buggy, and examined the feverish man. The doctor soon came to the conclusion that

Green Lee had suffered a heatstroke, due to plowing that hot day without the benefit of a hat to shade his head.

After a month in bed, Green Lee escaped the prospect of immediate death and rose to resume his life, although never fully recovered. He was given to bouts of uncharacteristic behavior. For weeks at a time he would seem normal enough, tending to his crops and preaching the Lord's gospel. Then, abruptly, his morals would become totally depraved and devoid of restraint. He would frequent a local roadhouse known as the Bloody Bucket and blow his earnings on whiskey, gambling, and whores. Soon, his behavior lost him the respect of his neighbors and the faith of his congregation. Gradually, the good and bad of Green Lee seemed to balance out and he grew more eccentric as the days went by, dividing his time equally between God and the Devil.

Before his illness, the man had been stubborn and headstrong. But in the years afterward, Green Lee became increasingly weak in mind and incredibly gullible. This condition was best summed up by the incident that led to the ghastly crippling of his left hand. Among his other afflictions, Green Lee suffered a bad case of arthritis in his wrist and finger joints, and he was always on the alert for some new medicine or folk remedy that might cure him of the bothersome pain. One night a couple of drinking buddies pulled a cruel joke on the man and suggested a cure that he had never heard of before, but one they assured would rid him of his agony. That night, after his family had gone to bed, Green Lee fired up the woodstove in his kitchen and set an iron pot of cold water over the flame. He immersed his left hand in the water and—per his friends' instructions—let the water come to a steady boil. Slowly, the nagging pain in his fingers and wrist disappeared until only numbness remained. Green Lee was sure that he had miraculously been healed of his ailment... until he withdrew his hand from the scalding water and watched as the meat slipped free from the bones and fell like a fleshed glove, into the churning currents of the boiling pot.

His unfortunate crippling made it impossible for Green Lee to sustain the rigors of tobacco farming. He began to make a meager living as a handyman and an errand boy, working for a man named Leman McSherry who owned a number of itinerant farm camps in Bedloe County. To that day, Green Lee helped out the farming families that plowed, planted, and harvested the fertile tobacco bases along Old Newsome Road. He harnessed mules, went into town for supplies, and helped chop and split tobacco when the crop was mature enough to be readied for sale.

The old man's behavior was endured with a grain of salt. Most farmers thought of him as nothing more than a harmless imbecile. But the women and children of the camp felt differently, especially the handyman's own family. Sometimes he would approach the children, his bony hand outstretched and the menacing words of "Which one must I kill first?" quavering through his whiskered lips. As of yet, Green Lee had harmed no one, had not even lifted a hand to his own young'uns, but there was some talk that he was a man to be watched, especially when the menfolk were busy laboring in the far reaches of the tobacco field.

■■■

The sweltering days of summer soon passed and with the cooling of autumn came the time of harvest. The ripened leaves were cut, lashed to long poles, and fire-cured in the tobacco barn of a local landowner, Harvey Brewer, whose structure was large enough to prepare four crops at one time. Toward the end of September, Rebecca's father and some of the other men planned to load the cured tobacco into mule-drawn wagons and make the long trip to Nashville to the big auction house near the Union Station railroad tracks. During Will Benton's two-day journey, his family was to stay the night with their next door neighbors.

They were to stay the night at the house of Green Lee.

At the mere mention of such a visit, Rebecca felt as though she were being cast into the prelude of some horrid nightmare. Both she and her brother were deathly afraid of the lanky man with the skeletal hand. Several times since that day in the tobacco rows, the Benton children had been aware of an unwholesome interest that Green Lee seemed to hold for them. Sometimes he would simply stand beneath the hickory tree and watch silently as they played. Other times, as they walked along the winding bed of Devil's Creek, they would see him following at a distance. Once, when she and Ben were sleeping near the open window of their bedroom during a particularly hot night, Rebecca had awakened to Green Lee's whispering voice. She sat upright in her bed and saw the skeletal hand, blue-white in the moonlight, snaking through the open window and gently running its bony fingers through the hair of her sleeping brother. Rebecca had unleashed a shrill scream, but by the time her parents awoke and came to them, the intruder was long gone. Her mother and father had insisted that she had only been dreaming, but she knew that had not been the case.

And there was one other thing in connection with Green Lee that made her uneasy. Sometimes, at the hour of midnight, she would awaken to a peculiar sound, a harsh and unnerving sound. The sound of grinding. Sometimes when she looked from her window, Rebecca saw nothing. But on other occasions she would see a weird glow coming from the back porch of the Lee house. It was the spray of fiery sparks, the kind generated from the clashing contact of steel against whetstone. The grinding would last for only a few moments, then the sound and the strange light would cease, once again surrendering to the nocturnal symphony of crickets, toads, and lonely whippoorwills.

Much to the dread of Rebecca and her brother, the night of their visit to the Lee house finally came. Will Benton had left with the other farmers for Nashville with the dawn and, when the dusk cast its shadow upon the rural countryside, Sarah locked up the little house and ushered her reluctant children to the residence next door. Charlotte Lee and her two children welcomed the Benton family in their customarily quiet and nervous manner. Suppertime was long since over and the women sat around the long eating table, talking and drinking coffee, while the children played with a well-worn set of ball and jacks on the dusty planks of the cabin floor.

Green Lee was there, sitting in a cane-backed chair next to the potbelly stove. He sat there moodily, smoking a corncob pipe and staring intensely into the hot, red slits of the grate. The crimson glow reflected on the whites of his eyes and sometimes he would chuckle, as though he had glimpsed some mysterious revelation within the crackling coals. Fortunately, Green Lee seemed to pay neither Rebecca nor her brother any mind during the course of the evening. He merely sat there hunkered over, indulging himself with his smoking and fire-watching.

Eventually they all settled in for the night. The Lee family retired to their own beds in the back room, while Sarah Benton and her two children slept on pallets on the bare boards of the floor. When the candles had been extinguished and the last creak of bedsprings was heard, Rebecca lay there next to her brother and stared into the unfamiliar darkness. She strained her ears for the first sound of Green Lee leaving his bed and making his way to her pallet. But after a half hour of fearful anticipation, she heard no such move on the old man's part. Fairly exhausted by her anxiety, Rebecca was soon claimed by slumber, joining the realm of the sleeping forms around her.

Later on that night, Rebecca was awakened by the sound of harsh grinding. She rose and looked at the old German clock that hung on the bedroom wall. The ornate hands read five minutes past twelve. Rebecca's eyes searched through the darkness. She found the place where Green Lee slept to be abandoned. Quietly, the girl left the blankets of her bed and padded from the room into the adjoining kitchen.

She hid behind a kitchen chair and stared through the interlaced bands of cane weaving at the strange sight that revealed itself beyond the back door, which was open despite the coolness of the autumn night. The lank form of Green Lee, clad only in filthy longjohns, hunched over the big grinding wheel on the back porch. His bare foot worked the pedal furiously, sending the circular stone whirling at a steady pace. The man giggled and cooed softly as he worked. First, he pressed the edge of a hatchet to the stone, honing its breadth with expert precision. Shavings of hot steel glanced from the hard surface in orange sparks, then died as they cooled to dark cinders in the September chill.

When Green Lee was satisfied with the job he had done, he set the hand-axe aside and took up a straight razor. Again, he hunched over the wheel and went to work. Back and forth he drew the wicked blade of the shaving implement across the whirling flat of the wheel. When the razor was finally lifted away from the stone, Green Lee held the blade aloft. In the faint moonlight outside, Rebecca could see that its edge had been ground to a thinness that bordered on transparency.

She was about to duck back into the bedroom, when Green Lee twisted his grizzled head around and stared straight at her, as if he had known of her presence all along. His snaggle-toothed grin grew wider and his eyes wilder, and he asked in a rasping voice, "Is this the one Lord? Is this the one that I seek?"

Rebecca broke from her hiding place and ran back to her pallet. She burrowed beneath the blankets and pulled them up over her head, shuddering with the fear of having been discovered. She waited, listening for the old man's approach. It came moments later, the creaking of floorboards beneath bare feet. She pulled herself into a tight ball, expecting the edge of honed steel to bite through the cloth of her blankets and find the tender flesh of her body or the fragile shell of her skull.

But it did not happen. She peeked from beneath the covers and saw the shadowy form of Green Lee next to the big brass-framed bed. The old man lifted his pillow and laid the sharpened hatchet and razor underneath. Then the sleeve of cloth and goose down obscured the weapons from view and, with a soft prayer on his lips, Green Lee settled into the sunken spot next to his wife and soon drifted into a snoring slumber.

■■■

After that night, Rebecca never strayed far from the Benton farmhouse. Life went on in the farming camp as the colorful fall stretched into a bleak, gray winter. Most of the men, her father included, found jobs at a sawmill in a neighboring county to make ends meet, while Green Lee did odd jobs in town, toting firewood and cleaning out chimney flues.

But, at night, she could still hear the urgent sound of grinding.

Then, in mid-February, horrid screams roused the farming camp at the hour of midnight. Will Benton and a few of the neighboring farmers armed themselves and went out to see what the commotion was all about, while their wives and children watched fearfully from the frosty panes of the windows. They could see fleeting forms running across the barren, snow-covered tobacco field, frantic forms that wailed with shrieks of laughter and terror. Then there came the sound of a rifle shot and, soon, Rebecca's father and the others dragged the weeping form of Green Lee back across the road. His right leg was bleeding from a gunshot wound and in his hands he held the weapons that Rebecca had seen that night in September. The hatchet was clutched in his good hand, while the razor was wedged tightly within the bony fingers of his skeletal claw.

After Green Lee had been tied to a rocking chair on the front porch of the Lee house, his family was brought to the home of the Bentons. They were distraught and trembling, bearing a few shallow wounds, but nothing worse. A while later, the county sheriff arrived and took Green Lee with him. It was the last time that Rebecca ever saw the madman with the bony hand and the heavenly plea of murderous intention on his lips.

Not long afterward, Rebecca and her family moved on to another farming camp, for her father was a man who wandered from one community to the next, searching for a life he was never destined to find. A few years later, Rebecca heard that Green Lee had died in an insane asylum. According to the stories told, the lunatic had lain thrashing on the dank floor of his solitary cell, bound in a straightjacket and screaming for the Lord to "answer the riddle of my madness."

He had screamed long and loud, until his brain exploded with the strain of his hysteria and his eyes grew dark and bulging in their sockets, like blood-engorged ticks on the point of bursting.

■■■

In the year of 1923, Rebecca returned to Bedloe County, Tennessee. With her was a husband, Jasper Howell, and two young children, Mitchell and Millicent, who were barely of school age. Like Rebecca's father, Jasper was a tobacco farmer by trade. When he had told her that they would be moving once again, Rebecca had really thought nothing of it at first. She had become accustomed to the nomadic ways of the itinerant farm family during her childhood. But when they arrived at the farm camp and Rebecca realized exactly where they were, she felt a wave of cold dread engulf her like the treacherous waters of a swollen stream.

413

The four drab tin-and-tarpaper houses, the stone well, and the vast expanse of prime tobacco land across the dirt road—it all came back to her from the year of her eighth birthday. She was back at the farm camp that had served as her home fifteen years before. It was the place where she had first been introduced to the emotion of sheer terror, in the form of a crazed cripple with murder in his heart and stone-honed steel in his grasp.

Rebecca said nothing to her husband about her sudden revelation. It would have done no good. He would have simply called her foolish and refused to move on. There were two other families at the camp when they arrived, which meant that two of the shabby houses were still vacant. Luckily, they moved into the same house that the Benton family had occupied when she was a child. That left the ramshackle structure next door empty and dark...the house that had once been the uneasy home for the family of Green Lee.

They arrived in early spring, in time for Jasper and the other men to set about the task of furrowing the vast field and planting the shoots of young tobacco in orderly rows. The first few weeks passed without incident for the Howell family. Jasper worked the fields from sunrise to sunset, Rebecca busied herself with the chores of a homemaker, and Mitch and Millie spent their days studying at the one-roomed schoolhouse near the forks of Old Newsome Road.

Then, one night, Rebecca woke at the hour of twelve. She sat up in bed and stared into the darkness, trying to determine what had roused her from her sleep. It had been a noise—a coarse, monotonous sound that rang with a disturbing familiarity. She strained her ears and heard the sound again. It echoed through the blackness of the outer night. From the direction of the old Lee house.

She rose and walked to the window at the far side of the room. From that vantage point she could see the southern face of the abandoned house. The moment she looked through the dirty panes of the bedroom window, the puzzling noise ceased. She peered at the shadowy overhang of the back porch, certain that she had glimpsed a flash of fiery sparks a second before the sound of grinding had come to a halt.

Which one must I kill first? echoed the voice of Green Lee from the far reaches of her mind, as chilling now as it had seemed fifteen years ago. *Tell me, Lord, which one shall it be?*

Rebecca stared out at the darkness for a while, then returned to her bed. She lay awake for a long time and listened for the haunting clash of steel against stone, but the only sounds she heard were the chirping of crickets in the dark hours of the night, as well as the soft snoring of her sleeping husband.

■■■

Spring stretched into summer, and soon the tobacco grew lush and chest-high in the hundred-acre field. The men spent their days weeding and hoeing, while the children played hide-and-seek amid the thick stalks and pretended they were explorers in some great and mysterious jungle.

Rebecca and the other women of the farm camp had planted a small vegetable garden behind the houses and, by mid-July, the patch was ripe with fresh tomatoes, snapping beans, and corn. On one such summer day, Rebecca was digging taters and picking roasting ears for that night's supper, when the sound of youthful screams cut through her ears like shards of broken glass. The sound froze her heart and, at first, she was sure that one of the children had fallen down the stone well or had been bitten by a copperhead snake.

She stepped from the garden and watched as Mitch and Millie ran screaming from the dense growth of the tobacco rows and ran across the rural road as if Old Scratch himself was fast on their heels. "What's wrong?" she asked as they clung to her gingham skirt, nearly in tears.

"It was a man!" sobbed Millie. "There was a man in the field!"

"What are you talking about?" demanded Rebecca. "What kind of man?"

"A crazy man," said little Mitch. "A man with bones for a hand."

Rebecca's heart grew as cold and heavy as a winter stone. She grabbed a hatchet from off the chopping stump near the back porch and—despite their squalling protest—made the children show her where their frightening encounter had taken place. She felt her skin crawl with gooseflesh when she discovered it to be the exact same spot where she and her brother had first known the horror of Green Lee.

She walked up and down the adjoining rows, but found no sign of anyone having been there recently. Her husband and the other men were working at the far end of the property that day, a good distance from the spot that Mitch and Millie had shown her. Although she hated doing so, she assured the children that it had merely been their imagination playing tricks on them. They looked doubtful at her explanation, however, and felt that she didn't believe their fantastic story.

But, secretly, Rebecca Howell had good reason to believe every word of what they had told her, even though it was impossible to consider such a thing actually happening...especially with the culprit long since dead and moldering in the dark depths of his grave.

■■■

As the summer months slowly gave way to autumn, life in the farming camp continued uneventfully. The routine of each new day remained the same as that of the day before.

The children seemed to have forgotten their harrowing experience in the tobacco field, but Rebecca hadn't. The screams of Mitch and Millie still lingered in her mind, as well as the distant image of a claw of gnarled bone and the memory of a malevolent whisper from her own childhood. She attempted to drive those thoughts from her mind, for it seemed foolish to linger on such things.

Then, toward the end of September, thoughts of Green Lee resurfaced. Rebecca was awakened by that peculiar sound of metallic grinding. Swiftly, she left her bed and went to the bedroom window. This time she saw a faint hint of irregular light coming from the back porch of the old Lee house. Intrigued, she felt her way through the pitch darkness of the room and made her way to the kitchen for a better view. From her own back porch she saw the flashing bursts of orange sparks and heard more clearly the distinct grating of steel against stone.

Curiously, she padded with bare feet across the weedy stretch of yard that separated the two houses. By the time she got within thirty feet of the rickety porch of the deserted house, both the noise and the light had vanished. Cautiously, Rebecca stepped onto the bowed boards of the porch and approached the old grinding wheel that still sat where it had fifteen years ago.

She put her fingertips to the wheel and immediately jerked them away. The stone was hot to the touch. She crouched down and found that tiny bits of newly-ground steel were scattered upon the dusty boards underneath. But there was no sign of the person who had done the grinding, or the instruments that had been subject to the stone's whirling edge.

Could he still be alive? Rebecca wondered. *Could Green Lee be alive, despite what I heard before? Or could his ghost be haunting this place after all these years?*

As if in answer, the sound of heavy footsteps on aged floorboards echoed from within the darkness of the open door. Rebecca found herself rooted to the spot as a pale form slowly emerged from the shadowy kitchen beyond.

"What are you doing over here?" someone asked her and Rebecca felt her fright melt away at the sound of her husband's voice.

"I thought I heard something," she said, catching her breath.

"So did I," replied Jasper. "A noise and a light. But doesn't look like nobody's here now. Must've been an old hobo messing around or something."

Rebecca crossed her slender arms against the night chill and was escorted home by her husband. When they finally settled into bed once again, Rebecca glanced at Jasper's pocket watch lying on the bureau and saw that it was only a few minutes past the stroke of midnight.

■■■

During the next few weeks, Rebecca couldn't shake the dreadful shadow of that night on the back porch of the Lee house. During her daily chores she found herself casting an uneasy glance at the dark, empty windows, as if expecting to see a wild-eyed, whiskered face leering out at her from amid the broken panes.

And it was even worse at night. Her dreams were filled with the threat of Green Lee. Sometimes she would find herself running across a snowy field with Mitch and Millie in tow as a dark form pursued them, fistfuls of honed steel flashing wickedly in the cold, winter moonlight. Sometimes she would dream that she heard the whimpers of children drifting through the ebony night, along with the smell of cooking meat, and she would go into the kitchen and find Green Lee standing over a vast iron pot on the wood stove. From the boiling waters he would drag the bodies of her children, holding them aloft and cackling insanely as the blistered meat slid limply from their naked bones and fell like pale suits of dead gristle into the steaming cauldron.

As if the horrid nightmares weren't enough, Rebecca began to have suspicions that her husband might be playing a part in her sudden uneasiness. She came to the realization that he was acting strangely and not at all like the man she had married.

Lately, Jasper had chosen to spend his evenings sitting by the door of the big, iron cook stove, smoking his pipe and staring into the glowing slits of the grate, as if searching for the clue to some inner mystery. He also began to talk in his sleep. Not coherently, but in low whispers, reminding Rebecca of the breathy pleas of that lunatic handyman she had once known.

And objects around the house began to mysteriously disappear. One morning in December, Rebecca noticed that Jasper was shaving with a new razor. When she questioned him about the whereabouts of his old one, Jasper grew defensive. "I reckon I just misplaced it, that's all," he said curtly. Also, the hand-axe she used for chopping kindling vanished without a trace from the stump outside.

There was the matter of the bed linen as well. Sometimes when she did her washing, she would find some of the sheets filthy with mud and dank leaves, as if someone had gone for a nocturnal stroll and then climbed back into bed without wiping their feet.

■■■

It was on a cold and snowy night in the middle of February that all of Rebecca's fears and suspicions suddenly came to a head and she found herself lying awake in her bed, filled with a sensation of overbearing dread.

Her hand moved to her husband's side of the bed and found the space unoccupied. She rose and instantly smelled a sickening scent in the air. It reeked like spoiled meat cooking in its own fetid juices. Uttering a silent prayer, Rebecca stepped into the hallway and checked the bedroom of her children. Mitch and Millie were both gone. Their beds were empty and their blankets had been violently flung across the floor. She looked down the dark corridor and, from the kitchen, thought she heard the boiling of water...and the low, giggling mirth of an unsound mind. Then came the sharp slap of the back door slamming shut.

Bracing herself for the worst, Rebecca Howell entered the kitchen. Despite the cold winter night, the interior of the room was sweltering hot. The stove had been stoked. A crackling fire raged within its iron belly. The narrow slits of the grate winked at her like crimson eyes, privy to some evil knowledge that she was thankfully ignorant of. But not for very long.

As she walked nearer, Rebecca saw that her largest iron pot was on the stove and that plumes of acrid steam drifted from the bubbling waters within. The odor of cooking meat was stronger than ever and Rebecca fought the sickness that threatened to seize her. Taking a step closer, she peered through the warm mist and into the torrid waters beneath.

Something danced in the dark depths, a couple of small, pale objects rising and falling amid the swirling currents. At first she didn't know what they were. Then, as they rose to the boiling surface, she recoiled in horror.

They were clumps of flaccid skin. Pale blossoms of lifeless flesh that had slipped from the understructure of human bones. The objects waved at her like disembodied gloves. Tiny nails, bitten to the quick, graced each fluttering finger.

Rebecca moaned with terror. "My babies! What has he done to my babies?"

She recalled the slamming of the back door and, from the darkness of the night beyond, again heard the low chortling of maniacal laughter. She grabbed a heavy stick of firewood from the box, then opened the door and stepped out onto the porch.

It was a frigid night. The ground was inches deep with fresh snow, and moonlit icicles hung like jeweled fangs from the eaves of the overhang. Rebecca breathed frosty plumes of winter air, then, raising the stick of wood overhead, stepped off the edge of the porch. And instantly felt her bare foot sink into the cooling sludge that had once been her husband's brain.

Before Rebecca could give way to the scream that rose in her throat, she heard the rasping sound of tiny voices.

"Which one must we kill...next?"

Then, from the dense shadows beneath the back porch, came the flash of sharpened steel and youthful bone.

RONALD KELLY

AFTERWORD

'VE been gone for a while...ten years to be exact. So I have a lot of folks to thank for kicking me in the seat of the britches and urging me to give this storytelling gig another try.

First and foremost, to the good Lord, through whom all things are possible. Thank you for blessing me with this second chance.

To my wife, Joyce, who has been my strength and comfort for the past sixteen years. Thanks for your love and support through the good times and bad—especially those post-Zebra years—and for showing me that there is much more to life than sitting behind a keyboard.

To my precious daughters, who God has gracefully blessed me with. Reilly, my superhero and monster-loving buddy, whose interests in art, music, and writing show great promise. And my little Chigger, Makenna, a bundle of energy with fiery red hair and an Irish temper to match; a lover of baby dolls and fairy princesses, of which, in my eyes, she is both. And to our newest addition, my son, Ryan Alexander.

To my good friend, Mark Hickerson, who stuck with me throughout the years and, eventually, won me back

AFTERWORD

to writing. I'll be forever grateful for your friendship and tenacity. Most of all, you were influential in orchestrating my comeback. And to Shannon Riley, my small-press pal, who went to bat for me and got the wheels turning. Much thanks to my present and future publishers: Richard Chizmar at Cemetery Dance Publications and Stephen Lloyd at Croatoan Publishing, for your confidence, friendship, and support, and for presenting my work in a way it has never been presented before. I look forward to many wonderful projects together.

To my biggest fan and best friend, Rob McCoy, to whom this collection is dedicated. And to the following folks: James Newman, Katie O'Neil, Mark Johnson, and Alex McVey, for regarding me as much more than simply a name on a book. Thank you for blessing me with the privilege of being your friend.

To my good friend Hunter Goatley, whose generosity and expertise has been phenomenal in bringing the Ron Kelly website to life. Thanks for making this dream a reality. For more info on me and my brand of Southern-fried horror, y'all stop on by at www.ronaldkelly.com and make yourselves at home.

And, last but not least, to my fans, who never forgot me and forgave me for going AWOL for a while. I promise you, folks, the twilight only gets darker from here on out.

Y'all come on back and see me. There is always an empty rocking chair on the ol' front porch and plenty more tales to be told.

Ronald Kelly
Brush Creek, Tennessee
July 2007